WILLIAM SCHLICHTER

SERIAL KILLERS ANONYMOUS
A NOVEL

OPEN WINDOW
Livonia, Michigan

Edited by Kathryn DeJarnette and Kristi Martin

SKA: SERIAL KILLERS ANONYMOUS
Copyright © 2018 William Schlichter

Published by Open Window
an imprint of BHC Press

Library of Congress Control Number:
2018930157

ISBN: 978-1-947727-32-8

Visit the publisher:
www.bhcpress.com

Also available in ebook

ALSO BY
WILLIAM SCHLICHTER

NO ROOM IN HELL
The Good, the Bad, and the Undead
400 Miles to Graceland

THE SILVER DRAGON CHRONICLES
Enter the Sandmen
The Dark Side

Thanks to Katie and Kristi for your editing.

I utilized a few beta readers and I appreciated all your insight.

Thanks to BHC Press for all you do.

As I completed this book I lost my father to cancer.
His support will never be replaced.

FOR HEAVENS
SAKE CATCH ME
BEFORE I KILL MORE
I CANNOT CONTROL MYSELF
– THE LIPSTICK KILLER

SKA

were obvious, at least to me, but something deeper wanted me to keep this girl.

She prattled for minutes about trivial subjects in her own attempt to play me. After all, I appeared an easy mark. Not on purpose, but over the years I realized people glance at me—pretty girls especially—and think because I have a protruding paunch and a nerd vibe I can't get dates. Because of such misconceptions, the opposite rules true.

"I'm Courtney Lynn." She offers her hand with the same limp-wristed handshake I've gotten from guitarists. They have a grip as if they are a dead fish.

Self-aware…she wanted to play me. She asked if I had a wife.

"Yes," *of course*, "I'm married," I lied to her. She was hinting she would gratify me and I knew if she thought I was dissatisfied in my marriage she could manipulate me easier. What I'll do to this girl will scare people, but I think terror lies in the number of people falling for her shell game.

"I really need a shower." She cuddled up against my arm. Smooth, warm flesh sent a surge of precum into my tighty whities. She *did* excite me. She was attractive, despite babbling how she needed to fix her face for me. Be a doll for me. It was all for me. How many men was she a doll for?

"Why were you hospitalized?"

"I had this boyfriend…"

"And he hit you." It wasn't a question.

"Yeah." She fidgeted with her cigarette box.

I can't read the brand.

"I just spent six days in the hospital."

With no marks. A beating putting you in the hospital for six days would still have fading bruises.

"Where can I drop you off?"

"I could use a shower. Is your wife home?"

"Yes, with the kids." She wasn't my planned target. For all I knew, the gas station had cameras recording her getting into my vehicle. Her

SKA

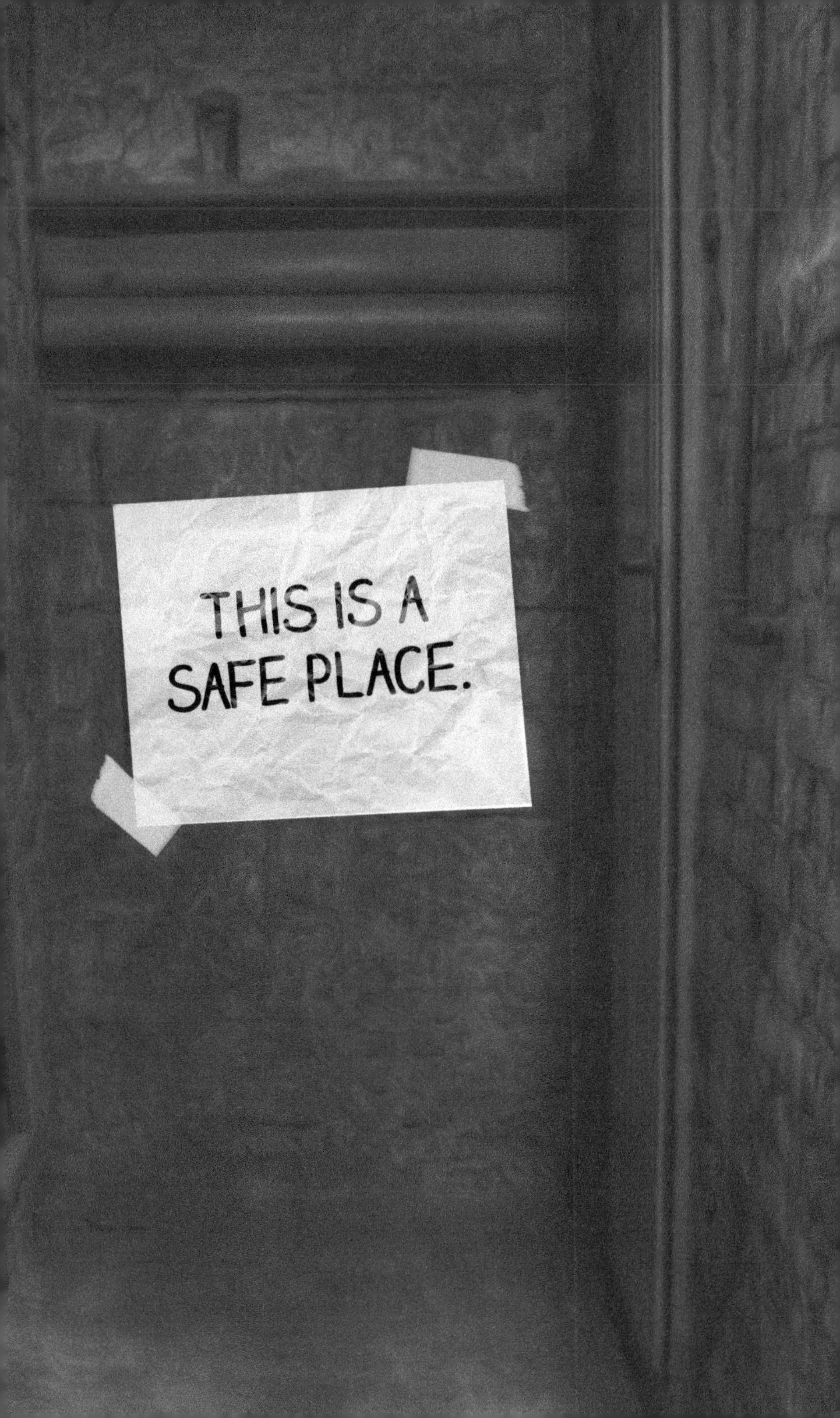
THIS IS A
SAFE PLACE.

ONE
SKA: FIRST MEETING

I

"THAT'S A LOT of money—do you want me to do something for it?"

Even on my limited salary, a Jackson wasn't a grand gesture. I've bought books costing more. The girl was messed up, and not just for thinking the twenty dollars I handed her was worth her doing *something*, but she had a hospital ID bracelet and a red medication allergy band on her wrist.

She asked me to watch her bag while she bought cigarettes—one of those plastic clothing bags hospitals give out. She'd be back, then I could take her someplace.

Despite her haggard appearance, her round face was pretty. Hospitals tend to fatigue people. They want you to rest, but constantly wake you up to check your vitals.

Returning with a green pack of smokes, she bubbled with excitement. The cheap pint she tried to hide might have helped. The seal already busted, she didn't notice me observing her slip it in the hospital bag. If I wasn't convinced she was an addict, I knew now. Curiosity overtook me. Stirring overwhelmed me. The sexual ones were obvious, at least to me, but something deeper wanted me to keep this girl.

She prattled for minutes about trivial subjects in her own attempt to play me. After all, I appeared an easy mark. Not on purpose, but over the years I realized people glance at me—pretty girls especially—and think because I have a protruding paunch and a nerd vibe I can't get dates. Because of such misconceptions, the opposite rules true.

"I'm Courtney Lynn." She offers her hand with the same limp-wristed handshake I've gotten from guitarists. They have a grip as if they are a dead fish.

Self-aware…she wanted to play me. She asked if I had a wife.

"Yes," *of course,* "I'm married," I lied to her. She was hinting she would gratify me and I knew if she thought I was dissatisfied in my marriage she could manipulate me easier. What I'll do to this girl will scare people, but I think terror lies in the number of people falling for her shell game.

"I really need a shower." She cuddled up against my arm. Smooth, warm flesh sent a surge of precum into my tighty whities. She *did* excite me. She was attractive, despite babbling how she needed to fix her face for me. Be a doll for me. It was all for me. How many men was she a doll for?

"Why were you hospitalized?"

"I had this boyfriend…"

"And he hit you." It wasn't a question.

"Yeah." She fidgeted with her cigarette box.

I can't read the brand.

"I just spent six days in the hospital."

With no marks. A beating putting you in the hospital for six days would still have fading bruises.

"Where can I drop you off?"

"I could use a shower. Is your wife home?"

"Yes, with the kids." She wasn't my planned target. For all I knew, the gas station had cameras recording her getting into my vehicle. Her

DNA could be explained in the seat, but not at my home. More importantly, I had not prepared it for my next guest.

"I need to go to this guy's house…"

"Your boyfriend?"

"No. I'm done with him."

"Good. You don't need people in your life who abuse you."

"I'm done with him. I just need to get this backpack."

Full of drugs I'm sure. "You shouldn't get into cars with people you don't know. I could be a serial killer." Yes, I said it. It's actually a disarming statement. Why would a serial killer announce who they are? Technically, I wasn't one—yet.

She cuddled against my arm again. "I trust you." Her warm breath on my ear surged straight into my cock.

"I'd rather you just slit my throat than go back to him." She leaned back against the door all business jonesing for a drag on a cigarette. I wouldn't let her light in my car.

"Since you're doing this for me I won't charge you."

I'm sure my eyes screamed, 'Charge me for what?' As they grew large at her remark, it also killed the growth in my pants. I wasn't about to pay—for her.

As I just drove, she prattled, "Do you know how much I make a night as an escort?"

Was this supposed to impress me? Maybe it was part of her sales pitch to worm more money out of me. Or cement the fact she would perform for money. She wanted me to take her to buy a cheap sundress. She had an insane notion of being dolled up for me because she appeared awful. She didn't.

"How many times have you been in jail?"

Silence.

She got quiet for maybe a full minute.

"I had to think about it."

"That many?"

"I was fourteen the first time. See, my dad was dating this real bitch. She was going to call the cops on him for raping her. They fucked all the time, it was no rape. I was going to say so. She hit me. I hit her. He hit her. I was in lockup for five hours." She patted my arm. "See, I had to think about it."

"What's your drug of choice?"

"Meth."

"Smile," I commanded.

She did. Her teeth were coffee stained, but no meth mouth.

"See, I don't really do drugs." She cuddled my arm again.

I know better.

"It's so nice just to talk and not be expected to do anything."

The part of me wanting her naked body deflated. Compounding the abuse she's experienced was not my original intention.

"I really need his backpack. Can I smoke in your car?"

"No."

"Can you pull over up here so I can step out? Then we'll go get my backpack and I'll shower." She stroked my arm, "You can shower with me."

I pulled onto gravel along a gate for entrance to a pasture. No traffic. She didn't get out.

I wondered if she thought I might drive off.

She lit up, rolling down the window and sticking her upper body outside enough to allow the wind to catch the smoke. Her long drag failed to dent her body's jittering. Days in the hospital failed to fully detox her.

"Tell me about being an escort."

"I don't always have sex. There was this one guy who gave me two-hundred to put on his dead wife's dress and wear her perfume. Then he just held me all night. Wasn't that weird?"

"I don't think so," I mused, "he missed her."

"I think he just wanted to say goodbye to her."

"It could be his way of dealing with her loss," I agreed.

"You're so nice." She flicked half a burnt cigarette out the window. "See, I respect your car. Guess how much I smoke a day?"

"A pack."

"Just five a day. And you saw I don't even finish them." She unbuckles her seatbelt.

The seatbelt warning alarm beeped and flashed.

She buckled it with the strap behind her. "I'm sorry. I need makeup, so I'll look beautiful for you."

"I think you're pretty right now."

"We could go get a sundress and shower." She shifted her loving tone, "We could just leave this town. I need to get my backpack first."

"What's in it?"

"My important papers. If you don't want to do anything, could you at least give me twenty more? I need to get my prescription. Those pills are worth seven dollars each on the street."

I slid the car into gear and rolled up her window.

"I need a shower. We can get my backpack and there's a room in the back of my friend's house where you can shower with me...but first I need a sundress. I want to look nice for you."

My assurances she's pretty enough were unconvincing. She didn't need makeup. And I doubted this mythical backpack existed—drug house for my money.

Her self-importance might draw in other men who lacked the ability to translate her playfulness for what it was. I, however, knew what she was. Her desires to run away with me may actually be genuine, but she'd rather self-medicate than escape with a man who wouldn't use her for sex—or a punching bag. Admittedly, my plans to use her for my pleasure were not what she expected.

She had me turn down street after street into neighborhoods where my newer car stood out among those on blocks.

"We can just go in there."

"Where?"

"The resale shop." She pointed to a store in major need of renovation, "I'll get a dress in there."

She either didn't know what street this backpack was on or it's just a ploy to worm little bits of money out of me as we went. A stop here at the thrift store to buy her new clothes to appear nicer for me cemented she believed I could be played.

"I could really love you."

No, sweetheart, you love the medication or meth. You sell yourself. If you think twenty dollars is a lot and are willing to do 'something' for it then the four or five hundred dollars you earn as an escort creates an algebraic formula if I was concerned about your past numbers or partners.

It was a chase around the clothing racks. I paid for the hat and the jeans and bag. She changed into the jeans with sparkles on the pockets. She shoved her shorts into the large purse and showed the lady. The cashier never investigated the bag or she would have found a black party dress. Even I didn't spot her snatching it.

Her chattering about how she wasn't sure if she appeared attractive enough for me in the sparkling top allowed me to turn out of the city.

"I think his house is back that way."

"Trust me." I drove on. No more backpack scavenger hunt.

"I do." She cuddled up against me. "I love you. Let's just run away. We can go away wherever you desire. I'll be your girl—be whatever you want."

"I have responsibilities. I have a job." *Should say wife.*

"I don't date many men with jobs."

"Could be a start to fixing your life."

"If you go down that street my backpack should be at that house, and once we get my stuff we could go shower together."

I ignored her pleading to turn down a street to a known drug house. Despite her anger with me, she turned back into a lovebird within a half-breath.

I parked under a highway bridge next to a river. It's private enough for four in the afternoon. Not many people even knew a gravel road extended under the bridge.

"Why don't we sit in the back for a while, then I'll take you to whatever house you want so you can shower."

She crawled over the captain seats to the back. I got out and climbed in the second row. Cheap seat covers didn't hide the squeaking plastic seat cover underneath. I had planned only so far.

Courtney straddled my lap and griped my face with her hands. Her gray eyes had so much life stolen from her—by her choice.

"I don't want you to think of me as some whore. I have a degree. I was a radiologist."

I could have guessed medical field. Many people I know involved in drugs have worked in medicine. I know more nurses who smoke than any other group of people. It explains the lack of track marks on her arms and her teeth. Meth must be a new thing—if at all. She may have gone into the hospital just to get narcotics.

Her tank top rolled right over her head, allowing her hair to splash down around her shoulders. I was sure she felt a surge from my lap. One snap of my thumb and forefinger and the two hooks released her breasts.

White.

I expected more tan skin like the rest of her.

"Don't say anything about my body. I'm no anorexic."

Another sign meth doesn't yet rule her life. Conflicted—saving her could mean I came home to a house where all my belongings were at the pawn shop. I ran my index finger over the left underside of her breast, tracking a stretch mark most likely from rapid engorgement due to breastfeeding. "How old is your child?"

"Seventeen."

"Do you want me to be seventeen? I can be anything you want…"

Say 'Once I get my backpack' again and I'll bludgeon you with a tire iron.

Her hands fumbled with her pants buttons. She never broke eye contact, a flicker of life hid behind her pain.

"How about I just take you back to where I found you? I'll be the one man who doesn't use you."

"Makes me want to ride you even more."

Her lips had no taste. No sweet or even morning breath. Just lips. Her tongue had all the flavor of cheap rum. She must have been nipping off her bottle—I was driving, I couldn't watch her every second I drove.

Performed with skill not learned in any school, the numbing presence of latex slid over me. She worked it down, before clamping herself on me.

"You feel so nice."

Good answer. I hate lies about my manliness.

She ground her hips until she took me all the way inside her. I didn't think she's wet. Impossible to tell with the condom on, but she worked her hips slowly as if she didn't want to tear herself.

"Do you want me?"

"Of course, I do."

I force myself not to bite her hardening nipple. The slightest teeth marks could haunt me if *CSI* is to be believed. Each grind worked into a longer thrust up and down until I heard her wetness.

I reached into the map pouch behind the front seat and slid out a sparkling pair of lover's handcuffs covered in fur to prevent chaffing.

She smiles. "I usually charge extra for those."

"I thought you wanted to run away with me?"

She held out her wrists. "I do."

I cuffed her right hand. She giggled as I drew it behind her. She dropped her left arm and I tightened the bracelets behind her back. Now the novelty cuffs I bought with the pink leopard print fur had a safety catch so the shackled person could free themselves if a lover's game got uncomfortable. The police-issued cuffs I paid cash for at an army surplus store didn't unbind without a key. With the fur covers no one could tell the difference.

She shifted her thrusts into a fast-forward speed as her body accepted she wanted to have sex. Her face glinted at enjoyment.

I needed more than a shimmer to achieve my own pleasure.

I slipped a dog collar around her neck.

She ground away, trusting me as I drew the collar strap through the securing buckle. I didn't latch it like this was some S&M game. I pulled it tight until her breathing was disrupted. Her body constricted as air failed to fill her lungs. Putting forth all her effort she ground her hips quicker. She must have thought I enjoy this. I did. Consumed by the swelling power I exerted over her life, I drew the strap through the buckle until it caught, unable to go deeper. She gurgled from lack of air. Her hips ground faster. Her last gulp of air was used to pleasure me.

Silk tie choking was first introduced by a girl I defined as a passing fling. I had no idea how exhilarating total control over a life could be. Not many women trust enough to let you choke them. I found a second one. She liked it so much it scared her. I tried to have normal relationships after her. I couldn't perform—normally. Not like with the next project I assumed. I find those urges returning now. The power. The energy. The control over her and her insignificant life.

As I exploded, filling the condom, I gripped the collar itself with my left hand and pressed, still holding tight to the strap with my right hand.

Life vacated her eyes.

Her lack of fear startled me. My first victim fought with every ounce she had when she realized I wouldn't let go.

She slipped into a sleep state. Having experienced autoerotic asphyxiation before. She trusts me to release her.

Stopping then would have allowed her to live. Keeping my fingers on the dog collar, my vice grip closed both her carotid arteries preventing blood flow to the brain, and then sealing off her throat and stopping all air into her lungs.

Her chest heaved—three quick jerks failing to draw in any fresh air. She shuddered a full body shiver and she went limp.

She's broken.

She would've let me do this every day if I had kept her, but she'd never give up the drugs. I wasn't ready for the kind of guest my desires required. What I did, I do as a mercy for her. I kept my grip on the collar.

I slid out from under her. I disposed of the cheap seat covers and vacuumed out my car. It would eliminate most of her DNA. I should've toss the handcuffs, but buying too many pairs may have sparked notice.

Cinder blocks would weigh her body down in the river, and since she was homeless, I doubted I'll be connected to her.

I must make sure when I selected my next project I had no direct connection to her, either.

II

WITH HIS STORY complete, the speaker glances at the six faces hidden by the dark—judging. Not just him, but each other in the circle. None of them should be here. Not just in an abandoned boiler room, but gathering in a group. Everyone joining a support group for the first time, or the fifth, finds they doubt belonging. Being here marks the first step in admitting a problem, admitting everything they have done in their life has been wrong. Who is to say what is wrong? Why does doing what feels good to a person, makes them complete, must be labeled as wrong?

Most drug addicts would say it's not. If they stay home and draw their coke lines, they harm no one but themselves, so why is it a crime?

Addiction harms everyone around you.

Addiction is uncontrollable.

Addiction makes a person do uncontrollable acts against others.

Maybe it is an addiction. Addictions have cures.

How does anyone ask for help with this?

Who would even help such people?

All these question race through each of the seven's minds.

"You're the Dog Collar Killer!" The excited voice in the dark celebrates his own revelation.

"This is a safe place. We must follow our ground rules," the woman's voice breaks the cold. Warm, not motherly—not auntie—more like the kind nurse before she jabs the needle in the meaty part of the ass voice. "Your outburst is unnecessary...and not acceptable."

"The papers have labeled some of my killings as such. A bit pedantic. It's not what I do."

"None of what the newspapers describe is who we are," the woman assures him. "We did decide to choose pseudonyms as part of our protection. What moniker will you choose to be referred by?"

"Albert will suffice."

Excited, the young man pipes up, "DeSalvo!? You chose the name of the Boston Strangler, because you too strangle women."

"We're not here to judge, kid. We are here to help one another. In what we've done certain anonymity must be maintained. What we share, we do so under a blanket of trust. If you lack such abilities, we will end the circle with nothing more than a scary campfire story to go home with."

"I, for one, am here to prevent what I do. So, shut up, kid. I deal enough with stupid teens; I don't want your crap." One of the dark figures scolds.

"I'm twenty-two."

"I've never been to an AA meeting, but I'm sure they don't sit in the dark with a single light suspended over the podium," another figure says.

She snaps her neck with a dark gaze toward the voice. "If this is to work we at least have to make the attempt."

"But follow the rules—our rules."

"Are those rules enough?"

The voices bombard her from the gloom.

"AA is about building a support network, and our group needs support."

"Our group needs to be locked away."

The remark brings a chuckle from the assembly.

"Levity might do us some good. The major focus of group therapy is to share, to discuss and work out our shared problem, to explore and overcome our urges. We're here to stop killing. Who would like to tell their story next?" She asks.

The self-appointed hostess faces the man who stifled the kid. "You said you worked with teens. Would you like to go?"

"No one even knows I'm a killer. The victims are all taken by a ghost. People actually believe my victims are the product of a spirit from beyond. What do you have to say to that, kid?"

The young man keeps quiet, hearing the entire story before passing judgment on the meek man now speaking.

"My tale begins before I was born. Cliché as it sounds, the location is key to the events I perpetuate."

"Wherever the starting line is, we need to have an understanding of who you are," the woman says.

"Where I live, the American Civil War was just a chapter in history class. We were too far North for redneck southern pride, except among those few pickup drivers too stupid to even understand the flags they put on their bumper stickers. We were too far West to have much of a minority population, but what we did have was an impressive home lost in the woods at the edge of town. The dream house of a southern lady built for her by a gentleman."

"The house was grand and out of place. Despite ample farmland, it was more cattle than cotton. A home with Grecian pillars and a mint julep-sipping porch was an oddity among an original settlement of log cabins. The best version of the story was the gentleman who inherited the family property while prospecting for gold in California. He used his stake to build the dream house of the woman he loved. Despite all this she still spurned him returning to her family in Georgia.

"Only she never made it home. Her body was found in the cellar. Her lover had shot himself as she swung from her neck."

"We are not here for grand fairy tales."

"It's more than a fairy tale, and even if it is, it's part of who I've become."

"Continue. We all must learn to respect the sharing process," she says.

"With all my research, I've been unable to turn up the original family to confirm the story or who even owns the property, but no one wanted the home after the grisly deaths. The story persists how during several Civil War battles the home was commandeered and used as a field hospital. Confederate and Yankee soldiers alike died there. The lovers' deaths and so many wounded—dying—the home was considered cursed—haunted. No one wanted to live in such a place. And it remained vacant."

"You've set the stage for a nice twisted horror tale where the dumb blonde with big tits dies first. Is that what you do? Kill blondes with big tits?"

"I told you knowing the background of the house was important." The speaker spins his tale while Al and the other five attendees listen.

III

"RUN!"

"Run, you little shit! I'm going to cut off one of your tiny balls when I catch you." Allen stops. The bulky crop-top teen pounds his right fist into the meaty palm of his left hand.

Freshly cut grass butts against overgrown dead weed stalks, signaling the edge of a property line.

"Why only one ball?" the jocular Scott ponders.

"Give me something to cut off later."

"Call him one-ball Magee."

"Little fucker ran onto the Carson property," Scott says.

"I thought the city owned it?" George asks.

"Who gives a fuck who owns it. We got to get him," Allen says.

"Go across the property line?" Scott asks.

"You telling me that fuck tart is braver than your pansy ass? I knew you wanted to lick my balls in the shower after the game, you pussy mouth," Allen says.

"I ain't no pussy," Scott says.

"The runt's got more balls than you, even after I cut one of them off." Allen flicks open the gleaming razor edge of a switch blade.

"I'll find him." Scott marches through the grass and years of un-raked leaves.

Allen stays close on his heels—committed—unable to admit in front of his teammates he's uneasy by all the stories of the house on this forgotten land.

George scoops up a branch and whacks at grass as he follows.

• • • • •

The bravest action I had was to run onto the property no one traveled even when triple-dog-dared. I was forever on the receiving end of the jocks' abuse. Children today whine about bullies and feelings. What those boys did bordered on criminal, and there weren't any anti-bullying laws then.

• • • • •

I ran. I had to escape. Thing is, when propelled by fear, a person doesn't gaze at his feet and pay attention to where he should be placing them. A wrought iron bar tripped me. My own momentum betrayed me. I tumbled over hard stone. I scraped up the untouched earth as if I were a tractor plowing the field, and nothing I could do would undo the path I left. They would know I fled this way. I had no doubt I would lose a nut.

I got up, not bothering to clean off the black, rotten muck smeared on me from under the leaves. My mother would rage about the stains more than what I had landed on and how it road-rashed my arms.

Any other situation and I would break down in tears from the pain. I could afford no time to cry. Instead, I kicked away some of the dirt.

Tombstones.

Maybe those cowards wouldn't chase me into cursed land and a cemetery. It wasn't big, most likely a family plot. The names and dates were long faded, but there were enough knocked over limestone to reveal a family once resided here.

"Where are you, you little fuck!"

I was dead, or soon to be forever marked as half a man. Trees were thick, and an old, rotten oak had collapsed under its own weight in some thunderstorm years before I was born. Rotten branches and no foliage, it offered no protection. Then I thought it might.

Since it was rotting, maybe it had a hollow spot in the trunk. Leaping onto it, I found more stone was underneath the tree. It had collapsed on a limestone hut, leaving a gap between the stone roof and the stone wall. I wormed my way through, scraping and cutting up my belly to match my arms. It stung, but not like a knife to the balls would.

"Where'd the fucker go!?"

They had reached the cemetery. The sun beamed into the crypt. I had no idea they buried bodies this way. I was trapped if they found the ceiling gap. They might decide to put some weight into and close the hole. I would die in an unknown grave.

Frantic, I searched the chamber. There were alcoves in the wall where folded bodies rotted to bones. In the center was a rectangular stone platform. Covered in a moth-eaten shroud was a body reduced to black bone. I don't know what made me think of it. A body interned out in the open was normal in the middle ages. Some fantasy adventure I read once might have had a body displayed like this. It was to ensure no one touched, not the dead but the dais. I was motivated. I pushed past the skeleton on the bier and I found it. My escape. A tunnel. It didn't matter where it lead, or even if it didn't go anywhere anymore, as long as I traveled far enough down that the jocks didn't spot me.

My escape was short lived. They taunted me every day in school. They never admitted they lost me on the Carson or Benson or Watson property, or whatever name this year's class gave to the forgotten piece of land. Only it wasn't forgotten, it was just never spoken of. I had been on it and used it as an escape, learning a secret.

Not the secret everyone in town knew. The property was now more a location for hazing of the unsuspecting, 'I dare you to go inside' shit. Now I knew one truth, and it meant nothing. And I would not share because it was the one item I held over the whole town.

• • • • •

High school taunting was worse.

Allen stepped up his abuse—from the classic verbal, skipping the bathroom swirly, to the worst humiliation performed on any prepubescent boy. I was on my way to class doing all possible to avoid him when I found hands pushing into the sides of my pants. The fingers tugged and despite the cloth gripping my hips, my Walmart specials were around my ankles.

Everyone laughed.

"For so much hair, how do you find your dick?"

"Tiny dick!"

"With a dick that small your mom won't even go to prom with you."

Prom was the furthest thing from my thoughts.

"Tiny dick!"

"How do you find it to pee?"

Laughter. Haunting laughter and knowing even my classmates who never openly taunted me would speak of my miniscule penis. It was small—and I was insignificant.

I hurt. I would blow my brains out right there if someone handed me a gun. My diploma wouldn't say my name, instead it would read Tiny Dick with one Ball.

My older sister raced to my rescue.

For about half a second.

"Do you know how fucking embarrassing you are? Oh my God! Pull your pants up. You are the most embarrassing thing to ever happen to me! I have a senior reputation, and you'll ruin it. I hate you!"

Fuck. My own sister. I don't know what I expected from her, but whatever it was it wasn't her berating me on top of my mortification.

A teacher herded me from the hall. "Don't worry, Mr. Colson, it's not big enough to be offensive."

More laughs.

My shame was complete, and I had no one. No girl would desire a tiny dicked man. Even once I hit my growth spurt—now my nightly prayer—girls would forever speak of what I lacked in manhood.

Even if I ran away and found a new life in a new town, how could I ever be with a woman?

No, I would tough it out. I'd show them—him.

No longer having to worry about attracting girls, I was left with more free time and I would use it to extract revenge on Allen.

The interesting dynamics about high school was the way in which the social hierarchy worked. My sister, senior cheerleader, was expected to date college boys. Allen, senior jock, would chase freshman girls because they were too stupid to understand he would use them only for sex.

College boys used senior girls for sex, but somehow that was okay within the confines of the dynamic, even though both college boys and high school senior boys would leave the girl when a more prominent prospect of sex entered their lives.

Now Allen dated Melony—a freshman. Cute as a button, tight ass, no tits, could have passed for a sixth grader. Melony was a cheerleader and, therefore, my sister reasoned it was her duty to train her in the ways of social interaction.

Melony—dumb twat—who was so happy that seniors wanted her in their circle she had blinders on.

My sister had the smart habit of stealing one of dad's beers every time he went on a bender. He drank all the time now. Since my humiliation at school the town branded me a fairy—leading to his silent shame. Men were to be men, and not have pansy sons. If I had fought back and gotten my ass kicked at least it was masculine. I never understood how I went from being the brunt of all school bullies to homosexual. Dad wasn't a mean drunk, he would just drink until he passed out in his recliner. Gillian, on a good night, cleaned up Dad's empties and grabbed a full beer. With so many smashed cans in the recycle box, he never knew how many he drank.

Gillian and her friends held little séances. They loved to bring the new freshmen cheerleaders to the front yard of the plantation house. Kids built bonfires there for years and drank, fucked, tormented the unsuspecting freshmen with ghost tales and dares to venture inside.

I would sneak out. It was easy to witness the parties I was never invited to from the woods. Then a short hop to the cemetery and through the underground railroad tunnel when they were inside the house.

Karen popped a beer. "No way. You don't just sleep with any boy."

"Yeah, you're not a slut when you're popular. You only give yourself to one of the jocks and only when they win games." Carly chugged her beer.

Karen passed a fresh beer to Melony.

"I don't know."

"Besides, jocks are the best way to escape this town. They get a scholarship, or a pro-team snatches them. You're set with a meal ticket."

"Even if they dump you later for some other slut you'll have had his baby and he'll have to pay you child support."

"Who was the last player from our school to go pro?" Melony asked.

"Doesn't matter." Karen pushed on the bottom of Melony's beer, tipping more of the liquid into her mouth. "Drink up. You can't be a lightweight. You have to be able to outdrink them or they will take advantage of you."

"You have to be in charge of the relationship."

"You got to get used to beer with us or when you drink with the boys you'll pass out."

"Then you never know which one you'll wake up with."

"I don't want to wake up with any of them," Melony said.

They ignored Melony's protests.

"I don't blame you there. You don't want to start out with Trent, boy's going to be a porn star."

They giggled, except for Melony. She sipped her beer, unsure why they laughed.

"If Allen didn't already have his name on you, I'd say start with George."

"Or your brother," Karen laughed.

"My brother will never be a jock." Gillian opened her second beer, "It's not like Allen is all that impressive, but he'll do nicely for a first time."

"Have you girls slept with all the team?" Melony asked.

"No, just the players we think will have a career. You don't open your legs for just any one," Gillian said.

"Maybe not, but what about the new coach? He's like fresh out of college, and so hot." Karen melts.

"Gross. He's a teacher," Melony finally disapproved. Holding her beer at her side, she tipped it secretly, spilling the contents onto the grass.

"No. Teachers never end well, and even if he doesn't get caught porking a student, he's a teacher. He'll never leave this town," Gillian snapped. "Or his wife."

"Why not get good grades and go off to college?"

"Drink your beer, Melony."

"Liquid courage for what you have to do next."

"What?"

"You want to be popular, don't you?"

"Well, yeah. I mean, you girls are all anyone talks about at school," Melony said.

"Good. Then all you have to do is—"

"Go inside the mansion and snap a picture—" Gillian held out a Polaroid camera. "In the basement."

"It's haunted," she protested.

"You're just a freshman. You want to hang out with us seniors, you have to prove yourself."

"We've all done it." Gillian poked her in the stomach with the camera. "Flip up the top and press the button. It will flash. Just take a picture of the stairs so we know you are in the basement."

It was about time they got to the dare part of the party. Someone in the group always dared someone and they would eventually find themselves in the house. My sister's twist with the camera would force someone to go into the basement.

My sis had no idea how accommodating this was. Second, most helpful item was the town's lack of interest in the location beyond the *must be haunted* aspect. The crypt was an exit for the hidden tunnel to the root cellar. The plantation house was a stop along the underground railroad. It should have been a museum or at least a tourist trap with a gift shop. But instead it's a teen hazing hangout.

Poor Melony wasn't the focus of my anger, but she would do.

Closing the front door, her bold steps inside shifted to baby steps. She shivered, and I smelt her fear. I thought it was a movie cliché, but she was sweating and releasing a smell. It excited me. I had no idea I could become so hard. I thought I might stretch out my jeans. I wouldn't get any laughs if I was depantsed now.

The taunts from the group outside got louder and forced her to move faster to locate the cellar door.

It was impossible to move down them without a few creaking boards. I did so ahead of her as quietly as possible, praying it would only frighten her more—not scare her away.

"Old houses settle on the foundation at night," she whispered attempting to talk courage into herself.

She maintained her baby step stride. Each step creaked, and the ageing boards moaned when she lifted her foot. "Old houses make noise." The Polaroid quivered in her fingers.

Speaking aloud seemed to calm her. "The girls are likely in a shadow to jump out and scare me. I should have peed before I came inside."

Without the same care I displayed with my footfalls, her tiny feet released a wail of moaning from each ancient board on the stairs.

Her whole body just trembled. It crossed my thoughts to spare her. She had not laughed or tormented me—but she would. What I was about to do would spare her from becoming like the rest of them.

I heard the plastic camera split as it landed. She was too scared to struggle—froze when I wrapped my arms around her. Clamping a hand over her mouth, her breath warmed my palm. It even caused a tingle between my legs. There was nothing sexual about it, just my hand pressing down over her lips, mushing into her teeth, preventing a scream. She was tiny. I wasn't much stronger than her. I struggled to drag her. Had she scuffled she might have gotten away. I placed her on a rickety crate. Under her weight I thought it might shatter before I finished. She'd get away. So would I. She would think it was a trick by the girls and hate them for denying it.

Before she realized it was no joke, I had the noose over her neck. I jerked the knot tight. Pain from my pants broke my concentration. My engorgement would've made my classmates proud. I kicked the apple box from under her before she could squawk.

The rope rubbed against her neck, strangling away her life. She kicked, at first, in attempts to find footing. Her fingers, now contorted like talons, clawed at the rope. She wasn't able to slip any finger under the nylon. Panic. Her own nails marred her neck. I kept my eyes locked with hers. They rolled into her skull and only the white beamed. She gurgled and sputtered, her kick turning to spasmodic twitches. The seat of her pants darkened. The smell of urine filled the air.

My own heart beat faster. I felt it thump against my chest wall. The pounding drowned out all other sounds. I wanted to embrace her. I didn't have to fondle myself, I wanted to hold her as her life escaped. Life fled my erection. It was warm and soaked my jeans. Nothing like the wet dripping from her legs as they spasmed.

Even with only subtle moonlight through greasy windows her eyes glowed. With no air reaching her lungs her fear increased. I smelt it on her. The odor was stronger than the piss smell.

No one would laugh at me again.

I thought about using the Polaroid, capturing her death face. But no, I knew there could be no evidence. I seared the image of her face into my brain. I would forever remember it and her scent.

After her legs ceased twitching her bladder fully unlocked. I disappeared behind a shelf to a hidden room were runaway slaves were kept until it was safe for them to use the tunnel to the crypt and continue North. It was so well hidden had I not found the exit the day Allen chased me, I would never have discovered it from the inside of the basement. The door was meant to fool expert slave hunters.

Tomorrow would tell if anyone else discovered the passage with modern forensic techniques.

IV

"IF YOU'RE AMONG us then they never found the passage," speculates a voice in the dark.

Everyone meeting in the low light encourages anonymity.

"They never searched for one. My sister and her friends were the focus of the investigation. As we know, ghosts don't exist. The girls had to have something to do with it."

"I read once the perfect crime was one in which all evidence points toward someone more likely to have committed the crime.

"Pin it on someone else. Someone close to the victim. They love ex-spouses and spouses for most murders."

"Did the cheerleaders do any time for what you did?" The kid asks.

Al interrupts, "The perfect crime is when no one even knows a crime has been committed because of the cleverness and skill of the criminal, not because it has been unsolved."

"No, this death was ruled a suicide. Accident by drunken party game. Death by misadventure according to the medical report. No further investigation. It did cause my sister and her followers—even Allen, to an extent—to be shunned by the school and much of the town. It would follow them the rest of their lives. It wasn't my desired goal, but it moved much of the abuse off me. A few—a selected few—felt Melony had been murdered, maybe accidentally, as part of a hazing joke gone bad, but no one wanted to taunt the brother of a possible killer. People do believe in ghosts."

The woman's voice asks, "Have you selected a name?"

"The newspapers have never called me anything like Al, but I chose Kenneth. The Hillside Strangler."

"There were two men," the kid protests.

"I didn't care for the name Angelo," Kenneth says.

"Kenneth is acceptable," the woman's voice maintains kindness.

Al wonders if it's part of her arsenal to lure her victims into trusting her. He would trust her. He does trust her, or he wouldn't be here in a room of confessed killers.

"I'm impressed you were willing to allow your sister to take the fall for you. Perfect crimes occur when someone is imprisoned for what you did."

Despite the rules, and having gone first, even Al finds the lack of names frustrating. The woman and the kid are identifiable, but the other three men are still nothing...but faceless...dark monsters.

"I must remind—we are not here to judge. We're no better than anyone else here since we have all voluntarily taken a life, and now we freely wish to remove ourselves from this path. I want us to trust each other enough to return for a second meeting," the woman adds.

"As much trouble as it was to locate this little group and jump through the hoops to be invited, I'm in for making this work. But I won't apologize either. I'm a sociopath. No empathy. I'm guessing so are the rest of us, or we wouldn't be able to kill so easily," maintains the strong voice in the dark.

"We're still on Kenneth's time, but you may go next."

"I'm not quite ready to share, but I will. I'm more interested in you, lady." The strong voice continues, "It's all grand Kenneth killed a girl in the basement of a *haunted* house. One killing doesn't bring a person to the level of this group."

"We were asked to speak about our first, or at least an early killing to determine why we became who we are," Kenneth says. "Melony was my first. Her death prevented Karen from becoming the prom queen. Hell, she didn't even attend prom or her graduation. It broke apart the cheerleader click. None of them escaped the town. No one wanted to marry them, either. My own sister couldn't get into any college, and so the funds my family had so prominently saved for her rolled over to me."

"I respect the educated killer."

"You might respect me more when I share my second kill," Kenneth adds.

"How did your sister end up?"

"Today, old cat lady, without cats, would be the best description. She stocks shelves at the local grocery store, at night, when the store is closed."

The woman interrupts. Her voice raises an octave to display she is the group facilitator. "You'll be able to share more next time. Everyone must have a turn if we are to gain the trust we need to heal ourselves." She glances at three unidentified men in the shadows, "Who is next?"

"I thought this was going to be helpful. I seem to have more ideas about seeking my next victim than how to stop myself."

"You agreed. No killing while we are in this group." This time the warmth slips from her voice.

"Then I'll explain my fascination with Death. I was seven the first time I killed."

His statement hangs in the air, not as impactful among natural killers.

He mutters to himself, "Grandfather's voice was so soft I had to strain my ear."

Then like a voice actor shifts to an old man's voice, "You don't shoot where the deer is, but where he will be when the bullet meets with his heart."

"The rifle was so heavy. My little arms couldn't hold it up to keep in balance long enough for me to line my sights on the beast." He raises his arms as if holding a rifle. He pulls the imaginary trigger, jerking back.

"I missed. The bullet struck into the ground a few feet in front of me."

The kid breaks in, "You missed a deer. Not the same as a person."

"You need to hold your tongue," the woman scolds.

"This will help you understand, like Kenneth's depantsing." He shifts his voice back into grandpa's, "You missed. When you miss—we don't eat."

"I couldn't hold up the rifle, my only defense."

"March back to the cabin. Move the wood pile from the west side of the house and stack it next to the entrance," Grandpa's voice ordered.

"He never beat me. I'm sure some saw child abuse in the manual labor I performed, but it strengthened my thin arms. Once I had the stamina to hold up the rifle—we never had a night without meat. Hunting was my life, but after a while hunting for dinner never fulfilled me. I lacked the ability to travel and hunt in darkest Africa. I found a better animal than a majestic elephant."

V

CHERRIES FLASHED, PROVIDING the only illumination on the black-tar road.

Any time after midnight people fill their shorts when those cherries pop in their rear view. They panic, most having no idea what they've done. They don't notice the silhouette of the vehicle, just the pulsating red light.

I shone my light through the window, catching the blonde woman struggling to get her panties back under her dress. I rapped on the glass. She jumped, unable to restore her underwear to its proper position. She reached for the switch, rolling down the fogged window.

"Hi…Officer."

"You okay, miss?" I shifted the flashlight beam to the eyes of the male next to her.

"Everything's fine, Officer," her face brightened, full ruby in the Maglite beam.

"You're a little bit older than the teens I normally find out here. You sure you're okay?" I shifted the light back into the face of the man.

"We're sorry, Officer. We'll move on," He raised his hand as if to swat at the light.

I jerked the flashlight back into her eyes, "How about your license and proof of insurance?"

"We're parked, Officer," the man protests. He had yet to do more than untuck his shirt.

"For some indecent fun. Not many come out here for legal acts."

She found her purse on the floorboard and fished out a plastic-coated index card.

I took her insurance card, glancing at the name while waiting for her to dig through her purse for a pocketbook.

"Gabriella?"

She jerked her head up, shocked he used her given name. "Gabby," she corrected.

I shone the light in the back seat, searching for any paraphernalia like a real cop would.

Gabby tugged at her license to get it from the plastic cover in the wallet. Once free, she poked it toward me.

I snatched it. Before marching back to my patrol car, I warned, "You two stay right here."

I pretended to run her information. Instead, I listened to their panicked words. Even the most innocent of people try and figure out just how they are guilty when a cop has pulled them over.

"We didn't do nothing," he said.

"He caught us with your hand in my cookie jar."

"We're not sixteen anymore. We're both consenting adults."

"Consenting adults use bedrooms," she snapped.

"Your husband doesn't like to share." He smiled.

Alarmed, he lost hold of his own bladder when I tapped on his window before opening the door.

"I need you to step out, son."

"What did I do, Officer?"

"Please step out, sir." I put my hand on the Glock to enforce I meant business. People are so trusting of cops when they are innocent of any wrongdoing.

"May I put on my jacket?" he asked.

"No. Keep your hands where I can see them."

The man followed me toward the patrol car, a mistake a real cop wouldn't make. They would stay behind the perp, but this dude was so scared he must concentrate on not losing the rest of his bladder.

It just proved he wasn't much of a man—he would have to do.

I turned.

Gabby adjusted the rearview mirror in time to spot her date slammed onto the trunk of her car and cuffed.

I dragged him toward the cop car. She lost sight of us in the halogen headlamps. I had installed extra lights and increased the wattage.

I returned to her door, "Please step out, Gabby."

"What did we do, Officer?" Before she got her second foot on the pavement, I grabbed her by the arm and drug her to the back of her car. I shoved her face down down on the trunk, my hands clamping around her neck—soft permeable skin.

"Spread your arms out." I kicked her ankles apart, off-balancing her physically.

The snap of a rubber glove on my fingers caused a hard swallow, cutting off her breath. Beads of sweat dripped down her forehead.

She'd never been patted down before, but from what she watched on television she knew my touching of her breasts was intrusive, with no reason to search her at all. Maybe no reason other than her maracas were heavy as pumpkins and could smuggle a lot in the cleavage. I pulled her left arm back, snapping the cuffs until they pinched her wrist. I dug my pelvis into her rump as I cuffed her right arm. My rough fingers tickled up the inner calf to her thigh. I pinched her. I cupped the bottom of her ass cheeks—squeezing ripe melons.

"Please. Don't," she implored, expecting an assault.

Mentally off-balance. "Shush." For a woman in her mid-thirties she had firm, muscular, dancer legs, just what I desire.

When she learned of what I planned to use her for she would wish I had raped her. Before it's over she might even beg to be penetrated if I spare her life.

The man thrashed around in the back of the patrol car in protest of me fondling his date what he was just enjoying.

I took her purse.

Gabby rises. She found courage when she comprehended this was no routine traffic stop, "What are you doing?"

I drug her back to my patrol car. The flashing cherries were police issued, but the car remains unmarked.

She struggled against my grip. "You're no cop."

I shoved her into the back seat, her moist skin sticking to the plastic seat covers. Tossing her purse onto the floorboard, I drew a gun from a plastic case I left open on the roof behind the lights. I slid what most people would mistake for a shuttlecock into the chamber. At this range the near fifty caliber projectile would bruise the subject. Now, what most people believe, thanks to Hollywood, is that sleep from a tranquil dart is instantaneous.

Not true.

Fact is, a dart should be calibrated to a person's weight. The wrong amount will kill. I set the dosage low for about a buck ten female. She was a little more. It would take her man bun-wearing date longer to pass out. Her too. No way with those tits was she anywhere near a hundred and ten.

The first shot punctured the man's stomach, screams permeating the night from both.

Gut shots hurt. He's lucky I didn't put one in his groin. I didn't want to impair him for what I wanted.

Gabby cried, "Please let us go!"

I must reload the gun. I swiped it from a vet truck. Again, tranquilizer guns are one shot.

I put the dart into the meatiest part of her hip as it had more adipose tissue than her stomach. She screamed a single, never-ending scream.

• • • • •

I whittle away at a birch branch, making arrows just as my grandfather taught me. No forensics lab will trace a manufacturer. They might determine a general forest area where this type of birch tree grows, but I've learned to take care not to soil my nest. Not to mention this was not my hunting cabin, I just assumed ownership.

Thanks to my use of homemade arrows, the newspapers labeled me The Bowhunter. I'm guessing Miss Gabby determined who I was when she woke to find a table covered in homemade arrows. I had national fame.

"Please, let us go," she begged, her words muffled by the bandanna tied around her mouth.

"I'm going to let you go." My well-honed hunting knife caused more screams as I shredded her dress from the crotch to the bottom hem. She would need full motion of her legs.

I slipped off one of her shoes. They had enough heel she would twist an ankle running in them—such tiny feet. I peeled off her white lacy ankle sock. She was being naughty-sexy for this loser. Fucker had said nothing in protest to protect her. At least he didn't beg for himself over her.

The bottom of her feet were so soft. Her toes were painted. I pinched each one. Not my fetish—a woman's feet should be soft—but she had cute toes. She could afford weekly pedicures. I love those kinds of women. They panic so much more. She struggled against my touching her in such a private manner. Despite her detesting the touch, I could tell she wished loser boy had caressed her feet.

So would the boy. He'd wish he'd done a lot of things.

She struggled as my touch tenderly attempted to relieve her anxiety of being a kidnap victim. She chewed at the bandanna gag, screaming at her boyfriend with her eyes to save them.

I slipped off the second shoe, "You see, darling—your lover—I'm going to let him keep his boots on. He'll run better in the snow."

Her face melted with confusion. I spotted in her eyes she wasn't sure I meant to release them, or where she was at. Her part of the state wasn't calling for snow. Maybe I was taunting her as I did when I touched her feet. I stuff her socks in each shoe before placing them on the burning log in the fireplace.

Flames melted the material into wisps of black smoke.

I went through his wallet and tossed credit cards and an unused condom into the flames. I snagged his identification before adding the cheap pleather to the flames. Her purse was full of the usual female junk. I cupped her driver's license in my hand next to his. They went in my front pocket, so I wouldn't lose them. Her bag burned.

It signaled to them the finality of their situation.

I flung open the front door.

The cold shivered them both.

Snow blew into the cabin.

"I hate for your lovely feet to contact the burning cold. If you head south..." I used the hunting knife to cut through her bonds. "Take a right off the porch, run the two miles to the highway. If you make it to the highway." He placed a metal object in her fingers, cupping her hand tightly, "Start your car and live."

I dragged her to the door. She had a mild shock, confused by the major change in the weather.

She glanced back at her boyfriend.

"Don't worry about him. I'll cut him free. He'll have his boots on. You'll have the key. Does he love you enough to help you to the car?" I shoved her into the snow. The torn dress offered no protection, exposing her legs to the bite of the ice crystals.

I cut the boyfriend's bonds, clicking back the hammer of the Glock, "Don't be a hero. You'll have until I reach my bow to run. If you make it to the car and drive away, you live."

I had the bow in my hand as he reached the door. I slung the quiver over my shoulder before flipping up my hood. I hated the snow on my freshly shaved neck.

Yeah, I do clear excess hair. DNA has impaired my hunting.

Gabby must have had the willpower to ignore the stinging pain of the mid-calf deep snow. Her brawny calves tasted every bit of the cold. Fear carried her to the tree line or she didn't love the boy. She didn't glance back. Her athletic legs propelled her to the edge of my range to effectively hit a target where I wanted.

I notched an arrow.

The boyfriend caught up with her.

I drew my bow.

The arrow zipped between the couple.

The whistle of my warning shot caused Gabby to stumble into the snow.

The boyfriend, at least, cared enough about her or maybe he just wanted the car key. He scooped his arms under her pits, lifting her into the air. She may have been shapely, but she's heavier than he had strength to lift easily.

The struggle slowed them.

I drew the bow. "Don't make it so easy!" I waited. Before they left the light of the cabin, I noted her reddening feet. She wouldn't make it to the car at full sprint.

I loosed the second arrow. It sank into the boyfriend's shoulder. He sprawled into a snowbank. The arrow shaft sealed the hole, so little blood dribbled out.

She tugged at his arm. "Get up, motherfucker! I'm not going to die out here!"

I took a few more paces. I didn't want to lessen the distance. Killing them then would have destroyed the challenge—the hunt.

Gabby needed a reminder her life was more important than his, and she was destroying her beautiful toes in the snow while she stood there tugging on him.

My next arrow cut open her arm. She tumbled back into the snow when the pain forced her to release the boyfriend. Blood spurted from the gash torn across her bicep.

Just a reminder.

Adrenaline kicked in. She dashed in the direction I said her car was in. I couldn't slow my pace any longer. If I reached the boy, I'd just end him. So much for him being a challenge. I thought he'd do anything to protect her.

He forced himself up and I let him, only to put an arrow through his calf. Now he crawled away, trailing a steady line of blood drops mushrooming as they hit the snow. I might have let him run a bit had he shown any stones to help the woman. The next arrow severed his spine between the fifth and sixth Thoracic bone. He might live, but he'd never use his legs again.

I reach a man in tears. Snow, blood and snot covered his red face. I considered scalping him. I put my boot between his shoulder blades and reached for the arrow. I jerked the shaft from his shoulder. The wound bled. If it tore anything vital he might have bled out before I returned.

Playing with the boyfriend gave her a chance to improve her escape. She found the road, more a deer path to the cabin, cleared with mashed snow from the tires of the car. I had to drive them up here. Even barefoot the impacted snow would allow her to gain speed. I strolled from the boyfriend knowing he was minutes from death.

At the mile point, I realized she found her legs. I picked up speed. Snow boots weren't meant to race in. She sprinted at full tilt and there was enough snow to keep her feet from the painful gravel. Fear helped her ignore the cold.

Even in the dark the moonlight reflected off the car. Whatever part of her thought I might be lying about escape now filled with hope. Even if her brain should wonder if I had sabotaged the engine.

I loosed another arrow.

I missed.

She shifted her gait into a zig-zag pattern. Something besides her lizard brain pushed her.

Gabby reached the car. I was shocked. Many never made it to their car. They just didn't have the physical stamina. She fumbled the key into the snow drift blown against the car door. Forced to kneel, the cold finally stiffened her joints once she ceased her sprint. She raked her fingers through the drift, slinging snow, having lost sensation in her frozen fingers.

She scooped the key in her quaking palm unable to make her fingers grip the metal.

It had keyless entry like on the fancy luxury cars, but I kept the fob.

She did make it to the car, but wasn't inside. I respected this woman. She was stronger than any other I tested. Rules are rules. I put an arrow in her thigh. Again, little blood. She must have been so cold she didn't notice the puncture. Fear pumping adrenaline allowed her to ignore the stick as she jammed the key in the lock.

The next arrow penetrated her lower abdomen, sinking to the shaft's halfway point. It slowed her.

She fell inside the car.

I took aim. I lowered the tip so as not to perforate her neck, instead. putting it in her shoulder. I thought she earned the privilege to escape, unlike lover boy.

VI

"YOU HUNTED THEM like that *Most Dangerous Game* story I had to read in school," the kid says.

"What—yesterday? You're a dumb kid. I'm not imaginary. I kill for real. Call me Robert. But I'm better than him. I won't get caught."

"There are several killers named Bob," the kid says.

"Robert. Robert Hanson. He was different than most. He'd fly people into the Alaskan wilderness and drop them off into the forest to hunt them."

"Careful, kid, I think he means to hunt you if you insult him again," Kenneth warns. "You let your prey live in your story. It could lead to your capture."

"I don't hunt in just one area. And Miss Gabby lived, unable to give a proper description of her assailant. She was too traumatized after multiple surgeries to remember much. And I kept her driver's license. I could find her anytime I wanted, but I wouldn't. If I did that the game had no sport."

"The police said she didn't identify you," the kid points out. "It could be a ruse to draw you out."

"I don't agree. Cops will keep information sequestered, but not an identification. They want someone to report spotting a red truck or a man with a tattoo, even a face with a mole. She doesn't remember what he looked like or it would have been on the news," Al says.

"You seem to think you know a lot about how cops think, kid," Robert says. "You're young too—clean cut—you a cop, kid?"

"What's your story kid?" Al demands. "You're just old enough to be out of the academy and might jump at a chance to work undercover over traffic stops."

"It's your turn to share with the group if we are to build trust," Kenneth says.

"Everyone remain calm," the woman keeps her loving nurse voice. "The Internet security measures I enacted might be traceable, but the actual chat room conversations are not. I stole a page on how to use the deep web from ISIS."

"After I hear the kid's story, I think we'll know if he's killed or not," Robert says.

"I'm not a cop," the kid says.

"Prove it. Tell us about your murders."

"I'm not as adept as some of you. I haven't even developed my MO, but I know—and after hearing what I've heard today—I don't want to be like the rest of you. I'm here to stop any more deaths..." His pause could cost him, "at my hands."

"We all want to stop," Al says. "Something mental compels us to do what we do. If I could cut it from my brain to prevent me strangling another innocent girl, I would. People are disgusted or don't understand how anyone could do such things. I wonder myself. Something's wrong with me, but how do I ask for help? Anywhere I go for treatment places me in prison with no assistance to recover. Tell us your tale, Kid. If this group does nothing else, maybe we'll find solace in saving one life."

"Fine," the kid blurts more like a three-year-old.

VII

SHE DIDN'T EVEN know I was alive.

I tried to speak to her. The one time I attempted—I was nothing—a tongue tied mess.

How does anyone speak to a girl so pretty? Her hair bounced around her shoulders when she moved, and she had this bronze skin. Those chest balloons always popped out the top of her buttoned-up shirts.

She had worn such garments on purpose.

Never did a mean word come out of her mouth. Even when she was angry she never berated anyone. Kind words for all. She was a dream. Maybe she was. Maybe I saw her different than she was because I desired her.

I spied on her all my freshman year. Amylyn hadn't developed any curves then. It was never about her breasts. I thought if I could just see her topless then I could die happy. But she just was so nice. She would say hello. One day in science class she spotted a *Dungeon's Masters Guide* hidden among my notebooks.

"You shouldn't read those books, you'll get possessed."

She lacked judgment. It was one-hundred percent concern for my wellbeing.

Amylyn didn't understand. There had been some news stories, but she cared. She had started her warning with my name. I bet half of science class didn't know my name. She cared about me. No one ever cared about me.

I studied her from afar. I couldn't speak to her, and she thought I was some devil worshiper because I gamed. Nerds were frowned upon then—bullied mercilessly. Targets for the jocks. At least they still were in my school.

• • • • •

It wasn't the impact on the locker that bruised me, it was the combination lock handle.

Chaz drove his palm into my shoulder, pinning it against the molded vent. I couldn't wriggle free. He maxed out at three-hundred on bench and was every bit the linebacker with enough sports medals to have single-handedly taken Iwo Jima.

"Listen, worm, I saw you staring at her tits again. I warned you. They are round and firm and…" he raised his palm to my face to illustrate size, "when free don't fit in my hand. You're never, never going to get to touch a titty."

"Not what your mom said." Nothing could take back the remark before he broke my nose. It might have been worth it, but the varsity star didn't even get a lunch detention.

He had to go.

Too many sacks to the head or just a natural brutish male, I knew in the end he would be a wife beater and Amylyn would never leave him. She'd wear long sleeve blouses and be a klutzy girl who bumped into tables. No, I had to protect her.

No matter what, I had to stop Chaz—even if I never got to be with her.

I put a lot of thought into how I could protect her.

Most of the town's recent housing developments were planted in wooded areas outside the city limits. In fact, never were there so many tree names. Woodland. Oak Tree Acres. Whispering Pines. Maple Valley. It was crazy. It made people forget they lived next a city. The forest provided cover. At some point, I never understood why some burglar didn't figure out he had backdoor access to half the town in these residential areas. But I guess it's hard to carry a plasma TV through the thicket.

Amylyn had a perfect body. I'd snooped on her while she swam. She had this…ritual…before she dove into the water; she'd twist and tug at her stomach as if she had a paunch. She didn't, but her esteem must have told her she was fat, or Chaz told her she was. She'd swim so many laps.

Chaz wasn't the macho stud he'd bragged about in the locker room. Amylyn would barely kiss him when he'd visit. She'd never close the pink fluffy drapes of her bedroom. Why would she when only the trees beheld her? Chaz would watch her swim only dangling his hairy legs in the water. I didn't understand what she saw in him. They shared nothing in common.

She did stroke him off once. Just a hand job, and she remained fully clothed. She didn't want to, but he pressured her. It was funny. Not the masturbation, but how Chaz was as close to nowhere with her as I was. He only got to fondle her breasts on the top of her shirt.

Not that I observed her 24/7, but when I did witness them together—alone—they had no chemistry.

The problem was Amylyn was also an athlete. She had the most powerful serve ever in volleyball. And, because of this, she was expected to date a jock. I don't know who made this rule and why it's enforced—it ruins lives.

After spending my afternoons in the trees before my own parents got home, I learned none of the neighbors paid any attention to what occurred in their back yards either. They cared only for their manicured front lawns, ignoring the forest butting the property line. I built a nest to scrutinize Amylyn's window.

My mother was happy I attended school functions. Mostly I appeared at the games Amylyn played. When she wasn't on the court, I attended other games, too. While she sat in the stands witnessing Chaz smash into people, I observed her. Mom never knew I would spend some of my time at Amylyn's window. Even on nights she wasn't home, I'd wait—just in case. When she was gone I cured my boredom learning other homes weren't out of view of cheap dime store binoculars.

Two houses down I spotted a kid who kept a twenty-two-rifle hidden in his closet. He didn't want his mother to find it, nothing too abnormal about it. He had an older sister, and she was clearly of high school age, but didn't attend mine. There may have been a few hundred in my grade but I would have remembered if I had passed her in the hall. She could go to one of the three religious schools in our town, but I never saw her in her uniform to confirm my theory. She spent most of her time in her room strutting around nude as if defying the Lord.

Never did she even once move my cock. I loved Amylyn. She was the only woman I desired. I needed Amylyn to notice me.

I would watch the girl sometimes only when Amylyn wasn't home.

The night came when there was commotion from the other girl's home, enough racket some neighbor should have called the cops, noise enough I shifted my binoculars off Amylyn.

The father left a crying mother on the living room floor with a bleeding lip. She blubbered as he marched up the stairs.

He broke open the daughter's door. I knew she protested from her movement. I knew she screamed at him to leave. She even tossed stuffed animals at him, but I didn't hear the words. Surprisingly, I knew what was going on from their actions. He ordered her to turn over, tossing a leather-bound book from her night stand at her face.

She opened the super thin pages—a Bible, the golden cross emblazoned on the cover. I thought she attended a religious school.

He drew his belt through all the loops in one whip-snap. She was too old for a spanking.

He whaled on her backside, mostly striking her ass. Tears filled her eyes as she reads from the Book. If she stopped reading, he whapped her arm with the belt. I didn't know how she would move her legs from the beating.

The mom just cried downstairs. She did nothing to protect her child.

I lost count of the thrashes.

Mom's trembling fingers fumbled with each button as she unbuttoned her dress. Allowing it to drop on the floor, she never exposed her naked back in my direction. Whelp scars wrapped around her ribs. She took the stairs with baby steps.

Upon entering the bedroom, he flung the mom down next to the daughter. The flogging ceased and he undid his pants. His assault on his own daughter was brutal, then he violently fucked the mom. During the whole fucking, the daughter never stopped reading aloud biblical passages.

It left me sick. My stomach burned. My bowls tightened. I thought I might soil myself.

Never aroused by what I saw, I was angered. It was necessary to protect this new girl like I was compelled to protect Amylyn. Why did these men have to be so cruel? This girl did nothing to earn permanent scars.

I knew what I had to do.

I would protect Amylyn.

To prove myself, I would defend this unknown girl.

The mother was rarely home. Sunday, however, they all attended religious services. I had my window. The younger brother wouldn't report the missing twenty-two. I wondered if he got it to protect his mom and sister. His room was always dark during the assaults.

I cut the screen on a downstairs window, just a slit to allow me to slip the lock with a metal wire hanger. Once inside, I raced up the stairs. I entered the boy's closet. It took a bit to find it. He hid it behind a ceiling slat. Then I discovered why he had yet to use it to save his sister. He had no ammo.

I would have to find some, and fast. A good beating was overdue. The dad seemed to like to let the women heal just enough then go at them again. Always after church, he had to cleanse them of their sins.

Then the night came and I knew what I must do.

I changed trees for a better angle. Only these branches creaked as if ready to crack under my weight.

I aimed the rifle.

I had shot pellet guns before but nothing like this. It cramped my arms to hold it so long pointed at the house.

The ritual always began with the striking of the mother.

Tonight, his anger supercharged, he flung her onto the couch. The mom didn't move as he trudged upstairs. Normally, mom undressed. He hit her so hard she never moved.

The daughter's beating ended and with no mother in the hall, she kept reading from the Bible.

The dad marched into the hall, screaming downstairs. He spun back toward his daughter. Before he takes a step into the room I jerked the trigger.

I missed.

Other than the cracking glass, I doubt he realized what had just happened.

My heart was beating in my throat, sweat beading along my hair-line. My palms also marred the rifle with moisture.

I fired again, but the center of his chest didn't explode. I thought it would be like the movies. I fired again. This time red blossomed near his navel. Not much blood. I thought it would waterfall like in a Tarantino movie.

I'm not sure he felt it.

I needed to breathe slower.

Still naked, the abused daughter actually jumped, concerned about her father. She was worried about him. He had been ass raping her. I saved her from another evening of sodomy and she was concerned about him. I'm not sure if he hit her or threw her to the ground to protect her, but once she was behind the bed, I emptied the gun. Bullets tore apart the window remains. I don't know how many hit him.

As I climbed down, the branch snapped. I landed on the rifle. The smoking barrel burned my side. I had the wind knocked from me. I had to get up. The shots would surely cause some neighbor to call the cops this time.

My heart raced. So did I. I would have to dispose of the rifle.

VIII

"NOT MUCH OF a story, kid," Robert says.

"What he did doesn't make him a serial killer. Hell, some police departments might hang a medal on him," Al says.

"I wanted to know if he shot Chaz," Kenneth says.

The delicate tone of the woman interjects, "One story per meeting. Unless we reach a breakthrough, and we don't have the trust for such a display yet. It's not the number of kills. It's the desire. The need. Killing fills a hole inside us. We're here to plug that hole. Al, you should be asking if the father survived."

"I doubt this kid's taken a life." The older, unnamed man demands, "Did this bastard father die?"

"No, I barely got the gun tossed in the lake. I forgot to wipe off my prints," the kid admits.

"Dumb ass kid. I bet your fingerprints were all over the brass. Did you police up the casings?" Robert scolds.

"I'm not perfect. I didn't have some elaborate hunting plan. I wanted to stop the fucker from raping and beating his daughter." The kid rises from his chair, his testosterone in overdrive.

"Sit down, kid. I doubt you'd take him," Al says.

"How would this impress Amylyn? She couldn't know you shot this father to protect a stranger."

"If he killed once, he could get better with Chaz."

"Building trust is not easy for us, not with what we've done, but we don't need to criticize our techniques," the woman says. "This is about healing, not making him a better killer."

"I don't want his mistakes leading the cops to us. He's fresh out of high school as is. If he's captured he'd spill to avoid prison."

"I would not," the kid protests. "Any of you would."

"No. They wouldn't take me alive. I won't end up beaten to death in prison like Jeffrey Dahmer," Robert says.

"Don't eat your victims and you'll be fine," Al says.

"Cages are for animals. They won't get me," Robert says. "But I don't want it to come down to a gunfight. I want help."

"We are here to help. We might be the only people who are able to help each other," she says.

"I was in college," the kid pops up, "a criminal justice major. I was studying how cops think so I don't get caught. But I don't want to kill—not after the last time."

"Remorse is a good thing. It means you are reformable," Al says.

"We've all screwed up a killing—only we didn't have remorse about it enough to want to stop," She asks, "What is your nom de plume?"

"Hello, I'm...I'm Dexter."

Protesting grunts emanate from the dark. "You can't call yourself Dexter, he's a made up serial killer."

"Sounds about right for this kid," Robert says. "We know he didn't successfully kill the father."

"Dexter is rather amateurish. Some of us may have taken inspiration from other killers, but they were real, not some phony Hollywood imagination. The man would be caught after one kill attempting to dispose of all the plastic or raise suspicion buying so much so often."

"Fine. I'll chose a more appropriate moniker," with a long, drawn out breath he snaps, "Jesse."

"You're no gunman."

"Not James. Jesse Pomeroy. In the 1870s, in South Boston, Jesse mutilated several young boys and girls," he explains.

"It's better than Dexter."

"I did save the girl," Jesse says. "My actions revealed all the father was doing to all three of them."

Convinced, Robert says, "You failed to kill the father."

"I put five bullets in him."

"And he lived?" Al asked.

It takes Jesse a painful second before he answers, "Yeah, the neighbors did report the shots. EMS arrived and got him to the hospital in time, but the girl was found naked putting pressure on his stomach wound. The arriving officers saw her fresh whip marks, found the unconscious mother and her bruises."

"They removed the girl?" The woman asks.

"I'm not sure what happened, but the dad was arrested. For a time, they thought the daughter defended herself against him, but the broken window and bullet trajectory proved they came from outside. The little brother was cleared as well. He only had the rifle I stole and no evidence of ever having a weapon. I didn't police the brass, but I never held the rounds bare-handed. I had no way of learning what they did with the daughter. They didn't attend my school and they were part of one of those cult churches. I saved a newspaper clipping where they sentenced the father to twenty years. His wife pleaded with the judge at the hearing not to take him away."

"Burn it," the woman snaps. "Burn anything you saved from the crime."

"Not entirely his fault the bastard breathes," the older man says.

"He had intent. It might lead back to him," she adds.

"You going to allow him to call himself Jesse?"

"What is it that bothers you about his name choice?"

Robert throws his hands up, "Fine. Let him keep it. He's not much of a killer. Sounds like he fits with made up killers anyway. What's your story, lady?"

"I'll take my turn now. People should never be afraid to do what they ask of those they lead," she says.

IX

"IF I COULD just stay away from him, Miss Jane, I know I could make my life better," Lindsey pleaded.

I inspect the girl's arm—fresh track marks. Twenty-three and forever committed to the dragon.

"I have to report this violation, Lindsey."

"Please, no, Miss Jane. If you do, they'll put me back inside." Before the drugs her face would hold an innocent expression impossible to refuse. Now plagued with age lines, her begging incites no sympathy. "You don't know what's it like in there, what they make weak girls like me do."

"If I don't report you I'll be the one in trouble," I said.

"Please, no. I'll do anything you want."

It wasn't her pleading that convinced me to pardon her. She wasn't a bad kid. I had read her file and the boyfriend most likely used her to transport his drugs. He rewarded her with needle trips. She might have been able to turn it around if he would've stopped interfering in her life. To this day I don't understand why these women keep going back to the men that abuse them.

"This halfway house is all about second chances, but if they suspect you used or even spoke to this man again, I'll put the cuffs on you myself. You'll do the full stint of your time and no more chances for parole."

"Yes, Miss Jane."

I turned a notepad around on the desk around and put a pen in her trembling fingers.

"His address."

"No, Miss Jane. He'll kill me."

I picked up the landline phone punching in three numbers.

"Who are you calling?"

"His address before I finish dialing or you're back inside before I hang up on the officer."

Lindsey scrawled numbers and a street name down.

"Are you going to report him?"

"No." I hung up the phone. "But if I don't know where you are, I send the police there. Now you take a shower, go to bed and tomorrow you find a job. You don't find a job and it's out of my control. You go back in."

"I'll get a job. I promise."

"And?" I demanded.

"I won't see him no more."

Every few weeks I received a poor girl like Lindsey. Their stories were all the same. They were usually pretty girls with no self-esteem who got mixed up with a man who used them to transport drugs or punching bags. Some would sell them for sex. Most were all three. People think these girls are of low IQ, but many were smart. Some had earned scholarships to college, but not full rides so they didn't go.

Dumb as a post, little Jimmy got to attend university because daddy donated enough money to build a practice stadium. He won't contribute to society beyond a reality televised show about his drinking on a beach, while girls like Lindsey who have—had a brain—are tossed by the wayside because she came from a trailer park. Given the chance—should—would have changed the world for the better, even if it was just obtaining a degree and never having to rely on the system to support her. Now the system owns her.

Yes, I have a soap box—angry feminist kills!

I followed a detour to my apartment. There was a room for me to sleep at the halfway house in case I had to stay late or deal with an issue, but it had a night watch woman. I made sure the night staff was a woman. Some of these girls would convince a weak man with their bodies to do whatever they wanted. It was not a man's fault, he is designed to do whatever to get a pair of tits. It's why women have them.

Women have them to attract men. All other creatures only have breasts when it comes time to nurse. Not human women. We've got to deal with them being in the way twenty-four/seven. And they do so get in the way. Hell, when I was younger they would arrive five minutes before me. Now, give me some tassels and I'll sweep the floor with them.

No, I'm not angry about my sagging boobs. Sexual urges were a part of the human condition—one I lacked.

My side trip was to the address Lindsey wrote down. I didn't trust her. I half expected it to be a corner market. If it was I still had her pee in an unlabeled cup. Write her name on it and she twelve-twelves. Only I wanted to give her a shot no one else had ever given her before. I wanted to change the world. Or change her.

I was a bold bitch. I had heard it more than once. Why not? Middle-aged white woman decently dressed in a crime infested neighborhood. I exploded on everyone's radar and yet even the lowest street urchin never bothered to beg me for spare change. None of them even bothered to notice my latex gloves.

I marched right up to the boyfriend's door and pushed my way past the doorman—stupid lookout who answered it.

Amid their protests, I spotted only three men. I drew a pistol. I put the lookout down first. The other two drew guns. I had the drop on them. I shot the one from the kitchen next, betting he wasn't the boyfriend.

The third. Now he appeared the type I'd bet got Lindsey hot—total cartwheeling douse-goblin swinging a massive dick.

I didn't allow him time to consider why a middle-aged white woman was in his crib. I put two in his chest before words of protest fall from his mouth.

He chokes on his own blood. I slipped the Berretta from his waistband. The door punk had a gun too. I dropped both in my purse, nice clean guns for my next performance. And there would be one. Girls like Lindsey are a revolving door through the halfway house. I put one more round in the third man before tossing the gun on the floor.

I strolled down the street as normal as possible. No rush. Gun shots were rarely reported in this neighborhood and equally slow to be responded to when they did. White people all appear the same anyway.

I did avoid the cameras at the intersection—just in case. But I was in no fear of being discovered.

I lost any fear I had a long time ago especially when I graduated to guns. I always slept better after a cleansing.

• • • • •

Lindsey burst into my office the next morning. Now, how she learned of this so fast I'm not sure. I made a mental note to toss her room for a burner phone. Bet her boyfriend gave her one.

"Miss Jane. Someone shot up Tree-dog's house."

"Is he alright?" Someone shooting up your boyfriend's home should be reason to find a new boyfriend, but these girls never seem to *think* so.

"He wasn't home."

Damn.

"I'm glad he is alright. Was anyone else hurt?"

Damn. Damn. Damn.

"Three of his buddies were shot dead."

"Over drugs?" I was finished placating her. She was about to be last on a short list of people I helped.

Lindsey dropped her head in submission. She knew if she lied what I would do, or what she thought I would do, but she didn't want to rat out her man.

After she thought about her answer, "I'm sure they will say it was. That whole neighborhood has a gang problem."

"You have to stay away from there." This would be her test.

"I'm going to find a job today."

"Good. It will keep your mind busy and your body out of trouble."

I don't like not killing my target. I doubt I get another shot at this Tree-dog, not for a long time. Unfortunately for Lindsey, it means if she screws up I will have no forgiveness for her.

None.

"The diner down the street called to check Lindsey's reference. He gets a lot of business from the halfway house when the girls have jobs. Some nights I order as a reward after curfew. He needed a night waitress. I said I would file the motion to allow Lindsey a night job if he wanted her.

He thought she would work out and overnight the till had less money for an employee to steal. He liked that she was upfront about her living arrangements, and her reason for being incarcerated.

I would allow it.

Two weeks. Lindsey was a model parolee and then the honeymoon was over. She left work halfway through her shift, claiming her cramps were too bad to work. Men always fell for *my cramps are terrible today.*

She wouldn't be at Tree-dog's place, it might still have police tape on the door. Cops were looking at a gang hit since there were so many thousands in drugs left in the house.

I thought about it. Why wouldn't they go there? It would be private. Perfect. Cheap, unlike the no-tell motels. I would swing by. If no one was there I would deal with Lindsey when she came back. I hated to do it at the halfway house. Lots of paroled women failed there, but too many in the house caused investigations and oversight. I understood how too many in one location raised red flags. It was what brought an end to my first career. I'd rather do it outside my required duty station.

Damn.

There was a light on upstairs.

I found Lindsey only in her panties. She was alone. High. Tree-dog left her here after he gave her dope and his seed.

She was loopy, just lying in the bed floppily waving her right hand toward me.

I prepared another dose.

"Miss Jane," she had the giggles, "You know how to do drugs?"

She was in her own humor-filled world, but I felt compelled to explain myself to her. "Before I was your den mother I was an RN."

"You should still be a nurse. You're so nice." She slurred most of her words now.

"I would be, but the administrators felt too many terminally ill people were dying too soon on my shifts. If a dying person clung to life for weeks or months, the hospital made money. If they died it was over. No more medical bills." I prepared a dose of the *medication*.

"But they were dying," Lindsey floated into confusion.

"They were. I ended their pain. In the end they thanked me, but too many died, and someone questioned why it was on my shift."

"You wouldn't never kill anyone, Miss Jane."

I thumped her arm, searching for a useable vein. I didn't want to use her thighs. She reeked of jizz.

"My selections, at first, were simple and easy." I inserted the needle. "I tired so of wasting resources on those no longer productive in society. Do you know how many millions are tossed away on people who will never wake from comas?"

"I'm not in a coma?"

"No, but you've proven you aren't willing to be productive. I've no use for those who don't contribute." I depressed the plunger. To cement it was her doing I left the needle in her arm.

She would overdose and die in bliss, better than many of those in the hospital. They died still in pain.

I had reached the door when Tree-dog returned. I hated to spend one of the two weapons I had taken days before, but I was left with little option. Three in the chest caused him to stumble back and tumble down the front stairs backward right into public. I dropped the gun and just strolled down the street. This time I did hear sirens.

X

"HOW MANY HAVE you killed?" Jesse asks.

"They would have all died." Robert, smug in his assumption.

"You played God," the older man says.

"Don't we all?" Jane asks.

"You told the story as your avatar?" Al inquires.

"Yes. I choose Jane Toppan," she explains, "I play two roles here. One as mediator, the other as attendee. I want help, but I want to help."

"She was a nurse," Jesse says.

"She experimented on her patients during her training. She would bring her patients to near death states and revive them before killing them."

"You ended lives."

"I didn't take a sexual thrill in it, or get off on being the only person who knew how to save a patient's life at the last second. Because I secretly poisoned them, like most Angels of Death. I just eased them to the other side. Families are so selfish. They watch their mother live in pain just so she would be there for them because they can't let go. I did what was right and what benefits society. I had no sexual drive during what I did."

"Then why start this group? Why end what you are doing? If it is beautiful?" The older man questions.

"My last few killings did stir a strong sexual awakening. It never happened before. It's not right. I was never about pleasure. It was time to stop when murder left me wet," she admits.

"We all agree with you or we wouldn't be here. We would not risk the exposure attending such a meeting and admitting what we did, but stopping won't be easy."

"No, not even for me," the older man admits.

"Then you should go next," Jane says.

"Our other member has spoken nary a word. I want to know about him, what brought him here," the older man says.

The quiet man steps into the light enough to expose flaming red hair, "I've been contemplating how best to cook all your hearts."

XI

EVERY TOWN HAS its sex workers though regular people don't like to admit it. You don't even have to spend much time to find one. Even the family-oriented travel truck stops naturally have lot lizards, but a local bar will have some women willing to blow you for a few Jacksons.

Over my seventeen years as an over the road truck driver I have crisscrossed the country a few thousand times. No one cares for these women. I never tried a man, but they can be found too. Cops never check into druggy whores and barely do so if they have a family. Most bodies are Jane Does. Before the Internet linked many police databases, I would take one into the next county or a few counties over and with police always arguing over their jurisdictions. I mean short of them whipping out their dick to mark their territory with piss, they cared more about who was to take the hit on the unsolved murder than who killed the poor girl.

I got more pleasure from dumping the dead girl to screw with certain areas' murder rate numbers.

I fuck'n hate cops.

My first time I had been away from the wife for a few weeks hauling a load across country and back. Truck stop bathrooms were never clean enough to pump one out and I hated standing when I did, so the showers were out. I wanted to relax. I thought I'd get one of these honeys hanging around to blow me. It was safer than sex with one and getting head isn't cheating on your wife. Hell. If she won't suck it how can it be wrong to let someone else do it?

I brought one into my cab, squeezed a little boob through her sleazy dress and undid my pants.

She sucked really good. I came fast.

It was worth the money, but I wish I had lasted longer.

"My turn," she said.

"What do you mean?" I was confused. I mean, I'd pay her. Might pay her to hang around so she could do it again.

But instead she hikes up her skirt and whips out a dick tucked between her legs.

"What the fuck? You're a dude!" Those budding tits felt real.

"I take hormones, makes them grow." She juggled them in each hand. "But I know what you truckers like."

The hell I do. Pussy only for me. Never even thought about a dude.

"You're away from the wife," he pointed to my ring finger, "and like a little tube steak." She tugged at her foreskin stretching the straw to a length of three inches.

It was little, but it didn't matter. My dander was up. I was humiliated. Fucker. I ain't no fag.

"You want to suck it or just play with it when you slide it in from behind, Big Daddy?"

When the shock wore off I busted him in the face.

"Daddy likes it rough." He/she/it touched the blood dripping from its lip.

"Be rough. I like rough, but not the face, okay?" She touched my bicep. "Is this your first time?"

It was difficult to maneuver with my pants undone, but my anger moved me.

I punched and hit the fucker. She/he clawed at me. I'd have to take another load across country giving the cuts a chance to heal before I went home to my wife. I doubted I'd be able to explain them to her. She was a money whore anyway, loved not working and the extra cash I brought in.

I pounded the fucker.

My dick got hard.

I hit him more.

Real hard.

The cab rocked from the struggle, but any trucker strolling by would figure it was sex.

I don't think I'd ever been so stiff and standing straight up as I turned this dude's face into mush.

He was dead. I was left to fend for myself so I did. I stroked for an hour. Man, I had no idea the rush. It was better than the coke I snorted sometimes to stay awake.

If it hadn't been a man I might of—well—the bottom hole was still good.

I left the truck stop after I cleaned myself up. I dumped the body in a roadside rest stop. DNA wasn't as big a deal then. I cleaned the cab. Not as well as I would later when DNA became a thing.

It was a thrill. Man, I wished I had a woman to pump after I beat that Fag. I might have lasted for days.

XII

"I JUST WANTED to get your attention. I don't eat people. But I will be called Ed."

"Gein?" Jesse asks.

"He inspired more movies about serial killers than any other, except maybe Jack," adds the trucker.

"Ed is acceptable," Jane says.

"He did eat people," Jesse points out.

"Well, I never fucking ate anyone beyond licking pussy." Ed raises his voice, "You're such a shit, kid."

"I'm not a homophobe," Jesse says.

"It ain't homo-what's-it if I don't want a fucking dude to grope me. I don't know we must accept those people. It's not normal. If you're born with a dick, then you are a man. If anything, I should be chastised because I beat to death the mentally ill."

"That's the pot calling the kettle black. We are all mentally ill or we wouldn't enjoy killing people," Kenneth says.

"I'm just saying if you cut on yourself with a razor blade or a compact disk they lock you in a mental ward. Pump up the Thorazine. But you go to a doctor and ask for your pecker to be lopped off and they go *oh that's fucking normal*."

"Enjoying it is why I'm here," The old man shifts the conversation. "When I found I enjoyed it, it was time to stop."

"We'll get to you, old man," Ed says.

"Stop a minute. What do you mean mentally ill?" Al asks.

"I know everyone sees a dumb redneck truck driver, and you all figure I'm a bigot. Hell no. Some of the best blow jobs I've gotten are from black women. Hell, I'll kill a black girl, white girl, Hispanic, all the same to me."

"Asians?"

"Not many of those in the parts I drive. And they become coveted. Like a cupid doll from the ring toss at the county fair. Many a trucker would like to brag they nailed a dog-eater. Someone might miss a rice-cooker since they are so rare. But I wouldn't mind bagging and tagging one. It would make me rather worldly. Get me one of those Antarctica women and I'll have about got one from every continent."

Jesse opens his mouth and Jane waves him to shut it.

"I figure it's like this. Sure, those people are born gay cause they are mentally ill. You must treat them. Cure them. You are born with a wang then you are designed to like pussy. It's how we propagate the species. Cause if they are born a woman in a man's body then why is what we do wrong? I was born to enjoy killing. If they were men born to want to suck dick, it's the same damn thing. Nothing wrong with me."

"You want us to buy being born gay is the same as being born a serial killer?" Kenneth asks.

"Damn right. We were born to hunt our food. With the need to track and capture our prey removed we must compensate for it. I am never more at peace than when I hunt. A thinking person makes it a challenge," Robert says.

"More research needs to be funneled into human mental health, but being man and liking men is not a threat to society—not like what we do," Al says.

"There are scientific theories, most border on the conspiracy line, but humans were originally genetically designed for certain tasks. I've read about the warrior gene idea," Jesse says.

"I'd bet we all have it. And without a war to contain our urges we lose control."

"I would too, and perhaps because we are not in a warrior cast and being warriors, we're left to proceed the only way possible, by acts of murder," Jesse says.

"So we do need mental help?" Kenneth ponders, "or gene therapy?"

"Your saying it's aliens that made us like killing people?" Robert laughs.

"Whoever, but we may be predisposed to be killers and have never been trained on how to properly deal with it," Jesse says.

"The kid's smart, but I was never a warrior. Not until the accident," the old man says.

"Are you going to tell us about it?"

"Once our non-bigoted truck driving friend confirms his name choice. Or do you have more to your first killing to share?"

"Nope, call me Ed. Even if I never ate someone I admire his gumption. He, like me, was just a good ole boy. Never meant no harm."

"We all mean harm. I started down this path with nothing but reasons to harm," the old man says. "Call me Jack."

XIII

MORE TUBES ARE connected to Nina's little body than I thought a living person could possibly accept. Did it make me a horrible person thinking her surviving the car accident wasn't the miracle everyone else bestowed upon the comatose child? Thirteen—possibly brain dead, lacks the finality the rest of my family has now. To bury them…

I've cried enough. Grieve too long and no healing occurs.

"Jack," the nurse startled me, as she touched my shoulder. "You've been here five straight days. You should go home, shower, eat some food besides the garbage they serve in the cafeteria. I'll call you if anything changes."

"Would you go home if your only surviving grandchild was in a coma?" I asked.

"I doubt I would leave her side. But I also know you do her no good if we must put you in a bed down the hall because you don't take care of yourself. It would be just for a few hours. A shower will rejuvenate you. You have to stay healthy for her," she lied next.

"When she wakes, she's going to need you. When people come out of a coma after this long they don't remember and sometimes their bodies don't operate like they should. You may have to reteach her to tie her shoes."

Wouldn't it be nice…nice if that was all I had to do if she came back? But I knew. The doctors still offered hope, the worst thing ever, Pandora's curse. Myth says she saved hope for humanity, but hope is a vagrant—a tease. Hope is worse than all the other evils released.

Reluctant, I gave up my vigilance to just go home and shower. Throw out all the food people dropped off after the funeral. Nothing wrong with its quality other than it sat on the counter too long. I kissed my granddaughter on the only patch of flesh on her face not bandaged, promising I'd return quickly.

While scribbling down my cell number at the nurse's station I noticed a woman too old to have green hair, but too young in her appearance to have a child approaching puberty. The little girl could be my

Nina. Only Nina had yet to blossom into womanhood. This poor girl was too young to…She was too young to have the body of a woman.

Two female officers, one in a uniform the other in plain clothes, interviewed the green-haired woman and the young girl. Too far away to understand their words, I knew enough to recognize the little girl's trauma. I feared how she was distressed. I would bet a million-forthcoming social security checks the mother allowed it to happen. Her left arm had track marks even I spotted them from down the corridor.

My grandchild was fighting for her life and this woman threw her life away along with a daughter who never stood a chance of a normal life. The officers were too preoccupied with their interrogation to notice how close I got to be within earshot.

"No. Nobody has touched her," the green-haired mother protested, her glassy eyes never focusing on the officers.

"We need you to allow the doctor to check her out," the uniformed woman said.

The plain clothed officer attempted mild threats. She worked an angle to be the heavy of the situation. "If we must get child services involved—" I guess officers do play good-cop, bad-cop.

It didn't take me long to decipher what transpired with the little girl. It angered me. I exercised every ounce of self-control. I want to fly in there and pound on the green-haired woman. I'm sure I was projecting my grief. My wife, daughter, son-in-law and new grandbaby were just killed in a car crash. They were on the way to set up a surprise birthday party for me. I blamed myself, but mostly, I blamed the inebriated punk who had nothing more than scratches from the accident. As much as I contemplated how to kill him it did my granddaughter no good if she woke up and I was in jail. I mustered a calming presence forcing me, preventing me from not placing the green-haired mother in a coma.

I don't know what drug this woman chose to self-medicate with. But drugs were the reasons for both of us being in this hospital.

Since I'd left my granddaughter's room the nurse assumed I drove home. The nurses returned to their station doing whatever nurses do at their fortress of counters and desks.

I was going to rescue this little girl. The cops didn't seem to have the evidence to hold the woman, but I didn't need the rules of law. I had the rules of what was right. Now to learn what I needed required a distraction.

I slipped into a room where an older lady slept. Tugging at the monitor cord until gravity took over, I had seconds to escape.

The nurses scrambled to assist the woman they thought had coded. I used those seconds to reach the nurse's station and memorize the address on the med form of the drug addled mother before I left the hospital. By the time they fixed the old woman and returned to check on my granddaughter, the nurse would assume I was long gone home to shower.

People who say they crossed to the wrong side of the tracks must have been in this neighborhood. I won't pass judgment on the people who lived there because the housing was income based. I saw no chance for any of them to escape. It was a Norman Rockwell scene if he were to paint crack neighborhoods. My two-year-old Nissan Rogue, still with original luster, didn't blend with homes ready to be condemned.

I drove past the address. Someone had converted it into a downstairs and upstairs two-family dwelling. The regulation iron fire escape explained as much. I sped away before my tires were stolen while I was driving.

I was forced to leave the hospital again to arrange the funeral of my wife—my daughter, her husband and the baby. My whole world was going in the ground. Nina being alive kept any heart palpitations in check. No father, grandfather, should ever have to do this—all alone. Nothing to do but ball up my sadness and push it down inside. After the funeral, I made a second pass by the little girl's house.

I didn't know what I was going to do. What could I do? I had one speeding ticket my whole life. I wanted to inflict agony on those causing my pain. I'd never get near the boy who stole my family.

I was not a gun person, but I sat all night holding the 9mm my son-in-law owned. If not for a comatose little girl, my Nina, I might have joined them.

I ignored my anguish, driving it deep down inside of me. Someone would pay. I would allow the courts to deal with the man. Going after him might place me high on the suspect list, but there was a grander problem I might address. I would start with the other little girl I saw in the hospital.

Nurses are not always careful about or forget about watching what they say around someone when they become a fixture in the hospital. They were pissed the cops had to allow the little girl to return home with her green-haired mother. They almost wanted to bet on how long it would be before the poor child would be back for more medical attention. They had other sessions involving her physical wellness. One had even hot-lined and—nothing. Mom would keep her from the doctor for minor events to prevent documentation of constant abuse. When she did bring her back the next time it would be horrid.

I left again. Retired, I had income and was about to have a windfall in insurance money.

Money wasn't enough. I wanted to use it to help this little girl, but she was a minor, so anything I did financially the mother would have access to.

I drove past the house on my way to the hospital. It was on my second lap the unshaven man in the wife beater on the porch spotted me. He must have figured this white suburbanite was wanting drugs, but hadn't the stones to ask. The shiny Nissan's a dead giveaway I didn't belong in this part of town.

Driving away made me question what I was doing. What could I do? If I protected her tonight what about tomorrow?

The little girl needed to be removed from her mother with no chance of returning or she would never escape her life.

Remaining vigilant over my granddaughter gave me thinking time. My thoughts now had focus. I formulated how to make it better for the little girl. To do so would bring her hardship but if I didn't she would forever be lost. If I did this successfully then I would take steps to make sure there were no more little girls in comas. I devised a brilliant plan even if it seemed a bit fantastical.

I didn't want to use the son-in-law's 9mm in case it was traceable. It wouldn't take more than an afternoon drive to locate a gun show and buy a gun.

I didn't want to use it, but I knew I needed protection. Next, I bought a junker car for three hundred dollars. It blended better than my Rogue. As long as it got me away from the house I didn't care how long it lasted. It may have even been stolen. The seller did have paperwork, but left the plates.

I acted that night before I lost my nerve.

"What the hell do you want, old man?" The bearded wife beater clad man demanded of me from the door of his house.

He wasn't expecting me to slap his face with the gun barrel.

With a broken nose, he dropped to a knee, blood pulsing from his nostrils. I kicked him and he fell inside the threshold. I followed the gun quivering in my hand. Luckily, the dealer's eyes watered badly, and he had no clear vision to spot my nerves.

The green-haired mother was sacked out on the couch next to a table of needles and what I assumed was other drug paraphernalia.

I'm not sure she even knew I was there.

The man lunged at me. My grip tightened. I cocked the hammer of the revolver. It didn't have to be cocked to fire, but the noise created the desired effect. The man dropped back to his knees begging for his life.

He offered me money.

I was glad I had remembered to buy a revolver, so I wouldn't have to police up any casings.

"How much more dope you got?" I'm sure I sounded ignorant.

"You want to score, you didn't have to hit me."

"I want you to inject her."

"Dude, she's had enough."

I found my balls.

"Inject her again or I inject you." My arm stiffened with no shaking as I pointed at the center of his forehead.

"Take it easy, grandpa." He prepared the syringe and stuck it in her arm. "She's going to die. Nice and blissful, but dead, just the same."

I didn't care. Worse, he didn't seem to care.

"Where's the daughter?" I poked his nose with the barrel.

"In the back bedroom. Are you some kind of pervert? You want mom dead, so you can foster the girl and have her all to yourself? Man, I would have sold her to you. No legal paperwork and no one checks on her."

"Are you related to her?"

"No. Just keeping Mom to fluff me. She makes a little on the side with her daughter. Bitch sells the little girl to get her drugs. Hell, some months she lets her stay with the landlord for the weekend to cover the rent. Guess I'll have to find another meal—"

Half his face painted the wall. I could take no more.

Glad some part of my brain stayed on its toes, I was against the wall just inside the hallway entrance when the naked man ran in demanding to know about the shot.

His brains decorated the opposite wall.

I knew what I would find if I entered the bedroom. A naked little girl not even old enough to have had a period. I couldn't witness it.

"Little girl!"

No answer.

"Little girl, you just stay in the room and you don't come out. Don't you dare come out!"

No one should have to witness what I did.

The car did get me to the playground park where I had stashed my Rogue. I wiped down the interior and the door handles to remove my DNA. I thought about burning it. If it was stolen maybe the real owner would get it back.

I returned to my vigil over my granddaughter.

The story was in the newspaper the next day. *Drug Deal Gone Bad During Child Sex Ring!* was the main assessment of the media. The girl who was left nameless was removed from the home her after mother's overdose. None of the facts were accurate. Nothing reported matched anything that occurred. It didn't even line up with the way the bodies were discovered. The two men were said to have killed one another over the drugs and the abuse of the little girl, all while the mom drifted to death on heroin.

Do you know how much insurance money your entire family is worth? I set aside an anonymous scholarship for the little girl. It wasn't much after I buried my family, but I figured her mother had nothing to leave her. Others added to the funds. She would get an education. She would need years of therapy to recover from how her mother used her.

XIV

"JACK, YOU ARE nothing like the master ripper."

"You're more Jack the Ripper than I, Ed. You do kill prostitutes."

"Did," the truck driver corrects.

"I was thinking Dr. Jack Kevorkian," remarks the old man.

"Dr. Death?" Jane praises, "Good choice. He helped people to the other side. You do rid the world of the unnecessary. But so did the first Jack."

"We no longer have the luxury of considering our victims unnecessary. They are people. People with family and names and we must no longer steal that away," Al says.

"I just sought to rid my town of those who took my family. To do so, I needed to remove the drug peddlers," Jack says.

"The cops never glance twice at an OD. Drug use rates just above prostitutes."

"The cops are understaffed, not stupid. When it quacks like a duck they don't check for feathers."

"You just saved a little girl from a terrible life," Jane says.

"Only if she stays in therapy," Jack hangs his head.

"Maybe you should be Paul Kersey," Robert says.

"Who?" Jesse asks.

"Now we know he's young," Al says.

"My youth has little to do with it. Our youth is when we killed insects first. A puppy. What did you go after first before you graduated to prostitutes?" Jesse snaps.

"You are correct. It is a deeper process than sharing a few stories the first time."

"I never harmed anyone. Not even when I served in the Army. What I did I did to avenge my family and to save dozens of others. It was when I enjoyed the killing, when I needed to kill that I turned to this group. God how I enjoyed ending such bastards. None of you are any better than those I killed. The problem is that I'm no better. No stones from this old man."

"At least you know you're no better than the rest of us, old man," Robert snaps.

Jane stands as if to interject her physical self between any of the others ready to get physical. She never expected them all to mesh and become friends during the first meeting. "We have gained some trust though this will not heal us after one meeting. And I know what we desire—to prevent another killing is a difficult monster to quell."

"It is a big leap, like AA buttons. We do this one day at a time."

"We have all shared, we should end our meeting. I want to build trust," Jane says.

"I ain't fucking holding hands," Ed says.

"We're drawing to a close. What you heard, and saw, and who you met here stays here. We must keep our trust," Jane says. "I will contact you with another safe location."

"How does this heal us?" Kenneth asks.

"Asking for help is the most difficult step. Your desire to be here is the start," Al says.

"Maybe we should come up with some guildlines like at AA."

"I'm not praying."

"And I'm not sure we should share phone numbers, yet."

"The chat room works if one of us has an urge and must talk," Jane says. "I will clear us another meeting time. Before you return to our next meeting remember to destroy your trophy collection. It will be difficult, but it is a major step in recovery."

"What if we're unable to?"

"If you can't then we must address it and help you. Let's process what we've heard today and next time line up how we help each other stay on this path of sobriety."

TWO

JESSE

I

"JOHN DOUGLAS, FORMER chief of the FBI's Elite Serial Crime Unit, and author of 'Mind Hunter,' says, 'A highly conservative estimate is that there are between 35 and 50 active serial killers in the United States.'" Professor Arnett allows those numbers to sink in. His back remains to the auditorium classroom full of innocent young faces. Unlike many in his fellowship, he doesn't make it his goal to scare students away on day one just to have fewer papers for some TA to grade. The career itself will weed out those who are unable to handle dealing with the dead. Writing implements scrawl on paper or fingers peck on keys to record the numbers he expounded.

He continues, "Many of these killers are difficult to track because they will exercise a 'cooling-off' period between kills. This period may stretch into years for some. As you study in this course you will find there are other experts who think the FBI numbers are conservative and there are many more active demented predators—a number reaching over a hundred—all actively and currently operating."

Pencils go down and laptops close. He's captured the class and he knows it. Arnett will separate those only fascinated with the macabre and those worthy of catching these killers. He over exaggerates his limp as he marches in front of the desk at the base of the curved rows of chairs with the half-folded desktops.

Jesse's pencil hovers over his note paper. Writing anything down might cause him to miss something pertinent his teacher reveals.

"Why don't we have an exact figure? Why don't we know more about these killers of at least three people or, in most cases, many more? A person can't be a successful murderer without being secretive, and often the successful murderers are nomadic. The most successful have never been caught, nor their true number of killings known."

Arnett again allows his inquest to sink in among the fledgling minds. So many believe killers are fascinating in books and movies. Some might even enjoy slowing down to view a car accident, but they have yet to understand the depth of conviction needed to examine a crime scene. To stand over a two-year-old with a slit throat covered in her mother's blood. To find a four-year-old with her genitals pried open with a screwdriver because she was too tight to be raped and then had her eyes dug out with the same screwdriver. To sit in an interrogation room while some father explains how his eight-year-old daughter performs fellatio on him better than his wife. No, they have yet to develop a stomach for such a scene. What he won't share—he never could stomach such tragedy. Somehow, he escaped his first career without beating one of those bastards to death for what they did to the innocent and defenseless.

His job—weed out those who will never handle it.

"More active killers won't even be identified. Get those *CSI/NCIS* fantasies out of your head. Real police work rarely reflects television. Sometimes you know who the killer is and the DA won't proceed because he fears a lost case. He won't risk tarnishing his perfect conviction record because some trailer trash whore was found bloody in a ditch."

Now some offended students grumble because they still view all people as human. "A killer never sees his victim as a person. They are disposable and easily replaced. Many killers live in a fantasy world and suffer delusion. Some believe their victims enjoy being tortured or enduring forced sexual congress. These are the people who selfishly believe their heinous acts are justifiable. Others murder the same person over and over and over again. Make no mistake, they have no remorse. Much like the wolf, the bear or the tiger, once they get a taste for human blood they never cease the hunt."

One female student leaves the auditorium. Arnett contemplated flashing crime scene pictures on the giant screen to sicken those who couldn't handle the carnage.

"Many killers are nomadic—truck drivers. At least four active serial killers prowl the highways in Texas interstates right now and they target lot lizards. Prostitutes are popular marks because no one cares about them."

He allows the usual affront to wash over the students. The female students especially are offended over his perception about sex workers having no value. Some students might even report their butt-hurt over his words, but as his Dean knows, as he also spent more than a decade on the force, prostitutes are not considered people. Not by cops, doctors, the johns or worse, many families forget them.

Reiterating his point, he speaks aloud his thought, "No one cares about a prostitute. Be offended all you wish, but they're never a high priority on anyone's radar for any crime committed against them. Even when they are runaways, and have a truly loving family searching for them, they are never going to top the caseload of an overworked detective. As long as this is true, many serial killers will continue to act with impunity. Before police departments were linked by national Internet databases, no one even suspected these girls were killed by mass murderers."

Arnett hops onto the desk to remove the weight from his bad leg. "Let's get to it. I was a police officer for thirteen years before I was shot in the line of duty. I have since earned my doctorate in criminal psychology and have worked on several FBI task forces involving possible serial killers. No, I won't speak on active cases beyond why information is pertinent to educating you in this course. I like to start day one with your questions. Tell me your name and your major and ask your question."

It's always a girl—pretty—and wanting to be in the FBI, no matter which one he calls on initially. Maybe he should select an ugly one, but they never stand up first. He points to the attractive brunette about five rows back.

"Sherly Nackberth, and I want to work for the FBI. Have you caught any actual serial killers?"

"I arrested three murderers when I was an officer, including the one that shot me. I've assisted on several cases involving possible serial killers. I'll share some of those cases throughout the semester."

More hands shot up. He'd bet now they will be about his wound.

Arnett diverges from his normality of calling on a male second. They want to know about guns and where they are allowed to carry. He calls on the masculine girl clearly into man-hating and questioning her sexuality.

"How can you say prostitutes are not people?"

He could have guessed her question.

"Right or wrong, you have to accept the stigma people put on someone willing to sell their bodies for sex. Even men who frequent brothels are ashamed. American society has branded them less than human. We have very childish and taboo views of sex. Ask yourself, have you ever considered a woman a slut because she enjoys sex, or had several partners she never married? You think she is immoral—evil—full of sin. Now, following such logic, a prostitute is a horrid creature. Even the most well-intentioned crime solvers sometimes don't see these victims as people. Or worse, because of a lifestyle choice they are less than human. Not every one of those girls...or young boys, had a choice. I've arrested many *boyfriends* of runaway girls who force them to turn tricks to show how much they love them. We will cover more of this as we progress. But when you think like our killers you will know, all of you in your seats right now, prostitutes are not human to them."

His answer never pacifies those who maintain a resting bitch face. He points a finger at a male.

"What's it like to be shot?"

Professor Arnett finds himself back on track. "At first I didn't even know I had been hit. My adrenaline was pumping. We had to stop this guy before he put any more people in danger. It was after we brought the guy down I noticed the wet—warm wetness. My leg was sticky and warm. Blood, as it coagulates, becomes gummy. And it's slick unlike any other liquid, even oil. At first, I actually thought the guy had pissed on me. When I realized it wasn't urine and wasn't a fluid from him I reported to the ambulance. They cut my new pants open and the white-hot burn overwhelmed me as soon as I saw the hole burbling gushes of red from this finger-sized hole in my leg."

Jesse soaks in the story, evaluating what kind of man his teacher is. Studying the criminal mind will better steer him towards his goal.

The professor continues, "I think I screamed. I know I screamed in my head though it may have been out loud. Memory is funny. It hurt. My leg was on fire like someone had taken a pot and dumped coffee all over it. The bone throbbed—vibrated. I was immobile on the gurney. The bone moved inside me as the muscles contracted. The tendons would twist and pull, but there was no bone to stabilize. I cried. Later, I learned the femur was shattered. The doctors had no idea how after being shot, with nothing supporting my leg. I was able to run this guy down. I don't have an answer, but I just knew if this guy got away someone would die. I could not live with that. It is some of the most difficult days on the job—when a suspect you know is guilty gets away. And kiddies, it happens—it happens a lot.

"Would I do it again…yes, but had I gone down when first struck by the bullet the bone damage would not be as severe and I wouldn't have a limp or the pain when the weather turns cold. Might even still be on the police force. I might have made a different choice. What we take on when we become protectors of society is not like it is on TV, nor not the way the news leads you to believe. We train because we make split second life and death choices and when it's over we pray those choices save lives. The killers we hunt—they plan and are fully aware of what they are doing. I'm going to train you so you are able to stop them."

II

THE QUESTIONS RUN the rest of the ninety-five-minute course and then a few students desiring answers, too afraid of ridicule in front of the group, wait until after the others have vacated the auditorium to ask individual questions important to them.

Jesse stuffs his laptop into his bag as he hangs back while other students ask foolishness about crime fighting. He waits until they are alone. "Professor, you said that before the Internet connected police files it was even harder to track some of these killers?"

Arnett notices this kid wasn't fearful of peer mockery, he carries a personal weight. Those people who seek entrance to the program to fulfil some Ahab fantasy should be expelled. They end up being trained and fired only to later shoot up an elementary school. "Yes. Detectives had to piece together MOs and other similarities between killings the old-fashioned way. Research. Questioning witnesses, newspapers. But even then, only surrounding counties would have access to newspapers. It was time consuming. It was why many missed the serial connection. Now all departments in different countries speak to each other through computers and several national databases. The FBI has the ability to search the world."

"Is there a way to go back, say twenty years, and get information on a murder?"

Twenty—about the age of this kid plus two or three years. Even when departments did connect someone still had to upload information from old cases.

"Depends on the case, the department and how high profile the killings might have been. If it was solved it may not have been a priority for someone to upload." Arnett assumes the kid seeks a case to write a book, or…the investigation is personal—Mom? Grandma?

"My sister was taken when I was two," Jesse deadpans.

Sometimes Arnett hates always being on the money when it comes to reading certain kinds of people.

"My family gives me no information. At a gathering one Christmas I overheard the discussion of her death being linked to a serial killer, but no one would share anything with me."

"You don't need my course to research."

"I read every paper in the local library," Jesse says.

Arnett has seen two officers with such a goal in their career and they failed at being competent police. Many take an unsolved case with them when they retire and continue to investigate it during their golden years, but it's not the same as those entering the police force to take down someone who personally harmed them. "I'd recommend you not become an officer if you're seeking a vendetta."

"I don't know how to convince you I'm not. I want justice for my sister. And no one in my family has the motivation to reopen the investigation. I have to know who killed her," Jesse pleads.

"I suggest you follow your family's lead and let it go." If they did, they have a reason. Families never let a death go—to do so means the answer's unbearable. "It's taken them twenty years to move on. Those wounds never heal and bringing this up will open a lot of hurt and pain. Pain you don't need to bring on them. Cases like this have to be relived every time they are discussed."

"But what about Victoria? Doesn't she deserve justice?"

Arnett explains, "All officers hold onto a cold case, some crime where the killer got away. because they all feel those people are deserving. You attend your classes, study and become an officer. Then you gaze upon this case with the eyes of a professional." Arnett won't expel the kid from the program yet.

"Each year the case is dormant is another year some killer goes free," Jesse protests.

"No denying your logic. I'd start in the local library. You said you read all the newspapers in it. What about the library in the next town?"

"I did. No newspaper articles exist on the event."

If true, this would be an interesting case. Someone must have powerful motivation to hide this girl's death. Arnett considers, but judgment of experience steadies his curiosity. "You complete the course and I'll take a gander at it." Sometimes answers end the quest, but often they only drive a person deeper into the search.

"It's not unheard of for a serial killer to be inactive. BTK was dormant for thirty years. Many other killers go years without seeking out victims," Jesse says.

"Most cops assume the killers are incarcerated for another crime which prevents their attacks. Once they are released they resume. The theory goes all the way back to Jack the Ripper." Arnett says. It is a terrible assumption and some serial murderers don't need a fix as often as others. "BTK also studied the police techniques. He even read books on himself. He got off on how wrong the experts were about him, contemplating how to entice the cops based on their analysis of him. He studied them in an attempt to beat them. It kept him dormant. In fact, their renewed interest in the case woke him up. Let it go, kid. What if your research brings this guy out of hibernation and he takes the life of someone else's sister?"

Jesse's quick retort smacks of being prepared, "What if that's a shit theory? Profilers examine predictable behavior, patterns. BTK deliberately broke with his patterns to confuse the cops. Many caught killers. When tested many are of slightly below average IQ. But what about the ones not caught? You said there could be as many as a hundred active killers some stretching back into the 1960's, which means dozens die never having been caught or even identified as mass murderers."

Professor Arnett runs the tip of his tongue against the right inside of his lip while his brain contemplates. "Thinking outside the box and new perspectives have caught many criminals, for they never follow the rules."

"What if instead of killing they attempt to seek help?"

This question was never a thought Arnett considered. "Doctors, psychiatrists, and even ministers would be required to report the admission of multiple murders. Many states now allow for this one breach of confidentiality, and make it a crime not to report."

"A professed serial killer wouldn't seek licensed professional help, but not all of them wish to keep killing. I've read some pedophiles are the same way. They don't want to crave relations with underage kids, but they don't pursue help because of the way society views them. We don't welcome those who will to seek healing for their mental problems. We punish mental illness more than provide support." Jesse jerks his laptop from his bag. "This is a risk. Maybe I should wait until I've been in your course longer, but…" he flips open his laptop and spins it around for the professor. "Exploring the deep web, trying to find a way inside the dark web, I discovered this chat room."

"I won't warn you how dangerous exploring these places are." Arnett glances at the screen and the flashing title. "Assistance with the Unusual?"

"A large number express…sexual deviancy…some with animals, sick shit, but a few mention a fascination with preventing planned deaths."

"The FBI has people who monitor this kind of website. You should leave this to the proper authorities, and delete your search history. They have the software to navigate and are protected from the type of people who utilize these websites."

"I doubt they have found this one. After I got in and mentioned a few *interests,* I was invited to another chat site. From there after a few chat conversations, almost as if the person was conducting a research project, I was directed to a link where I was asked to fill out a questionnaire with only a limited time to complete it. If I passed, then I will be invited into group chat which will help people with these urges and prevent *accidents.* I need your assistance, Professor. I need into this group. I believe my sister's killer joined such a group and that's why he's never been caught."

"You're reaching. This isn't even a grasp at straws. There was no Internet twenty years ago to quell his urges. You've no evidence supporting the killer is a part of this group—if it is a group—and the danger factor for someone untrained in procedures in dealing with these people doesn't rate on any chart. This should be explored by the proper *expert* authorities trained in dealing with Internet criminals."

"I agree, this is why I'm coming to you. Guide me. I'm in. I just need to pass this questionnaire with the accurate responses. Somehow, I'm betting only a person who has taken a life will know the correct answers. Or someone who knows how a killer thinks."

"No."

"Professor, if I don't utilize this link soon, I won't find it again," Jesse whines like a toddler about to drop to the floor in a tantrum.

"I have a list of reasons and all of them are 'no.' I am ethically required to report you," Arnett says.

"I'll do it anyway," Jesse says.

"Blackmail of such caliber only works in the movies. Go ahead and answer the questions I doubt if you get much further. If these people are embracing killers, you won't make the cut. You won't think as they do. I doubt I fully think as they do. Stay away from this, kid." *Don't make me report you.*

"But you can. You've studied—interacted with murderers. A profiler's job is to get into the minds of murderers."

"If you pass the test, then what?" Arnett asks.

"I attend the meeting and figure out who killed my sister."

"You're not Batman. You're not on some childish quest. You have evidence, you take it to the police. Allow them to process it. People in a chatroom are likely liars. You play vigilante or detective on your own and even if you find this guy, it's likely any conviction will be thrown out of court, because you didn't follow procedure."

"So you won't help me?"

"Not like this. You sit in my class and learn. You must be smart to be accepted into the program. It means you're intelligent enough to have passed the entrance tests. You learn, you become an officer, and as a trained agent, then you do this. You are not ready to follow some damn fool crusade that will ruin the rest of your life."

<h1 style="text-align:center">III</h1>

"WHAT!? YOU SAT in a meeting with seven confessed serial murders?" Arnett balls his right hand into a fist. Instead of punching Jesse he pounds on the table.

"Six," Jesse corrects the professor. "I am one of them. And they all shared a story of a murder they committed. These confessed killers forming a therapy group desire to get better. They crave a method to prevent their urges to kill. Many claim they don't want to murder anymore, but don't know how to seek help. A psychiatrist would have them jailed, and even in prison they would not be cured of their affliction."

The aging professor reaches behind him for the back of his chair to fall into the seat perplexed such a conference occurred. "In all my years as a police detective..." He shakes his head. The next few minutes of his life will travel a path he never knew existed.

"Even without your help I was able to complete the test and join the group. They all need to be in prison," Jesse says. "I was never so scared. If I fucked up, they would pounce on me. I don't know how they didn't know I wasn't one of them."

"You don't know that they weren't playing you. They are correct. Prison doesn't rehabilitate, not that any of them would ever see the light of day, but they would never be cured of their...dare I say *affliction*. I don't know how you aren't dead. They must have been too self-serving to notice."

"What do we do now?" Jesse asks.

"Contact the FBI," Arnett says without hesitation.

"If we do, they will scatter. The next meeting will be in a new location. I don't even know their real names. They all took on pseudonyms and some came in from different parts of the country. With a few more sessions I might be able to determine what killings they are known for."

"No way. No way I will condone you returning. If I allow you to go back I am negligent, and I won't be responsible for your death," Arnett says.

Jesse ignores the protest. "We might be able to determine who they are after they tell just one more story. It would give us their pattern and possible MO."

"No." Arnett pulls his cell from his pocket and flips it open. "You're going to share all you know with the police. Leave this to the trained professionals."

Jesse doesn't want to hem or haw, but he must uncover who killed his sister. "Most told first victim stories. You taught in class most serial killers' first victims are botched and don't match the pattern of future murders. I need the second meeting to figure out their normal pattern then we go to the police. What I have will give them nothing to go on and you know it." Jesse realizes one or two of the tales he heard would determine the killers involved, but The Bowhunter was not his sister's murderer.

"When is the next meeting?"

"Two weeks. With a new location."

Arnett jerks a yellow legal pad from his satchel. "Write down everything. Everything you remember. Every detail. Every smell. Every eye roll at a remark. We will check if the murders match the MO of known serial murderers." He claps the clamshell phone closed. "I'm still calling."

"You said in class early murders of serial killers don't match their later perfected techniques," Jesse repeats. He prays the professor's knowledge of unsolved murders might lead him to identify a killer besides the confessed Bowhunter. He will leave most of his info off this report. If Arnett suspects he knows one of the killer's identities and reports it, Robert would be arrested and the group may never meet again.

"Write it down anyway." He flips open his cell phone again. "The FBI will want to know—"

"Wait, Professor," Jesse puts his pen down, "I must attend another meeting. I need more evidence. If we report them now they will all get away. I doubt anyone will even be arrested. They brought no evidence other than their stories. The leader, this woman, strongly suggested each person return home and destroy any trophies they kept, remove any ties to the memories they relive through them." Jesse exaggerates slightly what she said. If the FBI interferes now he'll never determine which of the group members killed his sister. *He* might even face jail time for tampering, or worse, obstruction.

"Not good advice," Arnett ponders, "Besides the evidence standpoint, which we may need to prove they are killers, it's too soon in the recovery process to eliminate trophies."

"But alcoholics are expected to go cold turkey when they enter treatment."

"And about a third of alcoholics will remain clean for the first year."

"They have pledged to be abstinent since their addiction has deeper consequences," Jesse affirms.

"None of them plan to kill. In fact, they must avoid all temptations to kill. Admiring keepsakes of victims might encourage those emotions or prevent the necessity of more. But even the most determined addicts relapse. Without their trophies, some might have to go out and collect new ones to replace those they destroyed. This is not a good idea unless they are all supervised by expert doctors." Arnett loses himself in his thoughts. "No, we need to report what you've learned or we would be remiss in our civic duties."

"If you do the group will break up and six killers will be free. You know the odds are they won't all face charges. Let me attend just one more meeting. Tell me what I need specifically to learn so when we go to the FBI we nail all six of them." Not Jesse's real plan, but it will hold the professor off long enough for him to learn more to keep this dance going.

"Condoning your attendance is reckless and immoral. Putting you in danger is unacceptable."

"I put myself in danger. My choice. With your help I will stay out of danger. I must share another killing at the next meeting. I thought, with your knowledge, we could construct what I did so they believe and trust me. My first story was shaky, but they bought it."

"You want me to let you stroll into danger? No way. I must report this." Unsure why he hasn't dialed already, Arnett open the flip phone again.

Jesse grabs at the phone, pushing down the top on Arnett's fingers to prevent dialing, but in no way attempting to remove the device from the professor's hand. "You report it—I'll tell them I made it up."

Arnett jerks his hand away. "Are you blackmailing me? Unlike what those mass killers believe, *we* are not above the law."

"I'm asking—begging—for your help in one more attendance of their meetings. My sister's murderer must face justice. Help me."

"Your sister's murderer is not among this group. No. I must report this."

Jesse grabs at the phone again as it chirps in response to several numbers being dialed. He tosses the phone across the room, hoping the cracking plastic sound means he damaged it. Before the professor screams for assistance, Jesse shoves Arnett against the podium.

The older man may have been handicapped by the forced retirement, but his left punch has all the force of a steamroller.

Jesse reels back, but catches his footing. Even being young and limber, he quickly accepts he hasn't the power or experience to spar with the older man. He drops into tackling stance bolting forward. Using a desk as a backstop, he takes the professor over the desk landing on top of him.

He pounds on Jesse's back with his left hand. The right just lays there.

The kid knew he had been shot but never realized how useless the professor's right side had become. He grabs the man's tie—pulling it taut. The choking gurgle doesn't slow the pounding on Jesse's back. He jerks harder, bluing the old man's face. Without releasing the tie, he wraps it around his fist and wrenches the noose tighter.

No fight stays with Professor Arnett once his windpipe closes.

Arnett put everything into his first punch, leaving nothing for the rest of the struggle.

Jesse keeps the tie tight afraid the professor was faking unconsciousness in an escape attempt.

No, he was dead.

Lifeless.

Jesse clears the room of any evidence he remained to speak to Arnett after class. He'll leave the body to traumatize some freshman coed.

THREE

AL

I

RESEMBLING A CHUBBY faced Brad Pitt, Al sports a business suit, minus his tie. The jacket droops off his shoulders and the button up shirt hangs in wrinkled clumps, no longer holding back a wall of flesh. He marches through the woods, reaching a hand to hitch up his pants, his gut between belt notches.

He flips open his ID wallet.

The uniformed officer's response—lift the yellow caution tape for the plainclothes agent. Al places his boot carefully on a stone so he leaves no tracks in the mud. Never ruin a crime scene and never fuck up someone else's.

"Did you eat breakfast, special agent?" The man in a light tan trench coat asks as he steps from the dilapidated trailer door. He flips his left latex glove into the right and catches it like a baggie.

"That bad, Officer Chambers?"

"Detective, now." He ignores the barb at his rank, lashing out with one of his own, "You're having a wardrobe malfunction."

"Weight loss. Not buying a new suit yet."

"Good you didn't eat, you wouldn't hold it down. This one likes to cut on teen girls. I'll have to get fingerprints, but I think she's the Carmen girl missing from two parishes over. They both have the same Treble Clef tat on the middle thumb knuckle."

"Then this isn't an FBI matter. Why did you call me?" Al asks.

"You're the expert on dead girls. I don't think she is this one's first."

"Not what I want to hear." He puts weight on the bottom step with one foot, bouncing it enough to detect the rot in the wood.

"You have gloves?" Chambers asks.

"Never touch a corpse without them." Al slips a latex ball from his pocket. Fitting the gloves to his fingers he eases up each stair to the entrance.

A police photographer snaps pictures in some sort of twisted carnage photoshoot with a dead prom queen posed forever in her own twisted tableau.

Al kneels half a dozen feet from the body, "Beautiful…was the other victim this pretty?"

"She has the same long, wavy, corn colored hair," Chambers says. "And was a teenager. Late teens like her."

Cuts decorate her frame as if someone were slicing onions. First, he notes the lack of blood around her and, "No punctures?" And no pubes. Does *Cosmo* still tell girls her age to shave it bare? "How long has she been missing?"

"Two, maybe three days. She was supposed to be at a friend's house and didn't go. We are determining approximal time when she went missing."

Al rubs his chin. Stubble pokes sharp against his finger. "He shaved her. She has no body hair, but it's been two days, so she should have growth. He expended time on her before cutting on her. Check her for sexual assault but you won't find any DNA." With a backward step, he spins to the side, allowing a full view of the body.

"No stab wounds I have found—all slashes. A distinct lack of blood here means he performed this twisted surgery elsewhere," Chambers adds.

"This guy's new, but I agree, she is not his first. This *might* fall into the FBI's jurisdiction, but it might not land on my desk and I won't step on the toes of the locals," Al says.

"You said you were passing this way. This is your forte, and the Sheriff gave his blessing for me to have you give an opinion. There has been no murder here in twenty-three years. He has no idea what to do and doesn't want his men to know it. None of them have ever seen this. The town is one step above Mayberry. I'll get him to officially invite you."

Al snaps off the latex glove before rubbing the meaty part of his thumb against the bristling whiskers protruding under his right nostril as if to jump start a thought process. "Unofficially, I'd pull everyone back and get a full-on State forensic team out here. No matter how careful this guy was, he moved her here. He left something behind. I'm convinced she wasn't his first and if we miss a clue there will be more—a lot more."

"You ever encounter this MO before?"

"Not this guy, he's new to me. And I know many serial killers," Al grins.

II

A DARK MAN with a hooked nose sips his coffee in the back booth. A chambray button up shirt hangs open to reveal his tight Under Armor tank, showing off his muscular frame.

When the waitress, blonde hair in a bun stabbed with a pencil, brings a steaming pot to refresh his cup, he asks, "How old are you?" He notes the golden name tag with black block letters designating her as Mila.

"I'm seventeen," she beams having not been on her feet every day for years to embitter her.

"So you're married?" A logical explanation as to why she's at work on a school day.

"I don't know why anyone would want to do something they know would end in divorce," she smiles.

"Shouldn't you be in high school?"

"I had to drop out. I need to work to earn money."

Money—magic word.

She has not waitressed long enough to include a sob story to improve her tips.

Now he must lay his cards on the table with care. He needs a reason to open his wallet. He only eats eggs, no pork, but people tend to recall special orders. He wants no one to remember him. "The home plate breakfast will be fine."

"I'll get that in for you." She tops off his coffee.

After he finishes the eggs she returns to fill his cup. He opens the wallet. Fanning out seven Benjamins, his attention focuses on how wide her eyes grow. He speaks so only she understands him clearly, "Would you like to earn some money on the side?"

She salivates a yes.

"Traveling for business get lonely." Even an inexperienced girl would recognize his conjugal smile.

"You asking me on a date, or just for company, mister?"

"Private company," he smiles.

"Is it worth all seven of those hundreds to you?"

He slides out one of the hundreds. "The other six will be waiting for you at the Moose Lodge, room 207. But no one can know. I mean, I do have a wife."

She snatches the hundred, stuffing it into her shirt, securing it in her bra strap. "I'll be secretive for six more of these." Her empty hand slides across her stomach, pausing for a second.

• • • • •

As soon as he locks the door to the hotel room she asks, "Got those six hundreds?"

He nods and points to the top of the TV cabinet. She snatches them up. He checks the curtains for any gaps allowing a peeping tom to witness his infidelities. The setting sun bathes the cloth in orange.

"What do you want me to do? I'm for anything except in the ass," she says.

He tosses a packet of thigh high hose on the bed. "Put those on."

"You want to watch or what? You're paying for it, I figure I'll do whatever you desire."

"Change on the bed."

She pulls her tee-shirt over her head. Immediately he understands the hand-pass over her belly. He wouldn't need a condom. She has the mound of a girl in the earliest stages of pregnancy.

Once she has aligned the thigh high seams she stands before him, the rest of her exposed.

"You haven't shaved," he says.

"Sorry. I came here straight from work."

"No matter. You wouldn't have done it correctly."

"This what you want? I've never done it for money, I just screwed the wrong boy and he won't pay for the baby."

"I don't care," he deadpans.

"You don't have to be an ass."

"Lay down on your stomach," he orders.

"You know, I'm not sure I want to do this. You can have your money back," she reaches for her pants.

"I said lay down!" he growls.

"Okay. I'm just nervous. I've never…"

Straddling her midsection, pinning her to the bed, he reaches under the pillow, drawing out a leather restraint. He clamps it over her left wrist before she protests.

"What the fuck? I'm not into this."

He hooks her right wrist into a second restraint. She kicks and flails her legs. He mashes her face into the blankets. Despite her struggle to breathe she finds herself smashed against a hard-plastic cover under the sheet. When he lifts her head, she opens her mouth to scream. He jams a Jennings Dental Mouth Gag between her teeth, although it doesn't muffle her sounds completely. She's unable to clamp down or release an alarming scream. After tightening the leather strap to secure the gag he slides backward, keeping his weight on her legs.

Blood dribbles from her gums as she chomps on the metal. He banged a tooth as he shoved in the mouth gag. Reaching to his left he slips a leg shackle around her ankle.

Once he has her secure on the bed he undresses. From a fine leather case, he draws a straight razor. He waves the gleaming blade an inch before her eye. "I'm going to shave you. If you move I might cut you. Hold perfectly still," he warns.

III

"FOR A GUY who has Brad Pitt's face you sure don't date." Chambers tosses a wadded-up paper ball across the desk.

"No time. I must constantly solve crimes you country cops can't seem to." His cell chirps. He accepts the call, "Special Agent speaking." He waits for the confirmation and then the usual question. "No, not officially. Maybe not at all, but you know they love to consult an expert." He glances at Chambers. "But just not listen."

After a few seconds, "I agree…she's maybe fourteen, fifteen at the max, beautiful, killed elsewhere, but sliced—not stabbed."

A few seconds more, "Blonde…call me back."

"The sheriff needs to make my presence here official. I don't want anything I uncover to be inadmissible. They'll gladly loan me out, just have him make the call."

"You still pissing off the administration?" Chambers asks.

"They've never liked my profiles, not after the billionaire."

"The one who liked little girls?"

"Boys as well. He was a known contributor to the last President's campaign. Deep down I think they would just let him go on and do what he did because he was such a humanitarian. What did it matter how he ruined the life of a dozen children if he saved a hundred-thousand?"

"How much prison time did he get?" Chambers asks.

"The last case was a mistrial. After a second trial it no longer makes the news. His lawyers will keep the case tied up and he'll only be a millionaire when it's all over," Al says.

Chambers jumps to his feet when his office door swings open. Al rises, hand on his belt to keep his pants in place.

The tall, uninformed man holds out the hand of a former wrestler.

"Sheriff Mallard, this is FBI Special Agent Al. He's just visiting at the moment," the detective clarifies.

Emotion overwhelms his face as if tears will drop. "We've never dealt…with this before. I've never seen…"

"Sheriff, I've encountered worse. I assure it never gets any easier to deal with. When it does I need a new job. You need to contain the scene and bring in the State Troopers or the FBI. This won't be it for this guy, not the way he cut on her. He enjoyed it. He'll need to do it again."

"I'll make the calls. Get them down here."

"Do you know this girl?" Al asks.

"She's a freshman at Cedar Hill. Good kid. Already talk of her getting a volleyball scholarship."

"I hate to do this to the family, but get someone over there to interview them. Find out where she's been and how long she's been gone. You might get lucky. She's not old enough to drive so someone drove her to her last known location." He holds out a business card. "After you get the state forensic team on the way, you call this number and ask for Supervising Director Slincard. Tell him you want me as a consult, make it all official. I uncover some piece of evidence and you can't use it, this guy will escape the needle," Al says.

IV

"HOW DID SHE know this guy?" Al glances through compact binoculars at the small saltbox house.

"He graduated high school last year. Point guard. Lasted one semester in community college." Chambers smirks at community college.

Al keeps his attention peering out the passenger window of Chambers' car, "I started at community college. Beats keeping track of high school sports when you don't have kids of your own," he jabs at his friend. "Why did he drop out?"

"Grades."

"Still passing the high school sports stars in small towns. How did they hook up?" Al interrupts to answer himself, "He fails in a bigger pond, returns to the safety of home, where he still shines and impresses the younger kids. The senior girls understand what a loser he is, but not the freshmen. Classic story told repeatedly in every small, midwestern American town. Your town just happen to *not* have a store where I could purchase smaller pants."

"You read people pretty good, but stereotypes don't work every time," Chambers says.

"If I don't, someone else dies. And who do you pull over, the El Camino with the pot bumper sticker or the soccer mom Prius?"

"Soccer mom, she might be single," Chambers laughs. "We do tend to favor the paraphernalia. But you deserve to get pulled over if you advertise."

Al steps from the car, "How do you want to play this?"

"I'll follow your lead."

"It's your town. I'm here as an observer," Al says.

"You wanted to rule out the love interest first."

"It is best to start with the boyfriend, but with a pending near identical case in another county I doubt he is our suspect," Al says.

They march to the door. Chambers knocks.

Al tilts his body to hide his hand on his service weapon.

Chambers flashes his badge when shirtless Craig answers.

"When was the last time you saw Shelby?" Chambers inquires.

"No hi or a warrant?" Craig asks.

"Don't get smart, Craig. You lost any currency you had with the Sheriff when you dropped out of college. Now when did you last speak with Shelby?" Chambers demands.

"She dumped me. I sent her a few texts, but she stopped answering a month ago."

"Did she dump you for someone else?" Al asks.

"You know the legal age thing was an issue, but she was a little too churchy for me."

"A small town like this, I thought everyone attended church," Al says.

"We got out of practice early on Wednesdays so we could attend," Craig says.

"How was that too churchy for you? She staying chaste?" Al asks.

"She wanted to spend too much time with her pastor. I mean, I go to church, but this guy hung on her like a creepy uncle."

"Your mom home, Craig?" Chambers asks.

"Yeah."

"Why don't you let us in and go get her?"

"What's going on?" Sweat beads form along Craig's close-cropped hair line.

"When was the last time you saw Shelby?" Al asks.

Craig has yet to lose his athletic physique as he towers over the two. "I go to the high school games sometimes. You know there is nothing else to do in this town but park at the quarry or go to Friday night games. I see her there."

"So you did hang out?" Craig asks.

"There's been some parties, but she's jailbait." Growing sweat beads draw together.

"And the church would frown upon you," Al pokes.

"Not so much the church. I mean...she was all into the pastor. She hung on his words and..."

Al notes the change of story in the young man.

"They like boys as pretty as you in prison." Chambers steps away to answer his vibrating phone.

"I never touched that girl," Craig protests. Gravity now pulls on the sweat droplets. They roll down the side of his face. "She was under-age. We…were just…at some of the same parties."

"And?" Al demands.

"What and?" He wipes away the trails of sweat from his cheek.

"Just tell me, Craig. Let me help you."

"We made out a few times. And she'd stop it. Saying the *pastor* would punish her for such sinful behavior." For a second his nervousness abates to anger.

Chambers blocks them out focusing on the call. "Are you sure? Thanks. Send me a copy," he flicks off the phone, marching back to the porch. "Do you want to question him at the station?"

"Question me about what?"

"Down at the station. He'll view all the photos of her body."

Craig's stomach burbles loud enough for them to all hear it. "Body! You mean she's…oh my God…No. I mean…" His cheeks chipmunk out as he clamps his hands over his mouth to hold in his bile-filled vomit.

Chambers pats Craig on the shoulder, "Let's find your mom."

Al inspects the family photos hanging in the foyer as Chambers returns. He closes the door behind him as they step out. "You want anything from the kid? He was working at a choke-and-puke off the interstate the same time she turned up missing. The call confirmed it."

Al shakes his head, "Not now. I think you should keep him on your suspect list until he returns to college and finds a girl his own age," Al says. "I want to speak to this pastor."

V

"WORST PART OF the job." Chambers turns down the street, driving with one hand and failing to signal. "I hate to have to tell anyone a loved one is gone."

"It wasn't him, or it would not have been new information for him. Before he knew she was dead, he thought we were there about him having sex with her."

"You put the fear of God into him."

"Good. He needs it, or you might be arresting him for something statutory," Al says.

"You just know that's all he did?"

"Typical adult male behavior and she was young. I'd be scared, too, if I were him. But he had no *tells* about her being missing. He was a typical jock asshole, not a sociopath," Al says.

"You rode the kid pretty hard, suspecting only fornication."

"He has a small dick and chases the young, inexperienced girls because of his insecurities. He'd have knocked Shelby up and she would have been stuck here as a waitress, never getting a chance to live her dream, Now some other bastard used her to live out his fantasy. We need to find him before he goes dormant."

"At the seminar, you never said why you got into profiling," Chambers says.

"I just always thought like a killer. Leaves you with two choices in a career—I prefer to be on the catching end." Al shifts his focus onto Craig. "And I don't think Craig ever had sex with the girl."

"You a mind reader?"

"No, but he was mad he hadn't. This pastor was a cock block."

Chambers pulls into the church parking lot. "Pastor Paul has been an outstanding member of the community for…three years now."

"Craig said Shelby would blow off their dates to go pray."

"It's a small town. Church is important to many of these kids. Sometimes it's the only acceptable social activity some of them get." Chambers closes his car door.

"And she would be punished 'by the pastor, for her sins. An interesting word choice. Not him as in Him—God, but the pastor." Al pulls his pants up after stepping from the car. "It is not the place of a man of the cloth to punish—only God."

From behind the building puffs a thin stack of smoke. The black smoke signals something manmade likely burns. Al gestures to Chambers and they split, racing around each side of the building.

Al's Glock clears its holster as he spots the pastor dropping photo paper in a pile of cut brush. "Back away from the fire, Father. Put those papers down and raise your hands."

Pastor Samuel recognizes Detective Chambers. "Officer, I have a burn permit."

Each of Al's steps are taken with care so his pants don't drop to his ankles. He swings around the fire to get a clear view of the papers.

Chambers draws his weapon. "Al, I've got your back, but he is a respected member of the community." Translation: *You better not fuck this up!*

"Special Agent Al. Drop the pages and step away. Keep your hands where I can see them."

By the book, Chambers notes. "Father, do as he asks."

Pastor Samuel steps back.

Al kicks at the pages, scattering them away from the growing fire. One stack of photographs already turns black and crinkles in the bluish flickers. He glances down at the images consumed in flames. He raises his gun to center mass his target. "Your upstanding citizen enjoys personally consoling his parishioners."

Chambers scoops up an unburnt page. Grinding his teeth, he swings his right arm. The butt of his Glock breaks open Pastor Samuel forehead as the impact flings the man to the ground. "You have the right to remain silent." His boot impacts the Father's abdomen before Al slides between them.

"Not this way, he's not worth it."

Chambers waves the picture of Shelby clad in lacy underwear, sprawled across the church pew.

"This is brutality," Pastor Samuel protests, touching the dripping blood on his forehead.

"You resisted arrest when we informed you we were bringing you in for the murder of Shelby." Al slips his handcuffs from his belt pouch.

"I didn't harm Shelby, we just had sex."

Al deduces he will recant the admission after his Maranda Rights are read and before trial. Pleading to a statutory conviction means he will not spend the rest of his life behind bars or face the needle. Al considers, not sure if this state even has the death penalty anymore. He holsters his Glock. As he cuffs Samuel he says, "You are under arrest for possession of child porn and the murder of Shelby Mathews."

VI

AL PUMPS THE hand of the female officer. She has a grip firmer than most men he's encountered.

"Alisson Weber." She peers through the two-way mirror at Pastor Samuel. Even with his hands cuffed to the hook in the center of the metal table, he folds his hands in prayer.

"You're going to have more girls come forward. I don't know how many he molested, but a few will step up once they know why he's been arrested. And since the gossip wagon moves faster than the Internet in this town it may be soon."

"I trusted him with my own kids," Alisson says.

"Chambers has someone identifying the pictures we rescued from the fire," Al says. "They were all teens. I know it is no comfort."

She glares through the mirror at Samuel's bandaged forehead. "Should have shot him for resisting arrest. Those poor girls are going to have to relive what he did with them for months, and face years of follow-up therapy."

"We think one of his other victims heard we arrested Pastor Samuel and rushed down here. I thought it was better a local female officer spoke with this teenage witness. Once the identification of Shelby's body was released in the media and word we arrested the Pastor leaked, this girl feared she would be killed next."

Alisson nods, unable to remove her eyes from Pastor Samuel.

Al continues, "Fucker convinced them the normal teenage girl's confused feelings were sinful, and the only way they would be clean in God's eyes was if they did *things* for him."

Alisson raises her fist, holding back the urge to pound the glass and scream.

"Hard to believe in the age of the Internet those kids are still so Victorian in their knowledge," Al adds.

"The only sex education in schools is 'don't do it.' And parents don't say anything. Some even encourage early dating, so girls get pregnant and another welfare check comes into the home."

"It happens everywhere."

"You should have shot him while resisting arrest."

"I have to draw the line somewhere," Al says. He places a photo of a young girl in lace into a folder containing other pictures of the same girl. "You know you're going to have to show her these and make her confirm they are images of her in the photos. I don't envy you."

Sheriff Mallard enters the observation room. "He's my Pastor." He stares through the two-way mirror. This admission was one of shame.

Al recognizes the guilt from faces he's encountered before.

Mallard listened to the man preach for years and never knew what he was doing in the basement. In just a few years Mallard's own daughter would be in the age bracket of the girls in the photos with all his police training, he never noticed.

"And a man of God is less likely to be a killer? He's human and they do some bad shit. His collar doesn't prevent dark perversions; in fact, it opens the door. No teenage girl would go off with a forty-year-old man alone in any other circumstance, not without cash or force," Al says.

"So, we become a country where everyone is suspect?" Sheriff Mallard asks. "No one is left with good intention."

"There comes a point where people should ask more questions, or maybe the Midwest should come out of the stone age. Speak about sex with their children with proper age appropriate education and not an abstinence only policy. When some person attempts to harm them, children will know it's not healthy and be more likely to report it."

"Maybe I should speak with my daughter tonight," Sheriff Mallard says.

"If I may suggest, I would keep this man on suicide watch. He knows he's going away for a long time and what he has done won't place him in high esteem in prison."

"Let them have him," Alisson says. "He deserves every dick they stuff into his ass."

Al ignores the...irony...double standard. People abhor rape when it is a woman or small child, but deem it an acceptable punishment for convicted criminals. "Sheriff, I'm going to be gone a few days. I want to check some information where a body in similar circumstance as Shelby was found."

Mallard snaps from his depression. "We have the case files and those you dug up could be two more bodies."

"I know I've pissed some of your deputies off by my methods. I know Pastor Samuel was a hometown hero. It has hit Chambers equally hard."

"At least he didn't kill him," Sheriff Mallard says. "You're not wrong about small towns, but you're not correct about everyone. These are good people."

"I agree. I'm going to find Shelby's killer." Al chews his bottom lip.

"We have him," Allison says.

"I don't think Pastor Samuel is a killer. Sick, and a child molester, but not a killer. There is no evidence at his church where he keeps his trophies. And I suggest you get a warrant for any place he might have hoarded more—people like him never give up their trophies. In the age of computers and quarter-sized SD cards, he's stashed those photos electronically someplace. He was burning his collection too quickly not to have a backup."

"Who warned him?" Allison inquires. "How did he know Shelby was dead?"

"One of the family members, when informed of her body's discovery, called—hell, others may have called him asking for prayers," Sheriff Mallard says. "It's not relevant."

"Sheriff Mallard, I must examine the other crime scenes. If they are similar to Shelby's then we have a killer still out there."

"Chambers said you spot things others don't."

"Sometimes, but I think it is more I focus in on small details many people miss. But I must stand in the room. A picture doesn't cut it. It doesn't fully capture. Smells. The room's energy. I need to…feel… the place. I rarely admit it. Sometimes to catch these guys you have to assume their thought process."

"If you didn't have a high closure rate I'd question your sanity." Sheriff Mallard shakes his head. "Some people are just meant to do this. I'm already taxed on the cost of this case, the cost of the lab work for all of the DNA tests on Shelby. Nailing her killer will bankrupt the department."

"I want the correct guy in prison for her death. You have enough evidence to put Samuel away on kiddy porn. Trust me, Sheriff, I won't turn in a mileage report. No one need know I was gone."

"You want Chambers to accompany you—off the books?"

"No. He needs to run down Shelby's last few hours to tie together what I learned at the other crime scenes," Al says. "You pretend like I'm locked away in the back office sorting through those photos. I won't promise, but when I get back I'll have a direction—pointed toward Shelby's killer."

VII

"HOW WAS YOUR meeting?" she asks in the half-awake tone of a caring lover. She doesn't bother to cover her naked body.

Al crawls in next to her, already void of his clothes. Quickly he snaps the end of the handcuff over her right wrist, making sure it's just tight enough and the black fuzzy cloth keeps the metal from marking her cream-colored skin. She never protests or struggles against his control.

His hands slide down the curve of her back, over her teardrop rounded bottom to her legs.

Near the bed rests a stationary bike. Cables run from a turbine where a front wheel should be if it were a road bike. The wires run to a television. His fingers trace along the tight musculature of her legs. She must have watched many hours of television while he was gone for there to be no loose thigh skin.

With her hands secured behind her he undoes the ankle chain. It allows her to reach the bathroom and the small mini refrigerator, but not out of the bed chamber. No further than the bike connected to a mini-television.

Al tucks in tight against her, making them one person. Her smooth body excites him. Nothing like the touch of a naked woman to stimulate his blood. He yawns, too tired to extract enjoyment from her. Driving all night to be here has exhausted him more than he realized.

"Did you do any reading?" Silly question. He knows the television has limited channels and she must peddle the stationary bike at top speed to give it power.

"I didn't care much for the female protagonist. She was given everything and remained a whiny brat."

"I agree." He draws the alphabet on her tummy with his finger. She has a slight paunch even if her legs are hard as rocks. Al finds it attractive, as it makes her real. Not some airbrushed model—a real woman. He pinches the paunch of skin at the top of her navel where she had a piercing.

"Do I not please you?" She uses her nose to point at the leather dog collar on the nightstand.

"Yes. The drive took it out of me. I want to sleep a bit." He kisses her neck behind her ear. "After a nap I'll do you." Al yawns again.

"Good. I was afraid you no longer required me." She grinds her hip to stimulate him.

In a dream state Al thinks, *This is not love and no matter how much you pretend you're afraid I lost interest in you, I would end you. It's what I do. I have done. I'm trying to quit. I care for you. I know if I release you it won't be reciprocated, but if I kill you then nothing remains. I'll keep attending those meetings to stop being a killer. In the end what do I do with you?*

Al hugs her tight as she grinds. *So even if I succeed in overcoming my urge I will never be able to release you. You'll never be able to freely love me for fear at any day I would end you. Nor am I naive enough to believe you would ever be my lover willingly.*

She pretends so well. At times, when she begs I believe her.

Maybe she does mean it. She desires it, not for love, but for me to keep wanting her so I don't murder her.

She closes her eyes and keeps her hips grinding at a steady pace as if the bulge now poking the soft curve of her rump brings her comfort. Al fights off the sleep as his eyes roll back into his skull.

"NO!" He pushes her away.

Her twisting hips work his stimulation.

"I need sleep first." *I must think. How do I release her? Releasing her would be the only way to prove I was cured. The meetings mean something. Alcoholics get chips for sobriety. How do I earn a chip with this woman chained to my bed?*

"I did nothing but think about you while I was gone." *Not a lie. I have. I want...normal.*

"You know I only think of you," she mews. Her finger tickles him.

"I believe you. But your thoughts are not of loving me, but emblazoned in fear." He slides his finger he used to draw on her tummy up to her lips. "Don't lie. If I didn't know you feared me, I'd be a fool."

"I don't want to die," she pleads.

"You may not believe, but those meetings are about sparing you the fate I bestowed on—" *She doesn't need to know my number. I don't even know if the group will know my number unless I attend enough meetings. My story with many are the same once I finished this chamber in the basement. I explored a few I liked, but I had to develop the skill to perform and not accidently kill them. In the excitement of the moment, if I don't release the collar then I choke them out.*

Jordon enjoys it.

No predator bullshit. She enjoys being choked. She hates the confinement and I'm sure despises me.

Maybe if I figure out how to release her I'll find an Internet chat group for women who enjoy rough sex. The next meeting Jane will ask if we gave up our trophies. I will destroy all but Jordon.

"I do like it." Jordan returns the gentle touch of a teasing lover who knows the sweet spot to rub.

He slips the collar around her neck. Before cinching the buckle, he wonders if he will be able to release her.

FOUR
JANE

I

SHE TUGS ON the white stocking to remove any wrinkles around her exposed lower calf. Jane detests the hospital's traditional nurse dress code. Constantly buying bobby pins to keep the little cap secure is a wasted expense.

Where do the things disappear to? In some twisted Stephen King universe, the hair must be absorbing them. No, the hat—the hat eats them because the dreaded thing must be a gateway to another dimension like a Buick or the little boy who could flip from one reality to another to save his mother from her cancer. Only in this story when she flips to the other side she will find fields of bobby pins stuck in the ground in rows like corn stalks. Whole forests of the bent metal.

No snags tonight.

Another needless expense—white pantyhose. At least they are control top, as she wasn't born in the age of garter belts as a practical means to hold them around her upper thighs, though she doubts it was ever a preferred method. Nurses make so much money—only to buy clothes—useless bits of uniform for work. She lacks the education to understand how white hose and a hat that doesn't fit improves the health of any patient. Nowhere in any nursing text does it explain how her white stockings will save lives.

She could use them as an improvised coffee filter, instead of points of speculation from visiting husbands, whose main concern was if the white nylons went all the way up to her thighs over the welfare of their wife as she gives birth to their child. The worst were the jerks who, as their wives were giving birth, pressed her for a phone number.

Bastards.

No. They were normal behaving men. The bastards were the ones who, as the woman's water broke, had a lawyer deliver divorce papers. In this state a divorce is forbidden while a woman is pregnant.

And then there are the Nurse Ratched jokes. She has heard them all, especially from the male orderlies on the night shift. Fuck them.

She charts her patient's vitals. Better to do it now. She got this weird shift and a half today, covering for part of a dayshift girl, a shift she covets. Nursing is the only job where all the pretty girls work nights. The older—age worn—women have seniority and have earned the best hours. She's somewhere in the middle, and since she pulls the extra days it boosts her up the ladder when one of them finally retires—or croaks.

The day ones are all so bitter.

She hasn't reached bitter yet—cynical. Tired of the truth. In some far-off reality, like those fantasy books she reads on long nights, there is a place where patients get the help they require...more than require... and insurance claims. It's a world where only healthy people exist.

Placing her paperwork in a drawer, she makes her rounds. Everyone sleeps. She'll need vitals again soon, but she hates to wake people. Sick people require rest and yet they all get woken up once they finally fall asleep in a strange bed after being poked and connected to tubes.

Rounding the corner in the maze of corridors, only a long-term employee understands, she peeks in at Tawny. The sleeping girl will never get off a machine, doomed forever to have a tube pump air into her lungs. The poor thing was on the road to becoming homecoming queen.

She got into a car with her drunk boyfriend and he rolled the…Camaro. He got a cut—scratch on his left pec muscle—and she will forever be in a coma. Sadly, she had no alcohol in her blood work.

With her charting complete, the morning shift brings a full staff, including arrogant doctors and rude visiting family. Despite her being the charge nurse on the ward from eleven at night until eight in the morning, she sinks to the bottom of seniority by nine. Worst, the day shift doctors treat her as if she was just handed her certificate.

Jane opts for the easiest of tasks. None of the experienced real Nurse Ratcheds wanted the task with those kids and the mom.

The little girl was considered a middle schooler. Every underdeveloped limb, even her head strapped into a padded wheelchair. She has never even once fed herself. Science is to blame. Maybe mom was on meth. She appears to be a pill popper now. But this poor girl arrived mangled. Tests show she has a mind, or at least brain activity, but she's never spoken or been out of her chair.

Jane preps a syringe full of an oatmeal paste.

"They said not to feed her this morning until they drew blood," mom hisses. Her self-righteous demeanor is one of, 'give me everything free because my life is shitty. Just look at this helpless kid I'm burdened with. God hates me.'

Jane sometimes wishes she was afforded an opportunity to end others not worthy of life instead of those she chooses.

"They drew blood and now I'm checking how she takes the food tube." It progressed into her stomach. Poor child, doesn't even get the pleasure of enjoying an ice cream.

"Can you give her something to deal with the smell of her shit? That stuff we feed her. She stinks. Sometimes I can't stand to be in the room long enough to change her."

Jane slips the tip of the syringe into the food tube connected to a valve on the girl's side attached directly to the stomach. "They don't offer flavors." *She has no taste buds down here anyway.* "It gives her the substance she needs." Jane brings her eyes to the little girl's—lifeless orbs. "So, your little blessing remains with us."

"Nothing blessed about her except the government check and this summer school taking her for more classes and giving me a break."

"She is darling." Jane depresses the plunger slowly, easing the food through the tube.

"Change her after she shits, you'll smell darling. At least the welfare bought me a new van. The old one was difficult to get the chair in. They won't give me a motorized one, since she can't move her arm or even her fingers." Mom joneses for a cigarette. Jane recognizes the twitchy shake of the hand.

Jane completes the feeding. "I might have some samples of food flavors you could try to see if they help with the bowel movements."

"Perfect. Maybe I can stand to change her more often."

Jane opens a cabinet and removes several baby food jar-sized cans of the powdery mix. Her latex gloves still on from the feeding, she slips a needle under the seal of a can and injects a clear substance. Recapping the needle, she dumps all the food tubes in the proper disposal and the needle in the sharp's bucket. "I don't have a bag."

"One thing this little girl is good for is the storage on the chair." The mother kindly opens a pouch.

Jane places the doctored can in first and four more cans on top. "Try one a day. You should notice a difference in a day or two."

"Figures about the time she goes back to school and they get to change her."

II

JANE NEVER BUYS a newspaper. Usually one or two remain in a patient's room and the hospital gets several subscriptions, but by night shift they are scattered around the ward and waiting areas. Three days. No four. The third day the mom should have used the tainted food, and since the poor child couldn't speak, she had no way of expressing the discomfort she felt after being fed. By the time the mother realized something was wrong and called EMS, it was doubtful anything would save her. If Jane believed—the girl was an angel now. Truth was, she has no spiritual belief. In her heart the little girl is better off.

The news article would explain how police suspected the mother who, tired of caring for her invalid daughter, slipped something into her feeding tube to end her suffering. Toxicology pending and further charges forthcoming.

Jane smiles. The child was her mother's meal ticket, and due to her disability mom would get a check and services for the rest of the child's natural life. Her death is the last thing she would have wished.

No rush, nor orgasmic thrill, just satisfaction she had corrected a misstep in the grand scheme of the universe. In some other reality, the poor child grows up normal and is the first woman to reach the rings of Jupiter. But not here. Not now. Despite her lack of religion, Jane knows even the ancient Hebrews would leave deformed children to the elements or what they considered to be God's hands.

Now for her next project.

Tawny's recent brain scans revealed she will never wake. Mom refuses to consider pulling the plug even if dad likes the idea of his little girl living on in the bodies of six other people.

Angels of Death or Mercy, as killer nurses are referred to after they are caught, report getting a sexual thrill out of killing, or nearly killing, a patient and at the last second bringing them back—being hailed a hero. Jane's no angel. She gets no thrill. She finds practicality in what she does.

The family hasn't the means to support the medical expenses to keep a dead girl alive by tube. She is fifteen and might live a full long life. Now she considers how to end it without damaging the organs.

Dad has the right idea to save the lives of others. Seven, sometimes nine people, but her organ tissue must match six people in need on the list. This is society's problems. They don't focus on keeping people healthy or fixing those who are capable of being fixed, instead, hundreds of thousands are wasted on a dead girl because of mom's guilt.

If she had only loved her a little bit more her baby wouldn't have made a dumb teenage choice. Choices in life are like playing the lottery. Only a lucky few win big. Most lose and a select few break even.

The door to Tawny's room sticks as she pushes on the handle. It should not be closed at all. She'll call maintenance in the morning.

The fuck she will.

Charles, night orderly and god's gift to women hops off the bed. He towers over Jane by two feet and his rock-hard cock would cause a mare to cry. Why a man with such a proud member would need to result to rape she'll never understand.

"What the fuck?" Jane demands.

He reaches for her throat with fingers matching the thickness of his still stiff cock. Jane never flinches. Only her eyes shift up as if peering over the top of invisible glasses in annoyance. She uncaps the needle in her hand. Before he reaches her, "Touch me and I'll inject you."

He halts.

She only half bluffs. The syringe is empty of a fluid. It contains air, and she could kill him with air, but worst she would do is give a stick. He doesn't know that.

"Back over there and put that thing away." She points the needle at his member.

He does as ordered. No verbal protests.

Jane keeps the syringe gripped, ready to stab as she inspects Tawny. "You're fucking stupid. Have you touched her before? And don't lie."

He falls into a chair, struggling to tuck his stiff penis into his pants. "I've played with her tits a few nights."

"And when no one noticed you thought you'd rape her? She's fifteen and a virgin. you'd have torn her open. They'd know it was you." She pulls up the girl's gown, inspecting. "How far did you get?"

"I couldn't get the tip in. She's closed for business."

"No blood." Jane must relinquish the syringe to pull up the girl's panties. "You were going to rape her with her catheter in. You're seven kinds of fucking stupid."

"You going to report me?" He undoes his belt and pants button to get his saluting cock back inside his uniform.

"No. From now on, you are going to do exactly as I say, when I say it. You belong to me, starting with you never touching another patient unless I tell you too. In fact, I want your key card."

Charles struggles to refasten his pants. "If I'm caught without it they'll fire me."

"And what will happen to you if I report this? She's got her flower." The bitch mom actually had them check. Her daughter will never wake, but at least she was a good girl, not a slut. "Your horse cock would have opened her enough they would have proof." She doubts he got far enough to damage. "How about your precum? They check DNA now."

"All right." Charles unclips his ID from the belt clip. The hospital has yet to install cameras, but in a few select areas the identification cards substitute for keys—when they work.

The pressure within him subsides as he limps toward flaccidness. Charles adjusts his white pants and tee-shirt uniform top, finding some courage to ask, "Why aren't you having me arrested?"

The ten-thousand-dollar question at the top of the pyramid—What is a scapegoat? Wait wrong game show answer. What answer do I give not ending with his fingers around my throat? Charles would have no money, so not financial blackmail. I could make him think I want him for sex, but one time in bed, and he'll discover how not true that is. "I need an ally. I want off nights for a day shift."

"A few of the other nurses are ahead of you."

"Then you understand how seniority works, but it also goes by performance. What if those nurses had one or two little non-life-threatening mistakes on their shifts and I did not?" Jane almost winks at him.

"You would bump to the head of the list," Charles adjusts himself. "Where would that leave me?"

"Debt paid, you go on with your job and never touch another patient again, or you'll find out what I was going to inject you with."

III

BAM. BAM. BAM...BAM...BAM. BAM.

Jane lowers the Smith and Wesson .357. A bit too much gun for her thin arms, but nowhere near the kick the forty-four would have had. She has a vision of flames from the barrel and a gun flying back to impact her face. No, this will do. She'll do some of those therapeutic arm curls she instructs stroke patients to doto add strength.

The bell alarm alerts all shooters on the line to unload and place their weapons on the table. Charles joins her in the cubicle. He slips the gun by the warm barrel from her hand and places it on the table. "Want a clean target?"

She pulls the ear protection down to her neck. "I must know how I did."

On the range the paper silhouette of a man has six clear orifices. Three in the midsection group tight under the heart, one in the bladder and two in the throat.

"You're the quick learner, Annie. But I would stick to center mass if this is for protection. Avoid fancy trick shooting. You'd kill him with a throat shot, but you may miss if he is moving toward you."

"Show me how to reload it." She beams. It's been a long time since anything like a sexual stirring moved her, but the power surging through her with each trigger pull stimulates her loins. Orgasmic—if she knew what one felt like.

No wonder men must go out and kill things with such tools.

In the cubicle he flips the release and the cylinder pops out the side. "You do this as soon as you fire, and not only will the gun be hot. so will the brass. He dumps the six spent casings into a clean-up bucket.

"You just slide each new round into the empty holes. Some of these guns have a speed loader so you do all six at once."

"Just like you and little girls," Jane whispers.

Charles jerks his head around and no one is within ear shot.

"You ever notice," she holds up the shiny gold metal bullet between her thumb and index finger, thinner than the round itself, and twists it in the air as if peering into a soul, "How this is like a tiny penis?"

"No."

She slides the next round in herself. "Fits perfectly snug, unlike sex with a breathing man. Guns were invented by men. Was this a way to make sure you're always fucking with people?"

The bell rings.

"You got this?" Charles asks.

She nods, He steps from the cubicle. She pops her wrist so the cylinder slams into place. Now live, she places her feet shoulder-width apart. The bell chirps. She raises her arms level with her shoulder, adjusts her grip, left hand over right, and peers down the sight.

Thunder.

A hole magically appears three inches above her first group of three. She put the next five close enough to the first shot and the individual holes merge as one. Dumping the brass in the trash bucket, she reloads. This time five of her shots splatter what would be his brains. One round penetrates the white next to the left ear.

The bell rings.

She places the gun on the table.

Charles steps in. "That miss was the guy that kills you."

IV

JANE SLIDES CHARLES' identification card into the vertical door reader. A low *buzzut,* as if the buzzer is dying, whines to signify entry. Charles has been an angel at work. And he will be an Angel. She treads lightly, as she wants to utilize him for as long as possible. The burn ward houses three patients tonight—all long term but terminal. Sometimes the paramedics do their job too well and people should just be allowed to die on scene.

She hangs back just inside the door—studying. No one notices her.

V

"CHARLES, WILL YOU bring me those syringes from the top of the drawer?"

He complies. Rarely do they spend time near each other while on shift unless work requires the interaction. Big, strong men are utilized in the wards where patients must be moved often. He reaches in and doesn't think twice about the open sterile packages the syringes should be sealed in.

Jane takes them from him in her latex gloved hands. "Thanks." She places them on a tray with several vials of medicine to be distributed to patients. She hands him his identification card. "You'll need this. Go down to the burn ward. Tell them it's a slow night and you want to offer your assistance. See if they need anything."

His first response is confusion. "You going to do something to make another nurse appear incompetent like when I stole those drugs?"

"The less you know the better. And if they find out we *see* each other outside of work they won't allow us on the same shift. The deal was you do what you are told."

"I need to stretch my legs anyway," Charles grumbles.

As soon as he leaves, Jane pockets the drug vials and the syringes. She keeps to her rounds. Charles has been in the drug closet more than an orderly should, although no one checks the records.

They might one day and she will have a stockpile of meds. After Charles collects his unemployment none of those drugs will be traced back to her. They will deduce he sold them for street value. The prize is not the deadly medication it is his fingerprints on five unused syringes.

At the end of her rounds she checks on Tawny. She wanted to do this a week ago but thought better in case the family requested an autopsy. She didn't know if any form of sexual penetration would be detected. People believe during a rape a woman is scared and torn open—leaving a ton of evidence.

Untrue.

Women are sexual creatures. To the horror of the victim, sometimes her body betrays her and she enjoys the forced intercourse. Defense attorneys love to utilize that tidbit. Isn't it trust, little miss slut, the whole time he was inside you, you never scream no, instead you moaned like a whore, a whore who was asking for it? You wanted him, so this wasn't a rape.

Jane loathes the legal system and its maladjustment towards victims.

True, the body enjoyed it, but the mind didn't. The poor girl never asked for it. Tawny never asked for it—helpless in a hospital bed. Comatose—forever—never getting a chance to know love or be disappointed by a boy she believes she'll love forever.

Jane prepares the concoction of medications including Tawny's prescription pain killer. She's not the primary nurse for Tawny. The toxicologist might deduce Tawney was given a second dose of her meds by accident, which the hospital will cover up.

The other meds are counterintuitive to her recovery—if she were able to recover. The best part is nothing will damage a donatable organ and part of her considers they won't have time to run a complete toxicology if they want to save six other lives.

She drops the tainted syringe covered with Charles' fingerprints in the sharp's bucket.

She's back at her desk and charting for at least a half hour before Tawny codes.

VI

JANE LAYS OVER the edge of her claw foot tub, her finger slipping from the page she turns. Charles thrusts inside her, quaking jarring her vision of the book on the floor.

"Slow down, cowboy. First, this is all you get. Second, just because I have no nerve feeling between my legs doesn't mean I can't be hurt."

"Sorry," Charles grunts, kissing her shoulder as he draws slowly in and out of her. "You know it's hard for me to get into this when you don't seem to care."

"Fuck off, Charles. Tawny wasn't going to get *into you* while in her coma. You left precum on her thigh." Jane lies about that part. "Now finish. I want to soak in the tub alone."

He pumps his hips, his shutters informing her he completed his task. He lays against the porcelain.

"Want to cuddle?"

"No. I just allow you to do what you do because I don't want you touching any of the patients when I'm not on shift. And don't kiss me again."

"We had a deal. I won't break it," Charles says.

"Good. What I don't understand is how a handsome, well-built man doesn't have women lining up at his door."

"You're a woman who has no physical desires."

"The nursing gals always enjoy out-sizing each other's loves, boyfriends and husbands," she says.

"They lie, just like men. I've been with a few dozen women. Want to guess how long my longest running streak was with a single girl?"

She closes her book and twists around. "Besides me." She'd allowed him to relieve himself inside her for three weeks now.

"Twice. Two sexual encounters with the same woman. Girls talk about landing the huge one, and some do. Some want to know what it is like. But most see it and say no. Some, as it stretches them, say no. Most women are scared of it. Some tell you it will never fit and outright refuse. One or two try and then don't want a second date because it hurt so bad."

"Become a porn star. Those girls are smaller than me and take bigger than you," Jane suggests.

"I don't care what you think of me. I want a lover and partner," Charles says.

"You're right, but raping a comatose girl…"

"It was a moment of weakness. When you go so long without you get desperate. What about you? Why…well…why don't you work?"

"I never have. My plumbing has never worked. Never bled, never had any sexual desires. Part of why I attended nursing school, but there was nothing in the books about it. I was even a little slutty in high school and not one boy did a thing for me, not that any of them tried."

"You like girls?"

"Nope. I just don't have any tingle."

"We could get you a vibrator, try some clit stimulation," he offers.

"I have three. There is nothing going on down there. I allow you to do it in the tub so you don't tear me."

"I thought it was to keep me on your leash. Tawny's dead, so you don't have anything over me anymore," Charles says.

"Buy me another gun."

"I don't have the money," he says.

"I'll give it to you, I just want you to be the one to buy it," she says.

"You changed the subject."

"I don't want to speak about how I'm not normal, that every medical book I've read lumps it into female sexual dysfunction. I'll let you get your rocks off and you do what I want."

"I just thought you might want to make love over being a warm-blooded blowup doll," Charles says.

VII

IN FRONT OF her full-length dressing mirror, Jane flips open the chamber on the Smith and Wesson—empty. She examines herself—her body posture—her every nuance as she holds the gun to her temple.

Holds it under her chin.

Places the barrel between her breasts.

Her forehead.

She studies the angle her body would be in if she made such a choice to end her life with a gun. She memorizes how the elbow would be cocked if she jerked her head as if changing her mind at the last second, flinching as the hammer slams down. Finally, after she knows how she would be if she made such a choice, she places the barrel in her mouth.

VIII

WHEN JANE DOES work the same shift as Charles she uses her time to build a pattern, constantly dispatching him to the burn ward on slow nights to check on the patients. He builds a relationship with Chrissy, the bubbly girl fresh from nursing school. Coed with perky tits. The kind of breasts mothers with kids hate seeing on childless women because they believe their husbands will leave them for such younger, firmer girls.

Being friends with Chrissy, Charles visits the burn ward even on nights Jane is off shift. He must pass through the keycard required doors. No one checks the logs, but they are there—an electronic footprint.

He is a pawn. Jealousy in their interaction would overwhelm Jane if she had sexual desire for Charles.

She slips into the burn ward using Charles' identification.

Careful—Jane's mantra since Tawny.

The deformed baby coded, the ninety-seven-year-old slipped away. Both were cut short in life, unnaturally. No one even noticed. Jane's stockpile of medication, untraceable back to her, begs her to be used. Each death was weeks apart, leaving her with only one syringe left with Charles' prints. Victim number four had fared better. It lacked the maximum dose of her cocktail, but the levels in toxicology would have pointed to someone on her shift. The hospital will only cover up deaths for so long.

If Charles liked miss perky tits, and she wasn't scared of his dong, she might lose her control over him. Men are quick to chase sweeter smelling tail.

These poor souls in the burn ward have been suffering, but not from pain. The longer a person burns the less pain they experience. It is healing and recovery and the rule of nines. According to the math all three of these people will die, they just shouldn't in one night.

Jane waits until Chrissy goes to the bathroom. To save the hospital money she is the only nurse on the ward. Jane injects each well-done person with her concoction and drops the syringe in the sharp's box. She is gone from the burn ward before Chrissy washes her hands.

Jane offers Charles his identification back before the codes on the burn ward hit the interclan.

It's while everyone rushes to assist Chrissy that Jane slides into the room of a seven-year-old boy. He crashed his four-wheeler and the brain scan is inconclusive, but nothing happens when the doctor tickles the kid's left side. She removes the breathing tube and places the kid's hand as if he had a spasm and jerked it out. Jane rushes to the codes on the burn ward. Everyone knows poor Chrissy is alone and will need help.

IX

"IF YOU WERE the target of the investigation then they would have placed you on administrative leave," Jane assures Charles.

"I spent all day being questioned," he says.

"They were burnt on over eighty percent of their bodies. They were not going to survive."

"All three coded at once. They said they suspended Chrissy and they wanted to know why I go down there all the time."

"Suspending her is normal procedure. Chrissy works alone some nights shifts, you would do your rounds and then you would check on her. Also normal."

"I told them that. They also asked me about missing meds, and some other deaths. I was on shift during all of them."

She meets Charles accusing eyes. "People die. The bean counters are just trying to scare you to make sure they have their ass's covered. No one has died on this ward that wasn't natural. The little boy died the same night as the burn ward codes. He jerked his own breathing tube out and we were all on the burn ward helping. You were down there, too. You just keep your mouth shut," she says.

With a dry throat Charles blurts, "Murder is a little worse than an attempted rape."

"Why don't you go to the car. I'll bring you something to calm your nerves."

As Charles moves away from the nurse's station she whispers, "Hey, you got to pull your car around to the south entrance."

"That wing is closed for renovations."

"And no one is parked there." Jane smiles.

• • • • •

Rain. She hates the rain. It is proof she was outside.

Charles was smart, at least, in parking between two dusk-to-dawn lights, dark due to the remodel. The hospital expansion means more health care money and no room for a three-death scandal. Jane has yet to be questioned. Some repercussions may come from the little boy's death since she left the ward unattended.

Jane slides into the passenger seat, using her hands to towel the water from her face.

"What did you swipe?" he asks.

"I decided against medication." She reaches over and fondles his crotch. His member grows. "I thought I might…well give you something a little more therapeutic that won't show up if they do a piss test."

"You said you don't like doing that."

"Just put your head back. I don't want you watching me acting like some dog lapping at a popsicle." Jane pushes his chin up so his eyes meet with the ceiling.

Smiling, he likes how she fondles him through his pants.

Cold metal presses up against his chin. The pressure hurts—confuses him—in the second he realizes that it is his brains that decorate the car ceiling. Jane fumbles the gun into his hand. The haze of gun powder covers her and him in the enclosed space and her ears ring. She has to get inside, change and dry. She'd bet some blood specks her white uniform.

Charles' suicide will close the investigation. Either it confirms their suspicions of him or it cements it. She will have to wait a few months before allowing any unnatural deaths to occur on her shifts.

FIVE

PA EDGARS

THE SHIRTLESS EDGARS pulls Taylor's hair back behind her head. The girl's eyes stare at the floor refusing to glance at the reflection in the hotel mirror.

"You're pretty." He slips off her oversized glasses.

"I'm a bookworm." A funhouse version of herself now reflects back at her. She closes her brown eyes.

"And beautiful." With one hand he places the glasses on the dresser next to the mirror and with his other hand he strokes her long brown hair.

"All those women, there to get your book, they all desired you. Why did you ask me to stay?" Under his touch she trembles as his fingers brush the back of her supple neck cleft.

"See, women lack an understanding of what beauty is." He slides gentle fingertips along her neck and draws a line along her chin, easing her face up. "It's not just this pleasing flesh." He leans in to whisper in her ear. His warm breath tickles her. "It is what's in here." He taps her temple. "Those women all love the protagonist, my imagined hero, because of his suave demeanor, his conquering of women. Despite all their protests women love the dominating man with rippling muscles, but not you."

His warmth confuses her. "I…I like muscles."

"You gleaned deeper into the text. That excites me." His hand grabs her hip firmly, but not hurtful, pulling her back so she detects the pressure in his pants against her cheeks.

"I. I. I," she stammers. "I've never kissed a boy. Not really. I mean, this one touched his lips to mine, but no more."

"I don't want you to do anything you don't want to do."

His warm breath melts any forcefield she may have had.

He circles his lips around her neck, never touching her—just breathing.

"Why would you want someone who doesn't even know…"

"Do you know what to expect when you open a book?" His finger draws along the bumps of her spine.

Her bottom lip quivers. "I've read the book jacket."

"And I bet you've watched porn."

Taylor's china white skin reddens.

"So you have an idea what you desire, but viewing's not the same. Each new book is an adventure for the first time." His hands slip under the bottom of her shirt, his fingers exploring the slight paunch of her belly. "Do you like what you saw in the videos?"

A confusing mess of emotions churns her stomach. Taylor desires this, but she's never been asked such questions. Her time in front of the computer was private.

His fingers slip into the waistband of her pants, but before they creep too far south too fast she grabs his right wrist. "I don't…I do…I."

"Don't be embarrassed. It's normal."

Taylor knows him. She's read all his novels, short stories and blogs, listens to the radio interviews and clips newspapers. She knows and trusts this man. "I don't know how those girls do it. It hurts when they slide in a finger. And they take men. So big."

"Which finger?"

She extends her middle finger. He kisses the thin digit before exploring a more erogenous zone. His lips caress her neck at the same moment he slides her pants down an inch, exposing the top part of her lacy black panties.

"Did you wear those for me?" He tenderly massages her neck with his lips.

"Yes." Her mouth turns into a desert. "I just…never thought you'd see them."

He rubs his fingers along her middle extremity. "Did you think of me when you used this finger?"

Her knees wobble. He holds her up on noodled legs as she weakens in his arms.

"What did you want me to do to you?"

"I wanted to bounce on top of you." Her knees scream at her to sit down, "I like watching that." Her admission spills out having never even shared the fact with her journal.

He slips her pants down just below her thigh gap, places his right hand on top of hers and guides it toward her own crotch. She only resists once her fingers reach her mound.

"I've never…"

He overpowers her using her own fingers to rub her special spot. Her next gasp lacks protests as her clit swells. Never had it felt this good when she had touched herself.

He runs his left hand back to her chin brushing past her breast as he clamps tight pushing her face up again. "See your face. Your eyes. You're allowed to enjoy this."

Blurry both from her lack of control and her pleasure, she locks eyes with her reflection.

"You're beautiful."

She releases her first moan.

He drops his left hand and she keeps her chin in place. Her fingers move faster as she watches her blurry self.

The clink of his belt clasp fills her ears, followed by a zipper.

He slips the back of her panties down under her rump. The next part happens so fast.

His right hand leaves her fingers, but she doesn't cease her rubbing. Before the burning pain his hand seals her mouth shut with his palm. She must concentrate to breathe through the one clear nostril. At first, she swirls her fingers faster on her clit. She thinks the pressure was normal, now she knows. He opens her up from behind. Taylor's whole body presses into the glass—trapped. He sinks into her.

She didn't want this. With each push her ass burns. The first few slow thrusts—possible to get used to—swiftly turn into a jackhammer. Taylor's screams are blocked, but her mouth remains open.

As the surprise of this not being a session of lovemaking but a destruction of her, her vision blurs further as her eyes water.

• • • • •

Taylor draws her knees up to her chest. Her bra dangles loose under her shirt. Her pants and sexy panties still around her ankles would act as leg shackles even if she found the courage to bolt for the door. With her slightly off vision she spots Edgars next to the sink cleaning his dong with a washcloth.

It was never like that in any of the movies. Even when the girl said it was too big the dude never…

It wasn't gentle…but it wasn't…

Edgars moves around the room folding his clothes and packing his suitcase, as if this assault was normal.

Taylor wonders if it was normal. She fantasized about him being with her. She had heard it hurt the first time. No. He hurt her and it was…

She lifts into the air and he puts her on the bed so her rump hangs just off the edge. Grabbing the back of her head, he mashes her face into the sheets. The sting burns and she screams. He muffles her with the bed as he slaps her ass, one cheek then the other. When he releases her she gulps air. He tosses an empty condom wrapper on the bed near her face. The next sharp pain, at least, was in the correct hole.

• • • • •

Before the third time he slipped off all her clothes. Taylor just laid on the bed fully nude. Never has she been unclothed in front of anyone in her entire short adult life. He dropped the condom and then the wrapper into a sandwich baggie. The strong odor of bleach. Even if she wanted to understand *why bleach* her brain doesn't want her to move from the bed. The sex was rough. It hurt. He hurt her, but he has made no suggestion he wants to harm her. Maybe this is how he likes his sex. Maybe she will learn to like it. Sex hurts the first time.

He cleans the hotel room as she just remains on the bed—feeble to his commands. She did desire him. She did come up here with him.

As he scrubs down places they had been or touched in the room, Taylor wonders if that means he will scrub her down too. No, she just wouldn't tell. Never speak of today. Promise never to tell. She had come back to the room with him, and chosen to come into the room. She allowed him to caress her and… She never told him no. She wanted to be with him. She just had no idea it was like this.

He slips inside her again.

● ● ● ● ●

The fifth time of him being inside her ended as morning light peeked around the cheap hotel curtain. Taylor was numb—at least the husk on the bed was. She didn't know where she was anymore. Her abdomen burned. She thought she peed herself. He made her go potty after the third time and the warm jet spilled from her like glass shards. She held it in. The pressure was too much. She had to empty her bladder—worse than any cramp she ever had. Her grandmother's description of a kidney stone sounded about right.

He wasn't violent. He did those things she would consider part of the making love process, the way a first time should be. He lit a candle and kissed her body. She hated herself. When he propped her leg up she held it there for him, never removing her eyes off the flickering flame.

Sporting yellow rubber cleaning gloves, he pinches her nose, forcing her to breathe through her mouth. He jabs a hard rubber ball against her teeth, buckling the strap in her messy hair. She knows it's part of an S&M game. She saw it on one of the videos.

He shoves her in the bathroom where bleach fumes bring tears. He covers every inch of exposed skin in bleach. Rubbing her down twice he places her into the tub. Taylor moves as he directs. She lost control of her body hours ago. Her brain told her to allow him to do what he demands, and all will be fine.

The water's freezing cold. Needles sting at the burning between her thighs where he rubbed bleach. He pushes her head, so she lays down. It's only as her lungs lack air that she realizes he has her head under the surface. Her desire to struggle loses to his strength as he holds her down until stillness.

After the last air bubble burps from her nostrils he caresses her cheek with the back of his hand. She could have been a love, but instead she will fill pages. Shaking the water from his hand, he leaves her in the tub.

Flipping open his laptop, Edgars connects to the free WIFI from the hotel next door. He dips into a hidden folder and logs into the deep web to send a simple three-word message—I NEED HELP.

SIX

SKA: MEETING TWO

I

WELCOME TO SERIAL Killers Anonymous, a fellowship of people determined to prevent our urges to take another human's life.

II

JESSE RECONSTRUCTS THE tale of murdering his professor—exchanging his need for help in tracking his sister's murderer for his grades being too low, the danger of academic probation and losing his scholarships.

"Way to go kid," Robert cheers. "You're a killer after all."

"Not a serial murderer yet," Ed muses. "But I've more trust since you succeeded in taking a human life. I'm not sure the cops would do much to you since they caught the girl's father beating and raping her. You might be hailed as a hero in his case."

"We are not here to praise past action," Jane says. "It's counterproductive to reward negative behavior."

"Nor are we here to condemn them," Al says.

"I earned an A. I wanted my A," Jesse whines.

"Studying all those killers has been the brunt of quality education."

"Did it impress Amylyn?"

"I haven't thought about her. She attended some girl's college on the east coast. Even failing to kill, I protected the girl, but not permanently. The dad could get out of prison, based on his behavior, in a few years and go after her. I had to know what to do, how the cops thought. Some of you do the same. I wanted to be educated."

"Admirable, kid," the new voice completes.

"We have two new members joining us," Jane explains. "When we have new members, I believe they should start by sharing one of their early incidents, so we keep building trust within our group. At the end of this meeting we must decide how we will proceed in bettering our health."

"Then why did I go first?" Jesse asks, having shared he killed Professor Arnett to commence the meeting.

"You spoke of near murder, Kid. Some of us found you wanting of our little group," Kenneth says.

"I'm sorry I'm not on you guy's level. I never desired to kill. I never hurt puppies or wet the bed. Mine was a moment of passion, I didn't get my grade I earned. He was a stuffy old man who didn't understand. He said my analysis of the killer wasn't accurate. How would he know? He never killed anyone."

"Neither had you," Jane says.

"I'd been closer than he had been. My insight was accurate," Jesse says.

"Kid, I'm not sure you'd pass the psycho test to be a cop," Ed says.

"Many people would love to put us on their couch. Your efforts to prevent your urges are commendable," the new voice says.

"As they should be. What we do is wrong," Al says. "Even when some justification for killing a person is present we have to accept what we do is wrong. We're not elected as judge and jury. First step has to be accepting what we do is inhuman."

"In the self-help steps of Alcoholics Anonymous recover people must admit they are powerless over their urge to drink," Jane says. "Are we powerless in our urge to slaughter?"

"We form our own rules here, you said," Robert adds. "We keep anonymity."

"Maybe the final part of our healing is to reveal who we are," Jesse suggests.

"First are introductions," says the new voice, "in an AA meeting."

"True," says Jane, "but we have elected to assume pseudonym just like in the chatrooms."

"I live my life under a nom-de plume," says the voice.

"We thought as part of our advancement toward acceptable societal behavior we would create our rules to help us. Not everything in AA works for what we have done," Jane explains.

"We do seem to be powerless over our need to kill."

"Even I agree," says Jack. "I came here because I enjoyed what I was doing, after a fashion. When it stopped being satisfying revenge I knew it was murder."

"My need to kill has made my life unmanageable. Normally you get away from being sloppy, but my desires are causing more and more frequent killings. Cops would suspect I desire to get caught. I do. I don't want to be punished, but I want to stop. If your group doesn't provide relief I will have to surrender to authorities. I get up from bed and spend my day searching for the next victim. I must be stopped," the new voice confesses.

"We're all here for such a revelation," Jane says.

"You want rules for our meetings? New members speak first is a solid rule. Unless…what if you initiate with anyone who has killed since our last meeting?" Al suggests.

"What do we do with someone who has? We don't have chits to recant," Kenneth says.

"Ed, Robert, you have no option?" Jane inquires.

"I find this a waste of my time, but I don't have any other options. I've avoided killing for two weeks. I burnt my trophies. I slept with no lot lizards. I changed my overland route to attend this meeting. I don't know what else could I do?" Ed asks.

"Has anyone killed?" Jane asks.

Silence.

"No one." She nods. "Even for those of us with years between killings. We're making a start."

"If no one's killed, and we find ourselves comfortable with Jesse's confession, it's the new people's turn to share," Al says.

"I still don't like the kid," Ed says. "But let's get to know our new guests before I share anymore."

"We've explored early kills so we understand our motivations. We thought it might help to discover why we do what we do," Jane explains.

"A character's backstory is highly important to the teller even if he doesn't give up the imperative information to the listener."

"You speak like a writer," notes Kenneth.

"Because I am one. And before you ask, I write murder mysteries."

III

"IMAGINE WHAT IT'S like to stab a person."

When speaking to the public I prefer the cordless ear mike to easily pace around the front of the lecture hall. It creates the illusion my practiced speech was actually an improvised conversation. "Do you have the picture of the knife entering the soft tissue—splitting open the flesh?"

I make the *Psycho* downward knife slash motion, leaving out the Rer, Rer, Rer, sound effect. "Get a whole chicken from the butcher shop and be like Alfred Hitchcock. Who, for *Psycho* sat with his back to a table of fruit and listened for the sound he wanted of the knife going into the body. He chose a casaba—a Turkish melon—in case you didn't know."

Some of the audience scribble the melon's name down.

"My rabbit chasing has a point. Take your knife, as close to the one your character uses in the story and butcher the uncut raw chicken. Listen to the sounds. The serrated edge of the blade as it cuts gashes into the flesh. Rips tendons. Saws bone. Now write it down. Don't lose what you see, hear and your emotions as you murder. You won't get the blood blooms. Living blood never behaves as it does in the movies," I sipped from the water bottle left for him on a wooden bar stool.

"Now you have your notes about stabbing flesh you finish butchering your chicken and cook the meat. Don't ever let food go to waste. Makes you wonder if Mr. Hitchcock had casaba juice for dinner."

The following group laughs—relieves the tension.

"I know there are plenty of you who wonder of the sanity of an author who constructs such gruesome murders. Let me just tell you I was never abused as a child. Nor, do I engage in illicit substance abuse, beyond the time I attended a Sammy Hagar concert."

Laughs scatter among the crowd—the ones who know the Red Rocker's reputation.

"Beyond normal childhood, fresh from diapers and bedwetting, I have not peed myself in my sleep. I don't think masturbation is ever excessive." Self-effacement enamors one to the crowd.

More laughs. The crowd loosens up.

"And no animal has died at my hand, but I have consumed many. What does my list mean?"

A cute wavy-haired blonde jerks up her hand.

I call on her.

Her white puffy cheeks redden. Anyone who might have glanced at her would recognize she was infatuated with my work.

"Your list, all common traits of known serial killers," she ejaculates.

She needed to breathe. Her excitement gushed as she was actually recognized by me. Fan girls—better than hair band groupies.

"Correct."

People around her thought she was the next contestant on the *Price is Right*. She might have wet herself.

"I listed the common factors nearly all captured or known serial, or even suspected serial killers have in common. Which brings me to the point of my writing seminar for all you wanting to know how I capture such believable, if not frightening, killers on the page. I do research. Gobs and hours of research." I raise my voice, "And not on the Internet—in the stacks. More reading than any English teacher ever assigned you."

The preverbal groans roll over the group.

"Sorry to tell you, writing a novel takes lots of homework. I spend my time reading newspapers. Reading 'What makes me a Murderer' books. I might even have a copy of 'Serial Killer for Dummies'. They have one for everything else."

More chuckles.

"My point, fellow aspiring writers, is you must write, but you must know your topic. And if you wish to follow my path, make friends with the homicide detectives. Once in a grand while you might get a peek at the murder book, or at least when you buy them drinks you hear how cops sound and speak, so your characters sound accurate and speak correctly." Most cops I know don't talk like they do on *Law and Order*.

They clap.

The next forty-five minutes of Q&A the drone of my own voice, precedes the flash of my pen on title pages.

I signed books until no one was left but the little, cute wavy-haired blonde. She purposely waited until last. Clutched in her arms, as if it were a newborn, was my first book. It was awful. I wondered what the publisher who approved its printing was self-medicating with to have said yes.

"Would you like it personalized?" I smile.

"Yes, please." She freezes, mouth agape.

"Do you have a name?"

Timid as a field mouse she answers, "Zana."

I thought she might cry when I scrawled 'To Zana, my best fan' and my name across the yellowing title page.

"You have no idea what this means to me." She teared up.

I glanced around. No one was in the room with us. I had become a big name in the writing world, but not so big I have an assistant to travel with me and pack my gear. Normally I had few books left after a signing so most of the labor was bringing it in.

"Zana, would you like to assist me in taking my empty totes to my car?'

"Yes." She came close to bouncing up and down. She wasn't a fat girl, but more mid-western thick, which was attractive as long as she stayed this weight. Her curves were proportional and feminine.

I sent her ahead and waited enough time, exiting through a door with a security camera—alone.

She was so excited. I don't think she even asked me what took me so long.

I always choose my parking spot to be as private as possible, even if the distance is a bit of a hike. I never plan on enticing a victim, but one never knows.

"Would you like to take a drive with me? Discuss my writing more?"

"Really?" Zana melts.

"Sure, I don't get a chance too often to discuss my work one on one with just a real fan. It's always groups or editors, who *never* understand my process."

"I would love too."

"Do you write?" I ask.

She nods.

"Get in." I unlock the door with the fob, but I open it for her like a gentleman.

When in an unknown location discover the best secluded spot quickly. The difficulty lies in not knowing the region, but also not exploring it. With a plane to catch in a few hours I would be above the fly-over states by the time anyone found her. Doubtful I will be cast as a suspect. My mild fame, and not from being a screen actor, granted me an amenity. The keystone bundlers, called detectives, in Podunk Nowhere's Ville always assume it's someone in my audience—*always*.

Two men sit in prison for girls I killed. I state a fact—Cops get a hard-on for a suspect and make the evidence fit—watch *Dateline*.

Zana would be easier than many. Her eyes saw only the moon when she gazed at me. Of all my victims, I felt this girl loved me. She had an unhealthy attachment which gave her trust she should not have. It allowed me to find a secluded picnic area on the backside of a park and hiking trail no one had visited in weeks. Park services had failed to clear the weeds from the entrance sign.

I leaned against the side of the car, pulling her toward me. I twirled her in this romantic twist. We stood spooning, her butt against my crotch. She giggles as my left hand stretches around her waist, tucking her in tight against me. Zana was melting into whatever fantasy she designed in her head about meeting me.

The needle was in her neck before she ever felt the stick. The plunger injects the Neuromuscular-blocking drug. Within seconds she drops, having paralysis of her skeletal muscles.

Holding onto a struggling, meaty girl usually causes me a mild back spasm, but she wasn't as heavy as I thought she would be. She was nice and soft. I drag her to the picnic table, leaving twin leg trails in the grass, roughing up the sod. Not because I lack the strength to carry her, but I liked the idea the cops would think I was smaller if it was a struggle for me to get her to the table.

She does the standard pleading promising to do whatever I want.

I explained she was doing what I desired as I pull on latex gloves.

I cut off her shirt. She had on a black, lacy bra much too small for her mounds. Once the black thong was free, I noticed Zana had freshly shaved this morning. She must have had fantasies about meeting me. On the left side of her pubis a tiny tattoo rest where only a person allowed to know her personally will ever visit. A red heart secured by a closed padlock lacking a keyhole.

I palpate the tat. "What is the meaning of your ink?"

"Why are you doing this?" she whines.

"Remember what I told you about the chicken?"

"All those people in your books. You killed them."

Smart girl. "My research involves more field experience than book research." I tap her ink, "What does it mean?"

"When I got married I was going to have his name tattooed as the keyhole to my heart."

"Do you have a boyfriend?"

"Yes."

Liar.

Her answer was too quick, "And when I don't text, he will wonder where I'm at." She adds as an afterthought, "And I have tracking on my phone."

"This phone?" I pop the battery from the electronic device. "No one will find you unless I want them to."

"But I love you. I love your work. I would so be yours."

"You're going to be mine. I'm forever going to make you mine. Each of my books gets the love I'd give a child. You will be immortally eviscerated in print, my lovely."

"Please. Please don't kill me."

"You'll be happy to know you weren't planned. I won't get to try a means of death I have yet to attempt. You will, however, add to the quality of my work."

"What are you going to do to me?"

"Ask your questions." I smiled.

Even not being able to move her body she responds to stimuli. The chilling air hardens her nipples to little pink bullets.

I keep a notebook so I don't forget a detail in my writing. Her tattoo choice fascinates me. "Explain to me why you choose your ink."

"I wanted to be naughty. Just a little. I thought a tattoo with my husband's name would be our private thing. You're the second man who knows it's there."

"If I didn't have to catch a plane I'd take it with me." I never collected physical trophies, but this one was deeply personal. I wanted to fillet it off and frame it.

The knife I bought at the convenience store after I disembarked the plane was not sharp.

Pain from the sawing of the dull edge exacerbated the sensitive groin area skin chalked full of nerves to enhance sexual pleasure, insuring massive amounts of propagation.

She screamed.

Our seclusion was confirmed when birds escaped in the trees from the pitching yawl.

She had a pitched tone, high enough to crack glass.

After I disposed of the identifying mark I opened my notebook and made some notes about the cuts. "Tell me how it felt."

Through her blubbering, "Please don't hurt me. I'll do whatever you want."

"Tell me how the knife felt, cold against your skin. If you don't remember...I'll cut you again."

I was going to cut her anyway, but many people under torture believe if they give in the pain will stop.

She gave a decent description of the cut, the way the chiseling knife tip stung like bees. How she clamped her anus because soiling herself would be embarrassing. How the warm blood rolled down her groin where her thigh connected and pooled under her cheek.

Zana was a want-to-be-writer-fangirl-writer.

"Now, what to do with you. I've reached my limits with a knife."

"I don't hurt so bad. I could make love to you. I could—" Zana blubbers.

"Dear, I get no perverted sexual thrill from this. I do this to seek understanding of what a human body goes through." I stroke her hair like a caring lover. "You, darling Zana, are my casaba melon."

IV

"LOCKED HEART," KENNETH says.

"What?" Murmurs from most of the group.

"A few years ago it was popular among the freshman girls. It was a love story centered around the tattoo the female protagonist gets. BAM. They find her body. The perfect boyfriend spends the rest of the book attempting to prove whether or not he is innocent," Kenneth explains.

"Was he successful?" Al asks.

"Don't give away the ending or no one here will buy the book."

"Are you claiming to be world renowned Mystery/slasher writer P.A. Edgars?" Kenneth asks.

"I have had three best sellers, one reaching the top ten on the *New York Times* list."

"No wonder your descriptions are accurate," Kenneth says.

"I'm glad I have a fan among my new friends."

"Not a fan, I just like to know what my students follow in pop culture. They make side references or use insults from a movie people my age would never purchase. I stay on top of their attempts to insult me. Or they ask me if I've ever 'Netflix and Chilled' before. You lose control of a class quickly when you don't know what they mean and they all laugh."

"Still you've read my work," Edgars says.

"It's the most brilliant cover." Jesse's flabbergasted. He won't admit he has to rethink his suspect list. "How have the police never pieced together your presence in a town and the murders similar to the methods of death?"

"I don't kill in every town I visit. I'm well known for my in-depth research into murders, but I avoid putting a detail in my book the newspapers leave out of the event. I will mix and match my killings. My books come out years after a murder so most assume I stole the idea from the murder's reporting. And people never connect killing an old black woman in the ghetto to the same death of a white girl living with rednecks. Not in seventeen books has anyone connected they were actually true crimes. It would give me an entire new shelf at the bookstore."

"You know the rules. No killing while you attend our meetings," Jane says.

"Do you mean to stop writing?" Kenneth asks.

"Never. No author has that ability. I've enough notes to continue for several more books. I might even try my hand at another genre. Despite the career ending status changes brings. I'm not allowed to profit off the deaths of my victims if incarcerated. I assume, like the rest of you, I just find myself needing to stop. Cutting on different woman yields the same answers about pain. I don't need further research, I need to stop. My final murder book follows a man in his quest to prevent a killing. I don't think it will sell. People love the gore."

Jesse wishes he remembered what books his sister read. Did she meet this guy at a book signing and he gutted her? Having eliminated Robert and Jack, he now wonders if the professor was correct and her killer is outside this group.

How can there be so many!?

His brain screams at him to check his evidence, yet no evidence points to his sister's killer being in this room.

"You killed those twins," Kenneth blurts out.

"The twin murders, ah, yes. During the Nazi death camp experiments—a real event. No one caught on those book deaths were all taken from killings I did," Edgars says. "But Dr. Mengele makes us all appear amateurs."

"You killed a set of twins," Jesse asks as confirmation.

"They don't share each other's pain, but the anxiety and fear most certainly existed between the pair. It took some finagling to get them both together and carry out my test. It was one of the few killings I planned out completely," Edgars admits.

"You only share once at a meeting. If not, then it becomes about helping you and not the rest of us," Jane says.

"I'm sorry. You've all done as much as I have, except maybe the boy. I applaud you for murdering your professor. I never thought to do such a thing to improve my grade. Did you get an A?"

"Some universities have a policy to award automatic A's in the event of a teacher's death. If the college burns down all attending students earn their degree where I attended," Kenneth says.

Jesse blurts, "We all did." He hadn't counted on follow up questions. "The department head thought it best to help with the grieving process."

Robert laughs. "So you got a fancy degree you didn't earn."

"He earned it. If he was studying the minds of killers what better way to know one than to become one?"

"He wants to stop before he turns into us," Al says.

"There are worst choices," Ed says.

"Just because you find killing homos a benefit to society, you'd be wrong," says Jack.

"You killed those scums who caused your family's death," Ed snaps.

"Yes, but I didn't discriminate on birth. I desired the source of the problem."

"We're off focus here, gentlemen," Jane interrupts.

"Are you sure? We need to work through all this aggression."

"What, you want us to speak how we hate our fathers?" Ed asks.

"Not everyone hates their parents," Al says.

"No, but many killers have parental unit issues," Edgars says.

"At some point during therapy a person has to move away from casting blame on shitty childhoods and abuse," Jane says. "We have to own what we did."

"I own it," Edgars says, "Maybe we should move into why we want to stop."

"We have one more new member to speak as well as sharing from the rest of the group," Jane says. "I know I felt some release after expressing about what I did. Being unable to speak about it to anyone... makes recovery so difficult—now I find myself lighter."

"I may be a redneck, but I, too, needed to share. I was raised not to discuss my emotions, but I did, and something left me," says Ed.

"Agreed," adds Kenneth. "I say I've had no urges since the last meeting, which I didn't. I don't just get the need to kill. It never pops up."

"You don't have a set cycle," says Edgars. "Cops track repeat killers' cycles, every so many months, weeks or even years. Randomness helps. Travel even better."

"I find all of you fascinating. I'm not sure I'm able to follow your rules, even if you have yet to set them in stone." The mystery guest offers. "I will leave before I have compromised any more of you."

"You already know about this group."

"If you don't want me to reveal you, I won't," the new man adds.

"We need insurance."

"My word should be good enough, but I understand how important your autonomy is. I won't reveal what I've heard. I will even share. I'm just not sure I possess the ability to stop. I do desire to quit, but I don't know if I'm capable. With full disclosure, I'm known by the FBI as The Plagiarist. I emulate other serial killers. By listening to your stories, I don't think of how I must stop, but instead how to copycat your killings."

"Why is the first thought I have is you would keep the cops from ever tying some of us to the crimes?" Ed asks.

"Identical killings allow for alibies."

"Mine are location specific. I'd end up being blamed for mine," says Kenneth.

"You killed in the same location?"

"I perpetuated the haunted house myth. Didn't you pay attention?" Kenneth says.

"Tell us about it," the new voice requests

"He did." Jesse knows his dead sister didn't end up in the basement of the plantation house. He wants to know more about this Plagiarist. "We should hear from the new guy first."

"We did hear about Kenneth's first killing, but he has taken more and it's relevant now, if he wants to share," says Jane.

V

"MR. KENNETH, WHAT do you know about the plantation house?" The pimple cratered teen asked.

"Local history's not on today's class lecture," I said.

"But it's way more interesting than the Reconstruction Era. The South should pay for the war, it was their fault."

"How do you justify your statement?" I asked.

"If they didn't own slaves there would have been no reason to fight a war."

"Clearly, we must review the events leading to the war. You missed several important elements," I scolded.

"I want to discuss the plantation house," the kid pleaded.

On any normal day students attempted to get off subject. The plantation house was a common topic and one I dissuaded, which actually caused more secret discussion. Plenty of kids trespassed on the property based on the stories I refused to collaborate. I overheard plenty of plans to go and made my choice. I selected just enough targets every few years to propagate the mythos.

"I'll allow one question—if it *is* within reason—I will answer."

"Great. I want to know—"

"You didn't allow me to finish. You first must tell me why it's referred to as the plantation house."

"Because it was a southern cotton farm."

The kid in the seat next to him actually high-fived him for giving the correct answer.

"Incorrect."

"How do you figure, Mr. Kenneth?"

"Cotton has never grown here. You check with the science teacher, but the climate is not right. Therefore, we return to my plans of understanding Reconstruction."

Even I cared little for the Reconstruction Era lecture, but it was on the state test. While I proceeded with my lecture, my peripheral vision witnessed the passing of notes. I knew the discussion was to set a time to visit the plantation house. It had been three years since the last death.

Every three or four years students needed a reminder, as if every new freshman class had to be brought up to speed on what happened. Many snuck there without incident, but when I learned of their shenanigans I considered cementing the myth with a body.

I did have to pick and choose. If I killed too many, too soon, it might get me caught. I liked the terror the town lived under because, no matter what, no one had the ability to keep the kids away from the *haunted* house.

Most people had a morbid side. They wanted to stand in the spot where multiple kids had hung themselves.

I prepared a black powder pistol. I learned I needed to be armed, and I enjoyed adding to the myth. To me it was about the myth. The chatter about how so many kids would go there to hang themselves thrilled me. Because no ghosts existed, the deaths were classified as suicide. Part of me wanted to give the town something more to speak about.

I waited in the hidden room for hiding runaway slaves.

I found it so strange how my mind wandered away from my intended actions while I postponed. I had learned so little about my hunting grounds. And because no one in the town spoke of this place, I did not wish to tip my hand by actively researching the property. But even the elders at the local diner, when asked—only when asked, and pressured—spoke as if they knew no history of this place.

It sparked my interest, even more as I waited for the teenagers. The deaths should spark more interest not less. In this town they never spoke of it. I didn't share what I learned when students inquired because I didn't want to slip in some piece of evidence only the killer would know. But the lack of conversation about the plantation house might be why so many students kept venturing out here.

Prohibition did not work.

The stair steps were not strong enough for the bounding pairs of feet. I knew it was two sets of shoes on the rotting wood.

Damn.

If the stairs cracked people would stop coming down here.

I thought about it. I might have been able to find some lumber on the property to match and make a repair. If I used a crosscut hand saw and pulled nails from one of the beams no one would notice in the darkness. The cops brought portable lamps to focus on the body. I was never close enough to find out where they pointed them.

The voices were muffled. I needed a peep hole, but it might allow a breeze to flow and lead to the hidden room's discovery. I would lose my vantage point and destroy the myth.

I believed if the shelf disguising the door was jerked it would not reveal the hidden runaway slave room. In reality, the original owners did want to help, but their deep moral protection was about making sure they—white people—were not found out. Punishments were harsh for abolitionists—free state or not.

I strained my hearing. The clear echo of feet on the stairs, but the voices were more muffled as if in a coffee can.

Two voices.

I was prepared with the pistol. Every time I witnessed kids entering the house... I did so from the tree line, even when I had desires to kill. All shuffled inside alone—on a dare. Now there were two. I would need the gun to make them obey.

After my second kill was a struggle to get him into the rope I carried the pistol. I thought black powder would keep the Civil War allegory alive. I made the balls myself from a period lead bowl to keep ballistics from being able to track it—cash at a flea market. I kept my fingerprints off them as possible evidence.

It was a first and only time I caught teenagers in the house who weren't so pissing their pants scared, they were lip-locked. Maybe they forgot how terrifying it was to be in a room where three people had hung themselves, not counting the legend.

With closed eyes and sealed mouths, they never saw the hidden door open.

I cleared my throat.

They jumped.

She let out a little burble scream, clamping her hand over her mouth.

Even in the limited moonlight enhanced by two flashlights the kids recognized me.

"Mr. Kenneth!" It was more surprise than loud, as if he had just pulled the hood off the Scooby-Doo villain at the amusement park.

One problem about lying in wait was I didn't know how many more kids were outside.

"Shush your hole, Benjamin."

"What are you doing here?"

I cocked the hammer. "I said shut it."

I needed to be quick.

"On the barrel, Cindy." She was a cute young girl, not bright, but not dumb. She would make a productive citizen if she grew up. Benjamin was going to leave a string of baby mamas.

She complied without words. Many people did.

"I hate being called Benjamin." He had grown a pair.

I shot him in the stomach.

The lead ball tore open his flesh. I knew bullets entered differently than what I saw in the movies, but I never expected such butchery of his abs. No wonder so many soldiers during the Civil War just had to have limbs amputated. His stomach was now shredded brisket.

He cried.

I might have, too. It appeared bad enough I had no doubt he would bleed out. I think the ball broke apart and bounced around inside.

Cindy screamed.

I didn't know how many more students might arrive or how much time I had left, but I was committed now.

I pointed the gun at her. This is where people's logic leaves them. She did not want to get shot. Witnessing all the blood flowing from the sucking wound in Benjamin's center, I didn't blame her, but I was about to kill her, and she was compliant. She should have charged me, died in the process of saving herself instead of being a sheep.

"Get on the barrel," I ordered the now trembling girl.

"Please, Mr. Kenneth, we won't say a thing. He needs a doctor."

Maybe she thought cooperation would lead to her life being spared.

I ignored her wishes and whines. "Reach up and slip the rope around your neck."

Reality sunk in for both.

Her fingers found a rope tied to the beam. She slipped the noose around her neck.

"Now reach up and pull it tight."

She complies.

"If you don't struggle it will be over quick," I advised.

Her eyes teared until her vision became a kaleidoscope of the darkened cellar. "Why, Mr. Kenneth?" Her question turned to blubbers. "Why are you killing people?"

I kicked the barrel.

She hadn't the body weight to snap her neck. She kicked and struggled, chortled burbles gasping for air. Her blue eyes exploded from their sockets as her lizard brain fought for air. Too heavy to get her fingers between her neck and the rope to relieve pressure over the airway she dies.

"Cindy!" Benjamin should have saved his breath by not moving. Struggle brought more blood. His screamed showers blood droplets from his mouth, ending in a coughing fit.

She ceased her struggle. Twitching legs the last of her life leaving her body.

I would have to burn my clothes. I considered doing it after the last kill, but now for sure. These would have black powder and possibly blood specks on them.

Kids didn't have cell phones yet. I didn't hear more voices from outside. They could be there scrambling around. I never noticed my ears ringing from the enclosed thunder of the round I expended. In all the excitement I never noticed, which meant their screams might have been louder than I thought. I considered someone might have heard my name.

I weighed my choices. So far no one was racing down the stairs. Kids outside would have had to get in a vehicle and drive—at a safe speed—the winding road's sharp curves wouldn't permit fast. Seven minutes to a house with a phone, convince the neighbors to call the sheriff, and if he was available and on this side of the county at least ten minutes to respond— conservatively.

Once poor Benjamin slumped into unconsciousness, he wouldn't last twelve minutes.

I slipped back into the hidden room.

VI

"I TAKE IT the boy died?" Ed asks.

"Yes. He bled out. Double murder, or as the newspaper called it, a suicide pact. The reports conveniently left out there was no gun to be found. I did get some scuttlebutt from a few student conversations about the bullet taking Benjamin's life being from the Civil War."

"Someone in the police department had to have shared that tidbit. Cops are dumb."

"We know they have faults. We're not here to discuss their bumbling," Jane says.

"Why are we doing this if it's not to discuss how it makes us feel?" Al asks.

"We are, but the ineptitude of the police is not why we did what we did. It's why we're allowed to continue and brought ourselves together to prevent future actions," Jane says.

"I understand how Robert allows some to live if they escape his hunt after the way Cindy died. She just climbed into the noose with no struggle. Someone willing to fight to stay alive deserves respect."

"The hunt is important, even the killing. When the one victim refuses to roll over, I couldn't bring myself to kill," says Robert. "Funny thing, of all those I've drug into the woods to hunt, women are the strong ones. They transform into fighters."

"They have no choice. Men are expected to be the prize winners. Most are not gladiators anymore, but women who are expected to be docile have only one direction to go," remarks Edgars.

"Many of us stalk women because they are weak, easy to manipulate to our will. You, Sir Robert, reward when they prove to be worthy. Have you freed many?" The Plagiarist asks.

"You weren't at the first meeting, but I put three arrows in that Gabby-bitch and she kept going. Her lover just gave up. Died in the snow."

Jesse clenches the moment to gather the information he needs to track these people back to their normal lives, determining if one murdered his sister. The professor will demand more detailed information since several of these killers don't stalk in their home neighborhoods. "What happened after you let her go? How did they not find you?"

"It's not the direction we should be exploring," Jane says.

Robert speaks before there are any more shifts away from his methods.

"She was found a few miles down the road half frozen, nearly bled out. The paper said she needed seven surgeries to repair the damage from the arrows. When the cops finally got to interview her, she had forgotten much of the attack."

"Or she's afraid you'll intervene. Did you keep her identification?" Edgars asks.

"I burnt anything I kept from any of my victims, as Jane suggested."

"She has no idea you just severed your connection to her. She knows you have her license."

Jane refocuses the group, "Robert, how did it affect you when you destroyed your trophies?"

"I built a fire. I touched them and smelled them and soaked in every bit of memory from each kill. And I tossed each child in one at a time. Each burned to nothing before I did the same to the other children."

"You think of your trophies as your children?" Edgars asks.

"Yes."

"I don't collect trophies, unless you count the novels. They are my children," Edgars says. "I could destroy my notebooks."

NOOOOOOOOOOOO! Jesse screams in his head. *My God. The evidence and the uniqueness of each murder, he might be the one who killed her. He's old enough. He traveled and did not murder in a pattern. I need those notebooks. It may not be enough to read his novels. How many more murders has he committed that are unwritten?*

"It would be the start to recovery," Jane says.

"You have said so several times. What else do we do to quell our urges?" Jack asks.

"You killed to avenge your family. Why can't you just stop?"

"As I eliminated the drug trade in my town other crimes dropped. The town returned to the type where people didn't have to lock their doors at night," Jack says.

"But a murderer was on the loose."

"The targets were criminals. Much like those of you who choose prostitutes as targets, no one cared when the local drug dealers got bumped off. There were no signs of a turf war so the cops didn't investigate too deeply," Jack says.

"No one prays for a dead crack dealer."

"If the town is safe then just retire," Jane says.

"It's not safe—it will never be safe." Jack clinches a fist.

"Nowhere is safe. And even if you stopped those drug dealers and we stop killing, others will take our place," Al says.

VII

I CHOSE THIS mall because no cameras surveyed the parking lot. Security was more concerned with catching shoplifters over the safety of the female employees going to their cars after midnight. Most women would go in pairs, but once they were in their cars and on the road, they lost all the fear they had of being attacked. Most never noticed they weren't alone on the road.

I tracked a half dozen, but none of them matched my need. It was more than selecting an easy target—most of them were. One would stop to buy gas at a service station with only the pumps on and no employees around. They believed some crazed worker might grab them.

I had prepared my den. I needed a new play partner.

I thought about this one the second time she bought gas at 1:23 AM on a Tuesday. The place had cameras, but I could park out of range and drag her. All they would get was my build and height, but so many white men were five ten. With a jacket and rolled towel fitted from sleeve to sleeve I appeared super broad shouldered.

No—she wasn't right for me.

Then the night a man escorted this adorable redhead to her car, I knew I had found her. She was beautiful. So trusting of this man I'd never seen before. Both must have been new to working the late shift. He kept her talking, each by their perspective cars, until the lot cleared.

I knew.

I knew what he was.

He angered me.

He wasn't a true predator.

Not like me.

He was a jackal.

What I did was love.

At some point during their chatting he wormed his way around to the passenger side of his car and was within a few feet of her.

Amateur.

He tugged and pulled on her arm hard enough to dislocate her shoulder. Luckily, he didn't. It also gave her the opportunity to scream, which worked for my benefit because it scared him. He flung her into the back seat and bound her hands. He would pay dearly for bruising her skin with the second punch. I'm sure the first was hard enough to keep her from screaming further, but he had to have a second to prove what a man he was.

In his stupid panic he may have watched for cars when he fled, but his mind was only on avoiding flashing cherry lights not the UV lights of a mid-sized SUV.

I drove past when he turned off on a conservation road leading to a boat launch. I flipped the lights off and turned around. It had only one exit. As upset as he made me by harming my love, my calm must be maintained. This was a spontaneous action and those lead to mistakes cops uncovered if care was not maintained.

By the time I put my car into park he was holding open the back door. She had kicked him from the way he was doubled over and using the door to support his weakened knee.

I kept a gun with me. Normally, I didn't load it in case a feisty girl was able to get it away from me, but they never knew it lacked bullets. I chose not to risk it with a male. I knew nothing of him or his capabilities.

I think he wet himself when I stepped from the darkness, my hands covered by latex gloves.

The redhead thanked me for saving her. Fool had bound her with a necktie. I unwrapped her wrists and tossed it in the back seat. Her DNA was all over it. He protested. It was what she wanted.

"Drop your pants," I ordered.

"What?"

"Drop your pants around your ankles."

She snickered at this. He wouldn't be able to rush me without tripping.

The poor girl hugged me as if I was her savior.

"I'll show you how to do it."

Before my words sank into her brain, I had her pinned against the back of the car with my body and her wrists cuffed behind her with my free hand. I could tie up a woman in my sleep now.

"Move to the car," I ordered him.

He reached for his pants.

"Leave them." I waved the gun.

He duck waddled to the back seat of his car.

Her long hair was so soft in my hand as I guided her to her knees.

"You're a sick fuck," she berated me. Her protests were broken. "Oh my God, he's fucking hard. You're both sick fucks."

"You want to live, then I suggest you finish yourself off. Shoot it into the back seat," I instructed him.

"You fucking want me to jack off!?"

"Beats a bullet to your skull." I clicked the hammer—unnecessary, but it had an effect.

Men won't maintain an erection when in fear. I rubbed her face against his crotch to keep him stiff. I removed her, allowing him to work himself to climax. As he fondled himself I tore away the ginger's purple lacy panties. I tugged and tore until one leg was torn free. I hated to proceed with my inspection of her there, but I pushed the panties inside. Her protest of where my fingers were exciting her first attacker.

The dome light allowed a clear visage of sploodges as he squirted in the back seat. He painted it better than I hoped.

Spent he hung on the car door for support. She would give in or fight me, depending on what she thought I would do to her next.

I drug her to the passenger side of the car. Taking the keys from the ignition, I ordered him back into the driver's seat. This was tricky. I tossed her DNA soaked panties on a glob of splooge in the back seat.

The police detectives would have a field day with her disappearance. They would speculate sex occurred. I removed one handcuff and recuffed her pinioned arms in the front. Unsure of my motivations she followed my instructions.

I handed her a wooden hinged box and explained in baby steps the process she was to obey.

She tied a band around her would-be attacker's arm to raise the veins. I kept certain drugs on my person in case I flubbed an abduction and needed to dump a body. The cops never investigated too closely an overdose, even when it was mommy's perfect angel.

She injected him like a pro. "Leave the needle in his arm."

They would think he passed out from the high. It was enough to kill a horse. A minute passed. He convulsed once and aspirated a snore. I scattered the drug kit on the floor next to him and tossed the car keys in for good measure.

I drug her to the back of the car and bent her over the trunk. She had lost all struggle in her. Some people froze as part of their natural flight or fight response. Her rump was so smooth and soft. I pushed back my own erection, pinching her rump until a useable vein rose. It wouldn't. It might have if she was thinner. I didn't need much. The needle I jabbed into her forearm wouldn't scar her that would be later. I drew blood.

She wore these thigh high socks. It was sexy on her, and I would have to replace the pair. I took both off her after I placed her in my vehicle. She would be secure under the third-row seating I gutted to make a female cubby space.

I tore one sock up and squirted blood onto it before tossing it in the grass. The second I tossed in the trunk, not sure what detectives would deduce from sock actions, but the news shows would explain why he did what he did.

I depressed the plunger, flinging drops in the back seat. The remaining half tube I sprayed over his now flaccid cock and pubic hair. Damn. Many redheads avoided grooming their pubis due to the extra sensitive skin. I should have plucked some hairs. If the panties and blood weren't enough to convince the cops, a few pubes meant nothing.

As I drove away, I thought about his claiming he didn't hurt the girl would be the cornerstone of his defense. How some mysterious stranger stole her from him, but first made him jack off and take drugs. To be in the interrogation room as his story unfolded would be better than an amusement park ride, and the craziest story a cop ever heard.

VIII

"THANK YOU FOR sharing."

"Thanks for the share, but I want to know about the investigation. We've all heard what you do to the women, Al. What did the cops do to the man you doped?"

"We are not here to indulge—" Jane attempts to redirect.

"I followed the case constructed against him. So much DNA allowed for testing and a few hits on CODIS."

"His semen was in the rape database. You ended one of society's problems," Jack says.

"Your soul must be torn. You condemn such actions, and yet what you've done is no different."

"I don't rape. My crimes better my community." Despite his advanced age Jack vaults to the balls of his feet, hands drawn to pounce.

"Gentlemen. We won't be fighting here. It won't help," Jane repeats, now a broken record.

"We're all killers. There is no way to help us. I don't know why I bothered," Jack admits.

Jesse raises his arms like a referee. "I know exactly why I'm here." *Figure out which of you fuckers murdered my sister.* "I don't have remorse for the death of the professor, I liked it. But killing him was wrong. If I report myself to the police, I'll get no treatment program. I don't want to murder again—I enjoyed it."

"There's still hope for the kid. Not for me. Those I kill aren't even people," Jack says.

"Those you kill aren't people. Of all of us you are doing society a favor. How many people do you save when you take down a drug dealer? If we all turned our urges in your direction, we might be productive. More productive than police, we don't have to live by the rules," Jane says.

"A vigilante group of serial murderers who protect the neighborhood. Some Dark Avenging League. I do what I do, and it falls into your category of wrong," Al says.

"I can't stand to be in the same room as a man who chokes out women, even if some are prostitutes. From what I've seen most of those poor girls are forced into it. Some take the mantle by choice, but those pressed into service are victims and need to be defended, not have their life stolen," Jack spits.

"We are losing our focus." Jesse falls into his chair.

"No," Jane realizes, "We need to work out our aggressions. For group therapy to work we must come to terms with each other first."

"You want me to come to terms with a rapist?" Jack's fingernails dig into his whitening palms.

"Now we know your true sentiments," says Al.

"You saved that girl for yourself, not to protect her. What you did was the worst. When I kill, it sets people free," Jack confesses.

"Not your victims. And how free are they? Did you follow up on the first girl you saved? She would have been placed in the foster care. Most children don't fare well in the system. You know the ratio of those who turn to prostitution after being in the system. You protected her from one abuser, what about the rest she must face?" Al says.

"This isn't about the drug addicts I cut off from their suppliers. Not *my* victims," Jack says.

"But it should be. Even in the dark I detect your smug, self-serving, better-than-the-rest-of-us vibe you radiate. When we steal one girl our actions have consequences. What you have done is no different. And before you heal you must admit it," Al says.

Jesse considers the old man a potential ally. His sister was never a criminal, although she may have partied like any teen girl her age. He accepts she might have drank and fornicated, his mother never spoke about her. Sissy never did anything criminal to put her under Jack's radar. Jack might even help him. He despises these true killers of innocent people as Jesse does.

"I make my choices and weigh many factors. But those I kill are hurting their own families less by being dead than by what they do when they are alive," Jack says.

"You're a hypocrite," Al says.

"As are we all, or we would simply turn ourselves into the authorities. What we do here is getting to both have and eat our cake," Al says.

"Everyone, we clearly have a long way to go, but this is progress," Jane says.

"How is this progress?" asks Robert.

"It's entertaining, but I don't see no healing," Ed says.

"We are hitting the root of our problems. To overcome them we must understand why we do what we do. Jack couldn't protect his granddaughter from an impaired driver."

"He was high on heroin." Jack mumbles, "There are no more heroin dealers in my town."

"You killed them all." Robert seems impressed.

"NO. Some left before I could track them down," Jack says.

"How many did you kill to run the rest out of town?" asks Kenneth.

"It's not my turn to share," Jack stews.

"This is good. We're reaching to the core of our issues. Let's explore more. It may not be your turn, Jack, but let's explore while what you're feeling is on the surface," Jane says.

The old man huffs more like a teen refused the car keys than a man in his late sixties. "The second action was just as sloppy as the first. I used remaining by my granddaughter's bedside at the hospital as my alibi. The possibility of her awakening from a coma decreased with each day. So did the number of times the nurses checked on Nina. I think they tired of placating me with false hope. They only came in for the required bed checks or to turn her. Even if I wasn't in the room they figured I needed coffee or was in the bathroom. I'd leave the bathroom light on and door closed. They would hurry vital checks and get out so they didn't have to lie to me about her now impossibility of waking up."

IX

I'M NOT SURE I had a reason to drive in this part of my hometown since my teen years. It had been largely working middle class families then. Once the neighborhood turned questionable with petty crimes I never ventured back. New business always built new structures on the north end of town. They just kept plowing up farmland. No one wanted to be a part of revitalizing the decrepit south side.

Crime occurred. The south area just bred crime. You would think instead of dilapidated, peeling paint ruins, drug dealers would make enough money to have well-manicured lawns and a fresh coat of paint. They claimed to make so much money, but lived in squalor. No wonder the police watched these places. They scream drug deals.

I cruised by for three nights. The first night I nearly pissed myself, I saw so many patrolling cop cars. The second night I was able to witness from across the street, parked in a driveway. No one had been home or maybe living there at all. Not a single cop drove down the street. Dozens of people would pull up. Same event each time. A passenger would hop out and race to the door, hands shook and something was exchanged.

All I cared was there were no children inside. I saw no signs of any despite the overturned plastic tricycle in the front yard. It was a ruse, or the child had been removed by CPS. Either way, there were no children at the residence.

The third night I learned why the first night had seen so many patrols. I had arrived at dusk. A cop car was parked in front of the house and the dealer was leaning in the driver's side window. They slapped hands and bumped fists the same way all the drug exchanges transpired the night before.

He paid the officer off, in cash or drugs or both, I don't know which. This turned my stomach. No wonder some of these places operated with ease. Even one dirty cop allowed dozens to get their drugs. The rest of the night the officer avoided the neighborhood and drug sales occurred as normal.

I made a mental map of the house and yard then the ways each transaction happened. I had formulated my plan to end this place.

There were seventeen hardware stores in my town and none open in the drug riddled neighborhoods. I wondered if business returned to the south of town how that would affect the trafficking. Would places work to stop it? I'm old, maybe I'm out of the loop on how drug economics work. I bought a five-gallon gas can from several different stores. Paid cash. No one notices an old man—we are too invisible. I filled the cans at a few different cash accepting gas stations.

Drug trafficking had an etiquette. You didn't just pull up to the house if another car was there. If a friendly exchange occurred, you drove on past, circled the block and came back. No assembly line transactions, just friendly neighbors slowing down to say *hi* and going on. Where did people learn these rules of the drug trade? With these kinds of management skills this guy could do well in an office setting.

Too bad life didn't work out for him. I don't know if he sold the drugs to the man who removed my family from this earth, but he would pay for it, as would all the rest in my town.

Let me tell you. After this night was over I was going to hit the gym. Destroying drug dealers was physically demanding and I was healthy, but by no means in shape.

After a drug sale I knew I had five to ten minutes before another.

I opened the Rogue's rear hatch and realized I needed to remove the bulb from the dome light less I give myself away. I should have gotten a burner car or whatever they are called. My plans required a reliable vehicle.

Despite how heavy the gas cans were I managed to get them across the street unseen. I put the first gas can under a back window to mask the strong smell. I lost my ability to detect how strong after the second can.

I placed gas under each window. None of the fools inside noticed me. I had to make six trips and avoid about twenty transactions. My next action was tricky and time consuming. My plan was to make sure no one could escape and everyone was killed. Just burning the house down was not enough. Left alive, the guy would be selling out of the NoTell Motel by dawn.

What I did would convey a message. It may take several dope homes being removed from the map before someone realized it was a message, but I would get my point across—and remove my family's killer.

I ran oil soaked sheets between each gas can for a fuse. Long before 9/11 you could buy fuse cord at the local feed store without question. Now I would be put on a terror watch list. I didn't know, but after all those NCIS programs I figured they could trace back where I purchased the fuse. I would have to devise a better way of setting off the gas. I didn't want to pour the gas and cause more of a smell, people inside might investigate. I did have to stop seven times as drug deals went down, but no one noticed me. This was too time consuming and risky. I stayed in the shadows. People demanded their drugs too badly to scan their environment. As the night wore on I knew next time I'd need a new method.

Once I had the gas cans linked together I dumped a five-gallon bucket on the porch. The splash of liquid against the door and smell of gas did grab attention. Lighting a flare, I tossed it and ran. I bounced the flare off the porch ceiling so the fall gave me a second longer to be in the street.

The sparkling flare caught the fumes.

Whooshing gusts blew past me.

I was just out of range when the porch exploded in a fireball.

A hurricane of warm wind then perfect stillness left me cold, as nothing stirred for a breath around me.

I didn't stop to glance back. I knew secondary explosions should follow—they did—breaking the silence and lighting up the night sky. No one would escape the house on the ground floor. Flames covered each first-floor window and the back door. The porch burned hot—fast—the once beautiful gabled roof collapsed before I got inside my car.

The screams of those inside didn't bother me.

I never heard the sirens.

All three newspapers I found in the hospital lobby the next morning displayed pictures of a burnt house protected by police tape with the headline: Three burned to death in suspected drug house.

I kept an eye on the news. The police ruled it some kind of turf altercation. Nothing was investigated as far as what I read in the newspapers. I knew it wasn't totally true, but no one cared some drug dealers were dead.

No other little girl would lose out because of those people.

X

"YOU COULDN'T BURN down every crack house." Jesse admires Jack's accomplishment to rid his town of drug dealers. More impressive than kidnappings and murders.

"No, one burnt house…no one cared about. Two might prevent me from ending the dealer who cost me my family. I didn't know which one sold the drugs, so I would end them all," Jack says.

"How does his actions not make him like the rest of us?" Robert asks.

"I sought revenge, and I enjoyed it. It became my reason for life. Once I ended the heroin dealers I didn't stop. I didn't know which specific house it was. I sought to end all the evil in town, the cops on the take, rumors of the high school girls' basketball coach who gave extra attention to certain players. It destroyed all maliciousness," Jack says. "Somehow I thought, with each passing drug house gone, my little grandbaby would wake up." Sobs emanate from his darkened station. "I'm so sorry for what I've done. Nothing I do will allow me into heaven to be with her again."

"Beware that, when fighting monsters, you yourself do not become a monster. Nietzsche words are your truth," says Edgars.

"He knew of no other way to death but pain." Jane's tone finds pity for the older man.

Of all here, he wanted to protect. Could Jack be willing to assist? Jesse's brain whirls.

"Now you know why I'm here. Why I tolerate what you've all done. My motives, at first, were pure, but I journeyed beyond. I acquired pleasure in my killing. Because I enjoyed it—I'm a monster," Jack says.

"Why do we have to be monsters because we take lives?" Kenneth asks.

"You say it's an affront to a higher being, but if we were created in his image, we have the same desires as Him."

"He says to love one another," adds Jesse.

"Read your Old Testament, Kid. He was a wrathful and vengeful God. He extolled great punishments over people for disobeying Him and his favorite punishment was death. Jack, if anybody here doles out the will of the Old Testament Father," Robert says. "If he's checking at the gate, I bet you get in."

"How do you take God's will so lightly?"

"Because He kills and so do I," Robert says.

"A man professing to know God would not be such a killer," The Plagiarist says. "Your time in church—"

"I never was much for a God who took attendance. I read the Bible, unlike most who enter a building once a week. God is a serial killer," Robert says.

"If only your God would slay the wicked! Away from me, you who are bloodthirsty!" Kenneth quotes.

"Psalm 139:19," Robert says. "But you're not quoting from the King James version, God's true words."

"So now we justify our killing as being God's messengers?" Jane asks. "If I work for God then why do I have self-doubt?"

"You don't work for God. He works through us."

"So did The Christ. He doubted and rejected God, his blessed Father," Robert says.

"We aren't working for God. Many of the people I killed were innocent," Edgars says.

"Not mine. Whores and homosexual tyrannies, all affronts to God. Being a homo is wrong. I know it says so," Ed assures.

"It does. But it also places a higher sin on eating shrimp," adds the Plagiarist.

"God *will not* be our excuse," Jane snaps. "Even if in AA God is the answer—not here. We will not use an outside influence to justify murder."

"Another rule?" Al asks.

"We accept responsibility for our own actions. We don't blame God. We don't blame anyone. We admit what we did was within us and we ask for help in stopping," Jane says.

"How do I stop?" Even if the question came from just one person they all were asking it.

After several breaths of no banter Al speaks. "You asked what the police thought of the redhead's disappearance. The man's DNA revealed he was a serial rapist who would face charges for his other crimes. I only saw one news report mentioning the mysterious man who allegedly set him up, there identifiable blood and semen at the crime scene. And I left no evidence of me."

"You know police suppress information," Jesse says. "We all think we are so much smarter than the cops, but we all speak about how sloppy we've been."

"We have spoken of the early kills. The dozens since I have perfected. I don't leave anything behind I don't want found," says Jane.

"You have a confirmed rapist in jail. Why muddy the case by searching for a ghost? Besides, one psychiatrist at his trial strongly suggested there was a second man at the crime—a second personality who instructed him to perform the acts he did. The jury never bought it. He was locked away," Al says.

"Leaving you free to practice your sickness on the redhead," Jack says.

"No casting of stones, now. But you are correct—it is a sickness," Al says.

XI

THE REDHEAD FOUND some fresh fight within her as I opened the door to the basement. She squirmed enough I didn't risk carrying her on my shoulder and us tumbling. Placing her bare feet on the linoleum floor, I found green eyes wishing to harm me. I slid my arms under her pits to carry her in front of me. I should bind her feet. Every time she kicked I lifted her up to prevent her becoming my landing pad at the bottom of the steps.

Rescued her from a rape she now accepted her fate would be worse at my hand. She would be the first to test my chamber. I hoped I had thought of everything, but most likely not. A smart girl might breach my defenses before I broke her spirit. I didn't choose on brains, though sometimes I did consider ethnicity. Swipe a Hispanic girl or an Asian because true serial killers tended to stay within their own race.

Getting her down the steps alive to the family friendly living space halted her skirmish. I think the lack of torture devices startled her more. The upcoming bath would change her mind.

Her face was swollen from where her attacker punched her. I palpated the spot. Instinctually she jerked away. It would bruise, but no permanent damage to her freckled face. She was my first redhead. She had a natural fire within her and smelled divine. I was in love with her spirit—a spirit I would steal from her.

After killing a few girls in my car, I knew I sought a permanent partner, but I needed a secure place for her—inescapable. I had plotted my safe room for my guest. It had to meet my functions, and yet be a home to me and my love—when I found her.

I installed a four-person tub in the bathroom. Over its center was a hooking apparatus of my own design using sexual bondage tools. After all I did to prepare this basement I wondered why I didn't go to engineering school. I could have employed myself in a side career of installing S&M gear in playrooms for those adventurous couples.

My flipping open a knife blade freeze her. Slicing the cord, I replaced her wrist bindings in fur padded shackles.

She no longer feared the blade. She cursed and spit at me until dry-throated and hoarse. She did have a fire—I sought to steal it from her, make her mine. Breaking her into subservience would be pleasure. I felt she could be more to me. So than many women give in quickly to my will, not this one.

Lifting her up, I hung the chain between the shackles in the suspension hook. I pulled the rope attached to a pully system of my own design, allowing for the adjustment of a woman's particular height. I raised her until she dangled on the tips of her toes. She had long, freckle-covered legs. Her toes—thin and boney.

Her first and expected act was to struggle against the bindings by kicking at me. Losing her balance, her body weight would drag her down and hurt her shoulders. Quickly, without my correction, she learned not to scuffle. All her focus shifted to maintaining balance on those stretched toes. It strained her calf muscles until they cramped. She would try and lower herself to the flats of her feet, but it would shift her weight and overextend her shoulders, forcing her back to her toes.

She would hang in constant balance of pain, attempting to find a stance which hurt the least on her wiry frame.

I allow the first kick. It was expected even the most peaceful, docile person made one attempt. It was the second which cost her. I pulled on her rope a bit more, testing my theory of her having to struggle to regain her balance until it stung her calves from standing on her toe tips as if she were a ballerina. The discomfort must have been more tolerable than the agony from the weight on her shoulders. Allowing her to hang long enough, aching constantly, was part of bending her to my will.

I had thought about securing her neck, but some girls might give up on life and hang themselves. Body disposal was not on my agenda. This way a girl might dislocate a shoulder but still be breathing.

I cut her clothes from her body. Her shoulders were covered in freckles. They sprinkled all the way down to her breasts, which beamed china white without a mole or single blemish, the nipples—pink and poked hard as bullets. Under the right areola the breast had a divot. No amount of pressing or squeezing reshaped the cleft. A defect, but it only enhanced her beauty, a marring of the form made special because only a select few had ever seen it. Or would ever glimpse it again.

She protested my touch, snarling profanities and perfunctory threats with her hoarse voice. She needed water. Dehydration also my plan. She could scream threats about my future incarceration if I didn't release her immediately, but no one else would hear.

I cut away her skirt.

She had an orange muff—trimmed. Freckles dotted her hips. She was beautiful. She was mine.

Her clothes burned in the trash incinerator. I collected her earrings and navel piercings, replacing the belly button ring with one less adaptable for picking a lock. I should have checked her at the car and left the bobbles as more evidence.

I sponged off her body with warm water, careful with each dab against her skin. She struggled, but the shifting of her weight to shudder from my touch prevented her from keeping on her toes. Forced to allow my contact she relaxes.

"You're beautiful. I warn you, next will be the most unpleasant part."

She ceased her physical struggle, but not her verbal berating of me. I would enjoy breaking her. It was the breaking of her spirit turning her into mine. Making her desire to be my pet was the thrill which drove me. Failure would mean her death. Examining why I do what I do is part of my motivation. It was the breaking—the control—that excited me.

I unscrewed the cap to a glass bottle. The direction said to mix with a clear, carbonated beverage, but my goal was dehydration.

I raised the bottle to her lips. She refused to drink.

Breaking capillaries by clamping her nose shut with my left-hand forces her mouth open for a breath. I poured in the liquid.

I expected her to spit up some, but not as much as she did. I loved the fighter in her. I clamped her nose again, and this time I shoved a flexible, plastic tube down her throat. She gagged when it reaches her stomach. I poured the liquid slow.

The combination of laxatives caused terrible cramps, voiding her system of all contents. I needed her hungry.

Hungry, thirsty, tired, in discomfort and sleep deprived, removing any of these elements as reward for the behavior I sought. It slowly would place her under my control. I could have beaten her into submission, but she would never have become mine, not in the same way she would with the reward system.

Beating her into submission would have yielded similar results, but she would only give herself to me physically. I didn't desire just her body—her soul as well.

I kept her nose pinched so I could remove the tube with ease.

She cursed me again with spittle and some of the liquid choking up. I told her to save her energy for she would need it.

Satisfied she couldn't retch up the concoction, I pulled the vinyl shower curtains closed around the tub.

Since the hook allowed for a swinging movement of her body, I installed the curtain with suction cups to hold it in place to catch any fecal matter I knew would expel from her in about two hours. When it was over I would just hose her and the tiled wall off.

Leaving her alone to the cramps she would experience, I flipped the lights off—pure darkness. All worked her toward being mine.

I knew in two hours the medication would cause her discomfort and within three hours she would lose all control of her bowels. It would flush her system of any nutrition, making her hungry and thirsty faster.

With the flicking of the lights, she released a moan. I figured she had become used to the smell, but I gagged. I flipped on the vent.

Peeling back the shower curtain, I found a distraught girl who had lost some fight, but she still had her spirit and one green eye. She had colored contacts, or did. She was down to one. Green-eyed redheads are rare, still it was her fire I loved.

Caked around her mouth and streaming down her chest was dried vomit. Splattered shit sprayed around the tub and between her legs. She had nothing left inside her. She was the nastiest she'd ever been and we both knew it. Shame masked her face. Her arms hurt, and her legs cramped down to her toes.

I attached a garden hose with a pressure sprayer tip to the faucet. Taking care of the wall and the tub first I cleaned her mess. She struggled against my spraying her legs with icy water. The high pressure stung like cold needles. She would get warm water. I left her face and mouth dirty dumping a bucket of ice water over her instead. She shivered, but my goal was not to freeze or even water board her, it was to keep her from drinking.

After she was clean I rolled up the hose. It stayed secure in another room.

"Please." It wasn't begging.

My finger touched the light switch, I paused.

"My legs are cramping. Please let me down."

Interesting.

She hadn't asked to be released, just down. No girl begged in such a way before. She contemplated some convoluted escape plan.

I flipped the lights off.

"Fucker! Let me go!"

I twisted the deadbolt, the kind with a loud echoing click. I secured her in the black room.

There was an escape plan in her somewhere. I doubted she had the strength, but she thought she did if I allowed her down. And sometimes thought is enough. Hope is a lying mistress. People convince themselves their bodies are capable of achieving great feats. When they are successful it's usually to the detriment of the body.

I recalled reading of a mother who flipped an overturned three-ton tractor off her son. Later her arms and shoulders needed massive surgery, but she did flip the tractor.

I would add time to my check on her clock.

Without hydration her muscle cramps would worsen. I'm sure she cried, but losing extra water for tears only add to her dehydration. I realized I should install a night vision camera in the room so I could check on my girl.

I brought her a glass mixed with laxative and Sprite. She gulped it down.

She would need cleaning again in a few hours. The room had a strong asparagus smell.

"Would you like to come down?" I asked.

She thought about her answer. She still had spirit in her.

"I'm thirsty."

"You can go three days without water. Not counting what you swallowed when I cleaned you, it has only been some thirty hours."

The skin shrinks, tightens around the muscles during dehydration and her legs were taut and cramping. She must have had a high tolerance for pain or she refocused it into her anger and hatred of me.

"You're not ready. You'll become my work of art." A great challenge. I had no idea I needed such a project. I was happy with those who were subservient quickly, but not this fiery redhead.

"Don't you fucking leave me hanging here in the fucking dark!"

I did.

At the two-day mark she may not have broken yet, but she had no fight in her, not until I allowed her to suckle on a wet wash cloth. It wasn't enough to undo the chapping of her lips.

"Just kill me."

"Do you want to die?" I placed several heating lamps like farmers used to warm newborn baby pigs.

"I don't want to be your tortured plaything."

"If I kill you, I'll just replace you. It would be your fault another girl becomes *my plaything*. If you're here and pleasing, you spare another woman this fate." Physiological control.

"What kind of sick fuck are you?"

I knew she wasn't broken mentally. The girl who was not ready to beg for water was nowhere near ready to be mine. I placed a stool in the tub on top of a plastic pad, snaking the cable from the pad to an electrical box wired to the lamps. She could choose to stand on the stool to elevate her muscle aches. Her body weight on the stool would trigger the heat lights on. They would be bright, hot enough to slow roast a turkey, or she could dangle on her toes in the dark.

I gave her eight ounces of water, four of which her body absorbed before she could spit it back at me in protest.

I would install a camera. I never wanted to witness the struggle before, but with her I did. I wondered how long she left the lights on during the last twelve hours.

Her skin may have been a freckled mess, but white areas were pink. She had withstood the heat long enough to burn. He legs had relief. Her body was eating itself for nourishment and demanded water.

Her skin was warm where it had pinked. She was willing to cook herself to give her legs a break. She may have even gotten some sleep. Resting would screw with my plans.

"Are you ready to drink?" Now we played the game, moving her toward being mine.

"I won't beg." She still had her soul.

"You know what you need to do."

"What!" Her chest raised as her heart pace quickened, "I'll suck your dick if you give me water." Her tone had an attached 'Is that what you fucking want, bastard?'

We were a long way from the trust it would take for me to place my cock in her mouth.

"Ask."

She huffs.

"May I please have some water?"

Smart girl.

I had a liter sportsman squeeze bottle with an attached straw. She could save it up in her mouth to spit it, but she would swallow, and her mouth was barren. She needed the water or all the fight she had to live would be pointless.

She drank about half before I pulled it away. "Too fast. You'll get sick."

I removed the stool, but left the pad. It would boost her up an inch or so and provide some relief, but not like the stool. She would get no more chances to sleep.

"Please," this tone was more of a relinquishing beg, "please leave the stool."

She had gotten rest at the expense of a sunburn.

"Try and not piss on the pad. I'm no electrician, so I don't know if you'll get a shock if you get it wet. It won't kill you, just send a jolt through you—maybe burn. Imagine attempting to stand on blistered toes."

I left her in the dark. She could give herself light if she desired.

When I returned in twelve hours, I removed her from the hanging apparatus. leaving her hands bound. Her kick at me was pathetic. She had no muscle control from being stretched and baked.

I needed to put a hook in the floor near the tub so I could secure hands while I laid her out, in case there was fight left in the girl. A half decent shot to my nuts and theoretically she could reach the door. A spirited woman was perfect for my chamber's field test.

The upstairs door was bolted. She'd never get it open.

She had anger and it radiated off her, but she had lost the ability to move. I had to carry her from the bathroom. Her legs cramped tight. The muscle spasms bubbled the skin. Any movement radiated pain. If she behaved I'd feed her a banana, nothing sexual about it. She needed the potassium. Her toes curled, and she whined from the pain of touching her sunburn.

I watered her and allowed her a bite of banana after I secured her arms to the headboard. As I massaged and worked loose her cramping legs, she never lost her fiery hate of me. Her green eye glared along with the brown one. The chocolate brown seemed milky without the contact. They were beautiful. I had yet to admire them. Given the chance she would stab me.

I allowed her another bite of the fruit. Her stomach couldn't handle food yet.

She never asked. Never protested. She accepted the water and bites of food, yet her eyes never lost the 'I will stab you' stare.

She must have realized eventually I would assault her. I undressed and cuddled against her, her body rigid in resistance. I would have to pry her legs open when the time came.

I rubbed on her with some sex oil. Her body required moisture. What people don't understand is no matter how badly a person refuses a sexual encounter the sex organs will betray the brain with the proper body stimulation.

It made her hate me more. Her body gave way to my fingers and the pleasure they brought. Once she was properly prepared I slipped the dog collar around her neck. I had bought several of the same design. They allowed me to grip the strap and remove the hook. I controlled the pressure on the throat so no accidental latching would occur. No dead girls until I was ready. It was enough of a risk to choke her to unconsciousness the first time.

I slid inside her. The death gaze burnt hotter, if it was possible. She only resisted me in her mind. She hated me.

I found my grip on the collar and when the time was right I tugged taut against her thoat. I held it until she passed out. I would break this one. We had all the time in the world.

XII

"WHAT YOU DO makes you one sick fuck," Jack says.

"We don't judge," Jane defends.

"You burnt people alive," Al proclaims.

"Even in prison committers of sex crimes are the lowest," Edgars says.

"Gentlemen. We are not here to condemn each other. Remember, we're here to help each other. If we could have gone to a doctor in the real world maybe we wouldn't have done what we did, but it is not an option," Jane says.

"I may be a bastard for killing women, but no one cares about those girls. They're forgotten or ostracized by society. People claim it's terrible some young runaway sells her cooch to survive, but they do nothing to address the problem," Ed says.

"Enough soap box," Robert says.

"I'm sure I should have been caught. My first few killing, I left clues I didn't know I did, but no one investigated dead prostitutes," Ed reiterates

"If someone did care you wouldn't have killed them?" Edgars asks.

"I would have been caught sooner, maybe. Or they wouldn't be out there presenting themselves for payment. If the world cared I wouldn't have had access to them," Ed says.

"Nope. It's the world's fault?" Edgars asks.

"I'm not going to blame anyone. We have to accept responsibility. But society has a simple solution. You don't want drugs on the street, you don't arrest some dime bag dealer, you send in your troops and burn the poppy fields. If the country, you invade doesn't like it you inform them the next burning will be the entire country. You don't want these girls out there, you get them the help they need. Many use the dope. Start with ending it," Ed rants.

"We've been over this, we have a sickness. We know there is no help for us. The world sees us as monsters and won't cure us. I enjoy what I did," says Al. "How do we fix the pleasure we get from what we do?"

"Is it pleasure? You have the control of a deity over those women. It's the power you have over them. We all have power over our victims. It completes something we think we are missing in ourselves," Jane says.

"You need to replace what you do to those girls with something else positive in your life. AA members are to replace drinking with God," The Plagiarists says.

"I want no god."

Other murmurs emanate in the dark.

They know what I know, God doesn't exist. If He did, how could He allow us to do what we do to the innocent? "I think you're correct. What do we replace our urges with? When the need to do what we do overwhelms us, what do we do instead?" Jane asks.

"We use sponsors, a team member we contact," says Kenneth.

Damn. Jesse wishes he'd thought of it. He now must get Jack to work with him. He needs the older man as an ally. Jack would turn against this group.

"After this second meeting, we should pair up. If we have an urge we contact our partner. We still use code phrases," Jane says.

"Just call it drinking. All our urges are the same as alcoholics," Edgars says.

"Agreed."

"Are we concluding this session?" Robert asks.

"We haven't heard from everyone," Jesse says.

"Jane?"

"As your somewhat unofficial group trailblazer I've more stories to confess, if we go back to when I was still a nurse. I grew tired of watching people witness the suffering of their family members as they died."

XIII

IT ALWAYS AMAZED me how much waste transpires in the practiced medical field. Use a medicine, say one dose from a bottle, for one patient and toss the rest out. Yes, it had a shelf life, but it wasn't instantly ruined. Some could be used for patients with no money and offset costs. I would draw medicine from a vial that had five doses and use one. I was expected to toss the remaining four and the family with insurance ate the cost.

At first, I sought to help those who could not afford it. But I couldn't record the administration of the dose without billing noticing. If I didn't record it, and a doctor gave a contra effective medicine, it would kill the patient.

I faced a conundrum. Help people or help the hospital make money. The longer I nursed the more I understood cured people didn't receive bills.

I was promoted to charge nurse on my shift, a few pennies more an hour for a lot more responsibility.

I met a young girl, Sarah. She was fourteen, but still appeared to be about ten-years-old. Poor child would never blossom into a woman. Fucking cancer. It was her second bout. She'd won the first at age four, but not really. She had thought she had gone the distance, but no cancer got back up on the count of eight. It was eating her organs. She was the walking dead.

All the treatments did was prolong her pain. All life may be precious, but no one should have to live in a hospital bed.

One evening shift I found Sarah—the little girl—sobbing. Never allow her to have a name. A name makes her a person. To snuff out the light of a person was still bothersome to me at this point.

"Is it the pain?"

"No. Yes. I mean. I hurt, yes, but these tears are for my mom."

I sat on the bed, offering her a Kleenex. "She loves you." It was a stroke-her-hair-lovingly-moment, but she had no hair, just carpet-burn stubble.

"I know, she wants me to keep fighting."

"They make big strides in cancer research every day," I said. It was true. I left out *and your parents will never be able to afford them.*

"Can I tell you something, and you keep it private? Even from my mom?"

"I'll do my best." It wasn't a lie if it wasn't medical. I'd be able to keep such a promise.

"I just want to die."

I should have been shocked or said something nursey about how she needed to keep fighting—*do no harm* shit. But I didn't have it within me, because keeping this little girl alive was doing her harm. Sometimes keeping people breathing is doing harm.

"I've heard the doctors. I won't win this time. I'm being eating from the inside and it hurts. As an organ fails they'll hook me up to more machines. Mommy doesn't want to give up. She thinks the machines are fine to use. She loves me. Do you know she lost her job?"

I shook my head no, but as many hours as her mother was here, I suspected she didn't have a job.

"She lost it because of me. And when I'm gone, she won't have anything to do."

"That's love," I said.

"I keep fighting because I love her, but I don't want to fight anymore. I don't want to be hooked to a machine. You can't swim if you're connected to a machine."

"Have you told her how you feel?" I asked.

"She doesn't want to hear it. She has blinders on, whatever that means. She tells me to hush and the doctors will cure her baby."

I slid my hand over the sheets. I squeezed her fingers as hard as I dared to show comfort, because the poor girl's arms were purple with bruises.

"Is death what you want?" No sugar coating, I had to know.

"I want no more pain. I know it will get worse and never get better."

It wouldn't. Her selfish mother would rather watch her daughter suffer to keep her here than release the child.

"I make you no promise, but maybe if I speak to your mother," I offered.

"She won't listen," Sarah said.

"I just need to know if you're sure you want your pain to end." I would take care of her if she did.

"I ask God every night to take me into his arms."

I tucked the girl in and kissed her forehead. "He will have a beautiful angel when he does. Sleep as best as you can, child."

I would have to cause her one last pain. The medicine she was issued had specific doses, and too much at one time would finish her. But I couldn't blast her all at once. I upped her dose and Sarah weakened.

Was ending a terminal life early doing harm? Death in her case was too slow, and she was suffering more with each breath. It had to end quickly. I did not record her last dose on the chart knowing her doctor would spot how she was overdue for medicine when he did his morning rounds. Being a young man, and still hands on with his patients, he would personally give her the second dose. Older doctors would order a nurse to do it. With so much of the drug in her system it would shut down her heart.

She would detect the cessation of her heart. I'm sure it hurt, but she said nothing, knowing it was about to be over. She coded. Nothing the doctor did would bring Sarah back.

The mother demanded no more cutting on her baby, so no autopsy was performed. I'm not sure they would have caught the double dose. It would show up in her system as high, but hell, she had just been given her meds.

I caused the end to her pain. It was good.

XIV

JACK SHIFTS IN his chair as if he were going to pounce on Jane, "You would have taken my granddaughter's life."

"At the time, had there been no hope, I might have. It was staying by her side every day for weeks which drove you to kill. Had I been her nurse, you and she would have had your suffering ended. Jack, your healing process would have started, not your murdering spree," Jane says.

"I never took an innocent," Jack says.

Jesse notes how Jack morally separates himself from the rest of the repeat killers in the room. His targets in his mind were evil. The people in this room are evil. Most of the murderers stole the lives of innocents.

"People are selfish. Their loved one is dead, hooked to a machine. They can't speak, they can't think, they can't bake, they can't unwrap Christmas presents, they can't rebuild a fifty-nine Ford pick-up they've worked on for years. They can't play with their grandchildren or great grandchildren and yet the family demands, sometimes with court orders, to keep them living. Why?"

No one interrupts Jane's rant.

"So they feel good inside. I did all I could. Fuck you, Jack! That little girl was never coming out of her sleep and you needed to let her go. The EMTs did their fucking job a little too well. She did die in the accident. They brought her back. I'm sorry for your loss, I truly am, but these people need to pass on into the next life or be permanently at peace."

"What is waiting for you in the next life? If it is there, and you believe in it, how do you figure what you have done will let you pass through?" Jack demands.

Jesse realizes the old man still has a relationship with God. None of the others do. Even Jane, who professes to deliver her victims into the next life, has no faith.

"I have my convictions. What I did was right. The medical doctors who strung these people along to collect insurance money—they will go to hell, not me. I never chose anyone who wasn't dead. They just weren't allowed to pass on."

Even in the dim lights Jesse recognizes Jack's growing contempt for Jane.

"We leave our judgments at the door, Jack." Jane restores her calm.

"Is that a clubhouse rule?" Jack demands. "I don't know if I can live with it."

"Well you're here rather than out there killing. You and I remove society's problems. Our quest is noble," Jane says.

"No. No. No!" Jack shoves his arthritic index finger at her in contempt. "If it was noble I wouldn't desire quitting. I'd find some crack house and go out like John Wayne in *The Shootist*. But, instead, I seek forgiveness among a group of peers, people with sick, twisted hobbies."

Edgars stands. "Everyone calm down. We're here to work together."

"Jack should release his anger even if it's verbally hurtful. He needs the release to heal," Jane says. "It's all part of the process."

"None of us have any moral right to kill, even if you did your carnage to end suffering, Jack, to end society's ills. Neither of you should. It's not our place to judge and execute. If someone requests a tube to keep them alive then they have the choice, not you," Al says.

"This is why I'm not sure I can be a part of your group. I am not ready to relinquish the power I get," The Plagiarist says.

"I have a grander problem," Al admits.

"You still have a hostage," Robert deduces.

"Is that true?" Jane asks, before Jesse proposes the same question.

"I destroyed all other evidence except the den. I have been contemplating how to release her. If I kill her then I've learned nothing, but if I let her go then she might report what happened to her," Al says.

"Might? She fucking will!" Ed says.

"How did you know, Robert, I still had a girl?" Al asks.

"You and I are the same in our hunt. You couldn't do what you do to the girls frequently unless you keep one around long-term. Your body count would rack up, and fast. Why build your den if you didn't intend to keep a harem?"

"I'll remove her for you. I've not committed to your group or not to kill," the Plagiarist says.

"No." Jane's finality ends all chatter among the group. "You do her no harm."

"He should stop having his brand of sex with her," says Kenneth. "He could choke her out accidently."

"Agreed. If you release her you're closer to being cured than any of us," says Jane. "I don't know what to do with her, but you can never touch her again."

"Easy enough. It's releasing her that remains a problem," says Al.

"Don't touch her. We will consider how to handle her release," Jane says.

"Feed her. Make sure she is healthy," Jesse adds. He knows this revaluation changes the game. He not only must find his sister's murderer, but now he has a living woman to save.

"Ed?"

"You want him to divulge his dark secrets with Al's revelation on the table?" Jack asks.

Jane understands the chain of possible events. Al releases the girl, she turns him in. Al sells them out to reduce his own prison sentence. All her research goes to waste. She was too careful with the IP addresses, so she doubts they could be found through the chat rooms. If she doesn't trust Al the others won't. "It is why we are here. If we don't continue then this meeting serves no purpose. We all consider how to release this girl without harming our healing process."

"I'll share again, but most all my stories are the same," Ed admits, almost wishing his tales had more glamor to them after hearing the others speak about what they did. How their cases are high profile in the media and how they enjoy snubbing the cops. His counterparts here have big name agencies fooled. He does, somewhat, but only the local yokels.

"It doesn't matter. Speaking about it is why we're here. Even if you performed the same act, as you tell your story we learn about you and how to help you overcome your urges," Jane presses.

"My stories aren't as glitzy as some of yours, I'm just a good ole boy, most of the time never meaning no harm."

"Your story doesn't need a redneck theme song," Edgars chides.

"You do mean harm," Jesse adds, "we all do."

"What I do doesn't have to be flashed on a neon sign. I didn't do what I did to be famous," Robert says.

"Edgars did, or he used what he did to enhance his fame," Kenneth says. "You perpetuate a myth," Jack says.

"And you kill drug dealers," Kenneth snaps.

"Why?" Jane asks.

"What do you mean *why?*" Kenneth doesn't hide his confusion.

"Why do you kill in the basement of the plantation house?" Jane asks.

Kenneth ponders a moment. "Revenge for all the abuse. I hurt everyone in the town. I required them to experience the pain and fear I had—every day going to school, even from my own sister."

"You achieved it. Even if you stop right now your fear will live on," Jane says.

"How do you figure?" Edgars playing catch up since he missed Kenneth's first session story.

"I'll explain," Jane says, "But, Kenneth, think about it."

Kenneth wets his lips. His nervousness leaves him parched as all eyes beam at him from the shadows. Now center stage his breakthrough will leave them hopeful for one of their own. Part of his cure will be to reveal the correct answer. The pressure mounts.

"Okay. I wanted them to have the same fear I felt every day leaving the house. Um. Yeah. Okay," he catches it. "They have fear every time their kids leave the house. They might be the next victim. Everything is random. No set dates or socioeconomic class of kids. Totally random. Even my choices are. When I hear about it and it's been long enough to remind them, I remind them. Unless I'm caught, they will always have the fear of losing a child to the plantation house."

"It behooves you to stop. If you never kill again, the less chance you will be caught, and the fear forever clouds the town. If you get caught the fear leaves them and you lose."

"You going to find the rest of us motivation to cease and desist?" Robert asks.

"I don't know," Jane admits. "In Kenneth's case, what he desired will live on in his community. More killing won't change that fact."

"I understand what you mean by learning why we do what we do. The rest of us won't have such simple motivation," The Plagiarist says.

"I don't think my motivations were simple," Kenneth says.

"But the solution is, as long as you don't kill again or admit to crimes," Al reiterates.

"I thought about burning the plantation house down as part of my healing."

"Let it stand," Jack's tone demands. "It reminds you of what you're working for here. If you burn it, then people of your town will no longer fear the death of a child in the basement. It's like an alcoholic who keeps a bottle of unopened liquor in the house."

"Two meetings and you're willing to help someone." Jesse should be grateful, and the fact his sister wasn't murdered by Kenneth, he is. It means the others will keep returning to the meetings and he will track down her killer. Plus, if this group stays true to its self-imposed probation no others will suffer at their murderer's hands.

"We've placed Kenneth on the correct path. He will still need a buddy. He must resist future urges to kill. At some point a student will taunt him. Not directly, but something about how *those murders were so long ago or there is no ghost. It was made up* and the urge to prove them wrong will grow within him."

"Why are you not a psychiatrist, Jane?" Al asks.

"Who says I'm not?" she offers.

"You lost your nursing license. Does that exclude you from all future medical licenses?" asks Edgars.

"A degree in a field doesn't automatically assure you a license to practice, you do have to apply for it. Doesn't mean I couldn't earn such a degree. My knowledge base is no less valid than anyone who practices openly with a couch," she says.

"There would be regulations if she did attempt to openly practice and maintain her license. To help those like us, as she is doing under state regulation, means some of us would be caught," The Plagiarist says.

"We don't want jailed. Some of us won't be so quick to respond to therapy as Kenneth," Ed says.

"He's not cured. It was a breakthrough. And breakthroughs happen when we least expect it," Jane says. "What Kenneth faces now has changed from the irresistible impulse to an impulse he must resist."

"Then we help Kenneth stay on the straight and narrow as we continue. It was Ed's turn to speak," Robert says.

"I do see the value in what we are doing. But like I said, my story is nearly the same."

"Tell us anyway," Jane says.

"Tell us, Ed."

XV

I WAS OUTSIDE of Dallas.

Some 'choke-and-puke' off the interstate.

I could gas up, drop a deuce, eat my fill and scrub the nut sack all before the new place about three miles over on the interstate had a spot for me to park. You'd think we old timers wanted to help the place out, and we did. If it saw a decline in enough business, it might shut down. All us frequenters had a secret pact to not reveal it existed to newbies, which would end patronage. Besides, the new breed of truckers were beaners.

The new place's pumps would crowd, and the extra time would cost us road time. Less time on the road meant bigger paydays.

The Staties focused more on the new station. Busted, or so they thought, more drugs and prostitutes over the new Gas and Go. Actually, they didn't bust the prostitutes. They shook down the truck drivers for a few hundred in cash when they caught them soliciting. I'm sure a few bears got their knobs slobbered for free.

I was on my way to my rig when Big Rauf was being bothered by a girl. She couldn't have been more than fifteen in her Daisy Duke shorts and a tee tight under her tiny tits. She was too clean to be hooking.

"Please, mister, I'll do whatever you want. I just need a ride."

She had this catty tone. She was a fresh runaway, I'd bet my bonus. I knew she was fresh and clean and had no idea what *anything* meant to some of these guys.

"Hey, little girl," I had all my cash in a roll in my pocket so she saw it when I undid two Jacksons. "Just take these and take a bus somewhere. You don't want nothing to do with Big Rauf. He's got spots on his dick."

The twiggy bastard glared daggers at me. He did want the little twat, but his company was cracking down on picking up hitchhikers. Some guys who thought they would never get caught were recently fired.

She grabbed at the twenties. I held tight long enough. "Take the bus back home. Whatever made you leave is a much better life than jumping from truck stop to truck stop." I released the bills.

"Thanks, mister."

"Fuck you, man, I ain't got no spots. She had such a tight ass." Big Rauf never took his eyes off the bottom of her cheeks falling out of her shorty shorts.

She might have been worth being fired.

"She's a young one. Maybe she doesn't have to ruin her life yet," I said.

Big Rauf stormed off in a huff.

Now what I did didn't mean nothing. No moral compass shit. Nor did I care she was fifteen. I just liked the idea of ruining Big Rauf's night. Don't think for a minute I was having a lapse toward goodness. Not me, fuckers.

I was halfway into my cab when a catty tone screeched in my ear, "Hey mister, maybe I don't want a bus ticket."

Glancing down, I half expected her to have a knife. But she didn't. Next, I made sure there were no witnesses.

"How about just a ride to the next truck stop? The next bus doesn't leave until four AM and I got to get out of here."

I'd met plenty of runaways during my time on the road, and she just didn't behave like a troubled one. If I had to bet. she was punishing mom or maybe dad for not letting her drive or go to a party. Something simple. Something spoiled brats would do. She wanted far enough down the road to prove she'd run away and they would never see her again if they didn't give in to her wishes.

I glanced around again to make sure no one saw her. "Get in."

She climbed into the truck, over my seat, to the passenger side. "Slump down until we leave the parking lot, or I'll never hear the end of it from Big Rauf."

She complied.

Stupid girl. The parking lot was empty.

Once out of the lot she asked, "What did you call him Big Rauf? He's not fat."

"We've been encountering each other for years at truck stops. One night some lot lizard told everyone in the diner he had the tiniest cock she'd ever put in her mouth." I didn't excuse my language. Language would be the least worst thing this girl would hear if this was the life she was choosing. "We called him as a joke or a pun or whatever it is when you label something the opposite of being true. We all call him Big Rauf."

"That's harsh. I guess she would know," she giggled. "Does he have spots on his dick?"

"I don't know. I just said that to make you go home."

Somber, she even lost her catty tone, "I can't go back there."

I didn't care.

She perked back up. "Where are we heading?"

"You said the next truck stop."

"I know, but you already paid me. I could do things and you could take me out of state."

"How about you do things and I drop you off at the state line so I ain't transporting no minor across it?"

"What the fuck! You'd fuck my little eighteen-year-old pussy, but you won't take me to Nevada?"

"Who says I'm going to Nevada? And your pussy isn't anywhere near eighteen. You barely have tits."

She groped herself in protest, but even her small hands didn't find a handful. "Well, I'm going to Vegas to be in a show. I sing damn good. There are always entertainment jobs in Vegas." She squeezed both her apple-sized breasts teasingly. "They're perky for eighteen."

"You'll need an ID that says you're eighteen or no job. You're right, there are entertainment jobs for those girls willing to work a pole."

"I'll be on stage as a singer."

I kept to myself how that wasn't going to happen, how she was barely going to get a few more counties down the line.

She was a talker. Constant words fell out of her mouth about nothing.

I found a secluded spot I liked. It was on the service road that used to be the major highway until the interstate came through. No one would be on it this late at night, and truckers pulled over all the time to catch a midnight cat nap.

"I guess...I have to pay for my ride now?" Her catty tone reverted to a five-year-old who wanted you to play tea party with her. "Is it going to hurt?"

She didn't resist when I pulled her into the back of the cab.

"I'm bigger than Big Rauf, but not enough to hurt even a little girl like you."

"I mean sex. I'm...I've never done it."

You would think her confession would strike a chord either inducing sympathy for her and letting her out of it or it was more of her games to get a free ride.

I pulled it out of my pants and guided her mouth to it. If it was the first cock in her mouth or she just gave bad head, I didn't care. She gave me no thrill. She fumbled around with it in her mouth but I never stiffened.

I pulled her to a sitting position and she slipped off her top. Apples. Not even ripe.

"Take off the shorts."

She did as she was told. She'd lost her chattiness and maybe she wanted to cry. She'd want to go home next. It was too dark in the back of the cab for a clear view of her eyes. For sure she regretted running away. I bet she never imagined she would be naked as the day she was born before a greasy truck driver having her first sexual encounter.

I clamped my hand on her breast, squeezing to make it pop.

She shuddered before twisting away from my grip. She understood the cost of running toward an unrealistic dream. "I changed my mind I want to go home."

"You don't get to ride for free."

She jerked back. I caught her wrist, pulling her toward me.

"You understand something little girl—" I snapped her pinky finger like a twig. The blood rushed into my flaccid cock.

Her scream was high pitched enough to shatter glass, but she was too shocked to resist me.

I slapped her upside the head. I didn't want to ruin her mouth, not yet.

Now came the water works.

"Please don't hit me. I'll do what you say."

I did anyway. If I lost my edge I'd hit her. Pounding on her until it came back. I took her and took her and I beat her bloody.

When it was over, I had nothing left. I didn't care about her. If I wanted it again she would lay there and take it.

I had a bottle of bleach in a cooler to clean out the blood from between her legs. I sponged her down. I thought her moans of pain from the burning might bring me around again, but they didn't. I was done—spent all I had. After she was clean on the outside I drug her out of the truck. I had heard about this new thing called DNA and your cock was full of it. I took her into the grass and made her douche with the bleach. She was torn inside and howled and whimpered with pain. Refusing to continue, I shoved her down and forced the liquid into all her crevices. It was almost over.

She did say if I just left her there she would never tell. They all promise never to tell. I marched along the road to the bridge where I had parked before to catch some z's. The half-moon lit the blacktop, but not all the way down to the river. I heard the water moving swift in spots, but I couldn't see it.

She didn't even resist, just climbed over the rail, albeit slow as a snail.

Disappointed there was no splash, I could do nothing about it. It was a fifty foot drop, minimum, and onto a gravel bar. I was hoping for water. The current would carry her downstream, disconfiguring the attack location and destroying more of this DNA.

But she was dead.

I would still be early with my load and earn a nice bonus.

XVI

JACK FUMES IN his dark corner.

Information inundates Jesse.

He imagines Jack's emotional state. When the old man joined this group, he may have thought everyone else had motivations to kill like his own, but he is the odd man out in this group because he believes what he did was justified.

Jesse notes the way Ed says Dallas; he means the one in Texas. With the right details Jesse might have a way to figure out where Ed normally operates.

Edgars' killings intrigue him. They go back far enough for Edgars to have murdered her.

Ed could have snagged his sister and killed her also.

Jesse needs the police file on her death. It would provide him with evidence to compare with his notes on the meetings. His mother should explain what happened to her. So much guess work forestalls Jesse from discovering her killer.

"Was she dead?" Jesse asks. *Girl Attacked! Tossed off Bridge!* can't inundate too many newspaper headlines.

"I told you, I like to know when the cops fail. It was harder then, no Intrerweb or Wi-Fi. If I didn't pass back through the area within a day or two, the newspapers would have moved onto a new story and I certainly wasn't going to the newspaper office to ask for an old edition. They might remember the Mack truck parked outside," Ed says.

"In this case the little cunt survived the fall. She was alive when some fishermen found her the next morning. Her parents, some town's important rich folks, had kept her story running on the front page for two weeks. The cops had no evidence, and the police artist sketch printed in the paper was more like Big Rauf than me."

"Did you go finish her off?" Robert asks.

"No, she was dead. The fall did its job, it just wasn't instantaneous. Her insides had turned to goop on impact. Paper said she just lived long enough to put eyes on her momma one more time. The police got the sketch and she died. They never even questioned Big Rauf," Ed says.

"How do you feel about this?" Jane asks.

"I used to have pride in confusing the cops. And now, with blue pills, I don't need to beat on a girl to fuck her. But boy, the thrill!" He pauses, reminiscing. "Because I don't know what else to call it. It was better than any cocaine. I'm not sorry for what I did, I just don't want to get caught. Cameras everywhere now. Transfer DNA. It ain't like it was, I can't enjoy it if I have to be careful."

"You have no other reason to stop other than you don't want to get caught?" Jesse asks.

"It's a start," Jane says. "We build on it. Whatever keeps us from taking another life."

Waiting for the next speaker, Jane considers. "We should partner up now. Start with our screen names and chat. If we find comfort in the talks, we move to burner phones next time. We protect our anonymity, but we are there for one another if an urge nags at us."

"Before I commit to a sponsor I need to share," The Plagiarist says. "I'm not sure I have the means to stop killing, but I want to work with this group, work on getting clean, so to speak."

"Are you sure you just don't want ideas to copy?" Kenneth snaps.

"A fair question, one I don't have an answer to, but your group is built on sharing and trust. If I don't share you won't trust me and may not invite me back. It's not like you meet in the same location once a week or post it in the church bulletin. I don't attend with the intention of stealing your crimes, but like Ed, being caught plays into the equation of quitting."

"Tell us your story," Jane says.

"I had no intention of being a killer the first time, nor aspirations to copy the murders of famous killers. Like many of you, I found it to be a sick, twisted game which thrilled me. The set up for the deaths was what satisfied my urges, not the death myself. Even forestalling the cops was a part of my needs. I even contact certain cops before murders now, proof I wish to stop, but I don't know how.

"Strange how the desire to stop doesn't drive me to march into a police office and surrender. I know this much. After the first murder came my need to kill more. When the first crime was unsolved I had to know if I could get away with it again," The Plagiarist says.

XVII

AT SIXTEEN ALL I knew was I needed to be with a girl—physically. I may have tried too hard. Jana was the girl next door every boy desired. Long brown hair—always perfectly wavy. She didn't notice me beyond a morning smile at the bus stop.

I snuck into the barn loft next to her house. Its height gave me a perfect downward view into her upstairs window. Her parents were always gone for their jobs, Dad sometimes days or even a week at a time. I think when Mom wasn't at work she was out cheating on him, but I'm not sure. She didn't come home some nights. To make up for being gone, they just bought Jana stuff. They had a pool and when the parents were out of town she would sunbathe topless.

I'd stare at her for hours as she laid out. Even when I fondled myself she never heard me.

She sunned herself as two of the more jockular boys pulled up.

Jana lowered her sunglasses to the tip of her nose and lay back once she spotted who the two were, not bothering to cover those sun kissed orbs.

I could never speak to her, but for these two she lay exposed, round tits dangling.

"Hey, Jana. Nice tits."

"You've seen them before, Cody."

"So has three-fourths of the football team."

"If you're going to be nasty you can leave," she teased.

He scooped her up and tossed her into the water.

She hit with a squeal.

As she waded to the ladder the boys stripped. They both jumped in naked, close enough to soak her again.

She screamed at them, but it was only playful. They grabbed her. Cody kissed her mouth while Zeb kissed her neck. His hands disappeared under the water. Within seconds he brought Jana's right leg up above her head—she was so flexible. Her red bikini bottoms hooked between her toes. He grabbed them and flinging them to the deck.

"What are you boys going to do to me?" she teased.

Zeb pulled her so her feet dangled above the water, but she still faced Cody.

Her scream was one of pain. She slapped Zeb on the chest, one arm still around Cody.

"Fuck. That hurts. Zeb, you just can't go shoving that thing into a girl. I told you last time if you couldn't work it in slow, no more sugar puff for you." She jerked away from him, wrapping her legs around Cody. She kissed him, stirring the water with her hips.

"That's better. You'll loosen me up before he ruins me."

"You're so tight not even Zeb's tanker will ruin you."

I enjoyed witnessing each of them taking turns with her.

She must have been on the pill. They never used protection and only fucked in her pussy. Every time they tried to enter the back she protested and said nothing boys peed out of would go in her mouth. Man she took them each four times. Once she got comfortable with Zeb she did nothing but moan with pleasure.

Then they just gathered their clothes and left her on the deck—fucked raw.

"I'm going to need a week to recover from that." Breathless abandon flushed her.

The two jocks constantly high fived each other all the way to their truck.

Jana just lounged, contorted on the deck, her round bronze breasts glistening in the sun while her white ass beamed, having rarely been exposed to the sun.

I climbed the steps to the deck.

"You two want more? I don't know if my sugar puff can take another pounding."

She remained contorted—eyes closed.

I saw my chance. I dropped my pants. Despite my self-abuse I was instantly hard upon hitting air. I had her legs around me and slipped inside. It was warm and so wet.

Before she opened her eyes, she said, "Wow, you guys stretched me open, so enjoy—" Her eyes popped open and she screamed protests. Pounding her fist on me, I grabbed her wrists, pinning them to the deck.

"Let go of me," she growled.

"What's your problem?" I don't know why I asked. I did want to know. She fucked everyone else, why not me?

"You're scuzzy." She struggled. "Get off me."

My mind was blank. I had no thoughts.

"Get off me or I'll tell every girl in the school I couldn't feel it when you put it in."

I was taken aback. No screams of rape, no screams for help, even if we both knew no one would hear. She just laid there with me inside her. She was even going to allow me to take her, but ruin me after.

My reputation didn't mean much to me until her threat. Admiring Jana from afar, I had placed little on winning another woman. My focus on future choice she'd left me soft.

"You're done, now let me go. Maybe I'll just tell the girls you last thirty seconds. I won't even say what a rapist you are, just you have a tiny dick and don't last." She giggled. "No girl in this town will ever touch you."

Some say they snap before the first kill. I didn't detect a snap. I just let go of her wrists and cupped her breasts.

"Get a good feel, perv. It will be the last pair of tits you touch." She never ceased her taunting. I believe she enjoyed it.

She got off on this involuntary foreplay. Wet gushed around my crotch from her. I slipped my hand up, flicking her nipples. She let go a moan of pleasure. I slid my fingers around her throat, the genital caress turned vice. At first she liked the rough, but as less air filled her lungs, she struggled.

Her flexibility allowed her to plant one foot for leverage and kick against me. I lost balance and tumbled into the pool. I did catch her arm as I fell, dragging her top half into the water with me.

She had no time to gasp for air, instead gulping water. I lifted her by her hair. She choked, coughing water now. Her perfect hair—which she never got wet as she fucked the two boys in the pool—left her with a sad, soaked puppy appearance.

Wheezing breaths allowed her to spit, "Now I'll fucking report you."

I dunked her head under.

She thrashed her arms, trying to punch me. Her feet threw a toddler's tantrum on the deck, her heels impacting hard enough to break skin.

I was in control. I had the power, the power she had over men.

I lifted her up as her punching slowed. She sucked in air.

Once her lungs were full I thrust her under. Her struggle was at a faster pace. She used her feet to push her body up, attempting escape, not combat. Once she slowed again I lifted her head above the surface.

"Fucking let me go!" Her outburst cost her more time underwater without being allowed to refill her lungs.

Her legs had no fight this time. I kept her under. She was so tan except her now bluing white bottom.

I thought maybe she lost consciousness, so I jerked her skull. Water rained from her hair.

"Please." This begging tone was new. "I won't say anything."

I lowered her face to the water.

Her arms splashed as if she attempted a push up against the liquid. "You do whatever you want." She gulped air. "I promise I won't tell."

I lowered myself into the water to be eye level with her.

"I don't trust you. Even if I did want you I don't anymore."

She slips under the surface with little energy left to resist.

I lifted her head out again. Her eyes were draining of life. She had no strength to breathe.

A barely audible, "Please."

Her water soaked face made it impossible to tell, but I think she was crying.

I thought about flipping her around taking her from behind, making her take me in her mouth. Making her do what she wouldn't willingly do for other boys. I had accelerated to a new level of existence. I had unwavering control over this girl. The exhilaration was more than any self-induced sexual release. I doubt even her tight virgin ass—if it was so—would have matched how thrilling it was to shove her head under the water and control her access to her next breath.

She didn't move.

Panic.

I flipped her onto the deck.

This time my hand palpated her chest, not for some cheap thrill, but to locate the sternum and compress. I drove the ribcage down until water burst from her nose and mouth. Rolling her onto her left side, more water spilled from inside her.

I collapsed against her cold skin.

What had I done?

I transformed a masturbatory fantasy about the senior slut to attempted murder.

Was I a killer?

She coughed. Sluggish to rise, her first words were no praise for me allowing her to live, but threats. "You're so going to be someone's prison bitch for this. They'll ass rape you every day after I get done telling them what you did to me."

We were both back in the water with my fingers laced in her hair, pushing her to the bottom before I had a single thought. This time I held her under long after her last limb thrashed.

I left her floating face down in the pool.

Being in cold water prevented an exact time of death after they determined she hadn't just drowned. Better they would find two semen types inside her and not one was mine.

This was when I decided the thrill of being chased was greater than the kill. Physically ill—I waited for days for the cops to come arrest me. They never came, not even to ask questions if noises from her house could be heard at mine.

Most of what I learned next was from piecing together the town rumors, the persistent ones holding the most truth in them.

It was a fact Zeb and Cody were questioned multiple times by the police. They admitted to the intercourse, but she was alive when they left. They confessed—bragged—about the tag teaming. They didn't think it was rough enough to have bruised her ribs. The evidence of possible chest compressions blew the theory she had drowned.

I had controlled her with her hair and had left no other marks than the shoving of water from her lungs.

Zeb and Cody were also expected to be the winning stars of the upcoming fall high school football season. If they were arrested for Jana's murder there would be no leading the team to a state championship.

DNA wasn't a thing then. I don't know if they even needed it since they both confessed to tagging her and they would have only found their DNA anyway. Hell, the incident didn't even slow them from dating other girls.

The official report—

I did wonder if the sheriff thought they did it and couldn't take a chance of being the reason the football team had a losing season. After all, Jana was a little slut. She'd slept with so many, and not just her classmates. Her mother had taken her turn with many a man in town as well.

If not for the chest compression bruises she could have fallen in after and drowned—making the death an accident. She was under the water, someone pulled her out and revived her, only to submerge her again. The official report stated a vagrant attacked her. They even arrested this hitchhiking bum who hit town three days after the body was found.

He was railroaded as the perpetrator.

Somewhere after the hobo's conviction I stopped being nervous. I was in no danger of being caught. The police would never admit they made a *mistake*.

Getting away with murder was gratifying. But once interest in the murder faded, because a suspect was incarcerated, I lost my high.

I needed my high back.

Thus, I hunted. It couldn't be some run of the mill slut. Police didn't care. And I didn't wish my home town to fill with bodies. I wouldn't have a high if I actually got caught. Life before the Internet involved countless hours in the library. Nobody noticed me.

The library received the newspapers for most of the towns in the four-county area.

The adjacent county had two women murdered about three weeks apart. Both young women, in their twenties, found naked, but not sexually assaulted. Carved on their upper left thighs was a symbol. Now, this is where the Internet would have been nice. I spent a week going through texts for the symbol. A sideways backward L with the end pointing at the bend of a second tipsy L. Finally, in a book about

Vikings, I found pictures of carved stones. One of the stones had this symbol. It took another book to learn what it meant, but I found it.

Harvest.

XVIII

"HARVEST?"

"It made no sense to me either. I got my driver's license and I traveled to the next town. This was when I learned cops leave stuff out of unsolved cases so they can weed out the crazies who take credit for every murder. Dozens of people call to report they performed the crime. What a sick cry for attention."

Jesse bites his bottom lip. The convolution what these murderer's actions and their justifications stir his stomach. At least his made-up story was similar to The Plagiarist's. It should add to his credibility. In his research he lacks recollection of a mass killer who drowns people. He forces his brain from the sidebar, returning his attention to *Harvest*.

"I ate at a local café and listen to the indigenous patrons. I picked up tales from a few who knew—nothing stays secret in a small town. Hometown diners were better than any Instant flash messenger on the Interweb. Both girls were not sexually assaulted, but someone cut out their uteri."

"Jack the Ripper did that," Jesse says.

"The symbol? You meant to do what with it?" Jane asks.

"Throw the cops off. Both girls had been dating the same man in secret, or so the rumors flew around town. The lover had been only questioned and not openly accused, because during one the murders he had an airtight alibi. More rumors suggested both women were pregnant, and they had just found out about each other." The Plagiarist continues, "Some felt he killed them both and cut out the babies to prevent a blood test. They could do a blood type checking if he was the baby daddy. DNA was not in the police toolbox yet."

"The symbol was a ruse to make the cops think it was a cult or serial killer," says Jesse.

"I was going to steal it. It wasn't for my speculation as to what purpose it served other than a ruse for my actions. I hid my car well out of sight and waited for the diner to close. The waitress was older than the victims, but not by much, and was an acquaintance of the possible baby daddy, if the rumors of pregnancy were true."

No one in the group halts the second tale of The Plagiarist.

"No one told people in small towns to lock their car doors or check the back seat—yet. She nearly drove off the road when I put the cold steel to her neck. I made her pull onto a country lane about a mile across a field diagonally from where I left my car. I wasn't in tune yet with plastic gloves and disposable clothing. I also didn't know how he killed these women. If he killed them first and then cut out the uterus? I was totally blind here. The cops focused on the mark, so did I. I was going to botch this up.

"I had her undress. I whispered sweet nothings in her ear until she burst into tears. I told her if she just did what I asked I would finish quick and allow her to leave. Such power. Control. They all believe compliance will lead to release—unscathed. She did whatever I commanded. She touched herself when I said. She stopped when I said. "I told her I'd go quicker if she lie back over the hood. She needed it over. I stood before her. She never brought her eyes up to gaze into mine. Jana's breasts were nicer.

"My knife drank deep into her lower abdomen. Blood splashed everywhere as she doubled over. I thrust it in again, this time sawing across the yellowish underlying fatty tissue of her stomach. Helping her to her knees, I cut away her flesh.

"Her eyes explained she sought to hit me, but shock consumed her. As she lost more blood, I lay her down and pulled out as much of her internal sex organs as possible. They were reminiscent of the pig I dissected in science class. The blood covered my fingers, making my touch more slippery than a greased hog at the county fair. I dropped the parts of my version of a hysterectomy in a plastic trash bag, not sure how to dispose of it. She was bleeding out. I carved *harvest* on her left thigh in the exact spot as the other two. The newspaper pictures assisted in getting it correct.

"I knew I was covered in her blood, as she lost enough to end her life. I marched across the field to my car. Sirens. Fuck! I was going to get caught. I jerked around slapping the bag against the car door. Fuck me if it had busted. My chest pumped with quick breaths as my heart pounded. It was the rapid blood floor thumping my eardrums. The evening air was nothing but cicadas. I had to get cleaned up and home without being discovered.

"The key was the correct gravel backroads and avoiding any underage drinking parties. I drove slow until I reached the Old Mill Bridge. I disposed of the knife in the water. The area had a drop off and flooded frequently. It would never be found. Jasper's hog farm worked for the actual woman's parts.

"I still didn't know how to explain away the bloody clothes or the bloody trash bag if I got pulled over so close to home. I burnt the clothes and the bag in the trash barrel and scrubbed the car with bleach. Next time I would get a disposable outfit in case my mother noticed that some of my shirts disappeared. My success came two days later when the boyfriend of the first two women was arrested. According to the paper he had no alibi for the waitress's murder and one of the girl's. They would just have to convince a jury of those two. I might have to work a frame into my next killing." The Plagiarist smiles.

Jesse's first thought is a desire to know all this man's stories. He could have killed his sister and made it appear to be someone else.

"The thrill didn't last long?" Al asks.

"It lasted for a while. The third girl's murder and his alibi kept throwing a monkey wrench in the prosecution's case. The newspapers even claimed the cops were checking out other suspects. I lived on the thrill of this case for months. They finally prosecuted him on the one girlfriend and waitress since he had no alibi. Better to nab him on what they thought they could prove," The Plagiarist says.

"How many people sit in prison because of your interference?" Al asks.

"I said it before, cops get hard for a suspect and never let them go. At least with the waitress I know her death did not completely match the other two. I didn't know what I was doing then. Some forensic surgeon would explain how the cuts were different. How the angle of penetration was from a man of a different height. I bet I didn't even cut out the uterus the same. They didn't care—they had their murderer. And more important the closer rate. Departments are pressured to put a suspect in the hangman's gallows and the closest significant other is the most likely candidate. The number of closed cases and favorable crime statistics for tourist draw is more important to the government than locking away the correct person. Don't get me wrong, usually those people deserved to be locked away, but not always for the crime they are incarcerated for."

"They couldn't prove Al Capone was the killer he was, so they put him in jail on tax evasion," Jesse says.

"The greatest sin in the eyes of the government," Al says.

"Stealing's wrong. Unless you are the IRS," Ed says.

"Now we are getting off track," Jane redirects.

"Did the second girlfriend have an alibi for the first girl's death?" asks Edgars.

"What?" Confused by the question, The Plagiarist ponders a moment. "She was never a suspect, only a victim."

"If I was working it into a book plot I would make her so devoted to this boyfriend he would be able to convince her to kill the sister while he made sure he was alibied by a dozen witnesses. Later, I would end her in the same manner, believing I could never be a suspect in murder number two if I had not performed the first one." Edgar's creative juices flow. He wishes for a pen and paper.

"I wonder how many kittens he shit when that waitress wound up dead in the same manner." Ed laughs.

"He would know it was a copycat and he had nothing or no ties to her. Wow! He thought he was home free," says Al.

"Now you understand my motivation and my thrill. It has been why I have killed." The Plagiarist asks, "Now how do I stop?"

SEVEN

JESSE

I

EDGARS DRIVES THE cherry tip of his nubby cigarette into the brick wall, grinding out the flame. "You know, kid…"

Jesse jerks out of his skin. He gasps, not expecting anyone to be around the corner from the abandoned factory. Jane's choice of location was secluded, allowing the privacy they needed to be comfortable enough to speak about their issues.

"Never ended anyone with a jump scare before. Sorry, kid." He slips the cigarette butt into his front right suit coat pocket.

Jesse detects the crinkle of plastic. He naturally forgoes leaving behind possible DNA, another clue he's been active for a long time—twenty plus years. He draws in a breath to calm his heart. The man did frighten him, startled him enough that pressure builds on the inner wall of his bladder.

"I needed to ask you something. I didn't want to do it in front of the group."

Did you once have a sister…?

Jesse fantasizes the question he desires to be asked.

"When you choked out your professor, you got it over with pretty quick,"

"Not a question, Mr. Edgars, but allow me to deduce what you want to know. I had my body pinning the older man. He still had a lot of strength. I thought he'd be frail, but he had fight. I had him down and one of his arms pinned under my knee. He clawed at my hands with his free one. I had my fingers pressing down and he gurgled and spat. He choked for air forever. I had no idea a human neck was so taut. My fingers cramped. It was a long process. As strong as I am in the gym, no one works the fingers, which is where all the pressure emanates. I glanced at the clock on the wall. My fingers twisted in arthritic flares of spasm cramps. I needed to release, but he was still sucking in air. I thought I had every ounce of my weight on his esophagus. I squeezed tighter and the spongy windpipe caved. I glanced at the clock—three minutes. I had my fingers around a man to end his life for three minutes. I was terrified then. I was committed to the act and God help me if anyone had returned to the class because they forgot a book."

Jesse contorts his fingers as if he had them around someone's neck. "Three minutes to squeeze the life out of the old man. My fingers were frozen in a choking configuration. I had no idea how I would gather my belongings without disrupting the crime scene."

"I found choking to a be a slow process and you have to exercise those muscles."

It was a test. He doesn't trust me. None of them trust me. Jane screened the attendees. The professor was right. This is dangerous. Had I answered him wrong would I become a chapter in his next novel?

"You have to work at choking. While your hands are busy, theirs are free, allowing punches and scratches for those with the mind to fight back. If they claw you, they have your DNA under the fingernails," Edgars says. "I duct taped a few girls' fingers together when they had extra-long nails."

"They have to have you on file for DNA to work." And they preserved DNA evidence even before they used DNA. BTK learned of

DNA, changed his MO and, thank God, he wrote about how long it took to actually choke a person or I'd be dead. Is it Edgars who doesn't trust me or everyone?" *He spoke about it in his book, the long, tedious process in choking a victim. Glad I read non-fiction.*

"They always bag potential clues and now some are preserved enough they are able to test for DNA. I don't worry about it. Many of my victims have other suspects lined up first. Hell. Cops like ex's and drifters. No one sees a well renowned bestselling author as a vagrant." Edgars smiles.

Fuck me. Moonlight coated the pair in enough light to pick out facial features. *He's the only one who could view my face. We all know his appearance. His face covers the back of dozens of book jackets. They don't trust me. Recover the fumble, dumbass.* "Seventy-nine percent of all murders are committed by someone the victims know and half of those were spouses. I guess we threw a wrench into that statistic."

"Not you, you murdered your teacher," Edgars bemuses.

"This should be a group conversation, Mr. Edgars. We're supposed to meet in a part of town no one goes into, not even the drug dealers, and certainly not one in Armani."

"I don't sell that many books," he chuckles.

"I'm going to have to pick one up."

"Bring it with you and I'll sign it," he offers with the bright tone of someone still excited a person wants to read what they have written.

"I won't be able to have you dedicate it. No real names for the rest of us," Jesse says.

"True, kid. How about I dedicate it to a trusted traveler?" He pats Jesse's shoulder. "You're doing right by stopping now. The first murder is the hardest. And if you do two and find it easy, it's nearly impossible to come back from. And there is no help. It's not that I want to get away with murder, it's I don't know how to stop. Locking people away never fixes the issue." He taps the side of his forehead. "It's faulty wiring up here. It needs to be fixed before anyone kills."

"Many serial killers are conceived in childhood abuses. Identifying and restoring mental health before a rampage needs to be addressed. But people would rather have the stigma of being a mass murderer than a mental patient," Jesse says.

"It's a fucked up world, kid."

"At least we are trying to fix ourselves."

II

JESSE FLIPS ON the desk lamp. He slips an archaic letter opener into the end of the sealed manila folder mailed to Arnett. It was in the Professor's school mail basket. No one even questioned Jesse when he slipped into the faculty lounge and swiped it.

He dumps the contents onto the desk. Papers flood out, along with 8x10 glossies of a dead girl.

Jesse drops the envelope, shoving back from the desk as he tips the chair over. He crashes backwards, just remaining on the floor staring up at the ceiling.

I knew they would be in there. I studied murder cases. They all had pictures. I knew. How does anyone prepare for viewing their own dead sister?

He contemplates why his mother hid much of her death from him. He was four. She was seventeen. She always had good grades and was never in trouble at school.

Jesse ponders if it is true she was an angel or if he placed her on a unicorn carved pedestal.

Was there a boy?

Mom never spoke of a boyfriend. No signs of drug use at home.

Not until after. Mom drank. Maybe not enough to go to meetings, but more than she should.

He picks himself up along with the chair. Sissy is well into cold case status now after fifteen…sixteen years. It meant Jack didn't kill her.

Or did it? None of them have stated how long they have been operating. Ed's story has slang and remarks about this new DNA. DNA evidence has been a staple of crime shows as long as he remembers. Ed killed the girl as far back as the nineties, maybe late eighties. The story he told wasn't about his sister and they didn't ever live in Dallas, Texas.

Cops aren't as stupid as the group believes, but one thing for sure, they don't dig too deeply into dead hookers or runaways.

Sissy wasn't a runaway.

Sissy was accepted into medical school. Mom framed the letter. Jesse discovered it in the shrine that was once her bedroom.

Did Sissy prostitute herself to come up with the money to go? Dad had a college fund, but he said he didn't save enough to send her there, he would figure it out.

Once you eliminate the impossible, whatever remains, no matter how improbable, must be the truth. Okay Sherlock you have to start eliminating.

Jesse places a three-foot by three-foot cork board on an easel. It will be his murder board. He pins index cards with each group member's name along the top in black Sharpie. Next to Jack he draws a big red question mark.

Of any of them Jack is my ally. Even if he doesn't know it. I wish I had drawn him as my contact buddy over Jane.

I don't know how fast AA members get a sponsor, but Jane seems deadline quick to cure us.

Jack and Al were paired. Jane thought those two would counter each other better.

Jesse's murder of the professor wasn't up to par with the killings of the others. Professor Arnett was correct about this group seeing through him. He suspects they suspect him. He's not trained in undercover work. He thought being inexperienced would work as a cover and add to the character he played in front of them.

On an index card in green Sharpie he puts *Dallas, TX* by Ed's name.

Hospital deaths/Social worker in halfway house. Possible psych degree under Jane's name.

Recalling mental notes, he only writes down what he knows for sure in green.

In purple sharpie, he notes the 'they implied' information. He scrawls *never practiced* or *state licensed shrink* on Jane's card. He wonders how hard it would be to find out how many people have a degree and never used it.

Jesse laughs. *Plenty of Walmart door greeters who never used their degree.* The one checkout girl he flirted with told him once she, too, had earned a criminal justice degree, but there were no jobs and she didn't want to move away from where she grew up.

Maybe if he knew the state Jane killed in or attended school, it would narrow the list to maybe dozens after he eliminates any males in the same jobs.

The hospital would have covered up the deaths if they thought they were mysterious and how many fresh out of prison women go back to drugs? She's got her niche plotted well. With those kinds of search parameters, it would take forever to find her. *I need another clue from her.*

She is my buddy. Sponsor. Whatever the hell she labeled it. If the urge to kill blossoms, I contact her through the chat room. What could I say? What would make her reveal to me where she attended school? Just knowing the state she attended school in and I might locate her.

How do you even get there? I could mention there is this girl at college who frustrates me so much I want to choke her out. Ask her if she had these thoughts when she went back to school after she lost her nursing license. She implied she did. He writes in purple, *Psych degree? When?*

He chews the cap of the purple Sharpie. What about triangulating the distance between the meetings? We held two in different states. The third might be all he needs to determine how far she travels to officiate.

Jesse shoves the unseen photos of his sister under the envelope, so they fall behind the desk. He snags the police report:

The female, naked, approximately sixteen to eighteen years of age, was found supine, ligature marks and bruising at the wrist and ankles from being bound.

Jesse halts.

How can I read what happened to my sister? It's one thing to know she was raped and murdered. But to read about it? To read about the tears in her vaginal wall. Having pictures of the bruises the rope left behind. He falls onto his bed. The stack of documents taunts him from behind the desk. He closes his eyes. Sleep might help. Guessing about what happened terrified his sleep for years, but to know what they did to his Big Sissy? He knows it will haunt him. Haunt him beyond any story those in the group share.

His eyes scan down the Xerox of the hand printed text of the police report:

Dried blood surround both the vaginal canal and the anus.
Signs of forced trauma. Contusions line the inner thigh wall.

"Fuck!"

He crumples the paper. Rolling off the bed Jesse flings all the top of the desk contents to the floor. The cheap Walmart desk set and phone clang on the carpet. His class papers flutter harmlessly like leaves on the wind to the floor.

How do I read about her rape?

How do I not?

Jesse reaches for the fallen stack of papers.

If I want to find her killer I must read the reports. I can't use what I thought I knew before. I must know what happened to her in order to do this. The professor was correct, I can't investigate my own case objectively.

He picks up the house phone from the floor, still a hardline push button telephone in his dad's office. He must hang up and dial the number a second time.

"Hello, Professor Arnett. I thought about what you said, and I think it's time I speak to the FBI."

EIGHT
JANE

I

"I WANT POSITIVE references and your full support behind any new job I apply at." If she smoked this is where Jane would lean back in the chair and light up in defiance of the hospital's non-smoking policy.

The two fancy suited men are affronted by her bluntness. The one on the right with the poor combover speaks first, "I don't think you understand what kind of trouble you are in, lady. You're in no position to demand."

Jane imagines releasing a long puff with enough smoke to fill the room and flicking ash on the floor of the makeshift interrogation room.

"If we go back two years you were on the same shifts as Charles," the second man with dimples says.

Jane knows they have nothing. She never stole too many drugs or too often. It was the last one, the mentally challenged kid who spent his days drooling on himself and observing Clifford the Big Red Dog on PBS. Mom insisted it was his favorite because he blinked—blinked the most during the show. They brought in a VCR and a television so he could watch it while he was in the hospital for pneumonia. She had been giving him tapioca pudding through his feeding tube. It was crusted inside and likely was ripe with bacteria—and mom's fault.

It didn't matter. Mom and Dad were some big contributors to the church, and the church supported the hospital. After all, Jane was employed by St. Mary's. The parents demanded a target, someone to persecute for the death of their son. The hospital launched an investigation, and someone would lose their job because it was the fault their child died.

Jane thought it was ironic. What if this was a death she didn't encourage? Sometimes people get sick and die. Some people are meant to die. People worry about the growing number of childhood ailments and how it is an epidemic across the country. It's chemicals in the food. It's lack of clean drinking water. Mom smoked. Mom tried crack. Dad's sperm was weak. Fuck some of the dumbest ideas as to why so many underperforming special needs kids are being born. There are no more being born, it's medicine. Doctors are too good at their job. As much as people don't want to be the asshole who explains how nature already determined those kids should not have lived after birth, science trumped natural selection.

Nature.

Darwin's assessment was accurate and medical science pisses on it. Now these kids live and are destined to a life of medical issues because Nature had already determined they were to have died shortly after birth. Science and the money driven society screams NO! We keep the kid alive and you'll have to make monthly pilgrimages to the doctor and charge the insurance companies millions. How much is your child's life worth?

For such people who profess to live as God's plans, they sure don't follow it. God's determined your baby wasn't strong enough to be a part of His plan, so you turned to science to defy the law of the universe. And those professing to do His works demand payment. Jane laughs.

"This is serious, lady," Combover scolds.

"Why are we here, gentlemen?"

"To determine if any wrong doing occurred by our staff…"

"Fuck."

Both mousy men go into cardiac arrest over a professional woman using the word 'fuck.'

"Now there is no reason for a lady to use…"

"Fuck you." Jane's eyes flame. "Lots of nurses were on shift with Charles. And there was never any evidence of his involvement with the death of anyone, other than he was on shift at the time of some deaths of people who were already dying."

"Three codes on the burn ward at the same time was suspicious."

"And a good union defense lawyer would destroy the case with toxicology. I read the reports on all three *people*." Jane reminds them these were people, people who needed to be released from this world. "People. Unless the hospital lied on their own reports, they all passed from natural causes. One had lasted weeks longer than the doctors projected. But your investigation did cause a murder. You scared Charles into thinking he was facing triple murder charges. Triple murder! No wonder he blew his brains out."

Jane has a mild stirring in her sex drive. She controls the room and these two flaccid—impotent overweight middle-aged men know it. She would bet dollars to donuts Combover has pictures of underage girls on his computer. Not pedophile prepubescent shit, still illegal fifteen-year-old little girl shit. If not, he might, if she gets a chance to try all the computer shit she's been reading up on.

"I would bet you have a dozen nurses on the same shift as those deaths. All determined as natural—unless—the hospital has been covering up suspicions."

"Now…"

"Now, fuck you! Let me tell you what. Either I go back on shift cleared of all—whatever the fuck this is. Or if you're just fishing for blame to shut the grieving family up, keep their donations to the church and hospital flowing, I want references. My performance is impeccable. I demand fucking great references."

"Nobody said anything about anyone being fired. We are just making sure…"

"We had an old lady pass two weeks ago. She was in her nineties and there was no investigation." And she did pass naturally.

"There was nothing unusual about the boys…"

Jane rises to her feet, towering over Combover. "Then we. Are. Finished. This is a witch hunt and you have no witch. You're going to upset a lot of competent nurses for no reason. Upsetting them causes them to second guess all their choices and that causes mistakes—mistakes cause a death. If someone dies in the next few days it is on you two. You two are the cause because this little meeting jumbles some poor, young nurse's decision-making skills. You caused Charles to opt for a gun to his temple."

"It was under his chin," Combover corrects.

Jane knew. She just couldn't appear to know anything not in the newspapers.

The meeting ends.

Jane returns to her shift.

No more nurses are questioned.

Jane knows she painted a target on herself.

A target she could handle, since what she did was not for the standard hero complex or the sexual thrill. She would just have to witness people needlessly suffer so the hospital could bill eighty dollars for an aspirin.

II

JANE POPS THE door release bar hard. The metal rectangle misses the man approaching from the opposite side by half an inch.

"Whoa." His leap back lacks grace, but it keeps him from being impacted on the nose.

"Sorry." Her apology lacks any earnestness nor quells her anger.

"Bad day?" He does convey a tone containing mild concern.

"Even if I was I wouldn't discuss hospital matters with anyone." Jane recovers her composure. She discovered as a new nurse she had to quell her emotions. When a family witnessed a loved one in distress she never displayed emotion. She had to remain professional.

"I'm not some reporter," he says. "I hear they are roaming the corridors."

"Never thought you were." Jane flashes an eye toward her car, eighty-seven feet away, but her keys are in her pocket.

"I actually was waiting out here for you."

Some men have fantasies about nurses and sponge baths. Worse since female nurses convey a strong maternal instinct some men have a mommy fetish. No man has used an original pickup line in her last five years of sporting the white hat. The brashness of these men astounds her, especially when they're sick, or worse, their pregnant wife is in a room upstairs squeezing out their kid. The craziness of human behavior has led her to reenroll at the university and continue her education. She examines the man with her chocolate eyes. "I doubt it was me."

"I'm not making a shitty pass at you, Nurse Jane."

Shock should grab her, but her name, emblazoned on a golden bar on her chest, shines for everyone to see. "I'm sure your wife needs you upstairs."

"I'm not married, it's my father. He is hooked to all these machines on the fourth floor and my mother won't let him go. They are keeping him alive and I know he wants released."

She studies his blue eyes and even though it appears he might drop a tear, he forces the pain.

"That's between your mother, the doctors…and your God." But he doesn't give a shit.

"I thought maybe you might be able to assist him."

"When I'm his nurse, all I'm able to do is make him comfortable, to follow the doctor's directive for the best possible care we offer." This guy wants her to pull the plug, but he's no grieving son. He has more an ex-military commando vibe, and she'd bet her license the hospital employed him to scope her out. He carries his shoulders not quite as a police officer would. He might be a private dick.

Why risk it? Why end someone at this moment? She was just cleared of any wrongdoing. She doesn't have the desire. Nothing drives her to end someone. She has complete control...over...she contemplates. She desires to kill. No...she does it to help people, to keep the hospital from stealing. She protects families like a modern-day Robin Hood.

"But I can't stand him suffering. Mom would keep the machine breathing for him. He would never want to live as a vegetable."

Jane takes two long strides toward her car. "I'm not sure what you're asking. But as long as your mother speaks for your father we will provide all the medical care possible. I'm going to end this conversation now." In his heavy trench coat, he could hide a recorder.

"Would you at least check his chart? See he's not going to wake up?"

"I don't work on the fourth floor." Now I know he's a...plant. If they catch me investigating a patient on a floor I don't get assigned and he dies, then they might have a case. I know how to play the game. I did the same to Charles. She speaks plain so any recording device picks up her professional fuck off message, "I'm leaving now. If you persist, I will notify security."

He backpedals, but not because he believes she's not capable of being a plug puller, but more because she won't snap at his hook.

"I thought you were the person to help me."

"Not one nurse in that building will do anything to harm a patient." Her statement would have all the conviction of truth because it was true. Jane was outside. Enduring life is not always the proper choice.

Jane marches toward her car. She contemplates how to check this man's story. Is there a dying man on the fourth? Yes. They house most terminal patients on that floor. Should she carry this all the way and report the man for good measure?

Let it go.

He chases after her. A real distraught son might. Now she will report him just to cover herself. Because no random patient would have any reason to suspect she ends pain, they sent him after her. She fishes in her pocket for the keys.

"But Miss Jane, you are the only person who can help him." His pleas are disingenuous. She doubts anyone would fall for him.

"Leave me alone, or I will contact security." She fumbles through the keys until she finds the one for her car door. She flicks it at him as if she held a butcher knife ready to lacerate his throat. "And if you approach another nurse I'll...I'll make sure you're never allowed on hospital grounds again. How would your poor mother feel about that?"

He raises his hands in a defensive gesture. "Sorry."

"Back off!" She jams the key into the lock.

Mashing down the pedal she peels off, leaving a trail of rubber from one tire. Two blocks away she parks. Jumping the curb—frantic—she hops out, with every bit of her shaking she fumbles into the payphone booth.

"9-1-1 what is your emergency?" chirps the voice.

Jane quivers, "Yes...I'm..."

"9-1-1 what is your emergency?"

"I'm, a nurse...I'm a nurse at St. Mary's and this man in the parking lot he...he..."

"I have your location ma'am. An officer has been dispatched. Are you able to stay on the phone?"

"Yes."

"Is this man still there?"

"No. No. I left the hospital. He was...he was waiting for me out... the employee entrance." Keeping her voice trembling, Jane smiles to herself. Once clear of the hospital's radar, she'll punish them.

III

"IT'S YOUR DAY off." Tina, the thin as a rail nurse, points out as Jane reaches for a patient chart.

"They called me in," Jane says. "I guess Debora called in again."

Tina reaches across the desk, her uniform hanging baggy on her bony arms. She scoops up a disposable coffee cup marked in black Sharpie—Debora. "She's been sick a lot lately." Using just two fingers to hold the cup she dangles it over the trash. "She was up for a promotion. I think all these sick days will harm her chances." She drops the cup, caramel liquid splashing in the metal bucket.

Jane leans in so her voice doesn't carry. "It might if her sickness is a sign of a more permanent condition."

"What's wrong with her, do you think?"

Jane pats her own flat stomach.

"She's not married," Tina whispers.

"Women have been having children without being married for millennia." Jane raises an eyebrow.

The wheels turn for Tina. "But this is a religious hospital. If she is pregnant and unwed they might fire her."

Jane never understood how some people graduated nursing school. "They certainly won't promote her," Jane says. "You want to work the desk or do rounds?"

"Desk," Tina says.

Of course, because your bony ass can barely pick up a newborn. "I'm going to check the ward, then get some fresh coffee. Want some?" Jane smiles. *Maybe I'll add to yours what I gave to Debora.*

"Please."

• • • • •

Jane slips from the kitchen with a handful of new coffee filters in her hand. Someone just mopped the floor and her sneakers squeak. She chews her bottom lip at the high-pitched scrunch. Not even proceeding on her toes cuts out the noise. As she rounds a corner she ducks back into the corridor hiding from the two men.

She recognizes the combover and the man who she reported to the cops. They wrote down his description and assured her no one fitting his appearance had a father on the fourth floor.

The hospitable promised to add extra security. Vindicated he was a plant part of her wants to confront them both. She desires Debora's promotion. The medicine she adds to her coffee won't kill her, but it will damage her performance. She listens.

"She ran and called the cops on me. A woman willing to kill doesn't call the cops."

"You can't be on the grounds when she's on shift, but I've got two more nurses I want you to approach. I won't lose this hospital's five-star status and its place on *US News and World Report's* best hospitals."

Jane knows the combover man's motivation is financial.

"Sick people die."

"We just need to make sure our staff are on the up and up," Combover says.

"I'll check them out when this Nurse Jane isn't on shift. I'll get my coat out of your office and I'm gone."

The hospital administration wastes more funds to monitor her with this secret investigator.

Copper splashes on her tongue as she realizes she bit her lip in her anger. Fine. She understands the game being played, now to change to her rule book.

Swinging by the nurse's station, she checks on Tina. "Had to go to the kitchen to get filters. I ever figure out who doesn't replace them in the workroom…"

"You'll kill them," Tina completes the statement.

"I was thinking of placing them on permanent bedpan duty." Jane smiles.

"I'd prefer death. Some of the meds issued makes these poor people explode," Tina says. "You notice it's been slow since the incident?"

"Do you mean Charles' suicide?"

"I was told not to speak about it," Tina says.

"Next week when every bed is full you'll be praying for the night you only had three patients."

"And next week is a full moon."

Fuck it is. Tonight's my shot. I just need to figure out how to get back. Jane scoops coffee grounds into the maker. *Work remains an alibi. It needs to be tonight, before he goes.*

Jane kneels, opening the doors to the under-sink cabinet. She reaches behind the sink and removes an oil stained cloth. Unwrapping the rag, she finds a shiny thirty-eight. She knows even if the weapon was discovered it will be attributed to Charles. His prints are all over it. He bought it.

Slipping the gun in her waistband at the small of her back, she calls to Tina, "We're low on coffee too. I'm going back to the kitchen."

"It might be closed," she offers.

"Then I'll raid another workroom."

"Okay. I won't make it through the night without coffee," Tina says.

• • • • •

Jane wedges cardboard into the circular hole so the dead latch plunger won't catch, allowing her to slip back inside the hospital undetected through the fire door. She jogs across the parking lot, pulling on latex gloves. The dark dusk to dawn lamps have not been replaced. The only car must belong to the investigator. She reaches behind her back to keep the revolver secure in her waistband.

Arriving at the Buick as the rear lights blink on, the brakes squeak as he spots her. Before he opens the door, she brandishes the thirty-eight.

Opening the back door, she warns, "Stay in the car."

"You're a crazy bitch."

She slides inside. "Put both hands on the wheel."

He complies.

"Remove them and I'll shoot you. I bet you're packing."

"Look lady…"

She presses the barrel into the back of his head. "Understand, I won't warn you. I don't have need of macho bravado to exert my control of the situation. I am in control. And if you fail to cooperate the blood will spray over the windshield and I'll return to the ward still in a pristine, white dress. Now drive. Take a left onto the street."

He drops the gear shift into drive. "I wasn't stalking you, I work for the hospital. Private security."

"You're a spy and a waste of resources," she mumbles.

"You helped Charles kill patients?"

She presses the barrel harder against his skull. *He might have the recorder on.* "Take a left, next street."

She remains quiet as they travel down the two-lane blacktop. Two miles the constant row of houses turns to crop fields.

"Slow," she orders.

He does.

"Turn."

"There is no road."

"Gravel. On the left." She glances at her watch.

"There's nothing out here," he protests.

"Stop and put it in park. Keep your hands on the wheel."

He does.

Jane reaches for the doorknob. "You reach with your left hand— open the door. Move in any other manner and I end you."

His hand grips the door handle and he bolts, leaving the keys in the ignition. Jane flings open her door, keeping it between herself and him as a shield.

BAM.

She fires into the dark.

He grunts, falling out of the headlamp's light.

Jane fires where she believes he should be. The bullet skips through the grass. She slips around the back door to the front. Switching hands, she reaches into the car to flip the lights off.

"You missed, bitch."

Jane fires in the direction of the voice.

Miss.

He runs. She detects his shoes in the grass.

Jane fires into the air.

"You are one dumb bitch. I will be glad to attend when you get the chair."

Jane lines up her sight with the direction of the voice. The only disbelief she has is he is unarmed. He might be waiting for her to run out or reload. Everyone knows a revolver only has six. "Keep speaking. The light glare was throwing off my aim."

With only the ambient illumination of the dome light she detects his location. *Run forward a few more feet.* "I have two rounds left. You run away and I might miss." *Run away you fool.*

She flips the lights on, catching him approaching the car. Her left hand releases the wild shot, but it causes him to race away from the car.

Screams fill the dark until squelched by a splash. Jane jumps into the car and backs down the gravel road to the blacktop. She has been off her ward for twenty minutes. Tina shouldn't miss her yet.

She mashes the gas pedal until she crosses the city boundary line, slowing to the speed limit. She made up two minutes. Parking in the same spot at the hospital as when they left, she hurries inside.

She pockets the cardboard and allows the door to lock behind her.

• • • • •

"Where did you go to get coffee, Brazil?" Tina never leaves the desk.

"You wanted it fresh." Jane returns the pistol to its hiding spot under the sink. It still has Charles' fingerprints. Tossing the gloves, she scoops coffee grounds into the maker. She was here. Tina will vouch for her if the fall killed the man. She put a bullet in him and he fell five hundred feet into the shallow quarry.

She had thought about using the water to dump the meds she used Charles' ID to steal. But in the summer kids swim there and in drought years it does dry up. She would still have to dispose of the containers.

The hospital can't commit to knowing this man since Jane filed a police report on him. She's trapped herself here and won't be able to free anymore people of their pain. Jane considers it's time to vacate St. Mary's.

IV

JANE SNAGS THE crumpled rag from the adjustable table. Mr. Miller had finally fallen asleep after his morning perusal of the tabloid. His arthritic fingers were mangled, and no one wanted the furrowed mess after him. Three days and finally an article in the newspaper. In the bottom corner, front page, below the half page on the local Fall Harvest Queen winner announcement and a tiny blurb on how the high school football team lost again, was the mashed face of the male recovered from the quarry.

He was unknown and found by fishermen. Suicide was ruled out because of a gunshot wound across the top of his shoulder. CLEARLY FIRED FROM BEHIND, was the only comment of the Police Chief. No mention of his identity or his employment by the hospital. As the article drones on the reporter unprofessionally shifts into editorial mode and remarks on the growing hippies and their pot, and how more and more unknown people are moving into town.

Jane smirks.

A few Maryjane joints were never the town's problem. No one sees how the hospital and healthcare system gores people. 'Your blood pressure is a bit high—here is a pill.' The BP meds cause weight gain—here is a pill.' 'That pill prevents a boner—here is a blue pill.' All at the expense of the patient.

She scribbles on Mr. Miller's chart. What the poor man has never been told is there is a safe procedure to repair his fingers, only his insurance won't cover it and he hasn't the income to cover the out of pocket expense.

It's the people on the fourth floor who need a Death with Dignity consultation. The time come when life is over, and people need to be released from their earthly shell. She reaches into her pocket and slips out a syringe, dropping it in the sharp's box in Mr. Miller's room. The vial of medicine she'll use again—twice more. Glancing at her watch, the code should occur in about thirty-seven minutes.

She flips through the newspaper to the classifieds. Several hospitals—all short of nurses—advertise signing bonuses for those willing to work all hours.

Our Lady of Innocence Hospital two towns over would be a drive, but the increase in salary would be an easy explanation for her desire to move on. Some might know of Charles and be aware there were issues, but they would never inquire in an interview. But after such a tragedy many people shift jobs.

The code blue calls for a doctor to report to the fourth floor—STAT.

V

OUR LADY OF Innocence Hospital could not have checked Jane's references as fast as they hired her and placed her on shift. She functioned on both jobs for two weeks. Debora returned for her next to last shift and this time Jane lacked a desire to spike her coffee. What she had spiked were random bags of intravenous saline solution destined for the burn ward.

Doctoring of the bags would cause an unknown reason for an insulin spike in the patients. Since she chose the bags at random she doubts anyone will realize why these patients, some well on the road to recovery, code. If they do discover the tainted bags it will be weeks after she is gone and no way to tie her to the deaths. No fingerprints and the burn unit was not her department.

Those poor burnt souls need a quick end. The burn unit care wasn't nursing, it was dealing with the slowly dying. Few recover from massive burns and the cosmetic surgery to follow only lines the pockets of doctors. Burns leave a body without lingering physical pain. No one should have to die slow just to rack up hospital fees.

Jane cups the half-used vial in her uniform pocket. She could free two more. Three would be pushing it. They might live and be worse—worse, the hospital staff might save them. Life prolonging procedures are expensive.

No.

She must let it go. A cloud of suspicion might be over her, but it is not dark. She'll find people who need release at Our Lady of Innocence Hospital.

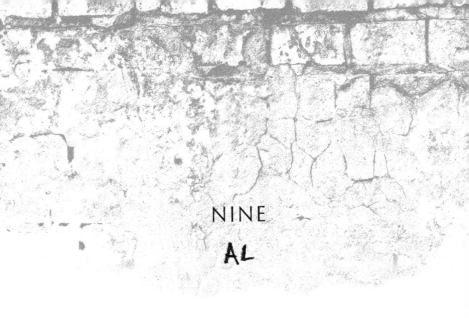

NINE

AL

I

AL'S BROWN EYES study every line of the painting. He notes details down a skin lesion on the chin. A deep shaving cut, which never healed, left a light pink mark. He admires the work. It may be of an Archbishop, but the masterful effort of the artisan always leaves him astonished. Why such a talented person would do unspeakable acts against society. If his own hobbies are ever discovered some might speculate on his own motivations and how he can track down people who have performed similar acts. It would become a television movie of the week on the wife-beater channel. They would not focus on him, but on the heroic efforts of the women and their many attempts to throw off his attacks and escape his basement harem. Only what those hard-core women-are-equal people refuse to acknowledge is, despite being forced upon them, some enjoy the domination. Not all, but some. Willful subjugation destroys their movement of women-are-equal in all places.

"He painted this?" Al asks.

"It was to be presented to the Father when he is promoted to Archbishop next month. It was commissioned by some diocese or something. I don't know, I don't care much for those idol worshipers," Chambers says.

"Good cops should consider the beliefs of those they serve and protect. It's not always a gang color issue. People of faith are just as prone to violence as any minority. In the last election many of the pro-testors had religious ideologies." Al asks, never removing his eyes from the painting, "What did your search yield?"

"You were correct. He was quick to burn his photo prints because they were not his trophies. We searched for a backup hard drive or disks with the jpegs and found several document-protecting fire proof boxes."

"The originals?"

"Not photos, drawings. He would sketch the girls. The first pages were innocent. You know, like on a church pew fully clothed. Then they got more revealing. Unbuttoned blouses showing some cleavage or in a bra. Same girl in each book. Each page showed more skin, but a trusted amount." Chambers hands him a spiral bound sketch book.

Al flips through it. "She was comfortable with what he had her do. This time it was an open shirt and nothing else happened. This time no shirt. He didn't touch her. Not until she was drawn naked, then her positions shifted to a sexual stance. He struck me as the type to use the sin as a motivating factor. I'll draw the devil out of you," Al's conjecture yields fruit.

"Not far off on some of the girls. Three have come forward and said as much. We know there are more, we have the pics. A couple have scars or birthmarks he would have had to have seen to draw with this detail. And I do care about my Bible thumpers. I care so much I don't want to put those girls through trial after trial. I want a clean confession from him so we end it. Allow those he hurt to heal."

"He didn't murder Shelby. It was someone else," Al says.

"Then we nab that fucker, too, but I need to close the book on this guy," Chambers says.

Al flips open a second sketch book. She was fully nude, legs apart to detect a bit of the pubis. It was a tasteful nude. No shame. A beautiful woman's body. A little less detail in the face and it could be any woman and the work worthy of a New York gallery showing.

Chambers hold up another pad, "The next one…gets a bit sick."

Al glances at the first image. "It's a simple square knot in a rope. The basic knot for beginning bondage. He undressed her and drew her tied up in a chest harness. Gave him an opportunity to fondle her—gain trust."

Al flips to the next drawing. The eyes of the girl have changed. She was anxious, frightened in the first picture, but in this one the eyes have changed. "He captured her fear. In this she is nervous, but the taboo act excited her. She enjoys the attention and for him to capture it with his pencil. The man's a Picasso." He flips up the third drawing. "He'd done something to her in this one. The eyes are afraid. He captures her soul. Some bondage enthusiasts believe by being secured by another they, are giving an understanding of their soul."

"According to the girls who came forward, he tied them up in sexual positions and drew them. It was after the third time. He questioned them about how they felt while bound and if it excited them. He used this advantage over them to molest them."

In the fourth picture the eyes are swollen, watery, and have blood vessel lines. "He has assaulted her and then drawn her in her pain. He captured it. A photograph couldn't do this moment justice."

"You sound as if you admire him," Chambers says.

"The work, not his methods or the use of his models. Have you interrogated him?"

"He won't speak. Sheriff wonders why he hasn't lawyered up. He knows there is no way he's going home."

Al fingers the sketch paper. "Is there an art supply store in this town?"

"Glenn's Hardware operates like a 5&Dime. They carry supplies for the high school kids' projects."

"Get me a tablet. This eggshell white color. I need it before I go in there."

• • • • •

Al places one of the drawings cut from the spiral bound sketch book on the steel table as he sits down. "You draw these? Maybe being a starving artist wasn't for you, but you spent hours tying the ropes. Does it take a long time to tie those girls up when they don't squirm against you?"

Pastor Samuel says nothing, just stares into his own reflection in the two-way mirror.

Al spreads out the prints of the girls—progressing from being dressed to bound and nude. The fear in their eyes beg to go home. Prayer filled eyes for hope of rescue—then pain.

Pastor Samuel refuses to examine the paper.

"You captured the moment. Perfection in the eyes. I'm no art critic. Sadly, despite how good you are no one will ever see these sketches. No one will ever know you did this for your art. They'll see the photos of each cut you left on Shelby, but they will never understand why. They will just remember you, a sick fuck, who cut up little teen girls and shot his cum all over their bleeding bodies."

"I never."

"You never what? Jerked off to these girls? We've got teams cleaning your church again. Every drop of your cum will be shown to the jury, every photo and drawing of these helpless girls you tied up." Al stands. He takes the hand-drawn sketch of the girl, arms tied to hide her crotch and her feet touching her ears. "Such detail. Such love in your pencil." He tears the paper.

"NO!!!" Pastor Samuel leaps to protect his work, but the handcuffs shackled to the desk keep him from reaching Al.

"They might understand why you did this, but I won't let them see the drawings. No, I won't let your work be glorified."

"Don't." Tears form and drip from Pastor Samuel's left eye. "Please. I didn't kill Shelby."

Al tears another one-inch strip from the drawing. "They begged. They begged as you tied them up. Left them for hours, body cramping in unnatural positions, all so you could get each speckle of the nylon rope correct."

Samuel gives a 'fuck you' stare.

Al rips away another strip. "Too bad they don't allow smoking in here, I'd burn the scraps. Let you watch." He selects another drawing.

"If you destroy them it was all meaningless."

Al grips the paper with both hands, faking a tear. "No one will know."

"I confess. Please don't destroy any more of my work. I drew them. I convinced those girls to allow me to draw them. And for them to expose themselves to God, to show them how they were meant to be seen in radiant glory. Please don't destroy them. I did it. When they were tied up I entered them, but I never killed them."

Al marches from the room, crumbling the pages.

Sheriff Mallard, thumbs hooked into his gun belt, fumes. "You got a full confession, but you destroyed evidence to do so. No wonder your boss is quick to loan you out."

"I hope you recorded his confession." Al wads the sketch into a ball. "The drawings were too valuable to take into the room. I made several photocopies. It was a pain to get your cheap copier to take the heavy sketch paper."

"He claims he didn't kill Shelby."

"He didn't. After visiting the other crime scenes, I have a better idea where to hunt our suspect, but Samuel did not kill. He raped. And you have a confession. Maybe with it those poor girls won't have to sit through a lengthy trial."

II

AL TACKS A picture of Shelby next to the image of two other victims on the cork board acting as a murder board. "The department would like to wrap this case up and hang Shelby's death on Pastor Samuel, but he was a no part of the death of these two girls." He faces the meeting room packed with every employed officer in the city plus a few reservists.

"Logically, he killed Shelby when she threatened to expose his sickness," an officer says.

Al doesn't recognize the young man in uniform. Such levels of thinking and quick human desire to assign blame incarcerates the innocent. "I am not unempathetic for the plight of this community, what you face in long term recovery. You could put Shelby's death on Samuel." Al forgoes the pastors title as he finds the man has lost his right to be respected. "I won't allow justice to be glossed over for those other women." He taps the board. "Jenny and Kathy." Names make them people. He warns, "And worse, if you do and they prove he didn't murder Shelby, a good lawyer will raise reasonable doubt on the other charges."

Al tacks up three more pictures, all teenage black women. He doesn't turn around. He knows the group exchanges quizzical and confused glances. He pins three more glossies, this time of three Asian women.

A murmur washes across the room, but not as loud as the rumble caused by the next news. "It's time to turn Shelby over to the FBI. You fine officers have done all you can for her."

"We didn't bring you in on this case to take it."

"I'm not assuming the case, but I will continue to consult and the perpetrator is out of your jurisdiction."

"Wait! You know who this perp is?" An officer asks.

Al shakes his head. "No. These nine women, and there could be more, all have the same MO. He targets them in threes."

"They are black and Asian. Serial killers tend to stick within their own ethnic line."

"True, normally, but this male has jumped the race line. He has an affinity for three and girls in high school, all with strong tendencies to attend college."

Sheriff Mallard breaks from his lean against the wall, uncrossing his arms. "Al, my office!"

The sheriff slams the door behind him. "I extend you every courtesy and you fuck us over without lube."

"No, sir. I did my job. I'm going to find Shelby's killer and make sure he spends the rest of his life in a cell."

"So, you do know who it is?"

"No. But all the victims, all nine I've discovered so far, attended a college visit day. The *same* event. It is their only connection."

"There could be hundreds of suspects," Sheriff Mallard protests.

"It wasn't a fellow student. I won't rule out a faculty member, but I believe it's one of the college recruiters. They travel across the states. They meet dozens of students. High school kids encounter so many they don't remember them. And it wouldn't raise suspicion to come across a student whom they could nab with a slight bit of coaxing. It's a perfect cover."

Sheriff Mallard rubs his bewhiskered chin. "You have to get this fucker."

III

AL WONDERS JUST how ancient he appears in his Guns and Roses tee-shirt. He blends in better on the college campus than he would a high school. Tons of hot young co-eds pepper the campus, and many of the most attractive ones are far from nineteen. A ripe hunting ground, Al suppresses his own tendencies. *I'm working. I'm no longer a person who stalks. Now would be the time to contact my buddy if I wasn't on the job.*

A woman's voice restores his attention. "Not many Hispanic students." In the radio earbud hidden in his left ear pops a woman's voice that continues, "Not many make it to college. Those here legally are lucky to be first generation high school graduates."

"True." Al nods.

"He's not touching those already on campus, he's targeted juniors and seniors in high school," Agent Smith's voice overlays Agent Shawna Sutherland.

"He may not hunt where he works, I just needed to follow him," Al says.

"Don't take too long. He visited all the high schools where the missing girls attended and there have been two missing Hispanic girls from Martin Luther King High reported," Agent Sutherland says.

"Girls who the cops believe are runaways," Agent Smith adds.

"Both girls are on the honor roll. Despite the bigotry of the local cops, not every Hispanic girl's a hoochie," Al says.

"Even 'A' students fall prey to a handsome boy," Agent Sutherland says.

"Too many girls fall prey to a boy, especially the bad ones." Al spots the white male. "He's exiting the building." A blond, handsome man in his mid-twenties marches along the sidewalk. Through his university monogrammed polo his well-defined, muscular frame reveals the kind of abs found on men in gladiator movies.

"Damn," Agent Sutherland says.

"Movie handsome," Al agrees. "Those teen girls melt for him."

"I'd melt for him," Agent Smith muses, *And I like girls*. "Now you've gazed upon Adonis, do we bring him in?"

"Not here," Al says. "If we are wrong we destroy his career. More important we have two missing girls and an alerted perp. The ME said they weren't killed immediately."

"Listen here, Sixth Sense, we need to collar this fucker," Agent Smith rants. The beep of a phone echoes over the speaker.

Al follows the college recruiter. He's easy to spot dragging his wheeled portfolio case behind him.

"We know he doesn't kill these girls where he leaves them. So he must stash them."

"We have his itinerary. He's got a high school appointment to meet with prospective students this afternoon at Northwest Academy," Agent Sutherland says.

"No reason for him to leave this early." No one must notice how he leaves early or takes time to get back to the office since he constantly travels. Gives the illusion of an alibi—brilliant. "I'm heading to the van. We need to follow him," Al says.

"Smith's on the phone with the judge," Agent Sutherland says.

Al hops into the passenger seat of the blue van.

Smith, a much older man with broad shoulders and a mustard stain on his tie, flips his phone closed before twisting the key. "We have the warrant for his house and property."

"Follow him. He has left too early," Al orders.

Agent Sutherland works a station of electronic monitoring equipment in the back. "Unless he added an appointment."

"We follow," Al instructs.

"You're the boss," says Smith.

"If we're wrong how we screwed the pooch will be all over the six o'clock news," Al says.

"You don't guess wrong," Smith keeps three cars between the van and the red smart car.

"Rumor at the office is you have the same mind as these men we track down," Agent Sutherland says.

Al and Smith connected with Sutherland after their first case together two weeks ago. "I do, I think like them. It's my curse and the day I'm wrong will be the worst. No one will remember the dozen I brought down, just the one who got away, or was innocent."

"I just figured you had some autistic tic which allowed you to notice a crime scene in a manner normal people don't," Sutherland says.

"Never been tested. Sometimes people are just one way in certain situations or given the opportunity," Al says.

"Is this your lecture on how people cheat only because they don't believe they will get caught?" Agent Smith breaks, forced to lag back as the traffic thins.

"People are never sorry they cheat, they are sorry they get caught. If they knew they would get caught they would not cheat. The basic idea behind sin in religion is to control the congregation. These killers murder because they believe they are above the law and won't be caught. They live in a delusional world where the rules of society don't apply to them."

"What about those who taunt the cops?" Sutherland asks.

"You're still new. That is Hollywood," says Smith. "Most criminals do all possible to avoid interaction with the cops." He changes lanes to follow the smart car onto a two-lane, lettered blacktop.

"BTK would send typed letters with lots of spelling mistakes as a test, learning what investigators knew about him. But he was one of the few who contacted the authorities directly," Al says.

"When they reach the point they're making contact with the police they have reached a state of arrogance, as if they were God and untouchable. Others have reached bottom and desire to stop murdering and seek out the cops. Both kinds do it to up their game," Al says.

"If they have chosen to halt killing, then why not just report to the police station?" Agent Sutherland asks.

"It could be like trying to quit smoking. It's an addiction. They need help, but part of the body doesn't want to quit. It needs the fix," Al says.

"Killing is not like jonesing for a cig," says Smith.

"From what we learn at Quantico the performance killings are much like a drug fix. Those that kill their abusive mothers over and over, or the girl who rejected them. The Angels of Death who cause a patient to code and revive then to play God or be recognized as a hero," Sutherland says.

"Al won't believe it's acceptable to kill because mommy didn't pay enough attention to some kid growing up." Smith slows the van just in sight of the driveway the recruiter turns onto.

The smart car parks before a small, saltbox farmhouse. The college recruiter glances around and then skips two steps to bound onto the porch. He disappears inside as Smith pulls the van into view.

Agent Sutherland peeks over the front seat. "Has all the hallmarks of an evil lair."

Her sarcasm annoys Al. "It's a house. It's difficult to kill in an apartment. Dahmer's neighbors smelt his cooking. This place has a basement, and in the dark no neighbor would see him move a body."

"You want me to call it in?" Smith asks.

"Put them on standby. Have them hang back. We should speak with him first. Smith, you cover the back. I'm going to knock on the front door." Al drops his legs out the door before Agent Smith has the van in park.

"What about me?" Sutherland asks.

"You have your firearm?"

"Yes."

"Chamber a round and keep it holstered until I say." Al marches to the porch.

His partners match his pace.

Smith zips into his stern, military precision mode. Gun drawn, he nods at Al as he slips around the house. Agent Sutherland slides to the right side of the porch door, her hand on her Glock, ready to draw.

Al pulls the screen door open and knocks on the solid wood frame.

With the second knock he announces, "Agent Al, FBI. Mr. Turner, we'd like to ask you a few questions."

Follow all procedures. A stray thought breaks into Al like the Kool-Aid man through a sunroom. *What if he is in the group? It's dark. People remain in shadow, but what if he is a part of the group?* Al cups the handle of his Glock. *Follow all procedures. The kill will have to be clean. Maybe Sutherland or Smith will tag him. In the inquest 'did he do all he was trained to do?' Smith can answer unequivocally, yes.*

Al nods at her. He knocks again.

Agent Sutherland snags the screen door keeping it clear for Al to enter. "We have a search warrant. Open the door, Mr. Turner." He should just burst in, but Al allows the vital seconds of warning. It's a risk, but he's in his armored vest and now the man has a chance to recover a weapon. Al reaches for the door handle. The guy didn't lock it behind him. Drawing his gun, Al sweeps in.

With the living room clear he states, "FBI, Mr. Turner, we have a search warrant." He waves the end of the Glock to signaled Agent Sutherland to follow.

She slides through the front door. Both swing guns towards Smith's entrance through the kitchen. He pauses and tilts his head toward a staircase to the second floor, next to it a reinforced steel fire door more expensive to install than the entire cost of the dilapidated house.

Al would bet it's not locked since the open hasps latch is on this side of the door, keeping the basement secure and whatever he keeps down there under key.

Smith pulls the fire door open.

Al moves in first. *Follow all procedures. Make it a clean shot. Someone in the group? Some of them travel several states to attend the meetings. None of these killings match the stories—yet.*

Al eases into the stairwell. Each step down exposes his legs to attack. He listens a moment for ambush.

So much to consume in half a second. The orgy of evidence in the torture chamber where he tied up, assaulted and killed the women before this one.

Shit!

The room reeks of feces and rot. Hanging from the ceiling are a hundred car freshening pine trees. Nothing in the room smells of pine. Al, sure he saw such a display in a movie, knew it wouldn't mask any smell. Plastic sheets, crusted in body fluid, cover the floor and stretch under a wooden kitchen table used as an operating table. It's too late for the girl on the table. Turner uses pinking shears to snip zip ties around her ankles. He left her for dead and allowed nature to evacuate her body fluids before he delivered her to the location of her discovery.

Al has the Glock leveled at Turner's heart.

Agent Smith's boots strike the top step, the stairwell too narrow for his wide frame to move swiftly.

Turner drops the scissors.

Al yells, "FBI! Drop the weapon! And step away from the woman!"

Before Turner admits compliance Al pumps two rounds into his chest. He was not part of the group, but it didn't matter. He prepared to kill and…the man needed to be ended.

Agent Smith reaches the step, allowing him to survey the basement. He gags on the shit smell. "Sutherland. Get an ambulance!"

Al lowers his smoking gun. "She needs a coroner."

Banging causes them both whiplash as they spin to a door in the corner. Inside a small closet is the second Hispanic girl. She scampers into the light and screams at the sight of the first girl. Al considers slapping her to break her hysteria, but she faints in his arms first.

Agent Smith kicks the scissors away from Turner's dead hand, "Clean shot, brother. He had a weapon and you had no idea from over there at the base of the steps the girl was dead. Not in this shitty light."

Sirens permeate the sealed basement.

Al places a foot on the bottom step. He dangles his Glock with his thumb and forefinger, handing it to Smith. "Clean shot or not, I still killed a man." He clumps up the stairs.

• • • • •

Outside, Agent Sutherland hands Al a Styrofoam cup of steaming coffee. He plops on the step of the open side door of the van.

"You okay?" Sutherland asks.

Al nods. "I will be."

"You saved the girl." Sutherland points to the stretcher being loaded into the ambulance.

"One."

She hasn't been an agent long enough to know the correct response. She hopes she never knows how to respond.

A black Lincoln joins the growing police parking lot in the field next to the house.

"Director Engström," Sutherland warns, as she awaits the man driving to approach.

"I wondered when the boss would get here," Al says.

Dew collects on Engström's expensive leather shoes, "Why don't these guys ever operate in nice neighborhoods?"

"They need seclusion." Sutherland doesn't care for the half-joke. She's heard recently promoted Engström hates to leave his desk or be too far from the ass he must kiss for his next promotion.

"I'm going to need your gun, Al."

"Agent Smith has it."

"Did he witness the shooting?"

"He was directly behind me." Al speaks the truth. No one will question...facts.

Engström flicks the tip of his nose with this thumb as if he clears any missed cocaine residue. Al knows he self-medicates, but he has no proof.

"It was clean?"

"He had a weapon and was over the girl's body. I didn't have time to check. She had been dead for a while."

"And you saved one. Sounds clean to me. Agent Sutherland, take Al home. You know you're on leave until the hearing, Al. Take three days compose yourself and come in for your deposition."

Al nods. Three days with his girl.

Director Engström offers his hand. Al grips it firm and pumps.

"Good job, Agent." Engström slogs toward Agent Smith.

Sutherland waits until her boss vacates earshot. "He gives me the creeps."

"Doubt he's around long. Bosses never want to work with me an extended period." Al rises, "Thanks for the coffee. You better drive. I'm not a Special Agent right now."

"You are to me." She smiles.

"After a shooting, it's SOP to be on leave until cleared. Better play this by the book. Just take me back to my vehicle," Al says.

"Why do you and Agent Smith keep quoting procedures to me like I didn't pass the test? Is it because I'm a woman?"

"I didn't realize you were a woman, Shawna. You're new on the job. Face it, newbies don't know dick."

"Fuck off."

Al climbs into the front passenger seat.

Agent Smith clamps his flip phone closed before handing over Al's Glock, breech open and in an evidence bag, to Director Engström.

• • • • •

"IMPORTANT?" DIRECTOR ENGSTRÖM asks.

"You remember a Professor Arnett?" Agent Smith pockets his phone.

"He speaks at some of those educational workshops I'm required to make you guys attend in order to remain up to date on being officers of the law."

"We appreciate how you value our education," Agent Smith says. "He has a student who has encountered a possible serial killer."

"He called you over the police?" Puzzled, Engström secures the Glock in his coat pocket. He won't lose an agent his first month on the job.

"I told him to do so, but he says the kid will retract his story."

"We are not here to work some criminal justice major's wet dream."

"Professor Arnett believes we should take a gander," Agent Smith says.

"Our task force is a shining example of investigation. With a gold star of a win we can't afford to deny any leads. File your report on the shooting and go check it out," Engström says.

Smith hands over a second evidence bag with the gun clip. "I could use Al."

"No. A definitive no. Don't even mention it to him. You go alone. I want this clean shoot to stay above board. It was clean?"

Smith sucks in a deep breath, "I was right behind him on the stairwell. I heard Al give the order to drop the weapon. A full second passed and then the two shots. It was dark. He couldn't tell if she was dead on the table." Smith adds, "From my vantage point he was going to stab her."

"We'll get Al reinstated in a few days, keep it all official. And if it turns out this Professor Arnett has a lead on a murder, Al will be cleared and ready to return to duty."

IV

"PLEASE. I'M YOUR favorite. I like when you choke me. Please." She reaches for the dog collar.

Her begging won't help. Part of the process to maintain control is to constantly remind them their place. Al slides a gentle hand over her naked shoulder. "I know you do." *I've never had a girl who was as willing and enjoyed being my lover.* "The way your body twitches." Al's eyes roll up as he fantasizes about his love making with her.

"It's not a trick. A woman can't fake that," she pleads.

"I know." *It's why I want to keep you.* He clamps his fingers until the pressure digs into her collar bone.

Her only struggle against him prevents his snapping of the clavicle as she maneuvers off the bed. Despite knowing what's coming, the fear of broken bones means death. No matter how much he enjoys her, Al won't keep a girl with medical needs.

He marches her from the bedroom to the living room. She pushes her urge of protest down inside.

Reminiscent of standing sweat boxes, without the sun to warm them, are three wooden doors built into the wall of the outer room. Each no wider than a person, all with bolts and reinforced in places with metal plates.

He halts her in front of the standing coffin and Al kneels before her. He taps her ankle and she lifts one foot then the other. He slides the adult diaper up her legs until it is snug against her crotch. She remains frozen as he opens the door. He spins her around fitting her in the custom-built space. Her neck locks into felt covered grooves, leaving her unable to move her head.

He places a plastic hose next to her mouth. Al pinches the big bite valve. Water drips. "Can't have you going without water. Hydration keeps your skin soft."

After she aligns her arms in the grooves cut for her frame he secures nylon straps to prevent her from clawing at the wood and damaging her fingernails. He checks her legs, ensuring her feet are all the way back to avoid harm when he secures the door. The stance leaves her knees slightly bent, uncomfortable, but necessary. He closes the door, securing the locks.

Al peeks in the eye level window allowing her a view of the living room. He slides the view port closed, entombing her in darkness.

She may be his favorite, the woman he enjoys best, but Al won't allow her to become comfortable. It would lead to a mistake.

Mistakes land him in prison.

Al unlocks the door of the second standing coffin.

After he hoses this woman off she will need fluids. *I had shared I still had one girl alive. It was detrimental to my healing, but my dirty secret goes further.*

Al places two fingers on her neck to check her pulse.

"I fucking hate you!" The redhead snaps, still not broken.

TEN
SKA: THIRD MEETING

I

Rule Three:
The only requirement for membership
is a desire to stop killing.
(Borrowed and modified from AA twelve traditions)

II

AFTER THREE LOCATIONS, I thought discovering the location of the next crack dealer's house would be easy, but it wasn't. Rumor was a few of the just *sell it on the side* dealers had ceased temporarily. I needed another major strike to make sure they knew drugs weren't acceptable in my town.

I was still too pure of an old man and lacked the swagger of a drug addict to be trusted. I was at a loss on how to find a supplier.

Days passed by and my granddaughter never got any better—she existed. I was dipping into depression. I bought a gun. My mistake was I legally bought one from a gun store. Loading it, I left it in the glove box of my Rogue. I thought about it. It was legal and never fired. I explained to the nurses I had probate matters to attend, due to the family, and would be gone two days.

They thought it a good to get me out of the hospital to regain some perspective on the world. They had seen more of me since two AM overdoses had dropped. I don't know by what percent, but from being at the hospital and with three less crack dealers in town, I noticed the ER traffic slowed down.

I wasn't as big on avoiding gas station cameras or anything to hide my trip as I should have been, but I did use cash. Especially at the Survivalist Gun and Event Show. I bought a few guns without having to register them. I did get smarter.

The one dealer I knew about was in an apartment complex. I wouldn't burn it down. It would leave a dozen single mothers homeless.

The depression worsened. I couldn't end my own life. It wasn't suicide if I shot it out with a crackhead and he popped me.

As I drove back to town, I realized there were still more drugs and I didn't know if I had gotten the dealer who sold to the man who stole my family from me. The apartment dealer could wait. In my time hunting the location I learned the town had its share of hookers.

I never knew.

Not once did I think there were prostitutes in my town. We weren't a community large enough to hide prostitution. I did know of one gentleman's club. It was known among those of us good Christians as a biker-type hangout. A few stabbings had even occurred.

Out near the county line there was this bunker of a building. And due to some fudged up laws and grandfather clauses the only titty—pasties required—bar possible in this part of the state.

Some twenty years before one county passed an ordinance about no booze licenses and the other county no bare titties, preventing a nudie bar from opening. Only this guy built his saloon smack dab on the center of the county line where he opened a bar on one side and girls on the other. Now there was no law stating you couldn't have a beer in the dry county or being inside strutting around with your titties hanging out. By the time the two counties figured out what the owner had gotten away with, he was open and licensed. Even by changing the laws he has protection by existing before the new ordinances.

I mention it, not as a grandfather telling long stories you don't care about, but I thought it was a safe place to pick up a prostitute and her not be an undercover cop.

Or at least a start.

The girls were so young.

I nursed a single beer all night, not knowing what to say to any of the girls who weren't much older than my comatose granddaughter. Finally, one woman who wasn't a stripper, but wasn't here with a date, sat down next to me.

"I've never seen you in here before." She flashed long inhuman eyelashes.

"I've never been."

"You lonely?" Her wink was full of twinkle and subtext.

"I've been alone for a while now."

"You looking for a friend?" She touched my forearm.

I guess she knew I was no cop at my age. I did wonder if she was. It would be my luck.

"My wife passed. She was the sweetest of church ladies. I want to do things now I was never allowed to do."

"It's never too late." She put her hand on my knee. "As long as you get *up* out of bed."

We left in the Rogue I asked her what she had in mind.

All the twinkle was gone, replaced by business. "I'll do anything, provided you have a fat wallet."

As we drove around and I was sure no cop car was following before I said anything she jumped in with, "We can drive around all night, but I'm still going to have to charge you. I don't come home with some bills and I'm in trouble."

"I've got a few."

"What is it you want to do?"

"You know, I mean. I want to get…I want to try something I never did."

She reached over and rubbed my thigh. "Why don't you tell me what you hunger for. I do everything for enough Grants."

"Drugs," it finally spit out.

"Take a left on this next street," she commanded.

No question. No hesitation. Just the way to go to my next drug house.

"Now, I'm sure you read the papers. With those fires, some of these guys are a bit jumpy around new people. You stay in the car. Trust me. Park, give me some cash and. I'll get what you need. They know me, here."

"Get whatever you like." I handed her three Jacksons.

She smiled. "Sure thing, baby."

The motel was cheap and accepted cash only. I'm sure my Rouge stood out in front of these A frame single unit buildings. nice and shiny as it was. I sure hoped it would still be in the morning.

She stripped off her shirt and was unclasping her bra.

"Leave on your undies. I like some mystery," I said.

"Whatever you like, baby." She used the nightstand to mix up the drugs. I still had no idea what she was doing.

"You go ahead." I sat in the wobbly chair across from the bed. "I want to stare at you."

She did her thing and was loopy within minutes. She danced around a bit and pressured me for sex, and to try the drugs since I ordered them. I resigned myself to spooning against her on the bed, explaining my recent loss. I felt I was still married and cheating on my life long love.

In the morning she washed herself in the bathroom. "I hate to do this, but I need a hundred and twenty dollars or I'm in for it when I get home."

I give her two Bens. "You keep it."

She reached her hand in my front pocket, fishing for my cell. She keyed in her number. "You call me anytime…Tori. Anytime you want to party or you need someone to hold." She touched my face. "I like you."

I knew she liked the two hundred I gave her, and the leftover drugs she pocketed.

I got what I needed from her and now I needed a shower—at home.

I drove past the crack house. I would have never guessed it was one. This was a better side of town and in a place where a prominent lawyer lived two doors down. I would guess, and I didn't know how it worked, but the quality of drugs was better here, therefore more expensive. Traffic was less frequent, and it catered to the college kid crowd.

This attack required careful consideration with Neighborhood Watch and lots of family homes with kids, I wouldn't want an explosion to hurt any of them.

I had no inkling how I was going to bring this place down. The families were upper middle class. I bet they had no idea what was going on in the house. I wouldn't have, either. These dealers were clever and kept evening hours, no cars stopping by during all hours of the night like in the poor neighborhoods.

It was harder to survey the house. Being upscale these people would call the cops because of a stranger. One night the man, I assumed the dealer, left the house at three in the morning. Was this dealer making a house call?

I followed him. At some point, I didn't follow badly enough, or I followed too good, but he was on to me. A car of men forced me to turn into the commuter parking. Blocked in, I had to pinch my ass cheeks tighter, for I was sure I was busted and was going to shit myself.

I was about to die. Three men, big burly lumberjack men, or should have been, and one short, thin motherfucker who made ninety-eight-pound weaklings appear tough.

I held the gun show revolver tightly. I would shoot the little guy first. Besides, the .357 bullets would splatter him over the others and the chances were good one bullet would wound two guys. He had to be the leader.

"Can we help you officer?" Joked the little man.

"Fuck, it's an old man." The biggest dude snapped my windshield wiper. He was also out of the line of fire due to the door frame.

"You used to be a cop?"

"What the fuck you want old man?"

"I just got lost."

"Oh, you're lost alright."

I was going to die. I would take as many as I could with me. I figured it would appear like a robbery gone wrong. Not having any family left to embarrass, I pulled the trigger until the chamber clicked empty.

They didn't expect it.

All four were on the ground.

The car from the dealer's house was gone. I was sure he was back safely in his bed.

I don't know how I thought so fast, but I did. I removed their guns. The little fucker was dead and I placed him into the car first. The big guys were heavy and breathing. I promised to get them to a hospital. They moved their legs, which assisted me in getting them into their car. I did all I could not to get blood in my Rogue and locked it up tight.

You know, a car window doesn't shatter easily. A few good whacks before I shattered the driver's side glass.

I couldn't trust these guys. I emptied one of their guns into them. I shot off a third Glock from inside the car, through the window, randomly at a field. The shell casings rained inside. My ears rang. It was painful. My head throbbed. I wiped the gun down and dropped it in the back. doing the same for a second gun.

My plan would shake up the neighborhood, but there was no chance of fire blowing up little kids. I drove their car back to the crack house. I parked it in the driveway at an angle so the car was unable to be rolled easily into the street, and put on the emergency brake. I got out. I had the .357 in my waistband, along with two unfired Glocks.

The thunder-booms were sure to make those little kids piss the bed.

I wrapped my handkerchief around the gun while standing at the car door. I fired into the high-class drug house. I dropped the empty gun into the car. Next, I bolted forward to the porch and fired the second Glock into the windshield, aerating the four men again. I wiped down this pistol and the .357, tossing them through the house's front room window.

I ran into the back yard, through another yard, to the next block. I stayed in the shadows. It was near dawn when I reached my house.

I burnt the clothes, showered, and slept until the alarm beeped. I got up, showered again, drank a coffee and stepped outside, to called 911 to report my stolen Rogue. The dispatcher explained no officers were free now. There had been an incident last night and unless there were drugs involved, or I needed an ambulance, I would have to wait.

III

"YOU SOUND MORE and more like those over exaggerated stories my own grandfather used to tell from when he was in the war," Jane says.

"It was all true. Thought I was going to have a heart attack moving those big dudes back into the car. I don't think the police cared enough to do one of those angle-of-the-bullet-tests, or they would have realized no one from the car shot at the house, and no one from the house shot up the car. Not after they found all the drugs and cash inside," Jack says.

"Maybe they did and were just satisfied they had one less crack house to deal with," Kenneth says.

"Were those kids in the neighborhood hurt?" Al asks.

"Not a one. It shook up the neighborhood, mostly because the next morning they couldn't leave the street to get to work. Hell, everyone they interviewed spoke of what a nice guy the dealer had been. He even mowed the widow lady's lawn across the street for free. He had a golden ticket on that block."

"And you punched it," Ed chimes.

"Did you get your car back?" asks Jesse. A reported stolen Rogue should yield search results in the police database. Didn't he say it was blue?

"It was late afternoon when a patrolman came by to take a statement. I explained how I woke up, had my coffee and when I stepped outside my car was gone. He wrote something up for my insurance. They, of course, found it. Damn window cost less to replace than my deductible."

"Wasn't there blood at the commuter parking?" Robert asks.

"Tons, but deer get splattered on the interstate all the time. No one connected the drug house shooting with the blood there. People assumed it was an animal. If they thought differently I never heard."

"You're one lucky *old* man," Ed says.

"No one sees him coming. It's like a movie: *Old Man's Revenge*," Jesse laughs.

"It only got harder to track down the next dealer after this success. I spiraled downward. I had to employ the prostitute to give up a location. Part of me sought to end my life at the commuter lot. I couldn't live with what I was doing."

"But your granddaughter needed vengeance," Robert says.

"You had the apartment, dude," Kenneth says.

"He was going to be the way to cash in my chips," Jack says.

When they repeat statements it assists Jesse in keeping track of facts for his investigation.

"You thought about killing yourself?" Al seeks confirmation.

"It was in the back of my mind, with all my family being dead. I was going to step into the drug dealer's apartment and draw my pistols. Go out like John Wayne in *The Shootest*, take as many of them as I could with me. I already shared my plan with you," Jack says.

"Beats the Hemingway cancer plan," Edgars quips.

"What's the Hemingway cancer plan?" Jesse asks.

"You had to ask, kid," Al chides.

"They don't do a good job teaching the classics anymore in school, do they." Edgars says.

"I never read him," Jesse says.

"Ernest Hemingway believed he had cancer after a visit to the Mayo Clinic. When he got home he ate the barrel of his shotgun."

"A shotgun is such a messy way to go," The Plagiarist says.

"They're all messy," Ed says. "Even passing away in your sleep, you shit yourself."

"You choke your victims," The Plagiarist points out.

"Still messy. People piss and shit. Some puke," Ed says.

"Little blood splatter. The tiniest of drops are what convict people on *Dateline* all the time," Jesse says.

"They don't show you all the evidence on TV news shows. They show you enough to make it dramatic," Al says. "So much is left out."

"Still the cops pursue one suspect."

"They check out a few and true, many cops chase down one guy or woman because most likely they had a real motive—money. A good motive is stronger evidence than a random stranger arriving in town and killing someone."

"It's what makes us—what we've done—terrifyingly fascinating," Edgars says. "The random nature. Husbands beat wives to death all the time. Wives poison husbands all the time. Most ingestions are even ruled as natural causes. But some crazed person driving through town killing and driving off—scary. Terrifies people."

"It sells books," Kenneth says.

"It does. Most murderers aren't repeat offenders. They have killed who they want dead and wouldn't kill again. But us? We live for the kill," says Edgars. "No matter what religious path you choose in the moment we take a life, we are Gods among men. We all live for the ultimate power over another living person."

"Taking a life isn't the ultimate," Jane says.

"None of that women create life shit," says Ed. "You grow it in your uterus, but you alone didn't make it."

"Women are vessels, a sacred chalice to nurture life. But Ed, you must stop with the neutral pronouns. It is a baby. A person. We don't kill people," Jane says. "From now on we must view living people, not objects, not *its*." She accepts they must cease dehumanizing their prey.

"I don't see how naming my victims helps, but I'll work with what the group wants."

"I'm never closer to God than when I'm inside a woman, not killing her," Al says.

"But to get there you bring them to the edge of death—repeatedly," Kenneth says.

"And each time you do you risk killing the poor girl you have locked away," Jane says.

"I have backed off. I've controlled my urges with her," Al says, leaving out he shifted to another victim. He won't admit her to the group, or how he's unable to give up his love.

Jesse requires more information, information useful in determining the home location of each group member. It is impossible to track them through the chatroom, so he needs a city as a starting point. With many of the facts they share, a city would allow a viable search yielding results. Maybe a state. It would determine where these killers operate. "Have you killed lots of people with shotguns?"

"I've killed with just about everything in my copying of murders," The Plagiarist says. "People will use anything handy when they are in a passion kill."

"I think you should share." Jane points to The Plagiarist.

"I have taken many lives, maybe more than I counted. After the Harvest killings lost their thrill, I made my next selection based on a well-known *inactive* serial killer, and that was my mistake. The cops knew instantly it was a copycat. They would be searching for me. Not me, but a fresh new suspect. I rethought my strategy."

"Wouldn't they have to be caught, and details of the crime scene released, so you'd be a true copycat?" Jesse asks. *He must be my prime suspect.*

"Correct. But I took the moniker The Plagiarist, who steals others work and claims it for his own. There is some leeway in how close it has to be." Even in the dusk of the room everyone detects the sheepish grin. "I was hard for the fame, not a hundred percent accuracy."

"Meaning you don't have to have every detail correct," says Edgars. "I knew my literary degree would pay off someday."

"I explored active serial cases where they had not caught a suspect and I repeated a similar murder. It was challenging. It did monkey wrench with what the police were investigating. It might have even pissed off the real killer, many of whom would take credit for the kill, anyway, if caught. Before switching to a current and active killer I was inspired by the master's first attempts."

"Jack the Ripper?" Jesse says.

"The first recognized modern serial killer, but in no way would the cops believe he was over a hundred years old and still killing," Kenneth says.

"I didn't take up his mantel," The Plagiarist says. "Carving out women's uteri is messy business and blood is slick. I knew personally. Before Jack, Jack the Ripper was news from Whitechapel there were murders in the United State. They didn't make the news nor gain the notoriety as they did in London. Sadly, the simplest explanation as to why the American Jack wasn't a household fear was because of his choice in victims—they were black."

IV

AUSTIN, TEXAS 1885

The thing about these murders was they were all black women, many who lived in a backroom servant chamber or on the property of rich white people. They were, by all accounts, well-treated house maids and paid until the last death fitting the pattern. I believe she was a copycat to get rid of this white woman for reasons unknown.

But again, despite outrage, no one suspect could be matched to all of the murders.

It wasn't even that the cops didn't care. Of the six one was a black officer. They were just overwhelmed. Austin had grown so big six officers weren't enough to patrol the streets and devote to a full investigation.

Our killer was brazen. He hacked one woman to death while her children witnessed, another while her lover was in the bed next to her. He lived with a head wound from the axe.

I read the newspaper accounts reprinted in several books and traveled to Austin.

I made several stops along the way to purchase an axe. The killer used a new—new—axe with each killing and left it at the crime scene. He also attacked barefoot and ran away, leaving tracks in the snow. With modern forensic techniques I'd not leave behind such evidence as telling as a foot print and possibility skin DNA.

Trolling Austin for the correct victim was not what I thought it would be. When I found a black maid who worked for an affluent household, it had security cameras and fences along with guard dogs. No strolling in the back door of those mansions.

I rethought my plans and followed my little maid home. She wasn't doing too bad in her quaint little house.

People, when home, make poor choices. People make poor choices anywhere, but at home they think they are so safe. They drop their guard completely.

This woman left her back door open at dusk. I stepped into her kitchen. Her scream didn't last long as the axe sliced off half her face.

The fleshy part at least. It stuck in her jaw. It was more a horror movie kill with skin peeled off the bone. Blood flowed down her face. I made the second blow to the back of the head. She crumpled to the floor in a heap and I ran, axe on the table. I figured her screams would draw attention.

The original killer had left his new axe at each crime scene. It amazed me in all the original reports how no one noticed someone buying new axes. There was no report of them even investigating the purchase of new axes in any of the literature. I doubt the killer bought it on credit and buying outright for the suspects would not have been easy. If the suspect was negro, like the one they arrested, it was reasonable he was impoverished. No one had lots of extra cash laying around to keep buying new tools. Who at that time would buy an axe and not use it?

He could have stolen them.

My copycat attempt failed. 'Jilted lover or hate crime' filled the modern newspapers. Not one reporter tied this kill back to those in 1885.

I scoped out a mansion next. The cameras were for show except those viewing the driveway. There was a surveillance hole in the back yard I could have driven a truck through and reached the back porch. I'm betting the wife didn't want their hot tub adventures on film.

The killings were at night, but then this maid wouldn't bet here, and the family would be home. I broke in. Sunk the axe into her skull until the face was unrecognizable then left it there.

Again, hate crime, though they arrested the boyfriend for a while. But they let him go—he was white. With two dead women by axe they called it a hate crime due to the massive attack to the head and the passion it must have taken to do such brutalization to another person.

I was sickened by no one even noticing the similarities to the murders in 1885. The liberal news media turned it all into a white-on-black hate issue. I had no idea how poor news reporting had become. In the original papers they spoke in detail about the attacks. Now it was simply black woman murdered in a hate crime.

Fine.

I showed them hate. I hacked the third victim into fish bait, then scrawled with her blood on the wall:

PIGS! WRONG ABOUT SERVINGIRLS! -THE PLAGIARIST.

I named myself. I got the point across. Someone finally investigated and rediscovered the murders.

I was now finished in Austin. I would not attack another. I'm sure it would have gotten me caught. I had plans to abscond into obscurity the same way the original killer had. I would expect notoriety later, the way he did when his second round of murders occurred in London two years later.

V

"YOU'RE SAYING THIS guy was Jack the Ripper? The MO is not the same," Jesse says.

Flustered, The Plagiarist clinches his fists, "I'm stating facts. One of the suspects in the Austin murders was also reported in Whitechapel at the same time as Jack was active."

"You're saying Jack the Ripper was an American?" Kenneth says.

"We do tend to export murder," Ed says. "We've grown more killers than any other nation."

"Europe," Kenneth says.

"Has the second most, but nowhere near the numbers of the good ole U-S-of-A," Ed says.

Jesse pops in, "But African warlords in Rwanda mass murder daily."

"War," Al says. "They are at war. Killing is not only acceptable, it's expected and rewarded."

"Joke all you like. There was circumstantial evidence that Jack was this man, and a more plausible explanation than many theories," The Plagiarist says.

"Personally, I like the one where Jack was a woman," Jane says.

"A woman?" Jesse, in all his serial killer studies, never heard this theory.

"One lesser accepted concept was Jack was a Jill. She was an abortionist who botched a procedure on one of the local prostitutes. Even uneducated she would have had some of the medical knowledge of women's parts the killer was suspected to possess. She killed several other prostitutes to cover her first accidental murder. A murder which, if it got out, would ruin her business. Which I'm sure in an age of no birth control and heavily active drunken courtesans was lucrative enough to keep her well-fed."

"It's a theory like several of the others which cannot be dismissed. Still, the Serving Girl murders occurred in Austin, and so did some similar brutalities over a hundred years later. Only the media didn't see them for what they were," The Plagiarist says.

"Gruesome copies?"

"Works of art!" The Plagiarist's passion matches his surge from his chair. "They cried *hate* crimes."

"Hate sells newspapers."

"So does the blood of innocents." The old man's accusing finger pierces the darkness.

"My failure with the Serving Girl murders sent me in other directions. Unappreciated, I sought out active serial killers or repeat murderers who had yet to be classified out of fear of terrifying the public and copying their killings."

This could be the guy who did my sister in, Jesse wishing he'd read the file on his desk.

"I found several more active repeat killers who target prostitutes," The Plagiarist says. "I added to their body count. The police should spend more time reviewing their deaths than ignoring them because they engage in the sex trade."

"We need to fix ourselves before we attempt to prevent others from killing," Jane says.

"And deal with them how? Kill them?" Jesse asks.

"It's the only way to stop some of them," Jack says.

"We haven't even figured out how to help Al with his guest or our own urges. We're not ready to save the world," Robert speaks out.

"Three meetings means we have spared how many people because we are here? We're communicating with each other. We have built trust. We will help each other." Jane dumps out a bag of sealed burner phones. "When we leave today we will share a single number with a partner and if we think of attacking we contact our sponsor."

"You ending the meeting?" Jesse asks.

"No."

VI

AL'S OWN THOUGHTS drift from the meeting to his fantasy harem collection. *Some women had a harem fantasy. No. Don't. Nothing justifies what you forced those women to participate in.* Not only does his brain shift focus, his body betrays him. He smashes his thighs together to quell his growing erection.

How do I explain…

No sharing. Not this time. This is how…who I am. The group should know. They'll understand.

The pressure builds against his pants as Al recalls the tale he refuses to share with the group.

My fingers were around her throat. I don't always use the dog collar, sometimes I enjoyed my hands around the soft flesh. This girl just laid back, elongating her neck, demanding to be violated. She rubbed her thighs against me. And I felt it. I felt her burst. She enjoyed the asphyxiation.

Al shakes from his memory. If he stood up to leave what would the group make of his full salute?

I released my fingers, allowing her airway to open. I never removed my grip from her tender skin. New energy surged in me. I pumped her harder. I pulled down on her to keep her from flying away as I thrust as fast and as hard possible. When I exploded, so did she.

I desired to lay next to her. I dared not. I got up, jetting across the room to my chair where I sat as the girls did what I commanded while I watched.

She had to suspect. I didn't hook her back in her collar right away. I let her lay there and enjoy the moment.

It was not love.

We connected. I connected with this woman. I could tell from her eyes, as she tilted her head to gaze into mine, that she felt it. Now she had a new fear. If she thought I was falling in love, I may kill her. Get rid of her to prevent my emotions from making a poor choice. I might love her enough to trust her. She would use that chance to escape.

Extra time in the box. I cuddled against her. Hold her until I got hard again. This time I made love to her. Made love.

Do I even know how? I never learned. I never learned what it was to make love to a woman. It's not an excuse, I don't make those.

I do what I do. And I like killing women from my sexual thrills. I don't care for disposing of the bodies. I don't—often. I built the three boxes so I could keep them around longer.

My loins stirred. No way. If I put it in her, I would make love. Love is dangerous.

My hand closed like a vice around her ankle and she was halfway to the floor before she even knew I moved. I jerked her to her feet, shaking her as a mother scolds a bratty child. I shoved her from the bedroom.

She came close to protesting, as I flung her hard enough it cost her balance. She skidded across the floor. Later, in the dark, her side was reddened from the carpet burn.

I wonder if she knew this punishment was is to protect her. Part of me wanted to slap her, beat the love out of her.

Sweat beads along Al's hair line. How no one in the room doesn't hear his thumping chest he doesn't understand. Throat dry, he gulps a breath.

"Al, you okay?"

Not sure who at the meeting inquires about his health, all he hears is her pleading.

No. Please. Don't lock me in there. I'll do whatever you want. Please. Chain me to the bed, but not in there.

Her pleading meant nothing. I threw her collar. It cracked like a soft-ball in a catcher's mitt against her abdomen.

Put it on!

Tears flowed. With shaking arms, she slipped the belt through the buckle.

She was mine. She slipped the metal tine to the tightest hole. It made it difficult for her to swallow, but she obtained air.

I secured the door and slid the bolts on three hasps to lock. I glanced at her eyes through the peeking window.

"Please. I hate the…" closing the sliding door didn't muffle her voice, but it finalized she must be in her box, "dark."

This was to protect her.

Al breaks from his memory.

I know people will say it wasn't about her safety, but it was. If I did love her I would have to kill her. I can't fall in love, not and keep her.

He reaches under the chair and breaks the seal on a bottle of water. Gulping down half, it breaks his fevered moment. "How did I get this way? What made me do this to women—a woman?"

"You explain it to us Al," Jane offers, restoring her non-judgmental tone.

VII

I WAS SIXTEEN. My high school hired a new female teacher. She wasn't fresh from college, she was a woman. She wasn't old enough to be my mother, but she was close. I didn't know if she had kids. Had the term existed, she would have been a MILF.

She wore conservative dresses, but they couldn't hide her massive bust. Proper church lady hair buns. Her horn-rimmed glasses, straight from the fifties, down to the chain necklace for them to dangle around her neck when she didn't need them to read, painted her as a respectable teacher. Only all the boys noticed the twitch in her hips signaling she was not Miss Appropriate all the time.

I had forgotten a book in her classroom. I snuck in after school to retrieve it and she was in her room grading. We chatted. She praised me for being responsible enough to come back so I didn't fail tomorrow's quiz. She asked if she could pay me to move an oak dresser in her house.

I said she didn't have to pay me. She insisted, to keep it a proper teacher/student relationship.

The dresser was in her bedroom. It was nothing like I expected. Just being there next to her four-poster bed, I was filled with dirty thoughts. I moved the dresser. It was heavy. I was strong, but it was a three-person oak mass. She offered to lighten the contents and tossed mounds of lingerie to the floor. I admit it excited me. She noticed. Those red nails pinched my little head through my jeans.

I had no idea what to do. She unbuttoned her blouse and had on a bra-corset contraption preventing a flood of flesh from bursting.

She ordered me to the bed.

I complied.

I'd kissed a girl, but…

It was a rough session. She tied each of my limbs to the four posts and assaulted me. It hurt. I had marks. And she never once said anything about not telling anyone. I thought no one would believe such a wild tale of domination. I mean, I didn't know sex was like that.

I was a sophomore. I knew what sex was. I might have known a woman would suck it. But I had no idea about anal. I was in gym one day when these boys were bantering about Tracy Pearlman and how they wanted to fuck her in the ass. At first, I thought they meant fucking her from behind. NO. They meant in the poop hole. The basketball boys all agreed her ass was her only attractive feature.

This teacher grabbed my erection and crammed it in her ass. With a historic gymnast move she turned our bodies allowing her to ride. It was so thrilling, even when I lost my load, I never lost the boner. Sex has never again been like the first time with her. Even though I visited her a few times, I never lasted with such passion until I shoved her down and forced her the way she forced me. It was the first step on the path toward what I do now to satisfy myself. She wasn't the first I choked to death.

VIII

"I DIDN'T MEAN to overstep my turn, I just had to share. I was compelled to explain." Al glances at Jane, masked in the dark. "As she pinched my cock, she told me the same thing you did when you formed this group. This is a safe place."

"It's a breakthrough for you, Al, not an interruption. She awakened something in you. It was the doorway," Jane says.

"Just close the door and he stops killing. Bullshit," says Robert.

Jane shifts into her therapist training. "Al's sharing excites his trust in the group. By releasing his deeper emotions, he has a breakthrough, and if he recognizes his self-destructive behavior then he has potential for recovery."

Al notes his erection has abated.

"You have made a big step. Soak it in," Jane says.

"Edgars, I believe you should take the next turn," The Plagiarist says. "Allow Al to marinate in his moment of self-discovery."

VIX

I HAD TO plan what I wanted to explore next. It was after a frequent stop on book signing tours. I had traveled several times in this state. I was no tourist to this place, knowing the secluded locations.

Don't think it happened after every signing, but there was always at least one obsessed fan. They fell into a few groups. Those desiring to be writers and wanting to know how to become published. Some believed by meeting me, I could get them published. The next group enjoyed the horror/thriller genre and wanted to thank me for my writing. No one touched them the way I did with my stories. Three, of course, was the fanboys or girls who, instead of chasing Brad Pitt, wanted an author.

These are the ones who could write the best blogs about your work and increase sales or stalk you.

These two girls, sisters, got a book signed and stayed after. They met me in the parking lot and were quite fresh. I didn't have to convince them to take a drive with me, it was their idea. I'd never been with two girls before. My thought was to forgo my carefully laid plans because, face it, without paying for it, when would I get a chance to be with two women at the same time again?

I had changed my mind about halfway to my *scene of the crime*.

The younger of the two knew what to do with her mouth. I never exploded so quick. I hoped I could recover—swiftly. I hated to believe my one shot at three-way was finished because she used her tongue like no other woman.

She sat back. Her sister, who had been kissing me, glanced at her sister's puffed cheeks.

"Did he?"

She nods, careful not to swallow.

"Good. Spit," she commanded.

The sister opened her mouth so all the white liquid ran down the front of her shirt staining it.

"Okay, Mr. Edgars. You just got a blow job from a minor. Or rather you forced a minor to suck your dick."

FUCK!

She hadn't appeared underage. As she was now, disheveled and her make-up smudged, she was done up to appear of age at least.

Somehow two women desiring me was too much of a fantasy to be true. These girls were here to roll me.

"What are you girls pulling?" I asked.

"We want your money, dirty old man."

Hell. I wasn't even thirty yet.

"You give us ten thousand dollars."

"Each," adds the younger one. She leaned back against the door face, a mess of smudged makeup and semen.

"Or we go straight to the cops and you go to jail for sex with a minor. She's covered in the evidence."

I had driven with them to my location of choice for privacy. I had considered it an alibi. 'Yes, officer, I was once with *two girls*'. They put no thought into the fact they were five miles from BFE. If I abandoned them, the young one had a shirt full of DNA evidence, and if I stole her shirt they could fight and gather more. This situation foiled my escape plan.

"I don't have that much on me. I'll give you my book sales for the day and you give me your shirt." I wasn't as desperate as I pretended.

"No deal. We saw on the news you just signed a book deal for three more books. You're loaded." She glanced at my limp manhood, "Your pocketbook is."

"It doesn't work that way. I have to write the books first, before I get the money," I explained.

"You've got the money."

"The money, or you'll be the one sucking cocks in prison. They like men who touch little girls in there," the younger one threatened.

The older one, and mastermind, was still in the backseat behind me. The young one had pushed herself against the passenger side door, her bare feet touching the central console.

If this goes south, I'd have some scratches to explain. I slipped my left hand into my sport coat pocket. I cupped the handcuffs in my palm so when I grabbed the young one's ankle I would clamp them shut around it.

At the same moment, I jerked the wrist of the older sister to reach the empty cuff, clamping it tight around her.

Amid the screams of confusion and protests I jumped from the car to avoid an instant, unplanned retaliatory attack.

They were too upset to figure out how to escape. The way I shackled them together they would not run, even if they could escape the car. One would have to carry the other, or they could try a wheelbarrow configuration, but first they would have to figure out how to get out of the car. They were too animated for rational thought.

I had only prepared for one test subject this trip, but I would make it work and last.

I folded my jacket and placed it in the trunk. I removed my kit.

Opening the passenger side door, I drug the backward little sister out so fast the older one barely had time to hop the seat to keep her arm intact with her shoulder. I heard a pop. Someone broke an ankle or a wrist—doubt it was the shoulder. They both were crying. It was difficult to discern who was hurt.

I selected this spot because of a tree. It had a low, strong branch and a root system which had been exposed. I looped a rope through, allowing me to suspend a person as if they were on a standing medieval rack.

I cuffed the older sister to a root. The younger one must have had the ankle pop. She stumbled on it and the pain prevented her from grabbing at me. She was crying too much to even listen to her sister scream a plan of escape.

They lost their chance. I got her secure and it was over. No amount of her cursing and threatening me would save them now.

I like those disposable rain ponchos they sell at baseball games. They cover a body, and no TSA agent thinks anything of one being in a travel bag.

Never again would I desire two women, either. I tied the young one's arms apart from the branch and then her legs spread eagle. When she did try and kick, I put a vice grip on her wounded ankle. I didn't detect a broken bone, but she howled when I touched it.

I cut off her garments to the tone of her older sister telling me what a sick bastard I was. I tied her limbs together, straight as an arrow, leaving her on the ground. I tossed her clothes in a garbage bag, using extra care in disposing of them—too much of me remained on and in them. There was an *SVU* episode where they typed DNA from a girl's stomach.

I noted her body size in my pocket journal. I had a code system for my torture research. Some TSA agent flipping through might find it suspicious, but I always carried on a copy of one of my books. After reading the back-cover notes on a brutal murder, I was waved on through with no body-cavity search.

I had a wooden bat on this trip.

Now the trick was not only in the exploration of body trauma, but to get the test subject to express the pain they experienced in more than screams.

"Please, we take it back. We won't say anything." The older sister now realized they had made a mistake.

There was no going back.

"Please, mister. She made me do it. I didn't want to blackmail you," the younger one's voice was soft and pleading.

"And you'll never speak of this or do it again." I didn't ask a question, even if she thought it was.

"No we—" Her lie was cut short by the bat impacting her thigh.

I didn't swing full force. It made a whack, like an extra loud wet towel snap in the boy's locker room after winning the big game. I did break capillaries.

She was a whimperer, not much of a howl-in-pain subject. Earlier, my grip on her ankle was for show.

As she blubbered, I asked her to describe the pain.

She responded with more tears.

I used this time to hang the other sister by her wrists. I looped the rope around her ankle to secure it.

"Please, don't hurt her, I'll tell you." She explained as best she could the shooting throbs, how her eyes saw a flash of lightening at the moment of impact.

I penned a note. People say they see stars. Lighting was a more forceful description. I patted her head, told her what a good girl she was. Then with all the force I had I cracked her right knee.

The impact was like a shotgun going off. And I conceived it. Bone didn't show, but her leg was like a broken stick figure cocked at a thirty-degree slant. The leg angel hurt me, bent opposite from the way God designed. She lost her bladder. No leg was meant to bend at this angle. If I stopped now she would need screws and a rod put in to repair it. When the air pressure rose, she would always have joint pain.

She blubbered louder—not a screamer, not like the sister. She cursed me, said she'd feed me my balls.

Once the little sister was calm enough to speak, she described the pain. She was sure it was like being run over by a bus. Upon impact, all air left her. Then she had no control over her body. She didn't want to pee, but she couldn't help it. Even though the pain was a thousand times worse than any menstrual cramp she was more embarrassed having to sit in her own urine. She had no control. Even if she tried to pinch it off it didn't work.

I noted every word. The fact she had the thought process to try and control her pee was interesting. I would work it into my next story. A story beat creating realism on the page. From all she described the impact and bone shatter lasted minutes for her instead of the quarter of a second it transpired.

I rammed the end of the bat into her stomach. She vomited.

I had to guess if I damaged the liver. Chances were I did. It was the second largest body organ and easily tore during abdominal trauma.

I cleaned her face with some bleach wipes, stinging her eyes. I should have done so right away because she had my DNA evidence on her face and neck. I added them to my bag.

I knew what I wanted to know about a beating from a bat. Besides head trauma, she may not ever speak if I bashed in her skull. I had a second subject—I swung away.

Three quick, full-swing shots to the middle of her back. It was with the third hit that I heard the spine crack. Her legs turned to a rag doll, her pee was red. I broke her back. She would forever be confined to a wheelchair.

Her head drooped. No explanation from pain other than the intensity rendered her unconscious. This gave me time to work over the sister. She wouldn't share what she felt as she witnessed her family mutilated.

I felt a need to make her session more torture than educational, hits to hurt, but not maim—not at first. I broke small bones. She wouldn't cooperate by explaining her pain, I noted sounds, how fast swelling occurred, any bruises.

When the sister came around, I poked on her lower body with a knife. She felt nothing. She could tell me when she was peeing. She still had some nerves in her sex organs, but none in her toes.

I found only one action left and I'd get no feedback from the blows. I made a shot to the teeth of the older sister. Fitting. She spits out her expensive orthodontic work, she may have even tried to spit her teeth at me.

I returned to work on little sister's skull, making my notes about sounds and what her body did. She spasmed and convulsed after one hit. I think I caused a seizure.

With little sister dead, I allowed the older one to hang next to her while I used the bleach wipes to sanitize the car. I always chose rental, as they clean them as soon as they are returned. I checked for any revealing evidence. The sun reached the horizon. I didn't want to leave anything behind in the dark. I ransacked their purses. Both had cell phones and together they only had about forty bucks. I kept the purse to throw off the cops.

"What was it like witnessing your sister die because of your greed?"

"Go to hell, fucker!"

With four blows to the skull before it cracked, I ended her.

Slipping the bat into a plastic bag and adding my poncho, I left. I drove for a while until I found a nice running river. Good-bye to the bat. I lost her cell phone in a sketchy area of town. I dropped my bundle into a burning trash barrel some homeless people blazed to warm the early fall chill. I waited to make sure the clothes had incinerated beyond useful evidence, and I left one purse, now with a few more twenties in it, near the fire.

The second phone I tossed a few more blocks away near some street kids.

Tracing them wasn't a normal police practice at the time or I would have jerked the battery first. I returned the rental car and got on my plane home.

X

"NONE OF US are text book traditional serial killers by our nature," notes The Plagiarist. "All those childhood norms most killers have—do we have them? I think not."

"Does it matter if I like to light fires?" asks Robert.

"It matters a great deal. We don't fit standard patterns, true. I believe because we don't fit into the mold we can save ourselves. No therapist has written books on our personalities." Jane explains, "Part of the questionnaire you each completed allowing you entry into our group was to determine if you had many of those common issues. If you answered honestly. Part of acceptance of who we are is honesty."

"I didn't bed wet and I'm no drinker. I just snapped," Jack says.

"I was a voyeur. Still am, I guess," Jesse says.

"It was in my nature—watching people. It brought about my use of the pen," Edgars says.

"Writers are isolationists by nature," Al points out before admitting, "I was abused, even if it was near adulthood. It lead to my auto-erotic adventures."

"Did any of you harm animals?" Jane asks.

"I smashed a few with my truck," Ed says.

"Only for food," says Robert

"Which is why we are curable. We're not fitting into the standard mold of the typical repeat offenders," Jane says. "Do you know how many hundreds of people contacted me through the chat room?"

She cut it to nine. A stone drops to the pit of Jesse's stomach. *Remove the blinders, kid. Listen. Sister's killer's not among this group. I just knew he was. I wanted him to be so badly.*

"I think what Edgars meant was we have our next purpose. We can't just believe victims are our test subjects, they are human. We must accept them all as living people, not playthings to dispose of. They have names. They have families." Jane repeats, "They have names. The difficulty level of killing raises when you know someone."

"Another rule?" Robert asks.

"You see them as deer, you hunt," Kenneth snaps.

"I thought you were cured?" Robert snidely asks. He tires of the group and desires a hunt. He wonders if hunting one from the group would yield a promising challenge, more than random people off the street.

"Kenneth has made progress," Jane defends, "and should we make it our rule. When we spot a potential victim, we must remember they are a living, thinking person. We won't visit the family and make recompense." She scoops up a burner phone package, waving it in the flecks of light in the center of the circle. "This might be the time to contact your buddy, ask for help to be reminded they are people, if you have an urge."

"None of us has killed since the first meeting. But in a six-week period it's not impressive. Not like a drinker. Even Kenneth abstained for years between killing? How long do we go before we earn 'days without killing' chips?"

"I desire to hunt right now. I'm itching for it," Robert says.

"Did you not speak to Ed?" Jane asks.

"We spoke a long time. He didn't go out hunting," Ed says.

"You have no idea. I'd gone as far as to prepare a motel room. Near one of my hunting grounds there's always a motel. Lots of couples use them for discreet cheating on spouses. The establishments take cash and keep no ledger, never have cameras and still use metal keys. Nothing electronic. Most barely have cable. I picked a room and waited then I called Ed. He got me to leave. It was no easy task. I needed to kill. He did good."

"So we are able to bring each other down from the ledge," Jane bubbles.

"You still have the urge?" asks Al.

"It's in me." Robert nods.

"Shouldn't we discuss this kind of back step first before we share past killings?" Kenneth asks.

"If the person trusts the group with the information. It is between him and his sponsor, but they should address it," Jane says.

"What do you do in these hotels? I thought you hunted them outdoors." Jesse says.

"I utilized this method to capture my prey when I don't employ my fake cop car routines," Robert admits.

"Tell us about it, more insight, help you not need to kill," says Edgars.

Jesse notes the writer's brain scribbling mental notes, like he does, only Edgars is constructing a new chapter in a book, not trying to prevent his own urges. Or maybe the group's stories will give him fuel enough he doesn't need to kill anymore. Unable to convince himself of his earlier realization, he considers, *Would my sister have read one of his books? Sis could have gone off to meet him.*

Robert sweats, guilt sweat dripping from his forehead. "I need to hunt."

"We'll help you quell this urge," Al says.

"You didn't swipe a person, you came back here. It means you're willing to stop. We will help you," Jane says.

"I don't know how," Robert admits.

"Go ahead, tell us how you use the hotels," Jesse says.

XI

NO-TELL MOTEL WAS not just a cliché for a location of illicit trysts. These off the interstate locations had little means to make revenue except by lost tourists and those couples seeking to hide affairs from spouses. If it weren't for the frequency of cheating couples these places would fold.

I discovered this one motel near a large woodland area. In the spring, it attracts few customers and operates only a few rooms—the ones with the kitchenettes. Those mini apartments all had sliding glass doors with a view of a little creek running behind the building. Nice, peaceful nature scene.

No one checked the backdoor locks. All of them opened from the outside. Even if the patron locked the door from the inside, one twist of the handle and the door slid open.

I waited for the room to rent.

The couple was a man in his thirties, she had to be twenty-five. They had a single overnight bag to make it appear as if they traveled, but in reality, I bet they met privately all the time. And this was just one of their frequent rendezvous locations.

People would bolt the front door, shut the shades on the road side, but leave the back vertical blinds to the patio door wide open. If a suspecting spouse hired a private dick, he'd have no issue snapping photos of the infidelity.

This couple didn't even set their one piece of luggage down before they were all over each other.

They were into each other faster than I was ready to move, no talking. And no wonder they came out here. She was a noise maker.

I slid the door open. Her pleasure moans masked the rolling wheels' squeak.

I had a fresh dart between my teeth and the loaded tranquilizer gun poised to fire.

I popped him in the chest.

She screamed. Even though her voice shifted from pleasure wails to terror, I doubted anyone outside the room would notice or care.

The medication acted quickly on him. I've had some people make it halfway across the room before they succumb to the juice.

I slid a fresh dart into the breach. She had ceased her hip swivel, but did not move from him. She submitted to her fate.

I think she thought I was there to kill them in the motel. She was prepared to die for her transgression. I guess she would rather be dead than explain why she was here with this man.

It saddened me.

Those who, in a high-pressure situation, freeze make for a shitty hunt.

Once she was unconscious, I laid her next to him on the bed so her legs didn't cramp from her odd falling position. I noticed she had the paunch most people get as they age, even when they have an almost flat stomach. She had a diamond shaped stretch mark pattern around the edges meaning she had kids—at least one. Maybe she thought her death would be better than getting caught screwing.

I packed them, one at a time, out the back door. There was a four-wheeler path most deer hunters used in the fall to reach a secluded camp about four miles into the woods.

At the manmade clearing there was fire pit. Even in the warming spring air a fire was nice.

I had put both back into their pants. She had rough feet and unkempt toenails. At least some of her young life she worked standing. She might have a good run on bare feet but there were too many pine needles. In her bag she had these soft soled moccasins, more like house shoes, but I slipped them on her. Him, I put in his loafers. No socks.

I tied them together at the ankles. A knot, time consuming to undo, but not impossible.

The meds may have knocked him down quickly, but he metabolized them fast and was wide awake when she finally stirred.

He pulled her in close never relinquishing his death stare at me. Now that she was rousing he hugged her, shielding her naked breast from my view.

I didn't care. Their exposed skin was actually a cheat. They were both so white and the forest was greening. I wanted to be able to spot them better.

When she peeked at me though his protecting arms I patted my gun as a reminder for them to stay put.

Every time I hunted was different. These people didn't even ask why.

A tiny part of me wondered who she was married to. I thought maybe she was more afraid of her husband or thought he was behind this. Maybe what I offered was a better fate than what her husband would do if he found out about this tryst. Some women cheat because the danger gives them a thrill.

I sat across from them, out of arm's reach, or a good lunge.

I held up their driver's licenses.

"Adam. Maybe I should have left you naked. And Shannon. Last names are different. I bet you two aren't married to each other."

"What do you want?" He still shielded her in a bear hug. She peeked through his arms at me with negotiating eyes.

"I don't care who you fuck. I care about—" I pocketed the licenses and waved one of my homemade arrows in their direction. "If you're able to get away. See, I hunt. I hunt for sport, but not little furry animals. They're for eating. I hunt people to test my skill."

"You're a sick fuck." Adam never raised his voice or dropped his protesting glare. Thing was he never even appeared to be searching for an escape, just held Shannon.

"This campfire is four miles from the hotel where I acquired you." I point the arrow tip at the path. "If you run the road it curves out and is four miles." I point in the 'follow the crow flies' direction. "If you go that way, it is three or so miles, a straight shot to your room through the woods. The back door is open and your phones are keyed up to 911. Just hit send." I made one of the horror movie pauses before adding, "If you make it."

"You'll just let us go?" Shannon didn't believe me.

"If you get back to your hotel room. I've got to make it sporting or there is no fun in this." I slid the arrow into my quiver, drawing a hunting knife. "Any questions?"

"Why are you doing this," Shannon pushes away from Adam. "My husband put you up to this. Scare me into not seeing Adam anymore." She spits. It lands a foot before my boot. "I don't care how powerful he is in the business world, he has no power in the bedroom. You tell him that when you collect your check."

"I bet I'd make a fortune at scaring wives into being faithful. I don't know your husband, I just hunt." I threw the knife. It digs into the log they leaned against. It severed the rope keeping them tied together.

Adam grabbed the knife, jerking it up and down to release it.

"I'd run," I suggested, notching an arrow.

Shannon bolted. the branches whipping against her naked skin and flopping breasts.

Adam hesitated a second as if my actions were a bluff.

I put an arrow across the skin where his neck met his shoulder. Blood pulsed from the scrape. His run—terror filled—caught him up quickly to Shannon.

I sheathed my knife. Wouldn't leave it behind.

I moved—in no hurry.

They made a beeline for the hotel.

Even if they didn't, there was a thicket of blackberry brambles to traverse, forcing most hiker to circle around.

Blood dotted the ground.

They gave a good run. I had to pick up my pace to stay on them. Once Shannon had given up attempting to protect her bare flesh and tore through bushes, she made over a mile before I caught up. Poor Shannon, it appeared as if someone had drawn a cheese grater over her exposed skin.

They had reached a swift moving part of the river. It was the reason the road was four miles and didn't cut this direction. There were plenty of stones to use to cross—all wet moss covered.

Shannon was wading out. Damn, the girl was going to die trying to make it. I'm sure she had some story cooked up in her head about how she was kidnaped and woke up next to the stranger and forced to play this little game. Or she thought I was working for her husband and was going get back so she could kill him.

I notched an arrow.

She was a good player. Time to keep her motivated. My aim was dead on. I would place it in the back of her left arm, right in the meatiest part of her triceps. The hit wouldn't affect her run, but the impact would distress her balance.

She slipped on the moss and fell into the river as the arrow passed.

It was luck she fell the direction she did. If she had fallen to the left it would have punctured her lung and it would have been all over but the crying.

She saw the arrow across the river. She was halfway across when Adam caught up with her.

I notched an arrow.

Adam grabbed her and flung her around as a human shield.

Fuck.

I had already loosed the arrow.

Not how I played this game.

She struggled to escape his grip as the arrow sunk into her breast. The thickness of fat may have prevented it from reaching deep into her lung, but not completely. She fell, blood frothing on her lips.

Adam, thinking it would save her, tore the arrow from her body. Blood mixed with the flowing water. She would bleed out now.

Coward.

I put an arrow into his thigh.

His death would be slow.

He slumped down next to her. Shannon clutched her chest. She stuck a finger in the hole, which might have plugged it enough to staunch the bleeding if the fool hadn't ripped anything vital. She was out of the game.

Maybe it was 'my women can't do anything men can do' upbringing, but in my hunts women turned out to be the survivors. I rooted for them to make it. I made my shots to prolong the chase, no matter the gender, but women made the best runners.

She wouldn't have made it to the hotel. The hillside on the opposite bank was too steep and wet for a half-naked girl in house slippers to climb, but damn this man who used her as a shield.

I put an arrow in his shoulder.

Shannon's coughing fit sprayed blood.

I remained on the river bank. My next arrow pinned them together. He would die with my next shot. He jerked, or the arrow didn't fly as straight as it should, because it pierced his jaw and I had been going for the neck. Adam died from the shot.

Shannon bled out from her wound, a livable wound had Adam not jerked the arrow from her breast. Who knows, she may have made it up the hill. I know I wouldn't have, and would have had to cut around the hill to stop them before they reached motel.

I don't want it impossible for my prey to escape, or I have no sport.

XII

"YOU SAID YOUR stories are the same, but they are not. You may hunt, but each time you hunt is different, even if your end goal is the same. When you have a victim who has spirit you change your strategy," Jane says. "You're willing to allow the strong to survive."

"Worthy," Al says. "Not strong. When Robert finds a worthy prey, he releases it. Rather Darwinian."

"I've committed many crimes. You've allowed some of these women to go, but you hunger for talented prey strong enough to escape. You need one final hunt with a worthy adversary," The Plagiarist assumes.

"Are you volunteering? Because unless you are we are here not to kill anymore," Jane snaps.

"I just understand his issue," The Plagiarist says.

"But saying one more killing is the same as believing 'I'll quit after one more drink'. It doesn't work," Kenneth says.

"Agreed." More than one member spouts.

"No one kills. No matter what," Jack says.

"What if I just leave the group?" Robert asks.

Jane never considered anyone would bow out of the group, proclaiming they would murder again. She selected those to attend based on their desires to quit killing. Unlike alcoholics, she thought these people had more willpower since their murders were all premeditated, involving more planning and execution than opening a bottle.

"I vote you allow him to go," The Plagiarist says.

"Plagiarist, you were never fully a part of our merry little band, nor have you promised to stop your killing," Jack scoffs.

"THE. My name is The Plagiarist."

Jack ignores the pretension.

Jane realizes she's losing Jack as well. Not to killing, but because the grandfather is disgusted with the acts the others have performed. Jack's killings were against evil, in his mind, and some of the murderers in this room have performed pure evil. *At least none of them have attacked children. No part of those…people. Even I didn't care to hear those stories. The rapes are bad enough, but children. I, too, might have to kill again.* "Gentlemen, we are here to discuss the driving force behind our impulses. We're far from casting a vote on anything. Robert, why do you want to leave?"

"Returning to hunting dumb deer will fill my belly, but not whatever satisfied me when I hunted people."

"We all have those emotions," Kenneth says. "Isn't this why we attend? We're trying to get over those incorrect urges."

"By whose standards? I, too, have been doing some reading. I read, you know. Humans were meant to hunt, not drive cars. I'm fighting against my nature when I don't kill," Ed says.

"Being able to fight against our nature is what makes us human," says Edgars. "We fuck when we want, and when we do we don't have to have offspring. We don't have to adhere to those primitive regulated urges. You enjoy tracking the gazelle because you are a lion, but humans weren't meant to be lions. We were meant for a higher purpose."

"I'm not going to church to praise some invisible being who takes roll call. And I sure as fuck don't buy into 'He is testing me' shit. If I wasn't meant to kill, then those urges should never be inside me. God is people's excuse for what they do so they don't have to accept responsibility."

Got him. His own words. Jane says, "Then if you leave the group you aren't accepting responsibility for your actions."

Robert pauses. He considers what she threw in his face.

"Why don't we speak of God? He is a part of the AA healing process, the most important part, and I was a regular church attendee before the accident," Jack says.

"And your loving God stole away your family for no reason. If he were just, and gave two shits about us, he would strike down those who harm those created in his image," The Plagiarist says.

"Don't they contradict themselves? Your beliefs and what you've done?" Edgars asks. "To claim belief in a deity who says *don't murder* and then you kill. You're unable to do both."

"Besides, the Bible is never clear on killing. God gives Moses his most sacred laws and then informs his people to go eliminate those on his sacred land promised to His people.

"I don't see it that way," Jack says.

"God was a vengeful, spiteful God long before he sent his Son to redeem us. And his Son was one way to ask people to forgive all the ills he wrought upon them," Kenneth says.

"That was the devil," Jesse says.

"No. There was no devil in the Old Testament. It's a common misconception made by those who don't read the text. It was all God," Al says.

"But the snake—" Jesse protests.

"Later, Christians claimed the snake was the devil. It's not written like that. Knowledge was the devil."

"Enough with the fucking Sunday school lesson. I want to hunt," Robert says, "The way God intended,"

"Then I say hunt. If you are not ready for a cure, hunt," The Plagiarist encourages.

"No. We can't go back and kill." Jane chews her lip to prevent a scream. *You'd like someone to relapse, Plagiarist, so you could keep killing. We must not stray from the path. We were doing so well.*

"There are bound to be relapses," Ed chimes in.

"Killing won't be the same for him. We've been working on understanding our victims are people. Robert may have been at the hotel, he may have picked out a couple to hunt, but Ed speaking to him reminded him they were persons. He'll have trouble hunting the next couple with a clear conscience," Edgars says.

Writers must have a functioning understanding of the human condition to create believable characters, but she hates how Edgars grasps the killing mind better than she does. So much for all her time in a text book. "Fine. Leave the group."

Robert stands.

"Now, wait. Unlike an alcoholic, who polishes off a bottle and must start over counting days, if you kidnap someone and then can't go through with your hunt what do you do with them?" Edgars asks.

"He's right. They'll have seen your face, or have valuable information to give to the cops which will lead to your capture," Kenneth says.

"And who's to say you won't give us up to lighten your sentence or at least earn yourself a ticket into a country club prison where they send the rich white-collar criminals?" Jesse chimes in, his chance to spill his plans and project them onto Robert.

"In this case a relapse would be bad if you can't complete the killing. And if you finish, you defeat the purpose of joining this group."

"We keep forgetting Al has a woman locked in his closet." Robert deflects the attention away from him.

"We'll deal with Al and his girl soon. We started this meeting by swearing we haven't killed," Jane seeks confirmation. "Is she alive, Al?"

"Yes." His answer has no hesitation.

No idea how to release the girl in his possession—alive, and not put the whole group at risk for prison. Jane adds to her rules for the group—Before you're invited to attend you must not have a current subject in your possession.

Maybe he should bring her to a meeting prepared to release her, allow her to meet the group. Inform her if she speaks of her captivity someone in the group will find her. It was a bluff and a strong one.

"Does she know where you live? The city, I mean," Jesse fumbles desperate for a clue.

"I didn't swipe her from the same town as where I keep her," Al says.

"Smart man. Since you use her in your sex game, she has seen your face." Not a question, The Plagiarist seeks confirmation.

"Even a bad sketch artist could do a proper rendering from the time we've spent together," Al confesses.

"Then we scare her into not ever speaking about her captivity," Robert says.

"Send a typed letter with lots of spelling mistakes to her family warning if she returns never to ask."

"After you clean her of all your DNA," Ed adds.

"How would you scare her, Robert?" Jane asks.

"He's got his hidey-hole in his car. He could drive her states away, maybe drug her so she doesn't know she was driven for hours. Then tell her if she talks to anyone you'll find her again."

"Plenty of people rot in prison because of people who promised not to tell," Kenneth says.

"Personally, I'd dump her in some neighborhood where someone else might end her," The Plagiarist says.

"I won't stand for that." Jack demands, "She gets to live, and Robert stays in the group."

They all detect the rest of his sentence, the 'or else I turn myself and all of us in'.

"Agreed, she lives," Jane's tone remains firm. "But the scaring her part must be effective. Bring her to a meeting. We allow her to know we're all killers and now we know about her. If she ever speaks of anything one of us will find her."

"I thought we were done with killing?" Kenneth seeks confirmation.

"She doesn't have to know why we meet, just that we know about her and we are all killers," Edgars says.

"What if she talks?" Ed asks. "One of us going to follow through with the threat?"

Why did he have to ask? The group was unifying, Jane thinks.

"They will place her in protective custody. I doubt any of us are good enough to get to her. Her threat would remain towards Al, but he would be the threat to the group," Edgars says. "And no telling what we might think when some of us are facing the chair."

"No state electrocutes anymore," Jesse says.

"Still, kid, someone in the room will squeal for a PC life in prison over a needle."

ELEVEN

JESSE

I

"ARE THE CUFFS necessary?" asks Professor Arnett, as he peers through the two-way mirror at Jesse alone in the Agency interrogation room.

"In what way is the boy not a criminal? Obstructing Justice. Knowingly consorting with admitted felons. Tampering with evidence. Maybe they are all misdemeanors, but there are enough to put him away for the next five years." Agent Smith clinches his fist, forgoing his urge to poke a finger at Arnett. "You're lucky I don't clamp you in irons along with him.

Arnett ignores the action movie bravado. "The kid has got himself invited to these meetings. He's a valuable asset to a case, Agent Smith, that you, and Agent Sutherland didn't even know you had. Busting six confessed serial killers would make your careers."

"Let's start back at the beginning." Agent Sutherland, playing the good cop, asks, "How are you involved, Professor Arnett?"

"The kid was in my class. He sought information about a family death. His sister was killed when he was four. Somehow he got it into his head she was murdered by a serial killer." Arnett holds out a sealed manila envelope. "I retrieved the file on his sister. Before you ask, an old friend owed me a favor. I get cold case files all the time to use in class. He did swipe a different case file I requested, but I don't think he's been able to open it or he would know it wasn't her."

"And he explored the dark web where this group meets in chat rooms?" Smith asks. "Why doesn't something like this show up?"

Agent Sutherland answers, "Because it's not a Homeland Security issue, and the FBI agents surfing the dark web are hunting pedophiles. Besides, I'd bet these people are smart enough to use the free WIFI at a Burger King. I'll spare you the technical explanation. Anyone can hook on and not be traced."

"This kid has an idea who some of these people are? He is for real?"

"He's gotten some good intel," Arnett says.

"He turns out to be some attention seeking, spoiled millennial and I'm jailing you both." Agent Smith flashes a smile.

• • • • •

"My older sister was murdered when I was four," Jesse explains, without having been read his rights. He wasn't under arrest—yet. If they do arrest him, he might have to lawyer up, and if he did he'd never get back to the group. Cooperate, and maybe the FBI will allow him to keep attending the meetings.

"My parents had the information kept from me. The investigation into her murder is a cold case, which means no one will be solving it. I've been unable to obtain anything from the local cops, but I've been able to determine it was performed by a serial murderer, or least not a onetime banger."

"And you *just* found a group of killers trying to gain information?" Agent Smith demands from across the metal table.

"I get the interrogation techniques, I was studying criminal justice. I used my knowledge to find the group. It wasn't easy," Jesse admits.

"How did you do find them?" Agent Sutherland asks. She leans against the back wall as if this is a waste of her time.

"Lots of hours on the internet. While researching killers, I uncovered several chat rooms. Mostly cranks claiming they had been a killer or knew who they thought Son of Sam was. But you find a few conversations with strange choices of words that at first you think may be typos or autocorrect. But then I discovered I had learned the code they used to speak to each other. The ones who might be killers or trolling for victims. And that lead to other chat rooms. Those conversations opened the Dark Web to me, along with deeper conversations about death. I found several who like to brag about their killings without admitting to them. One describes the skinning of animals, but there was something deeper. As I trolled those chat rooms I discovered one asking for means to prevent specialized addictions."

"You understood *specialized* to mean murder?" Agent Smith asks.

"I learned real fast everything was code in these dark chatrooms. You stay away from those offering Snow White or any other Disney princesses, unless your desires involve being a convicted sex offender. It took a lot of hours to even find a person with coded communication about their murders."

Agent Smith stands. "Just hold your thought." He stomps out of the room.

Jesse knows he is requesting a search warrant for all his electronic devices. They will keep him at the office until they get it. They will find his murder board with his guesses on who each killer is.

Agent Sutherland remains a statue. "How did you know your sister's killer was among the group's participants?"

"I poked around, inferring that I was having issues with my addiction. I said I could get no help. It was months of subtle hints to obtain an invite, take a test and pass, then receive an invitation to the meeting. I sought Professor Arnett's help to concoct my cover. He would not help me. He didn't believe my sister's killer would be in such a group." Jesse knows he just shifted some of the attention from him to his mentor.

"We've spoken to the professor," Agent Sutherland says, "He reported what you were doing."

Agent Smith returns to his seat, joining the conversation as if he never left the room. "He doesn't want a case against him. Former cops don't fare well in prison."

"Neither do young pretty college boys," Agent Sutherland adds.

Jesses ignores the prison rape threat.

"You're in live contact with these killers. You need to share all you know with us." Agent Smith leans over the table. "I'm putting you up on obstruction. So spill it."

"I know nothing." Jesse holds a card to play or they will place him under arrest. His information, vital to tracking down eight killers, would give a lawyer a great deal of leverage.

Agent Smith leans back. "You going to play this way? You sit in a room with six killers and say you know nothing."

"Eight. Two more joined. I know nothing because after three meetings I had listened to confessions about killings with no details to even lead me to guess where they occurred or in what state these people operate. I was collecting evidence. But not a damn one of them said I did this murder, in this town, on this date. Most of them tell the tales of early murders which were trial killings. They don't even match later MOs."

Agent Smith leans back, drumming his fingers on the table. The tattoo of each tip demanding information.

Agent Sutherland asks, "Did any of these killers mention they like to hack up pregnant women?"

"No. After three meetings not a single one said anything about pregnant women. Miss Jane, maybe, when she was a nurse, but she used medications, not a hatchet."

"No. We know it was a man." Agent Sutherland says.

"Love to get ahold of him. He murdered two FBI agents tracking him and escaped as if he never existed," Agent Smith says. "Anyone in the meeting ever mention Springwells, Missouri?"

"They have all been careful to not use names or locations," Jesse holds back his one ace. They could find P.A. Edgars through his publisher. He left him out of his notes. He doesn't want to turn anything cutting him from the loop and figuring out what happened to his sister.

"If we were able to catch that guy I might be willing to overlook your minor infractions."

"I won't make shit up. Those people have killed enough," Jesse says. "One guy calls himself The Plagiarist, he copies other murders. The dead pregnant women would be an easy one to copy. He likes those."

"Even if he did, I want this paramedic killer," Agent Smith says.

"Most of them kept their locations vague. They focused on their reasons for killing, not an address."

"Where did you go to high school, kid?" Agent Sutherland asks.

The question breaks Jesse's attention and disrupts his attempt to control the room. "Uh, Southwood High."

"Did you play sports?" she asks.

"Basketball. I wasn't much for crunching into guys bigger than me."

"Took you for the quarterback," Agent Smith says.

"I know what this is. You get me to tell the truth and then ask me questions to catch me in a lie. Then twist it all up and offer to help me. Fuck you."

"Don't help us, kid, and you'll never catch your sister's killer from a prison cell."

"I want to be a part of this. In the loop," Jesse says.

"It doesn't work like that," Agent Smith says.

"If we examine all the details of the killings we could match them in the database," Agent Sutherland suggests.

"Give us one with the most distinction in their killing."

"I want to be a part of this."

"Then you must cooperate," Agent Sutherland says.

Edgars. Again, they'll track the group through him. Jack? No. I might need Jack's help. He detests the group. Of all the killers, they wouldn't catch Ed. Lots of dead roadside prostitutes. Robert? The fucking homemade ar-

rows? No, not yet. I give them too much and they cut me out. Jesse explains the information he has displayed on his note board. If they haven't searched his apartment they will.

After an hour Smith never loses his bad cop method and demands, "Kid how old are some of these people? No DNA. Lack of cell phones. 'Hippies.' Fuck me. These people aren't that old. The problem is their stories have major time inconsistencies."

"Unless you're lying," Agent Sutherland adds.

Jesse realizes he might have lost Sutherland as an ally. "I don't agree. It would be their memories, and people didn't have cell phones in the Midwest, not at first. There are still rural areas today lacking coverage. Many people still have dial up Internet because it's all that is offered. I read there are still a million AOL users because it's all they've got where they live."

"And we know memory is shady," Agent Sutherland says. "They are telling their own stories the way they recall the events. The way they have relived them in their minds over and over to fulfill whatever drives them to kill."

"Even if their stories are embellished they are still evidence," Jesse says.

"Not enough, kid. You ain't got nothin'." Agent Smith draws his handcuffs from the pouch on his belt. "I think we'll just..."

"One of them called himself the Bowhunter Killer. His nom de plume was Robert after Robert Hanson. The original killer escorted people to the Alaskan wilderness by plane, dropping them off to hunt them."

Agent Smith snaps his fingers, signaling to whoever is behind the mirrored glass to confirm the information.

"The guy at the meeting used homemade arrows to hunt people. He would kidnap them, take them into the woods, release them with an option to escape. He told one story of a woman, Gabby. She escaped to her car with three arrows in her. He killed her male companion. There must be police reports on her attack, along with the arrows in evidence. Death by arrow can't be common."

"Tell us everything this Robert said." Agent Sutherland moves from the wall.

"From his first account, and other evidence, we might be able determine his home base," Agent Smith says.

"He says he changes hunting grounds. These people are not typical, you will have to write a new textbook for them. All of them are smart and they think cops are dumb."

"Underestimating us will be how we bring them down."

"I want my sister's killer," Jesse says.

"Did you read the file on her death?" Agent Sutherland asks.

"The pictures. I couldn't," Jesse admits.

II

PROFESSOR ARNETT PLACES a Styrofoam cup, steaming hot, before Jesse before he takes the seat across the table.

"Professor, I don't know how much more of this I can take. Day two. Non-stop interrogation. I need sleep, and not in the holding cell."

"They let you out of the handcuffs."

"I don't see how I am the criminal here." Jesse grips the cup with both hands, soaking in the warmth.

"I'll speak to the agents. You've been cooperating." Arnett asks, "You have been?" He flashes an accusatory eye. "You haven't left anything out?"

"Professor, there was so much. But I've said everything I can think of. I want these guys. I want my sister's killer."

"I know, kid. You didn't read the file you swiped from my office mail box?"

"I opened it. There were glossy prints and I couldn't." Shameful, Jesse drops his head.

"You're going to have to go through everything about Robert with the agents again and then you must read the file you *borrowed*. We need to discuss it. If you'd read the document on your sister I don't think you'd be in this mess."

Jesse raises the cup to his lips. "What do you mean?"

Before he clears the door frame, Agent Smith tosses three arrows in a plastic bag marked 'evidence' on the table.

Jesse immediately notices the brownish stains along the tips. He sets his cup on the table before he drops it. Had he drunk any he might have spit it up. "Are these? Is that…the Gabby woman's…blood?" Jesse stammers.

Everything spoken about in the group materializes into reality for him. All those people spoken about are gone, murdered in horrific manners, the same as his sister.

"These came from a woman who was kidnapped, drug into the woods and released by a man who shot arrows at her and her male companion. She did get away. Due to nerve damage in her leg she has trouble walking," Agent Smith says.

Agent Sutherland finishes Smith's statement, "And she seems to have no memory of her kidnapper. Not about any determining features."

"I told you he kept her driver's license," Jesse says. "In his retelling of the event he showed her he had it. He claimed he burnt them between the first and second meetings."

Agent Sutherland spreads out a map. "You claimed Robert had no pattern. He may have said so to your group. Maybe he believes he doesn't."

"It's part of the arrogance of the killers. They believe they are above all laws. Some even believe they are above God's laws," Agent Smith says.

"No. Through their killing they think they are God," Jesse says.

"When we mark the Bowhunter's attacks on a map," Agent Sutherland finds herself interrupted by Smith, thumping his index finger on Xs scratched on the paper. "They form a large circle over several states."

She continues, "We might be able to narrow it down. I think he originates from inside the circle. Maybe not the center."

"We want you to tell us again everything this Robert said in the meetings," Agent Smith demands.

"Reexamine these first." She slides a paper with eight black-n-white mug shots on it.

Jesse scoops up the images. "The meetings were held in low light, near blackness. Several kept their faces almost completely masked in it."

"Just do your best."

"How did you enter and exit?" Agent Smith asks.

"I told you all the locations were in abandoned factories and the buildings had multiple entry points. Jane always changed it up for our protection and peace of mind. It was about our anonymity, but later I felt like part of the healing would be to reveal our physical selves. She had a plan. How many times do I have to keep repeating the same information?"

"Until we are satisfied and have eight killers in a cell," Agent Smith says.

Jesse studies each pic in turn. "These three all have the same chin and jawline. Think of viewing them in the dark with the chin exposed like Batman. That is what I saw of him. He had dark hair so this blond dude is out. But the chin, he has this chin."

III

"YOU DON'T GET out of this car," Agent Sutherland commands, no longer speaking with her nice cop demeanor from the front seat of the cruiser. Even she doesn't like the idea of Jesse accompanying them. She wonders what Al would make of this kid. Still on administrative leave for the shooting, she'll run this case without him. "Once you ID him, we'll take him down. But if he spots you, it blows this sting and future ones against the others. If he gets away you'll be in danger."

"If I was raided and escaped, my first phone call would be to the group to warn them. You said Jane gave everyone a burner phone. Stay in the car, kid," Agent Smith warns. "Professor, you are here under the same conditions."

The agents leave them in the back seat. The door locks click.

Jesse holds the computer pad on his lap so Professor Arnett views the screen. It displays the video feed of a cabin.

"You marched into the lion's den and didn't even know how your sister died. Without knowing, you collected evidence, but not what you needed to narrow down your search," Professor Arnett says. "You should have completed the course work and learned how to be a cop. This John Wayne shit is only for the movies."

"I felt like I was doing something."

"All I taught you and my attempts to help. You should have read the file." Arnett shakes his head.

"I've put pieces together over the years, things people shut off as I came into the room. I knew for a long time it wasn't just a murder. Her death was a part of something else. The pictures fell out of the envelope and I just couldn't see her—dead."

"This Robert wasn't her killer. She was not struck with an arrow. You don't even know how she was killed to match her wounds with your perps. You're lucky we aren't zipping you into a body bag," Arnett says.

"I messed up. I've given them all I learned. We capture these people and it will make up for it."

"You better pick a new major. I doubt law enforcement hires you. No John McClains work long as an officer.

"As long as I learn who killed her." Jesse never removes his eyes from the monitor. The image bounces from the officer's chest cam. "Robert not returning to the group will disrupt their next meeting. Do you think they will know why he doesn't show up?"

"The FBI will try and keet his moniker under wraps. News feeds will report his arrest, no stopping it. If they use his real name and they don't release his method of killing it might not reach them. They do travel great distances to meet. Taking them all down at once would be optimum, but they are mass murderers and they all know at any time they are suspect to capture. Bringing them down one by one will tip off the others."

"But if I don't attend, two will be missing from the next meeting."

"I don't see Agent Smith allowing you to return," Professor Arnett says.

"Robert will be difficult to take alive. I doubt he shares anything to corroborate my version of the meetings." The image of the cabin door remains on the monitor.

"I wish you had read the file on your sister before you attended these meetings."

A military precise tactical team takes up position on the cabin porch.

The door smashes open.

Flash bangs brighten the interior. Jesse spots a collection of stuffed game heads.

Gunfire.

"I know they won't take him alive. This will be the ultimate thrill hunt for Robert," Jesse says.

Police and men wearing jackets saying FBI race toward the cabin.

Jesse and Professor Arnett spot white smoke from the car window.

"I believe your profile of this Robert was correct. They won't take him alive."

"It's not a comfort, Professor. You have no idea what is was like to be in the meetings with these people."

"You're not a trained undercover agent, which is why you may have slipped under their radar. You said they find police to be stupid. Even if the statement bothered you, you lacked the arrogance law enforcement agents get. Cops have a smell, for lack of a better explanation. You never asked or spoke out of turn and you didn't dig too deeply. You built trust with them. Undercover agents visit therapists to help them deal because to truly be undercover, you have to become like those you infiltrate."

"Anyone normal after those meetings needs a psychiatrist. I threw up after the first one. They speak about carving on a person the same as if it's like cutting the crust off bread," Jesse says.

"I don't know what was said around your house while you grew up to lead you to believe your sister was murdered by a serial killer. It may have been your family's way of coping with what happened."

More gunfire erupts.

"Robert won't be taken alive. This will be his grand hunt. He wanted out of the group, but wanted a final test of his skills. I didn't see it before now," Jesse admits.

"You didn't have a full profile picture. You didn't have all the evidence at your disposal," Arnett says.

A large caliber handgun reports, followed by a dozen short bursts of automatic weapons fire.

"If he escapes into the woods they won't find him." Professor Arnett keeps his focus on Jesse.

"He's going out in a blaze of glory," Jesse points at the monitor. Three agents in full tactical gear race from the cabin door. A fourth engulfed in flames flings himself onto the muddy earth attempting to stop, drop and roll. An agent in a FBI windbreaker and vest flips a blanket over the unmoving, burning man. As other agents drop to their knees to pat out the flames more fire erupts inside the cabin.

"He booby-trapped it."

"I'm going to have to retake your course. I missed so much," Jesses says.

"I doubt these individuals had enough trust in the group to reveal the critical information you needed to make a proper profile. Three group sessions were not enough to make a true breakthrough. Even Ed, the seemingly redneck trucker, was intelligent. You said all of them were smart and not like the average serial killers you've read about. You did the best with what you had," Professor Arnett assures him.

"It wasn't enough." The camera hangs on the unmoving, smoldering man.

More large caliber reports echo through the woods.

Heavy bursts of machine gun fire.

Silence—profound quiet, the only noise emerging the crackling fire inside the cabin.

It spreads.

The growing flames crawl around inside the cabin door. Pops, then bursts of growing, angry flames consume more of the cabin. Whatever fire trap Robert set was not meant to consume the cabin all at once. It grabs it in pieces, forcing further disruption and damage to the attacking officers.

More than one trap. A dozen small traps hidden throughout the home. If one failed or was discovered he'd grab an agent with the next one. A hunter until the end. Jesse shakes off his admiration.

Agents file from the tree line weapons holstered or slung at their sides.

Jesse doesn't need any further explanation. He knows Robert's dead. Inside he had no love or friendship for this man, but his death conflicts him. He didn't murder his sister and should be in prison for all he's done to those people. He's glad he dead. The Bowhunter needed to go. All the others do as well, except maybe Jack. He seeks retribution for his loss.

None of those people were her killer. Smith and the professor must be right. All this and he's back at square one. He doesn't know if his sister's killer is finished or if he is still at large. He may never know because if Robert did take her, and kept a trophy, it's burning now—no question.

Ambulances and fire trucks arrive.

"The water will most likely destroy any evidence the fire missed," notes Arnett.

"He booby-trapped all the evidence. When the cops found a clue they would burn it for him. I guess he was a bit of a fire bug after all. Serial Killers are known to have a propension for fires," Jesse says.

"You had access to eight killers all sharing stories of their crimes, some of them horrible enough the normal human brain would shut them out. You had no way of taking physical notes without being suspect. You brought to the table a lot more than these agents had before. Even if this operation turns sideways you did everything you could. And even if the FBA tells you otherwise remember you and I know you did your best."

But I didn't. I held back because I knew if I gave up certain bits I would lose the chance to get my sister's killer. Speaking about Edgars or Jack. Edgars is a celebrity. How many towns would have a half dozen crack houses burn in a few weeks? No, they could both be found instantly.

Fire fighters hose the flaming cabin. Behind the fire trucks and swarms of agents Jesse spots two sets of men, each helping to carry a lifeless person, on a stretcher, covered by a bloody sheet.

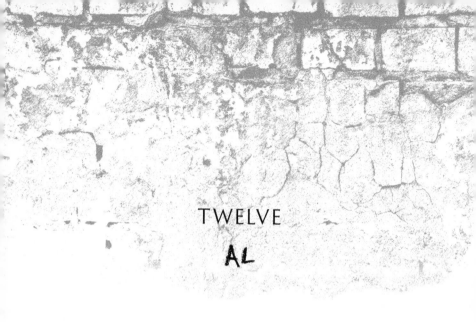

TWELVE

AL

AL LOWERS TO eye level with the autopsy table. Using an ink pen he flutters the end of snipped brunette hair. "Did you take a hair sample?"

The salt and pepper headed medical examiner places a human liver on a scale. "I wouldn't cut chunks out for any testing. As much I have to carve on the dead I attempt to leave some dignity on the parts viewed at the funeral. I would not ruin her hair. I need the root," the medical examiner says. "In her case the family will be able to have an open casket. People need proper closure."

Al glances at the golden name badge tarnished with decades of wear: Gordon. Small town MEs are never women, they all seem to be the same old man. He ponders if that is why cop shows always use the same guy to play the part. "Putting her attacker in prison will satisfy closure. It's what I will do for them. They were lucky to have a body to bury. Those without knowing the fate of a loved one have the most pain." He pockets his pen. "Any way to tell what he used to make the cuts?"

"Knife or scissors, but I'm doubtful about the kind." Gordon slips his left glove over the right, tossing the latex ball into the trash. He pulls on a clean pair before palpating her scalp. "He jerked her around by her hair." He rolls the cut tips between his thumb and first two fingers. "Before he whacked her with a knife."

Gordon points to her left side. If you recover a knife I'll match it to the hole in her left side. He punched through a rib to puncture a lung. He used a combat blade with sawback serration on one side and a razor-sharp edge on the other."

"Military?"

"No. He must have tried some move he watched in an action movie. He broke a rib, not stabbing between it. The result was the same, she could not scream. She suffered intense pain. It was not the fatal wound."

Al clicks his tongue against the roof of his mouth.

"He collects the hair as his trophy?" Gordon asks.

"Or it's part of his ritual. I haven't determined. This guy steals a car, uses it to stalk women and runs them off the road. He has an affinity for brunettes, but will take what he knocks off the road. He approaches them and might even demand to exchange insurance information. He drags her to the stolen car jabbing her in the side with a knife. He was not in the military, but had desires to be or believes by buying the equipment he is a soldier."

"He might have been discharged during basic," Gordon offers.

"Psychological discharge. Doesn't narrow down any list. Let's work the facts. I don't make leaps," Al says.

"He's strong. Once he stabbed her, she was dead weight. From the angle of the cut he has to be five-eleven or six-foot."

"Facts. We paint a picture of this man with what we know," Al says. "Did you examine the other victims?"

"This guy's operated in a limited area. It has the city on edge because no one is witnessing anything. All the women have passed through here."

"Share what you learned?" Al asks.

"The first victim identified was an Asian woman. The second was a young co-ed from suburbia."

"Your way of stating she was Caucasian?" Al asks.

"More his actions are random. The Asian woman was employed at a massage parlor and the second vic was a college student. The third was a brunette, but she was a mother of three, age thirty-four."

"And this poor woman. She seems young."

"Waiting on her identification to be confirmed, but from her teeth she's barely seventeen."

"No curfew in the city?" Al asks.

"We have an employment exemption. She worked fast food and was on her way home," Gordon says.

"This guy's all over the place in the city with his attacks, which means he is an opportunist. He doesn't stalk them long. He spots one he likes and follows until he's able to have a secluded fender bender. He won't tap her car hard enough to render his own vehicle useless, as he needs it to transport her to where he finishes his assaults on her. Then he dumps the stolen car elsewhere."

"Where he is close to his car?" Gordon offers, scribbling down notes about her organ weight.

"Or whatever his escape route," Al considers.

"He must be covered in the victim's blood. He slices them and they bleed all over him while he assaults them."

"Unless he's smart enough to cover his own car interior in plastic." Al's phone vibrates. He slips off his right glove. "Agent Al," he answers.

After a few breaths he answers, "No assessment yet. I'm here with the ME now."

Al nods as if the person on the other end of the line can see him. "As soon as I have a profile." He clicks the phone off. "I don't perform magic and without a proper assessment we won't have a proper profile to catch a suspect."

"Don't you have a perfect closing rate?" Gordon asks.

"Through careful examination of all information, not miracles or bloodletting. At this point if they want me to profile a suspect then I might as well use a bloodhound and a Ouija board. Guess is how a suspect escapes, or worse, the wrong person is incarcerated."

The phone chips again.

Al clicks *accept* on his cell phone. Before he even says hello,

"It's bad, Al."

He's never heard panic grip his partner. "Smith? What's wrong?" Never the buddy cop movie partners type they were paired for assignments together for four years. Director Slincard liked to pawn him off on other departments. His innate ability to solve cases freaked the man out. Director Engström hasn't worked with him enough to draw a conclusion.

Agent Smith was a hard nose. He fought everything. Growing up black he was never handed anything and worse, he's still pulled over by white officers. Al wishes it was just the backroads country troopers, but it's a lot of city denizens. What hurts Al is in many cases the local constables won't acknowledge Smith's rank. The first time Sutherland joined their team, Smith was driving through the Southern town. If Al hadn't been there Smith would have beaten that gold ole' boy to death. He didn't think it was proper a black man be in a car with a white woman in the front seat.

"She's dead, Al."

The phrase doesn't catch Al off guard, the crack in Smith's armor shocks him, the tears Smith holds back from him even over the phone.

"What happened, Smith?"

"We had a tip on a suspect and another task force to bring him down. It was a cluster."

"Sutherland?" Al questions, cold as ice. Unlike other serial killers he masks his lack of empathy. "How did it happen?"

"The suspect booby-trapped his lair. She was caught in an expulsion. I don't think she's going to make it. She's burnt on seventy-three percent of her body. What kind of fucking number is seventy-three?"

"Breathe…my friend…explain. You said she was dead."

"They revived her twice. She's in ICU. It's bad. While you were on administrative leave…"

Al detects the accusatory finger—*Had you been there this wouldn't have happened.*

"We received information on a man who had been in contact with a professed serial murderer. We followed the information to his cabin. Hell broke free."

In front of the ME, Al forgoes explaining that the second he was cleared of the shooting Director Slincard sent him on a shit assignment, his way of exacting punishment. "They've got me assigned to an active case. This guy shows no signs of going dormant. I'll…"

"Fuck the job. Sutherland may be new to our team, but you need to attend out of respect."

Tears must be streaming for Smith now. Al detects the pain in his partner. His presence in the hospital isn't for her, it's for Smith. He needs comfort. He has no idea how to ask and not appear weak. Nothing anyone does will change Sutherland's outcome.

Al's thoughts race to what Jane explained about the rule of nines. Body coverage plus the patient's age equals the chance of recovery. The formula eludes him, but Sutherland exceeds the percent needed to recuperate. Both he and Smith know it.

"I'm on my way." Al shifts into anger, "Did you get the fucker?"

"He's dead. The fire brought down a second officer. He'll need major skin grafts and some reconstructive surgery. Sutherland has little chance of using her legs again."

"I'm on my way, Smith." Al presses end, knowing he has two stops first.

THIRTEEN
SKA: MEETING FOUR

I

"We cannot change our past...we cannot change the fact
that people will act in a certain way.
We cannot change the inevitable.
The only thing we can do is play on the one string we have"
~ Charles R. Swindoll ~

II

"HOW LONG DO we wait for Robert?" Edgars asks.

"I'll tell a story, and if he hasn't checked in we'll decide what to do then," Kenneth says. "It was too long of a drive to this meeting location to not keep sharing."

"Just itching to relive your thrills." Jack doesn't ask a question, his statement was meant as a barb. Even in the dark the group tastes his disdain.

"I don't care for you, Jack, you still think you're above us, because of who you killed. Don't matter if it's helpless prostitutes or drug dealers, we both murder," Ed says.

"My choices were of a moral standing, Ed. But I know I'm the same as you. This group revealed to me what I was. I hate myself as much as you. My concern, at first, like many of you was being found out by the cops. If we stay active we run the chance of getting caught. Robert gets caught, he will sell us out. He wouldn't answer his burner phone. He desires to keep killing. I believe he's returned to seeking out victims," Jack reports.

"I believe he'll be reckless. Not his normal calculated performance because he's desperate to fulfil the urges he's been suppressing. He won't think straight," The Plagiarist says.

"Choosing to be dormant and forcing it are not the same," Al says.

"We don't know why Robert isn't here and we shouldn't judge him," Jane says.

"He could have a flat tire," Kenneth says, almost a joke.

"You think so?"

"No. Over my years of teaching it amazed me that the child who never did any work or cooperated was also the one whose computer never worked, or they sent the assignment electronically and it never showed up. Robert strikes me as one of those," Kenneth says.

"What if he did kill? Do we accept him back?" Ed asks.

"You return to an AA group and start over, with a chip representing hours."

"You're voting to allow him to return?" Jane asks.

Jesse jumps up. "He's not even here, and we don't know why. We aren't supposed to judge. So let's just see why he's not here before we all flip out."

"Why don't I tell a tale. If he hasn't joined we decide. Some of us do want this group's help," Edgars offers.

Jane grins. Two of the group are willing to continue forward. They do wish to quit.

"You think he's just running late?" Ed sneers.

"There are bound to be times we're conflicted. Some of us have a long rest period between our killings. When those times approach we will face our hardest struggles not to kill." Jane continues, "Even you, Jack. What happens when a new drug house opens? Someone will grow bold and open one. When it's not firebombed a second will return as long as there is demand."

"I haven't considered, anyone would want to return after I cleared the apartment."

"So you did finish him?" Jesse asks.

"I did more than finish him," Jack says. "It was why I'm here. I wanted to end it. I marched right to the door, and shoved my gun into the doorman's face. Those crackhead dealers were high on their own product, and had no response time. Even the ones whose guns cleared holsters had no speed. I drew on them as if I was Wyatt Earp. I desired them to end me, end my pain, and they were so high they couldn't fight back."

"I understand how the direct killing caused you to seek us out," Jane says.

"I took a rag and, using their blood, I wrote a message on the wall—"

No one in the group moves.

"*Fate for all dope peddlers in my town.*"

"After the fires and your cryptic message it will be awhile before too many sell drugs in your neighborhood," Kenneth says.

"Or they will remain on guard. The next house won't go down quickly, not unless you wait a long time. Maybe a year," Al suggests. He wouldn't miss the meeting, but he should be at Shawna's bedside. From the vague news reports and his job he knows Robert died. All the remainder of the group is present. Smith shared that someone met with Robert. Were they in the room?

"I'm done, dipping my hands in the blood. You're not wrong, I've thought about what I will do when the next dealer opens shop. I want to stop killing. I am here," Jack says.

"And we'll help you, Jack. We're all here because we're going to stop," Jane says.

"What if Robert killed?"

"Then we bring him back. We don't give up. It's a terrible relapse, but I don't think we'd all just say 'I'm not killing anymore' and go cold turkey. If we could do that we wouldn't need a group," Jane says.

"Then we continue with our telling of tales. Let me just inform you, biting hurts." Edgars rolls up his left sleeve, shoving his arm into the dim center light of the room. Two fading round scars dot his forearm. "Puncture wounds, when they hit a vein, bleed."

"Are those made by fangs?" Jesse asks.

"Yes. I actually became a Vampire to write, *Wafts of Blood. The Story of Victor Boudreaux: Vampire or Serial Killer?* Long titles are dangerous. People like them short so they remember them."

"You mean like *IT.*"

"Long novel, short title and people know of the text. Unlike *The Hundred-Year-Old Man Who Climbed Out of the Window and Disappeared.*"

"Never heard of it," Kenneth says.

"You may have, but people forget long titles *Hamlet, Fried Green Tomatoes* and *Wicked* all have much longer titles. They shorten them so you remember."

"This's not a book club," Ed snaps.

"Not a reader, are you Ed? I figured you liked something with lots of pictures."

"Fuck you."

"So you became a vampire to write this novel?" Jane refocuses the group.

"Yes. Yes, I did."

III

I DISCOVERED THIS underground group who felt they were real vampires. Not gothic people, but those who assume the lifestyle, down to the drinking of their partner's blood to enhance the sexual experience. It was like a twisted bondage club and many members had themselves surgically altered to become Dracula.

For those devoted, but not devoted enough, or still had to report to a day job where they had to appear as a normal human, there were removable prosthetics. I explored this world a bit, but was quickly unwelcome without partaking in the pleasures being offered. They didn't care for voyeurs. It was mandatory participation. I was shocked at how many demanded to be bitten and have their blood drank. One of the vampires was a dentist by trade and he gave me his card.

I visited him by light of day and discovered, for a nominal fee, I could obtain a set of off the books dentures turning my teeth into fangs. I paid cash.

Without them I could not continue to explore such a dark world where people were aroused by being bitten and having their blood sucked while fucking. Many times this was a private affair, but a few times some people performed at these group gatherings. It was all fascinating, and difficult to take mental notes as the events were sensory overload.

I kept my notes at home and prepared for my only leap into the supernatural as a writer. A vampire novel would lean toward an answerable mystery questioning if the blood suckers were real or not. I tended toward them being a man in a rubber mask or filled teeth to commit his crimes. It didn't detract from my experimenting. I could wound victims and not have to worry about dealing with the ramifications of body disposal.

The targets of women and men who wanted to be bitten lined up around the block. I knew I shouldn't do my deed at the party, but I could have without having killed. So many wanted to be dominated and bitten.

This may have been the moment I knew I had an issue. I basked in knowing about the biting and blood. People were lining up to be bitten. I had none of it. Somehow a willing victim was the last thing I wanted. Maybe it was my research methods, getting to understand the way pain was forced upon someone. It was honest. Those in the fang club craved orgasmic pain.

After the first willing bite I was finished. I would find a subject outside the club.

As I pushed through the overwhelming masses of dancing flesh covered in fetish wear to reach the door I spotted her. Librarian popped into my head at my first vision of the wrongly dressed woman in the corner. Down to modern horn-rimmed glasses, she was out of place, even more than me.

"You didn't look like you belonged, or was this your idea of a victim costume?"

"My college roommate swore by this place. I just wanted to understand what she raved so much about."

I slipped the teeth from my mouth to have a normal conversation because the dentures caused a slur. As loud as the music blared she would have had trouble understanding me.

"I understand." I didn't want to upset her already uncomfortable stance. "I'm researching a book. I couldn't get anyone to speak to me without the teeth. And even then, they don't speak...just bite."

She smiled. "What do you write?"

"Mystery/thrillers mostly."

"Anything I might have read?" She asked.

"The *Third Body in the Attic*," I smiled. It was a twisted romance, and if she was a reader she read romance. After attending so many book shows romance readers had a look.

"You're not P.A. Edgars."

She knew me by name. Good.

"Got Internet on your phone?" It was new at the time, but worth asking.

"It costs."

I slipped a twenty out of my pocket. "I'll bet you if you look up my books you'll see my picture. If I'm not who I say I am you keep the twenty minus what it cost to use your Internet."

"And if you are Edgars?"

"We go have a cup of coffee, and I'll sign the copy of my book you have."

"I have three."

I smile. "I'll sign all three."

She activates her phone. After about five minutes she glances up from the glowing screen. "I get no signal in here."

"Go outside," I suggested.

She turned to leave. "Aren't you coming with?"

"If you're asking. I wasn't sure you'd want a slightly older man wearing vampire teeth to escort you into a dark alley."

"Of all the men in this place, I trust you the most."

"Don't say because I remind you of your father."

"God, no. You aren't that old. Because of all the people here you haven't asked to bite me on my ass."

It was difficult to tell how nice her ass was even with the way she was dressed. But she was cute in her glasses.

The butt would not yield a large amount of blood, or would it?

Outside she pocketed her phone. "How about you just buy me a coffee. I'm not ready to take you back to my dorm."

"Smart girl. You may not get a chance to get my autograph. I don't normally make it to this part of the country."

"But I get to have P.A. Edgars buy me a coffee." She giggled covering her mouth with innocence.

It didn't take long. We were on a deserted country road in the back seat. She was quite forward. We kissed. I fondled her breasts through her clothes. I didn't move too fast in undressing her. I'm sure she enjoyed the slowness of the embrace but for me, as our tongues rubbed, I was considering if she was to be my next test subject. I rarely mixed my sexual encounters with my assaults.

I had to use the teeth. I figured I would be the last suspect and some regular attendee at the vamp raves would ping the radar. This girl was nice and quite the kisser. I wondered if she was as good with the rest of her body.

I considered my options, slipping off her shirt. No matter which way I chose she would be vulnerable naked. As I caressed her back, her arm reached to the rental car floor. Her body was off balance, which shifted our lips. Someone engrossed in the moment of passion might have missed it, but I, being more involved in my experiments, realized she had grabbed something in her purse.

I felt a sting as I exposed her nipple, but my first thought was she demanded to use a condom and was tapping me with a fingernail. Luckily, I wasn't distracted by the guaranteed prospect of fucking her or I would have missed catching it before she broke my skin. What she brought out of the purse, in a burst of a downward angry thrust, was a hunting knife. I caught her wrist, twisting it behind her back, before she even knew I was aware of the blade's attack.

She struggled, but I pinioned her other hand behind her as well. The next bit was difficult because I should have snapped her left wrist, rendering the knife useless, but a broken wrist meant my handcuffs would be escapable. I flexed and bent her hand until it hurt her.

"Let go, my kitten."

Her legs were pinned under her as she was sitting on her knees in the seat. I'm sure she thought about her position. As she raised up to stab down her legs were in a prime location, but only if I hadn't prevented her from stabbing me.

The knife clinked onto the floor.

She might have done better had she used her right hand since it was dominat. I used my weight to control her. It kept her locked in the position I wanted while I released her right hand and fished out my cuffs. She struggled, but with no way to surprise me, I had her shackled before she could scratch me.

"You some kind of cop?"

"No."

"Let me go and I won't claim you tried to rape me."

I was not expecting this from my little librarian. "You were going to stab me." I drug her out of the backseat.

"You were getting too forceful. I was just defending myself. Who do you think they will believe?" She jerked against her cuffs.

"You, ruining my reputation and book sales. And even if later you stab another man, and everyone finds out about the minx you are, my career will be over. And no one will care because I will have been judged in the court of public opinion and there are no retractions." I slammed her hard against the hood, kicking her legs apart to keep her off balance.

"You stab many people?" I wondered.

"Fuck you," she spits.

I flicked the first hook of her bra strap.

"Just put it in and do what you want. I won't even feel your limp dick."

I flicked the second hook, freeing her breasts. "I have no need to rape. Your taunting won't inflame me. Anger costs focus. What are you angry about?"

"Just fucking get it over with."

"Most women I've placed in this position do nothing but beg." I slipped the knife—her knife—between her ring and pinky finger. "Even when I cut off a finger they beg me not to rape them."

"What makes you different?"

"Cut me. Go ahead."

"You don't seem like a cutter. As you draw the edge of blade it over tan skin it leaves a trail of white. Then you press down and the skin layers separate until you open the capillaries. Normal instinct would be to jerk the blade away as pain strikes. But instead you apply pressure, cutting deeper, causing more pain, releasing a rush of endorphins to the brain, giving a pleasurable high."

"You're a sick fuck."

I cut a hole in her dress large enough to allow me to tear it off. The ripping cloth terrified most women, as they know it means they will be penetrated. This kitten seemed to want the process of forced intercourse.

I snapped the string on her black thong.

I'm sure the anticipation of me behind her terrified her, as she was just waiting for the hard thrust to separate her lips and violate her. The shock of the two fangs puncturing her left butt cheek sent her into a screaming fit.

"You bit me! You motherfucker! You fucking bit me!"

"Yes. You were going to stab me."

I pulled back her hair, exposing her neck. My hot breath caused her to shiver. I wanted the traditional vampire bite next.

I found the fangs must hit the vein for there to be a flow of blood. There was an art to it, one I wouldn't perfect here. I wouldn't need to. I gleaned much information from the neck bite and wouldn't risk swallowing too much of her blood.

I decorated her arms, with a single bite on each breast. The abdomen was difficult to puncture because of the angles of the teeth and mouth, but by the time I had reached her navel, her protests had shifted from verbal abuse to tears. I spread open her legs. She was nothing but a whimpering mess.

The inside of the thigh was the softest, best area to bite. I even hit the artery. She bled. I doubted she would bleed out from it, but it would be a large blood loss. As she lay on the ground riddled with fang holes and glistening blood, I wondered what else I could glean from her pain. I had not asked her about it, not like normal. I was more interested in how the bites appeared and felt from the vampire perspective.

She wouldn't beg me to stop. I didn't know if she would inform me if I did question her. Besides, I wanted her death to reflect the vampire fetishes. I palpated her clean thigh until I found the femoral artery. I bit three times, opening it up. The blood mushroomed from each hole.

She lasted an hour. I had to use her skirt a few times to unplug the coagulating holes. I cleared the location of as much of my physical presence as I could and waited. When her last breath wheezed I left her.

Part of me wondered at her motivation. Part of me wondered if she and I couldn't have teamed up. But in the end using her to learn of the bite and leaving her for the police to investigate the vampire cult was satisfying enough. A trusting partner who enjoys your passion is a keeper. I'm not sure she was such a person. She was sloppy. Her killing would lead to being caught. She could only claim in court the defense of her person once…no more than twice before a jury questioned her character. She would have drugged me down. She was a thought-provoking woman.

I wore the teeth through customs. No one asked me to smile nor expected one. Once in an airport stall, I packed them in my carry on. At home I reluctantly smashed them, scattering the pieces. The dentist who made them may have kept no record. I'm sure the bite marks could be traced to these teeth and since they were fitted dentures, custom to my mouth, to appear as my real teeth sans fangs. They were a major nail in my coffin if found by the police.

IV

"MAYBE YOU SHOULD have gone by Vlad instead of your pen name."

"I am who I am," Edgars says.

"Were you going to be the girl's first kill?" Jane asks.

"I did check the news on her. One reporter followed a non-traditional route with her story. Most papers were content to blame the brutal attack on the want-to-be vamps, but they were actually harmless."

"They bite."

"It was all consensual. The girl, however, was seen with another man a few weeks earlier who was found stabbed to death in the back seat of his car with the same hunting knife found next to her."

"She was blossoming into one of us," The Plagiarist says.

"She would have been on his lap or on her knees in the seat to make the downward thrusts the same way she was attempting to get to me," Edgars says.

"She was developing a pattern," Al says.

"She had anger toward your gender," Jane states, not sure if she is asking a question.

Edgars responds, "The odd ball reporter questioned this girl's attack because this would have been the third incident to occur while she was around. She jabbed a boy at her high school, claiming he was touching her. He swears he did but she asked him to. No one wants to shame the victim, but in this case she was asking for it."

"We all are," Kenneth mumbles.

Al notes how Jesse doesn't seem to be the enthusiastic kid he's been at the past meetings. "You okay, Jesse?"

"Yeah, fine."

"You don't seem yourself," Al says.

"Have you had a new urge, kid?" Ed asks.

"No."

"Something is bothering you. You should have messaged me," Jane says.

"I. I'm. Look, Robert not being here. It…really bothers me."

"Bothers you how?" Al asks.

Edgars picks up on Al's concern and the kid's nerves. "We're here to share our motivations, kid. Why does Robert not being here cause you anxiety?"

"I guess, if caught, you'd have the longest time in prison." Al adds, "Being the youngest among us."

"Hell, they'll tap his cute, white ass," Ed throws in.

"Enough. No one in this group is going to prison. We're going to control our urges and not kill again," Jane says.

"Not unless someone marches into a police station and confesses," Al says.

"Confession clears the soul, but not to the cops. This is my confessional," The Plagiarist says.

"Everyone here be clear," Edgars says, "If caught we are locked away for life. Pointing out other killers won't reduce a sentence, it harms the rest of us."

"Cops lie, anyway. *We only help you if you tell me.*" Ed mimics. "Bullshit. They want to close a case. Cops speak to you, I'd ask for a lawyer even if it was for jaywalking."

"Have you spoken to the police, Jesse?" Al asks.

"NO." Jesse blurts too fast for the room to remain comfortable.

Al stands. "I think this session's over, Jane?"

As reluctant as she sounds, Jane agrees. "You may be correct."

None of the group speaks any more. Al disappears into the darkness. After a few minutes Edgars slips away. One by one they all dissolve away until Jane and Jack remain with Jesse.

"Should I invite you to the next meeting?" She asks.

"I just got to work through something," Jesse mutters.

"It might be best you work through it on your own, kid." She slips away.

"Are you it Jack?" Jesse asks.

"I never can tell. This old factory has many dark corners. I would never speak privately here." Jack leaves.

FOURTEEN

JESSE

I

BUSTED—NOT BY THE therapy group, but by the FBI. Jesse left out facts, including Edgars. Once he listed the author's books in his report they would launch an investigation into him. He'd never get a shot at discovering his sister's killer.

Even if her killer wasn't part of the group, the group could lead him to her. Dozens of people had applied to Jane's quiz for help. He could have been among future addition to the group.

With Agent Sutherland dead and Agent Smith present at her funeral services, a new FBI agent was assigned to be his handler. Agent Thornton slaps a yellow legal pad down on the table.

"I don't know if you warned them on purpose, or why you would. Maybe you were nervous with the wire, but you didn't behave as you had before." He scolds with all the personality of a bobcat caught in a bear trap.

"Robert's failure to attend set them on edge. You weren't in the room to detect the tension. I don't know which of them didn't watch the news, but his not being there was the issue," Jesse eyes the paper. All meetings in the interrogation room are recorded. He ponders the purpose of the paper.

"You exacerbated it. I'm not going to treat you with kid gloves, the way Smith did. You may be cooperating, but you left out that one of the killers was P. A. Edgars. Pretty big clue, kid." Agent Thornton shoves the legal pad at Jesse. "Write down everything else you left out." He tosses a felt marker at him.

Jesse opens his mouth to protest, but Thornton cuts him off.

"Agent Smith just buried a partner. When he figures out you held back I doubt his badge will protect you from him beating the information out of you."

Jesse guesses if Smith got the chance he would swing on him. He glances down at the paper knowing he did have a part in Sutherland's death.

"Not revealing Edgars' name makes you an accessory."

No more meetings. No more chances to learn about my sister's killer. Jesse confesses, "He said he was an author. I didn't believe he was actually Edgars." He lies, but he knows since the group uses monikers it was a plausible lie. "I didn't want you harassing the wrong person and giving away my chance to uncover my sister's killer."

"I read about your obsession with her death, but she has been dead for two decades. I've seven killers, now and how many living people does that place in danger?"

"At least one. Al. Al collected his girls. He still has one. He was contemplating how to release her, but now if they find themselves compromised he might end her. Cover his tracks."

Agent Thornton wasn't expecting a confession. "Write everything or this girl's death will be, in part, your responsibility."

Jesse explains how Al framed the man and stole the redheaded girl. The raving of a perpetrator and how innocent he was happening a dozen times a day in courts across the country. "We must find the county with the missing red-headed girl. And Al never said what happened to the red-headed woman. She could still be his prisoner. She has to be on a missing persons list."

"No. If this perp was convicted of this woman's death then she may not be considered actively missing. But you are thinking, kid. Write it down. We have to find Al and save this girl."

Jesse uncaps the marker. He scrawls what he knowingly left out the first time.

II

THE MOMENT THE squeak of the tip on the page ceases Jesse hears Agent Smith ranting. Cramped from all the writing, Jesse drops the marker to free his fingers for flexing.

"He's my CI. You had no right to use him. You may have ruined all chances we have to capture those killers. What were you thinking?" Agent Smith says.

"I didn't want to miss the chance to gain an inside track to the meetings transpiring among a group of serial killers. You were attending Agent Sutherland's funeral. What would have happened if the kid hadn't attended this last meeting?" Agent Thornton asks.

"They would have been a lot less suspicious of him than they are now. He'll never gain back their trust."

"He may not need to. I've got him filling in any blanks now," Agent Thornton says.

"Now you scattered them." Agent Smith bursts into the interrogation room. "I just lost my partner. I've got another agent going to require multiple skin grafts. You're going to tell me everything that occurred in those meetings."

Jesse slides the legal pad across the table. Smith snatches it up and reads, flipping a page and reading more.

Agent Thornton slips inside. "We've got a possible kidnapping and I've put in a call to a judge to get a warrant to search the home of author P.A. Edgars."

Smith considers slapping Jesse with the legal pad. "I don't know, kid, if any of this would have changed Agent Sutherland's outcome, but you've allowed these people a chance to escape, putting them on guard against us. Some will elude capture and return to killing. And those deaths—those deaths will be on you. You'll have to live with that the rest of your life."

His words sting much worse than a slap. Jesse knows it's true. And even if some don't kill, those they track down will not surrender and more officers' lives are at risk. After all he went through he'll never learn who murdered his sister.

FIFTEEN

JANE

JANE PLACES HER cheeseburger back onto the plastic wrapper. A news story in the crawl at the bottom of the flat screen catches her attention:

> Police believe after a standoff the FBI has taken down
> a serial murderer known as The Bowhunter.

As she wakes from the moment, Jane realizes she has a mouth full of unchewed sandwich. She brings her teeth down to decimate the hunk of meat while she reaches under the table and into her purse. Hard, cold metal remains in its concealment holster ready for a quick draw. She laces her fingers around it to check the grip and a little tug confirms it will pull with ease.

Jane decides she won't be taken alive. She wouldn't share such a fact with the group, as her determination was not male posturing but rather a practical assessment. After all she learned about her halfway house girls' time behind the fence she wanted nothing to do with it. Besides answering for her philosophy was never part of her plan. She won't become the same burden on society she used to eliminate.

I did intend to start a group to stop serial killers. I wanted a PHD thesis never seen.

She scrawls on a napkin, *SKA Meeting Rules*.

Clicking on her iPad she connects to the mall food court WIFI the perfect camouflage to disguise her last messages to this group.

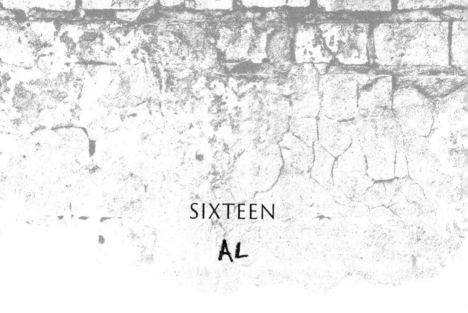

SIXTEEN

AL

I

AL GRABS THE small, brown-skinned man, shoving him behind a dumpster. The Middle Eastern man struggles, but is no match for the swift reflexes of a practiced wrestler whose normal fare is a struggling woman.

Al gets one bracelet around the left wrist. "Federal Agent, motherfucker. Abdul-Hamid, you're under arrest for human trafficking."

With the second cuff securing the arm behind Abdul-Hami's back, Al jerks the man to his feet and marches him to the back of his unmarked car.

"You're no FBI. You have no warrant. I want my lawyer."

Al shoves Abdul-Hamid in the passenger seat of his SUV before waving his FBI credentials in the man's face. What he refuses to explain that this is not his case, nor his arrest, or that he was to report back to his examination of the Car Tap Killer after Agent Shawna Sutherland's funeral.

He clicks the seatbelt into place. Glancing into the dark eyes he detects the anxiety and smells the fear. Al never gets this close to killer a when on a case.

Had he had light in the basements of the group's meeting locations he might have read Jesse better. The kid was green, but not working for the FBI. Al detected no institution vibe. Having access to active cases would have revealed an investigation to the group just like learning of this pending bust.

"This a, how you Americans say...a shake down?" Abdul-Hamid spits. "What do you want?"

"To see you in the same cage you place these women in," Al presses the push-start.

"No. You not behaving like regular arresting cops. Maybe you just want to harass an A-rab. Not enough blacks for you to bother. They riot now. Maybe instead of harassing, I pay you, make this all go away."

"Bribing a federal agent is a crime," Al says.

"Better to go to jail for bribery than for selling little white girls. Maybe you want...little white girl. I get you one. I guarantee she look just like your niece."

Al balls his fist, raising it to release a punch. He ignores the contradiction in his disgust of this man over his own addiction. He doesn't chase underage girls. The punch would give him an appearance of being normal. Normal, healthy people who don't choke out women should beat this man to a pulp. No matter what he does or what level of hell he'll burn in for what he does to women, they were all adults—no children. Al presses the brake and drops the vehicle into drive.

"Even if you are a cop, you want something, or we would be driving to your station. You want a little girl. I get you two. Whatever you want. Any age you like."

"Shut up." Al should cap him and drop him in the river. *Normal, well-adjusted people would. No, it's still killing. I'm trying to stop. What you want is death. Not by me.*

After a block of travel Al pulls over and cuts the engine.

Abdul-Hamid peers out the windshield.

Men in tactical gear marked in the lightening white S.W.A.T. BDUs attack an Asian restaurant next to an abandoned factory building.

"I know you operate your business out of there," Al says.

"I care not for Asian food."

"Not food, Asian pussy."

The SWAT teams penetrate the building, followed by men in FBI windbreakers. Lots of barely audible yelling reaches the car.

"Had I not arrested you, you'd have made it to your business to-day and be inside right now."

"As you Americans believe—I owe you," Abdul-Hamid says.

"All I have to do is pull up and say I caught you running away from the scene I caught you outside the perimeter where they expect-ed you to be."

"In a Post 9/11 America where cops are shooting people based on skin color, I'm fucking brown, motherfucker. My lawyer will claim I feared for my life. You've got nothing on me," Abdul-Hamid spits.

Al could never tell the age of Asian women. They never seem to grow old in appearance. All the long dark-haired females being es-corted outside to waiting ambulances appear to be young Asian girls, dressed the way they are in the kinds of pop-up ads on the Internet claiming they are ready for love.

"You're one sick mother, Abdul-Hamid."

"Then why aren't I with the rest of the men being arrested?"

"Because I'm one sick motherfucker as well, and as you said, I want you to owe me," Al admits.

"What you want? One of those girls? You have to wait until I get some new ones. I bet you want Asian girl with big tits. Those cost, but not for you."

"Abdul-Hamid, I don't need you to provide me with a girl."

"You Americans. If it's not sex it's money—usually to buy sex. How much do you want?"

"I have a problem only you can fix."

"If you want Arab boy…it take me a week."

"Listen motherfucker, my hands are no cleaner than yours and now I'm in a bind. You might end up in prison. But now you know they're on to you and I bet if I let you go you'll flee the country and not return," Al says.

"I have places to go," Abdul-Hamid says.

"If you leave does your operation shut down?"

Abdul-Hamid considers his answer, "As long as there is demand someone will provide a product. And there is a great deal of demand. Men always pay for sex. If not me someone else."

"Do you export?" Al asks.

"You've watched too many Liam Neeson movies," Abdul-Hamid says.

"Maybe I have, but I've been having a morality crisis. I need to get rid of a girl."

"Kill her."

"No. No killing."

"How old?" Abdul-Hamid asks.

"Early twenties. Pretty, still has spirit, red hair—natural."

"Too old. But red hairs becoming popular. I do this for you."

"Abdul-Hamid, they have you flagged. How will you leave the country?"

"My travel plans are none of your fucking business."

"Fair enough," Al says.

"Where is this girl?"

"Sedated in the back under the folded down seat."

"Show me," Abdul-Hamid says.

"Not here." Al drives from the chaotic liberation of the Asian girls. He wonders how many, once deported, will be smuggled back to be sold once again.

In a secluded parking lot Al exits his SUV. He keeps Abdul-Hamid in the handcuffs. Al flips the seat up on his side.

Abdul-Hamid twists to view the back chamber of the vehicle. Bound and gagged, the redhead sleeps spooned against a brunette.

"You didn't say you had two girls."

"Does it matter what the cost of your freedom is?"

"How do I know this isn't entrapment?" Abdul-Hamid asks.

"Then why would I bother snatching you before you were in your office? I need these girls gone and not dead."

"I export them to nice men," Abdul-Hamid smiles.

"I just don't want them dead," Al stresses.

"Lost the stomach for it? Or did you fall for her? Don't keep one too long, it helps prevent those emotions. But I make sure they are not killed."

"Good." Al knows they will be ill-treated compared to staying with him, but he must remove evidence.

"Then we have a deal, provided you drive me to the docks."

Al nods.

Abdul-Hamid leans into the vehicle, stretching out his arm signaling for the cuffs to be removed from his wrists.

"Which dock?"

"How about I sit here and tell you when we get closer."

"Fine." Al hands Abdul-Hamid a new, unopened burner phone. "In case you need to call your people."

"You seem quite the expert. These aren't your first girls," Abdul-Hamid guesses. "Why not kill these? The life you trade them into won't be pleasant. But you know this."

"They will be alive. I don't have the stomach to murder anymore," Al says.

"But you know they will be sex slaves."

"You will keep them alive? I want them to be alive," Al demands.

"You prevented me from being arrested. I overlook the way you put me in your car. I understand if someone spotted you, you needed to appear as a working cop. Protect yourself first. Consider their living a favor repaid. You will never worry over them again."

II

AL FLIPS HIS burner phone on. Jane paired him with Jack in case they needed a buddy to prevent a killing. To prevent his own demise, he must satisfy the hunt of the shattered Agent Smith. He may not have to bring down each group member, but he'll need a few for closure over Shawna's death.

He activates the only number in the phone.

After two rings, "I don't want to help you anymore. Just let those…"

"The FBI knows. The kid was a plant." Al's short expiation ends with a click. He snaps the phone in two, the pieces to be discarded along the highway in a few locations.

His best course of action would be to run, but he doesn't believe Jesse knows who he is. If he returns to his case and allows Smith to use the kid he may not have to interact with him.

Al activates his work cell. "Smith." The phone autodials the number.

"Al. I could sure use you, buddy," Agent Smith mumbles.

"Sorry, I had to leave right after the funeral. I've got an active killer and he's getting bolder in his attacks," Al says.

"I need you on this one."

"I'll clear this one fast. You be careful," Al says.

"I know Thornton is pushing me over the edge. Director Engström wants to run us as a task force and pad his resume. Fucker's got political aspirations. Rumor has it a new director may be assigned. Every agent's desires to make their career by being the one to bring down a half-dozen killers at once."

"Director Slincard hates my ass. It's why he keeps playing musical chairs with our supervisors. My concern is nabbing the Car Tap Killer fast. Sounds like the administration is more dangerous than a group of serial killers." Al ramps up his empathy. "Smith, you be careful. Just from the few bits of information I gleaned of your case I suspect none of those people are the type to be arrested. They will fight. Sutherland's death proves my concern."

"It's this kid. Your assessment of him might help. He's been withholding information. You'd see right through him," Smith says.

"I'll wrap up my case as fast as possible. Trust me, these people won't surrender." Al plants a seed. An officer on edge will more likely shoot first.

"I'll watch my back. We are serving a warrant on one of the alleged group members now."

SEVENTEEN
EDGARS

I

"HOW DO YOU want to play this?" Agent Thornton asks, staring at the book store across the street.

"From what Jesse said, Edgars always meets someone after the show. Sounds like a fangirl. He didn't carry weapons on him when he flew, but we are in his home town. We get in line near the end as the place clears, we get his autograph and we arrest him." Agent Smith waves a copy a of hard back book at his partner. "Just like our new task force leader wishes."

"Sounds all too easy. When was the last time Director Lawrence was in the field? I heard he met Hoover."

"Don't bet on it." Smith practices keeping the book in his left hand, allowing his right clear access to his service Glock. "I'm committed to this case. Agent Sutherland may have been a new partner, but she was mine and I will bring down this group to honor her. I ain't jumping ship because she died on my watch, nor am I seeking a multi-criminal arrest to make my career like all these new bosses we keep getting." Al knows the fool behind the wheel misses the jab at his own reason for being assigned to this case.

"We nab Edgars, we get this Kenneth, too," Thornton speculates. "It might lead us to this Jane who founded the group, but I doubt we figure out who Ed or this Al is."

"I've done this enough, you need to focus on one task at a time. We get this guy secure in a cell and we all go home before we worry about any other arrests."

"I know who Al is," Thornton says.

Smith slips his hand to his Glock, double checking. "Who?"

"One sick fuck. Choking out woman like that as he rapes them. He'll leave one too many bodies one day and we'll nab him. No one who does that will be able to stop."

Smith relaxes his hand. "You'll get no argument from me there. Why not this Ed guy?"

"Long distance truck driving killers are near impossible to find. The kid says he travels through Dallas. Texas leads the nation in unsolved highway killings. There are almost no clues and no telling how many are actively hunting at one time."

"You're correct as always, Thornton. When the kid said truck driver killer, I did a search and ran across the Highway of Tears," Smith says.

"Some forty reported young women have vanished on British Columbia Highway 16 over the last thirty years. I'd lay odds more than one truck driving killer hunts that stretch of ground," Thornton says.

"After this case you need to take a break. You've become way too engrossed in the subject."

"Only way to catch one is to become one," Thornton smiles. "Line's thinning," he says as he slides from behind the wheel of the car.

"Now you sound like Al." Agent Smith slams the car door behind him. "Are all you profilers this insane?"

Thornton jogs across the street, ignoring the question.

They reach the table. Smith places his book with the well-worn dust jacket before Edgars. He steps back, half into his gun drawing stance.

Edgars opens the book without glancing up. "You've read this more than once."

"It was good. I enjoyed it."

"I know you want it personalized."

"Make it out to Agent Smith, FBI."

Edgars flips the folding table into Thornton. He doesn't even wait to learn why the agents stood in line.

Agent Smith's gun clears its holster, but he balks at firing with a book store full of screaming civilians.

He makes a second rookie mistake that Director Lawrence will later chastise him heavily for. He digs Thornton out from under the table of books instead of immediately chasing the suspect. Once clear of the entanglement Thornton could call for backup and then follow.

Embarrassed, Thornton jerks away from Smith. "I'm good. Get after him!"

Edgars hits the fire exit door, activating the automatic alarm.

Smith doesn't know if the klaxon attaches to an automatic system alerting the fire department or not, but it will attract witnesses. In today's world of constant cell phone video he must make sure it is a clean shoot or none at all.

He barrels through the door. Edgars abandons fumbling with his car keys and bolts between two houses.

Smith pours on the speed, chasing after a man who's no spring chicken. The suit Edgars sports deceives the expected stereotype of a man who sits behind a keyboard for hours at a time.

Smith detects the swift footfalls of Agent Thornton behind him.

Edgars leaps a short fence tumbling through some staked tomato plants. A little old lady screams profanities no grandmother should use from her porch.

Smith yells, "Get back inside! The man has a gun. He's dangerous!"

Agent Thornton orders, "FBI! Get back inside!"

Smith knows Thornton has yet to witness Edgars brandish a weapon. But he planted the seeds in the old lady's mind. She saw a gun even if she didn't.

Thornton will be quick on the draw as well, believing there is a gun. He may fire on adrenaline.

Edgars darts across a street, nearly being hit by some soccer mom's minivan. Thornton waves his hand and screams for her to remain in her car. She wasn't going fast enough to kill Edgars if she had impacted him.

Edgars climbs a brick wall, tearing his suit jacket and pants on the barbed wire laying hidden across the top as he flips over.

Smith follows.

Thornton slips off his suit jacket, balls it before flipping it to shield his hands from the sticker points. He lands in the yard on overgrown grass, informing him no one has been home to mow in a while.

Agent Smith stands alone in the yard, gun in hand, no sign of Edgars, as if he just magically disappeared.

II

EDGARS CRANKS THE natural gas level in the fireplace. The flames crackle higher. He tears pages from a moleskin journal, the hand-written script having the gleam of an artisan. The grind of the cross cutting shredder pains him as if it were his own fingers slipping between the razors.

The banging on the solid oak door outweighs the whine of the whirling blades. Edgars knows the reinforced wood and steel door will take five or six impacts from the battering ram the SWAT team utilizes. A few years ago an obsessed fan kept breaking in and spreading her scent around the house. Edgars had bars, shatter proof windows and the reinforced armored doors added to keep her out.

She would have been an ideal research project, but her first break-in was while Edgars was on a signing tour. Her face was plastered in all the rag sheets when the neighbors reported her running around the yard naked.

Edgars made sure when her second break-in occurred he was home. He became the terrified celebrity, the kind of person too scared to venture out, but too scared to own a gun. He thought it might add to his alibi if a fangirl's death came into question.

The door opens with the crunching clatter of a bulldozer. He imagines the wood around the bolt splintering and stakes of wood impaling the Persian rug in the foyer. Edgars breaks the spine on an unshredded notebook before tossing it on the flames. The open pages, crisp with age, catch like fall leaves. He pops the spine on a second book. A closed book's inner pages are protected and will survive the mild heat from this teasing flame.

He jerks free the trap from the shredder and sprinkles the confetti reduced pages onto the flame. They grow and reach up for each fluttering square. Paper reduced to embers escapes the fireplace and reach the carpet.

Edgars doesn't bother to stamp the living beast posed to devour his study. If the fire reaches the shelves of books stretching to the ceiling, this end of the house becomes a tinderbox. He thought years ago to install a sprinkler, but the water chemical would damage books as bad, if not worse, than the flames.

The ancient oak desk would withstand a blast from a grenade. Edgars alone hasn't the strength to flip it over to use as barrier. He jerks open the center drawer and removes his legally registered pistol. He checks the clip and racks the slide.

He swallows, mouth turning to desert.

He glances down. A twisted mangle of multiple electronics scattered across the top of the desk. He won't make it easy for them.

The fire escapes the fireplace and crawls from the smoldering carpet to the books on the bottom shelf.

The movement of men in full tactical gear clearing the house room by room reaches the edge of the study. The doorknob rattles with two quick twists.

Edgars raises the Beretta 92FS squeezing off three nine mm rounds. The grouping scatter across the center of the door. He never practiced.

His thunder in the airtight concentrated space shatters an eardrum and halts the movement outside. He doubts the pussy 9s penetrated the door and any body armor, but it delays a charge while the men outside rethink their tactics.

A deafening blast stronger than the three ringing 9mm shots splinters the door knob. Some fired a shotgun.

The door flings open, followed by a hissing canister rolling across the floor. The powder blue smoke steams out—tear gas. It will stink and blind Edgars. Knowing he lacks the skill to target the broadside of a barn, he decides not to duck behind the desk as the chemical mixes with the growing black smoke from his books.

Edgars raise his right arm and tightens his index finger around the trigger.

Between the smoke and the gas watering his eyes black blurs cross his vision. He jerks the trigger as fast as he's able to flex and pull. The discharge is met with a hail of reports. Edgars' abdomen blazes with fiery pain, and in a quarter of a second he detects the bullet break apart and shred a kidney. He assumes it is his kidney, for warmth soaks his groin.

The muzzle flash penetrates his fluid filling eyes as the second bite thumps his shoulder. Edgars would never believe a bullet would bounce off flesh, but he detects the flick as if a fly landed.

His lungs burn. And his chest hurts. He attempts to bring his left arm up to stifle the blood oozing from the hole. The arm fails to cooperate. Through cloudy eyes he spots the waterfall of blood sloshing from the hole in his shoulder.

As two more rounds penetrate his chest, one shredding open his right ventricle, he ponders how the bullet felt like a fly landing on his shoulder but the ones in his chest and stomach were like being impaled by a flamethrower. As he loses his legs, he wishes he was able to record the experience.

EIGHTEEN
JACK

JACK MASHES THE gas pedal of his Rogue to the floor with a wrench, wedging the end against the seat to hold it in place. He braces himself for a leap backward before he flips the gearshift into drive. He barely lunges fast enough to escape the vehicle as it barrels across the street, hops the curb and smashes into the porch of the house.

"That will wake the neighbors!" Jack follows behind the car, brandishing a revolver in each hand. This time he'll give the crack dealers inside a chance to respond.

A man climbs through the front window of the house, screaming and cursing at the driver. Before he realizes there isn't anyone in the Rogue, Jack pops a round in the porch ceiling above his head. The man jumps back through the window, a strong indication he's been shot at before.

Jack passes the midway point of the street, still marching to his doom.

Bullets fly from the house.

Chunks of blacktop erupt, as their fear cost them proper aim.

A second man leaps through the window, diving for cover behind the railed fence running around the porch. It provides no real protection, except in his mind, as he raises his gun.

Jack's bullet embeds itself in the man's face. He has no idea where the dead man's bullet impacted. As he reaches the yard a jet-black SUV slams on its brakes, catty-cornered in the street.

Two suited men leap from the driver's side, using the car as a bullet stopper.

"FBI! Throw down your guns and put you hands in the air!" The driver yells brandishing his weapon.

Jack places a foot on the grass. He spots a third man at the window.

"Place your weapons on the ground!" Screams one of the agents.

Jack ignores the authorities.

Sirens wail in the distance.

Jack knows he won't be able to aim both guns. He raises both arms. The shots spew wild from his left hand at the house. The right gun releases two slugs into the man at the window.

Bullets tear open Jack's side. He left the FBI agents no choice. He knew as soon as he opened fire on the house they would have no choice.

Police are trained to shoot to kill.

Three. Four. Six. Jack loses count of the bullets puncturing his trunk. His thoughts—his last thoughts shift to his family and how he will finally be reunited with them again.

NINETEEN

THE FBI

"I'VE GOT TWO agents out on administrative leave because of this cluster." FBI Director Lawrence stews in his chair. "One dead agent and nothing to show for any of these alleged killers this kid says he's been holding a vigil with, except two more dead suspects, one who burnt up any evidence tying him to any killings."

"Therapy, sir." Agent Thornton says, resuming his role as a model agent.

Agent Smith misses Al's presence on this case. He needs his expert incite.

"I don't give a fuck if they were in a circle with their fingers up each other's assholes singing *Amazing Grace*. This kid's jerking us off and not giving us any satisfaction." Lawrence raises his voice the way the chief yells constantly at the heroes in an action movie where their misguided, non-regulation deeds yield results. "You have no evidence this old man ever went anywhere near a drug house until yesterday. The nurses at the hospital said he grew increasingly depressed over his granddaughter's condition and the fact she was never going to come out of her coma. More than likely he committed suicide by cop, leaving you with nothing but two less agents to work this cluster."

Thornton attempts to salvage his role in the investigation, "Jesse places the old man at the meetings. He would have no other reason to even be there unless he was attacking the drug houses."

Smith takes a shot at Thornton, "The kid never saw the old man's face."

"I don't care about what you know to be true. I care only about what you prove to be true. Charge the kid with obstruction of a federal investigation and put him in an actual holding cell with real criminals. He didn't give much on this Jack fellow or on Edgars and I think he's holding back even more. Someone, for fuck's sake, tell him what happened to his sister." Lawrence orders.

"Why? He doesn't exhibit any kind of Stockholm syndrome," Smith says. "Al needs to examine the kid. What if he is a groupie, or desires to become a killer and seeks a mentor?"

"No. Jesse desires information. He believes if we arrest the group he'll never get it. He's misguided. Put him in holding and let him have a taste of jail," Lawrence orders. "When you bring him out share the facts of his sister's death and see if he sings about the group then?"

Smith won't argue with his new boss. With any luck he'll be gone in a few weeks. They seem to be on an assembly line of supervisors lately. But none of them have entertained the kid might be a killer in training.

"He just wanted to know what happened to his sister," Thornton says, sounding more like he approves of the kid's action

"Then he should have read the file on his sister. For wanting to be a profiler he has not been too willing to examine all the evidence. It is clear what occurred. If he was decent at profiling he'd figure it out," Lawrence says

"I read through it. Parts are sealed due to the involvement of a minor. Did you read a page I couldn't, sir?" Thornton asks.

"It takes a court order to open the sealed sections, and despite this kid's involvement, the judge won't permit it. I, however, didn't make it to director by not knowing my shit. Read the file again. It is clear who killed his sister."

"How long do you want this kid in holding? As we speak we've got five killers going to ground. If they catch wind of Jack and Edgars being brought down they will disappear," Smith says.

"Is that what you would do, Agent Thornton?"

"Sir!?"

"To catch these people you must think like them. If you saw Jack's picture on the news what would you do?" Lawrence inquires.

"This is why we need Agent Al back," Smith chimes in.

"No. I'm not putting him back on, not as long as bodies are stacking up on the Car Tap Killer case," Lawrence says. "The kid said they held the meetings in shadows. He never saw a face clearly. Some of the MOs of these killers, take the one calling himself Ed, for example, are so—common—there is no discernable pattern to distinguish any of a hundred unsolved murders. Focus on this former nurse. The two agents now on leave for the shooting will ride a desk and sift through questionable cases to help narrow down possible suspect?"

"There could be a million. This Jane never even said a state," Thornton says.

"They need something to do. Maybe they will get lucky," Lawrence says. "I'm finished wasting hours on paid vacations."

"I could have the kid contact Jane through the chat room. We can't trace it, but maybe he could ask for her help, tell her he saw Edgars being arrested on the news." Thornton remains in his agent role.

"You'd tip your hand. If she didn't reach out to the kid she'd warn the others and they would all slip away."

TWENTY

JESSE

AGENT THORNTON SITS across from Jesse in the interrogation room. "We're spending a lot of time in this room on nonsense and I have killers on the loose." He holds a file folder down on the table with his fingers in a perprepared move to shove it across at the opportune moment. "How was the police department's holding cell? They filter through a lot more colorful characters than we do."

"I get it. If I don't talk I get to move in with a lot of guys who would insist on dating me. I get it. It's a reality for me, because I can't accept my sister's death."

"You're talking, but you're still leaving information out. Why?" Thornton asks.

"I don't even know any more. I was convinced I'd find my sister's killer among the group."

"Let's explore your theory a moment." Thornton drops his hand flat to the folder, but keeps it ready to shove across the table. "For someone studying to be an FBI profiler you have made some major mistakes."

"I can't read *her* file. I've tried a dozen times, but I just can't."

"You have to remove it from behind your desk first." Thornton allows the search of the kid's dorm to sink in. "How do you know what you are even looking for in a meeting where people speak of the killings they performed? You have no frame of reference to match up evidence. Some of the higherups in this office think you sought out a mentor to expand your killing," Thornton throws in to test for reaction.

Jesse chews his lip at the plaguing question. "I thought...I knew pieces of what happened. I have put together part of it from what my family has said in passing."

"Bits. I think you have misinterpreted. I have six confessed serial killers at large that you know more about than you have shared. I need that information to get these people off the street and in a cell."

"But they may not confess to my sister's murder." Jesse knows be should read the file, let his sister rest.

"You need to read this file." Thornton taps the folder.

"I won't."

"I need you to contact Jane. Tell her you saw Edgars' arrest on the news and you're scared and you want to meet with her."

"I'll do it. They ended the last meeting not trusting me," Jesse says.

"Any other piece of information on any of them useful to track them down?"

"Maybe, but let's try and contact Jane. Capture her and she'll lead you to all of them."

Thornton makes a hand signal toward the camera.

"What if you do capture all of them and none of them confess to my sister's murder? How will she get justice?"

"You want justice, but what about all the families of all the people this group has killed? Bringing them in will give dozens, if not a hundred, families peace. Is your peace more important than theirs? What about all the future families that will never know peace because you didn't help us stop these people? All of them, if you don't tell all you know, will return to killing. All of them will because you refuse to read this file." He slaps the folder.

Thornton leaves it in the room while he joins Agent Smith and another younger, female agent in the adjoining room.

"I miss the day of rubber hoses," Smith says.

Thornton's not sure Smith has a sense of humor.

Jesse pushes the folder across the table.

"He has no idea of the truth?" Thornton asks.

"No. We didn't know, at first, and he would not have a memory of the events being four." Smith waves his hand at the female agent. "This is Agent Nanami. She will be on a second computer monitoring what Jesse does and says to Jane."

"I've got the computer he is to use set up. Whenever you're ready," Nanami says.

"Why are we still fucking with this kid?" Smith asks.

"Because he still has vital information about the serial killers in the group," Thornton says.

"Cuff his hands to the table, he won't be able to stick his fingers in his ears. Just go in there and read him the file," Smith says.

"I've considered it, but I think he'll shut down and won't believe us. He's convinced he will find the killer among the therapy group," Thornton says.

"That kid's shut mouth led mouth lead to my partner's death," Smith says. "Prosecute him for obstruction. A few more days in jail and speaking to lawyers will shake loose the rest of what he knows."

"Nothing he gave us lead to Robert. And even if it did the kid had nothing to do with the takedown. The man who killed Agent Sutherland is dead and you have closure. Let's give closure to all the rest of the families whose lives these killers have ruined."

"Let's get him in front of the computer, contact this Jane, see if it yields any results."

· · · · ·

"Shouldn't you be in there monitoring the computer?" Smith asks. He leans against the wall, staring through the two-way mirror at Thornton and Jesse.

Agent Nanami holds out her phone with the image of a chatroom screen on it. "I am, but I don't think she'll respond to him instantly.

She may only check her messages at certain times. I doubt she requests message alerts."

"Why can't you just track her computer?" Smith asks.

"These chat rooms are set up for anonymity. It's complicated to explain, but they don't allow anyone to trace who is on them. It's why ISIS likes them. Anytime we figure out a way to track someone the chatrooms change. The users change up rooms all the time. The Internet is the perfect place to be someone else."

"Give it twenty-four hours. If she hasn't responded I doubt she will," Smith says.

"Then what?" Nanami asks.

"We give him one more chance to spill anything to keep him from being charged. Since its' frowned upon, me beating it out of him."

"If I might suggest, the kid smells," Nanami says.

"He has been in holding," Smith says.

"Move him to a safe house and I'll monitor the computer. Get him a shower and some real food," Nanami suggests. "A little comfort might loosen him up."

"I hate when we coddle criminals."

"We're not coddling a criminal," she says. "We've got a kid who wants justice, he's just going about it the wrong way. And you and I both know no prosecutor would have a real case against him, unless we could prove he left out something detrimental on purpose.

"I'll arrange a hotel suite and we'll follow your suggestion, Agent Nanami."

Her phone chirps. "Jane made a fast response." Nanami flips the phone screen in the direction of Smith. The message reads: *Final rule: What is discussed in group stays in the group.*

Jesse types before Thornton prevents him: *Jane, I need your help. You must assist me.*

Her answer—log off.

"She won't be back," Jesse says loud enough for Smith to hear through the mirror.

"Any way to trace her?" Smith asks.

"No, but I'll exhaust everything I know to attempt to find her," Nanami says.

Thornton jerks away the computer. "Wrong move, kid."

"She'll warn the others. I don't know how to reconnect with any of them. She was my buddy if I felt the need to 'murder,'" Jesse says.

"I don't think this Jane trusted anyone."

"She was taking a great risk creating a therapy group of killers."

Agent Smith bursts into the integration room. "We've no more use for this kid."

"Wait," Jesse protests, "let's go over my time in the meetings. There has to be something I've missed."

TWENTY-ONE
THE FBI

I

"I DON'T LIKE inheriting this mess any more than you want to turn it over to me. But I just got word from the higher-ups. They don't want the public to be made aware of a group of confessed serial killers banning together and how we keep losing agents failing to capture them. It's a PR nightmare as is. I'm shutting this cluster down," Director Lawrence says.

"Then Shawna's death means nothing," Agent Smith responds, his tone smooth, no hint of his normal anger. He has no idea what brought an end to the investigation. He's never known any inquiry to be shut down before.

Lawrence sucks in an offended breath, "Don't ever think an agent's death doesn't mean anything to me. I know I never met her, but we did get her killer. My hands are tied. They want the investigation ended."

"I don't like it," Agent Thornton says.

"It doesn't matter what you like." Lawrence waves a file folder at Smith. "You're off the case. Better, there is no case. This group doesn't exist except in the mind of that messed up kid."

"You close this case now, and you close on a win," Smith realizes.

Before any more protests ejaculate from Smith, Lawrence adds, "But those two agents reduced to desk duty after the Jack shooting uncovered some suicides in a local haunted house in Kentucky. Now, if you two left before I had a chance to recall you. Maybe the cell service sucks in that part of the South. Those people just got indoor plumbing so use your time and capture this guy. Maybe with a living suspect I'll resuscitate the investigation."

Smith's response—exit the office without a word. He has a new respect for his boss, thankful he didn't deck the man. Thornton jogs to catch up with him before the elevator doors close behind Smith.

"Didn't think you could move so fast," he huffs a breath.

"Lawrence offered one more shot to make sure Shawna isn't forgotten as just a name in the Hall of Honor. We don't have much time before we get official word our case is closed." Smith presses the ground floor button.

"This the teacher…Kenneth, you think?"

The elevator door shuts.

"Yes. If this is the correct location he won't be hard to find, unless he has gone off the grid. We snag him alive and we bring down the rest of this *group*."

"Thought you weren't into being three chess moves ahead on a case?" Thornton says.

"No choice. We keep this case open and then we slow back down to one clue at a time."

II

THORNTON FLIPS OPEN his ID wallet, "Special Agent Thornton, this is Special Agent Smith."

"The FB-fucking-I all the way out here in our little hick town." The man whose paunch proceeds him sports a greenish polo shirt as a uniform top, his gun belt buckle hidden under his hanging gut. He sneers more at Smith. "There have been twelve deaths in this house, nine by hanging. Even when hangings were popular, never once has the FBI seen fit to send an agent down about them."

Smith ignores Sheriff Delmont's condemnation and the implication the man has a white hood in the top drawer of his file cabinet. "Twelve? Our reports have only eleven deaths."

"Our Internet runs a bit slow around here, but yesterday we recovered a body."

Smith worries *Could this mean he didn't go to ground but remained active?* "Another teenager?"

"No. This one was more of a shock."

Thornton shifts a brown eye at Smith. "Anything different about this hanging, Sheriff Delmont?"

"It was a teacher. Worked in the district for seventeen years, local man, grew up here. It's never been an adult before, always teenagers." Sheriff Delmont adds, "Funny, his sister was present when another girl died some twenty years ago."

"Why doesn't someone tear this place down?" Thornton asks.

"It's been tried, but the question of who owns and is responsible for it is a legal torrent," Smith says.

"That's correct. People fight over this place every time there is a death, nothing gets resolved and no one wants to pay to figure it out." Sheriff Delmont eyes the black man, curious why a clear urban man has interest in his community.

Thornton debates if he will defuse the pissing match brewing. Part of him wants Sheriff Delmont to be put in his place. Racists rate right above child molesters in his book.

"I'm surprised no one ever snuck out here with a match and corrected the problem." Smith's eyes scream 'you boys, when in your hoods, love to light fires.'

"I'm sure you federal agents think we're backwards around here, but most people fear the Plantation House. And since there has been no rhyme or reason as to who gets hanged, people just don't want to risk stepping onto the property. I've got two sick officers, as soon as the call came in we had a fresh body at the Plantation House."

"If no one goes out there how do you know to search for a body?" Thornton asks.

"Usually, when its kids, they've dared each other and when one doesn't come back we check. In this case a note was found stating a history teacher was coming up here for some picture taking. He wanted to write some paper for his master's thesis. Maybe he'd figured out who owned it," Sheriff Delmont says.

"And you searched when he didn't return."

"Sheriff Delmont, I'd lay off thinking your ghost has claimed its final victim. We'd like to look around this teacher's house before we leave town," Smith says.

"What for?" Sheriff Delmont asks still befuddled at the last statement and his attempt to decipher its meaning.

"We had a couple of questions for him on a case we're working on and just because he's dead doesn't mean he didn't know the answers," Thornton says.

"I'll send a deputy with you, if you don't mind. I don't need nothing sprouting legs until I notify the next of kin." Sheriff Delmont gives Smith the *don't steal now, boy* eye. "I'll get you a deputy."

Smith nods.

Sheriff Delmont leaves his office, not wanting any more to do with the politically correct FBI.

"He must be afraid we're here to take over his investigation," Thornton says. "Too many people get hung up on jurisdiction."

"Smart killers will dump a body where jurisdictions overlap. Agencies spend more time arguing over whose numbers must take the murder hit instead of attempting to solve it." Smith then wonders, "Is that what you'd do, Thornton?"

"If I was plotting a murder I'd fuck with the investigation as much as I could. But if I was that smart why would I need to kill?"

"Glad you're not that smart," Agent Smith laughs.

"You think this is the hunting ground of the one calling himself Kenneth?" Thornton asks.

"Our two desk riding agents searched for unusual or unexplained deaths by hangings. Would you believe they got a hit on this location quick? Short of some Hanging Trees in the South where many black men were lynched, this was the only location to ping."

"With a fresh murder it was all over the wire. Why didn't Director Lawrence mention it?"

"It may be why our case is over. He wanted us to confirm they are killing themselves. Give the brass some comfort to pad their pillows when they shut us down.

The string bean of a deputy with a face too young to shave approaches.

"Could he be any more Mayberry Barony?" Thornton jokes.

"Sheriff Delmont says I'm to accompany you FBI agents to the Plantation House grounds and to the home of the teacher. Make sure you don't touch anything."

• • • • •

Thornton reads the man's name badge. "Deputy Grenard, is there a graveyard on the property?"

"Family plot." He waves haphazardly toward a tree line. "Stones have all worn due to time, part of the problem with identifying who truly owns this place. Like Sheriff Delmont keeps saying, no one wants to pay the thousands of dollars to sort out the property mess." He rants on, "The deaths every few years renewed interest. People demanded it get torn down then someone says that will cost the city some ungodly tax number. House stays up."

"Or be the person who inherits the house of hanged teenagers," Agent Smith bemuses.

"Agent, you may have hit the nail on the head. Someone might fear they are liable for not boarding the place up correctly and get sued," Deputy Grenard says.

"Have you worked an incident here before?"

"No. The last one was before I joined the force, but the girl before that, I went to high school with. Coming out to this place was always a big *truth or dare* situation. I'd bet about a fourth of the class had tramped into the basement and nothing. Then bam!" He slaps his right fist into his left palm for effect. "One of them is found hanging."

They reach the tree line.

"The graveyard's over in here, but the stones are faded."

"You said you attended school with one of the victims?" Smith asks.

"Do you remember if she was depressed?" Thornton asks.

"I don't see how. She was a cheerleader, and smart. She had a full ride scholarship. All the boys wanted to…date her. I don't see how anybody like her could be depressed." Deputy Grenard adds.

"Because, like ninety-five percent of the people, you don't understand depression," Thornton says.

Figuring he's just been insulted by the big city agents, Grenard points through the trees. "Graveyard's through there, but I's too terrified to go into them woods."

"No need for that, Deputy," Thornton says before Smith jumps on the officer for his insulting action. "We get we're not wanted around here."

"Why's the graveyard important? The only bodies here have been found in the house's basement. Sheriff Delmont says you aren't allowed down there, but to take you to the teacher's home."

• • • • •

Agent Thornton buckles his seatbelt before turning the ignition. "You didn't tell them about the tunnel."

"What tunnel? I didn't see a tunnel. Did you find a tunnel?" Smith deadpans.

"I get it. It's not what you know, but what you can prove."

"Sheriff Delmont is a competent investigator. They should tear the basement apart and find it. If we find evidence this teacher is our killer Jesse spoke with in the group, we'll check on this tunnel later. Besides, we give them the tunnel they may not let us search the teacher's house."

"It would collaborate the kid's tale. But the graveyard was there. It matches up," Thornton says.

"Many homes from before the Civil War and even after had family plots especially on farms. I don't want to besmirch this teacher's name until we know. Our suspect may have killed another to throw us off," Smith says.

"I just want to leave here with this being our guy. It'd be nice if one of these murders came wrapped in a nice bow and without a shootout."

"If he is Kenneth then Director Lawrence will fight to keep the case open. We'd be able to bring down more killers from this group. If not, I think we're finished with the kid and the investigation," Smith says.

Thornton considers, "Kenneth ensured a legacy by being his own final victim."

"This was a career making case for both killers and agents. If we don't collect all the suspects then Shawna died for nothing."

"Agent Smith, did the wizard finally give you a heart?"

"Fuck you, Thornton."

· · · · ·

Inside the home of the last victim Deputy Grenard reminds them, "Sheriff Delmont said not tolet you guys mess with nothing."

Agent Thornton pulls on a pair of latex gloves. "We'll make sure you get credit for anything we find."

"I don't know what evidence you guys would search for. We combed through the house for a note. Found nothing. This guy was a clean, upstanding citizen and teacher."

Agent Smith sits down before the computer. "We should have brought Agent Nanami. She's quite the whiz with these things."

"I'm sure he wiped anything useful." Thornton sifts through a shelf of books. "Deputy do you have the teacher's cell phone?"

"Sheriff has it."

"Both of them?" Thornton asks.

"Only one."

Without touching, Thornton kneels and points to an outlet with two different gauged chargers plugged in. "He had a second electronic device."

"Is that important?" Deputy Grenard knows people keep dozens of chargers even when the device is gone.

Thornton some days never questions why he and the other members of the group were never tracked down. "Maybe he left a note on his iPad."

"I'll tell the sheriff."

Like that redneck knows how to use anything other than a rotary phone. As a millennia Grenard should have thought of that. And Kenneth was a teacher. They are expected to use current tech.

Thornton inspects a bookshelf, the top row filled with high school yearbooks. He follows the dates. There is a four-year gap from what Thornton guesses was Kenneth's junior and senior year editions, followed by seventeen consecutive years' worth of books. "Grenard, what year was the death when you were in school?"

The deputy rattles off the year.

Thornton pulls out the corresponding book. While flipping through the pages a browned newspaper clipping floats to the floor.

"What did you find?" Grenard asks.

Thornton unfolds the clipping. "It's an article about the murder."

"Trophy." Smith didn't ask.

"Arguably, but being a teacher at the school he could have just saved a clipping due to it being the loss of a student. Not a smoking gun," Thornton adds.

Grenard's confused gaze presents a dumb question.

"Smart. If they are a trophy collection even a shitty defense attorney could convince a jury they weren't a way for him to relive the event. Not without other corroborating evidence." Thornton opens the first yearbook. Another clipping rests inside.

"We should have Agent Nanami check out this computer. Are those newspaper clippings enough for a warrant?"

"Along with what the kid has told you, yes." Thornton makes a call on his cell.

III

AGENT THORNTON AND Smith once again sit before their current boss.

Director Lawrence hangs up the landline phone. "Sheriff Delmont wants to file a complaint about you, Thornton. Says you should have told him about the underground tunnel. He feels you kept vital information from his investigation."

"Just me?"

"This is just my interpretation, but the good sheriff didn't want a race card to be played by pointing a finger at Smith," Lawrence says.

"We equally withheld the information. We felt if we revealed the tunnel they wouldn't let us check the teacher's home," Smith says.

Thornton changes to the *we* vernacular. "We had a reason for a warrant. We wanted access to the teacher's computer first."

"The tunnel would have confirmed Jesse's story better than the yearbooks, but the clippings were his trophies."

"Sheriff Delmont didn't want our assistance and told us not to muck up his investigation. I was merely respecting his jurisdiction," Smith says.

"Until it wasn't."

"Correct, sir."

"You'll get no commendations for closing the book on this one. I'll bat it back to the locals, but it doesn't mean you'll have another run at the kid. This is over."

"We still have a missing girl," Smith protests.

"We're done. Unless you have some evidence, I'm forced to close this case."

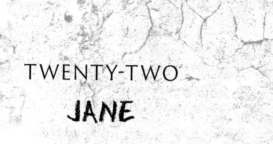

TWENTY-TWO
JANE

I

"MYSTERY/THRILLER AUTHOR P.A. Edgars was killed today in a shootout with the FBI. Edgars has been implicated in nine deaths where he brutally tortured and murdered his victims in the manner characters would later die in his books. The number is expected to climb as more evidence is uncovered."

Jane chucks the remote at the television. It bounces off with no damage to the screen, but when the flicker strikes the floor the battery cover splinters off and the twin AAA Duracells roll across the floor.

"Now you're being paranoid. The kid doesn't have enough to lead them to you."

"But Edgars," Jane protests.

"Edgars was a dumbass for using his pen name in the group. He was a braggart. He wanted us to know who he was. Male vanity. I doubt he was in the group to heal, he wanted another novel."

"I think you're right."

"They will come for you next."

"What do I do?"

"Finish it."

"It means killing again."

"You have no other options. They'll come for you and it all means nothing. You clear up one girl and a few of her worthless boyfriends and society receives no benefit, but this. This will change society."

"There's no coming back from this."

"You don't want to come back. If you did you would never have planned it. You hated the way insurance companies raped families— keeping loved ones alive, stringing them along. They will recover. No, they had terminal illnesses and all medicine did was keep them alive longer. And not for a better quality of life. All those you ended were bedridden. How many of them couldn't even speak or write a note to say goodbye to their loved ones?"

"I know. I only ended early those who were going to die."

"And the girls at the halfway home. No matter what you did to help them they all ended up back in prison. That is $40,000 a year, average, per inmate. A crappy amount, but a salary for another teacher to make classroom sizes smaller. Once they are in the corrections system they never leave. You studied. Recidivist rate is in the ninetieth percentile."

"People with addictive personalities never truly get over their addiction. The only way is to never start. But people don't know they'll become addicted until they are."

"Society wastes money on those who will never benefit from it. You recycle, but you alone will never stop the climate change. This. This you do, and it will make society better for a little while. The cost in savings will resonate on some chart and someone will ask why. Then they go oh, well, maybe we should have eliminated these social burdens. And in the end, no matter what. you will make America better for people."

"Everything I have done was to make the world better. People just don't see it." Jane opens a box of rat poison, dumping it into a mixing bowl. She crunches the green pellets to a fine powder with a pistol.

"Is that going to be enough?"

"I think so. I want the brownies to taste like brownies."

"Just tell those junkies you supervise that they are special brownies."

"No. They might suspect something. I finish them then precede to step two."

"You'll have to be quick. Once you enter they will send security to prevent you from completing your task."

"I will complete it. I have no intention of leaving until I do." Jane flips the oven knob to four-hundred-twenty-five degrees. "Maybe I should eat a few of these before I enter the ward, Just in case."

"If they cramp your stomach you may not be able to finish your task. If you pass out they may revive you."

"You're correct." Jane removes the baking ingredients from the cabinet. "You know, I never thought I would end this way."

"You've considered it for years."

"I know. But the group was a driving goal not to finish as I had planned."

"Exit strategies are always good when you do what you've done."

"End game more than an exit." Jane coats her brownie pan with non-stick spray. When done she places the can back in the proper cabinet.

"You're never coming back, must you clean the place one last time?"

"I must be insane to not only be speaking to myself and answering, but to nag myself about clearing away my mess."

II

JANE STROLLS THROUGH a side wing door of the St. Mary's Medical Facility. Even if the main entrance has security and a mandatory sign in station, in the seven years since she worked here, they still don't bar the side doors to the grounds. She wonders if, after this, they will increase the security, spend more money on those who will remain a burden on society.

In her handbag she carries all the guns she recovered from the boyfriends of the women she attempted to guide back toward being productive. Sometimes what is best for people is not what they should be allowed to do. They send those women back to the halfway houses close to their homes and the people they know, in most cases the people that got them sent to prison in the first place. Maybe they should do an exchange and send them to the other side of the country where they are forced to start fresh and not mix with those people who ruined their lives.

Too late now. After my stop at the halfway house I'm committed.

Once in the hospital corridors no one bothers to ask about her presence. One arm in her bag, hand around a gun with a finger on the trigger, Jane marvels if the families will ever appreciate the burden she releases them from. Maybe not in this first ward. Many of these people keep the state money gifted to them for the brain dead, those unable to feed themselves. They send these children to school where they have a nurse and a personal staff member to basically watch them vegetate. Most aren't people trapped in a body that doesn't work. They have no brain functions, either, the kind of children in the Old Testament that would have been left outside to God's will. Or in Athens, chucked off a cliff. But none of them would be allowed to burden society. Why is she the only one who sees this?

Staff members dive for cover. No matter how much they pretend to care for these individuals they won't take a bullet for them.

Jane keeps a running total in her head of her bullet expenditures. Three directly in the chest at close range, four more at a distance, with one getting a second shot since as she did not strike the heart. Eight rounds.

Screams in this room. Not much commotion elsewhere. She grips an extra clip in her left hand. As people rush toward the noise, none notice the smoking gun in her right. Scream filter behind her as she passes into the next wing.

More special needs. A nice polite way of speaking because no one wants to be the one to do what she does. She has a fresh clip in the gun before the empty one pings on the ground.

Two emboldened male staff members charge her. Two in the wall above their heads send them to the floor, scrambling to get behind tables for cover.

Some of these residents are so oblivious to their surroundings they never even bother to cease eating their pudding as bullets end them. Jane tosses the gun, pulling a second from her bag. A few wild shots keep the staff on the ground.

Now panic ensues as the corridors. People race past. most seeking exits, abandoning the patients, to whom they swore an oath—do no harm. Jane needs past them. She fires into the air.

They all drop, none in this corridor brave enough to grab at her feet. They don't know she won't shoot them.

The next ward she has to reach keep those in comas alive by machine. Most here are in long term care. Not a few days or *there is still a chance*, but will never wake up. Marching down the corridor, firing into each room as she passes, she drops the gun to draw a third.

Two security guards order her to freeze, drop her weapon and lay on the ground.

Jane spins to face them, stepping so she has a shot into a room she hasn't fired into yet. She raises the gun.

She ignores security's repeated warnings.

She fires.

They fire.

Jane only detects the burning fire from each impact for a second. Her organs fail before she hits the ground.

TWENTY-THREE
THE FBI

I

"CURRENTLY, THE SECOND worse mass shooting seen in America surpassing, Sandy Hook," the news anchor speaks with no emotion. "The alleged assailant, reported to be a middle-aged woman, was shot by security personnel. No word on her condition or of the dozens of people in the path of her rampage."

"The local field agency will handle the shooting." Director Lawrence dials down the volume.

"I know sir, but there is more relevant information," Agent Smith says.

The crawl along the bottom of the screen reports eight females were rushed being rushed to the hospital.

Lawrence hits the mute button.

The reporter continues, "...girls in a halfway house. Three dead. Five more sick. This emergency pulled away needed emergency personnel from the hospital where the shooting occurred minutes later. Authorities won't comment if the two events are being connected, but—"

"The woman calling herself Jane worked in a halfway house and also claimed to eliminate those whose time was near the end, but machines kept them alive. The shooter was taken down in the long-term coma ward, or whatever the medical term is for it," Smith says.

"You think this is Jane giving a last hurrah?" Lawrence asks.

"I think we need to check into it before all those local cops destroy evidence when they search her home," Smith suggests.

"It would close the case. I have doubts we find the truck driver, but this shooter might have something on this Al and we might save a girl's life."

"The brass may want to put a lid on this case but it just won't shut," says Lawrence. "Get on a plane."

II

AGENT THORNTON EXAMINES the hand-written note encased in a plastic evidence bag.

"It was the only thing on her," Agent Smith says.

Thornton nods. "I think she wanted us to figure out she was part of the group without giving it away."

"She fit the description of Jane. She was a nurse who was dismissed under unspoken circumstances. She worked in a halfway house and now seven of those girls are dead." Smith continues, "Jane was enrolled at university and was working toward her doctoral degree in psychology of the unstable." He half jokes, "Murdering twenty-six people who were unable to even run away from their attacker, she could have been her own case study."

"People she felt were a drain on society." Thornton asks, "How did the last girl at the halfway house survive?'

"She was trying to lose weight and ate one of the rat poisoned brownies. The other girls scarfed down two or three, according to her. She had enough strength to call 911. They got her stomach pumped or whatever they did to stop it," Smith says. "I figure it was part of her plan to tie up emergency services. In case her shot didn't kill a victim, there would be limited medical staff to keep them alive. She shot wild to scare staff, but shot so many who couldn't run, people who couldn't even feed themselves. They were innocent."

"Not to her. These people were a waste of hundreds of thousands of dollars, in her mind. If you are ever going to profile you have think like the people you chase. To her, she freed those people of a worthless life and the system of their burden. In her mind, she was doing the best for society as a whole," Thornton says.

"But we are a society of the individual."

"Maybe that is our problem," says Thornton. "This note confirms she was in the group. She addressed this letter *To The Man Who Was Holding The Girl.*"

"The group rules. I wonder why? He will never see this paper. No one outside this office will view it."

"She may have written it for him before the group fell apart," Thornton says.

"The note may spark something with the kid."

"We'll make available all the evidence to any agency that believes they have one of the three killers, but we are finished. Director Lawrence ordered us to release the kid," Thornton says.

"I can't believe you're willing to stroll away."

"Maybe if the murdered agents weren't avenged. But they are. With no leads on their locations or identities the case is closed. Truck driving killers are near impossible to catch and this Plagiarist changes his MO. He hides among other murders."

"What about this girl in the basement.?"

"He kidnaps women, but with the group decimated he will stop, maybe for years. I would bet my next paycheck he disposed of her," Thornton says.

"The kid claims he still had one he...*kept*," Smith says.

"We wait for a strangled body to turn up with his MO."

"You're cold, Thornton."

"Sometimes it helps...deal with the job." He reads the note one more time.

Printed are the rules the group was constructing to help each of them not return to murdering.

My Group

Maybe you will complete the list and restore yourself.

SKA MEETING RULES

Before you're invited to attend you must not have a current subject in your possession.

The only requirement for membership is a desire to stop killing.

No names.

New people must share first.

We leave our judgments at the door.

God will not be our excuse.

We must accept responsibility for our own actions.

We must change from an irresistible impulse to an impulse resisted.

When we see a potential victim we must remember they are a living thinking person.

Final rule: What is discussed in the group stays in the group.

Thornton hands the note to Smith. "Let the kid read it. Unless he has an address of another perp, we release him and close our investigation."

"No charges? Kid got lucky."

"You've spent the most time with him, try and convince the kid to read his sister's file. Or better yet, you read it to him, put an end to chasing down these killers. Dealing with what he learns will be enough punishment," Thornton says.

"He was attempting to do good," Smith muses.

"The road to hell is paved with good intentions. Read him the file. Or just tell him. But he doesn't leave until he knows who killed his sister."

"Is that your directive or Lawrence's?" Smith asks, dreading this task.

"Mine, but you know he needs to know in order to end this."

"I think I'm going to hate you when you are right. Glad I get my old partner back tomorrow," Smith says.

TWENTY-FOUR
JESSE

AGENT SMITH TAKES a seat across from Jesse in the interrogation room. "Don't remove it." He slides the bagged note toward him.

Jesse picks it up. On cursory examination he says, "It's the support group's rules. Jane wanted to create a real therapy group and help people."

"She was writing her doctoral thesis on active serial killers. She was using the group to earn her PHD." Smith adds, "Not sure if she was helping or studying them. Not such a noble person now."

Jesse gets excited at the prospect, "Then you should be able to use the information to track down Ed, Al and The Plagiarist."

"No. Nothing in her work gives clues to anyone's hunting ground or identity. In fact, she went out of her way to hide who people were. We're closing the case."

"I never figured out who my sister's killer was."

"After I leave this room some agents are going to process you out and drive you wherever you want to go, but first I have been ordered," He knows they record the conversation and wants to place on record it was Director Lawrence's idea in case the meeting ends badly, "by Director Lawrence to inform you of your sister's murderer."

"I could never read the file," Jesse admits.

"Why do you think that is?" Smith asks.

"It was my sister."

"I've read it. More than once. If you still want to be an investigator sometimes you have to examine evidence that makes you sick. Personally, as much as I hate the sick feeling. It reminds me I'm human. If you didn't get sick you've turned psychopath," he says.

"I'll listen."

Agent Smith opens the file. "I don't need to read it. Like I said, I've read it multiple times."

"Give me the highlights."

"This will be difficult. Director Lawrence has offered you the use of our therapists. Even though you are not an agent he finds your involvement and cooperation in this case has entitled you to a few sessions."

Jesse nods.

"You were almost four. Your mother believed you were rummaging around in her closet for Christmas presents. No one spoke of children and gun safety much back then. Your father had not locked up his gun, nor was it up high. You found your father's pistol and came out of the bedroom like you were John Wayne. You watched all those westerns with your dad. You just made bang-bang noises, so your sister got the bright idea to rush over and grab the gun before you got hurt."

Jesse's brain processes the event in a quarter of a second. "Oh my God. Did I?"

"When she grabbed for it the gun went off. It was an accident," assures Agent Smith. He remains stoic allowing the information to sink in.

"But there was all the talk." Denial coats Jesse's face.

"Your mother took you to this hospital where they thought it best if they pretended something else happened. The doctor was sentenced to prison in some malpractice suit years later, but he wanted your family to treat it like a murder caused by someone else to stop your nightmares."

"Your mother told me after you grew out of the nightmares they tried to never speak of the incident. She had no idea you harbored any belief she had been murdered or the little lies spoken about your sister would lead you to chase down serial killers."

"I should have read the file." Jesse shakes his head.

"It was a terrible accident. If you find yourself washed in guilt over your sister remember you brought justice to her death when you helped bring down a group of serial killers. The lives you have prevented from being taken and those dead you have avenged have insured your heart is lighter than a feather."

"Is that your way of saying God has forgiven me?" Jesse asks.

"Finish your degree. Report to the counselor. What you did on your own was impressive. The hours of trolling chat rooms to find Jane was remarkable. We've got trained agents who are not as patient as you," Agent Smith says.

"My resume highlight with have occurred before I had a law enforcement career. My life was driven by a lie."

TWENTY-FIVE
AL

BLUE EYES PEEK from the bedroom afraid to upset Al. He returned home and unshackled her leg, just leaving her free in the room, Something he's never done before. The man always follows a routine with any of the women he keeps. She knows it by heart. Some girls are afforded a different routine, but each one has one and he never deviates from it.

She hangs in the doorway of the bedroom as Al uses a pry bar to disassemble one of the homemade wooden boxes where he stored his women. He stacks the lumber in the fireplace. When he has enough wood for a nice roaring fire he lights it.

With the flames burning he collapses on the couch. "Come here, baby." He pats the cushion next to him.

He's never invited her. It's always been commands.

She hurries to his side. He's always been gentle with her, treated her kinder and better than the other girls he kept in those boxes. He chokes her, but she knows it is with love. Yes, he has forced her to do horrible things, but he touches her with a kind hand like no other lover ever has. She cuddles next to him, pulling her legs up underneath her body, nuzzling her face against his chest.

He strokes her hair as he explains, "I've been attending therapy, a special group which deals with people with similar tendencies."

Knowing there are other poor women trapped the way she is should terrify her, but in a manner, it comforts her knowing there is a strange sisterhood among them. The kind she felt when he had other girls here. She knows they are dead. When he removes one they go to die. She needs him to be happy with her. She desires her family, her old life back, but mostly she wishes to live.

She only listens. He'll let her know when she's allowed to speak. She recalls before when she fought with him, he punished her. She should have never made him punish her. His touch is so gentle when she capitulates.

"I don't want you to worry, I released the other girls. They aren't free, but they won't be killed. I kept you because I love you."

His heart thumps faster in his chest. Somehow it gives her comfort, comfort she won't die at his hand. She just won't anger him.

"I want to take our relationship to the next level of trust to show you how much I love you. No more locked boxes. I'll burn them, and we'll make love in the firelight. And no more leg chains. You're free to go anywhere in the basement. If this works out, and I know your love and trust is genuine, maybe in a year or two I'll bring you upstairs."

He moves her to the floor. She goes limp. She's learned it's better if he places her where he desires. His warm, wet lips on her neck match the heat of the fireplace. For the first moment in all the time he has kept and touched her, he makes love without wrapping the dog collar around her neck.

ABOUT THE AUTHOR

William Schlichter is an award-winning author and screenwriter specializing in the phantasmagorical world of the undead and science fiction fantasy stories. His popular No Room in Hell and Silver Dragon Chronicles series are fan favorites, and he enjoys spending time on the convention circuit.

His full-length feature script, *Incinta*, is a 2014 New Orleans Horror Film Festival finalist, a 2015 Beverly Hills Film Festival full-length feature finalist for a full-length feature, and an Official Selected finalist in the 2016 Irvine Film Festival. William also placed third in the 2013 Broadcast Education Association National Festival of Media Arts for writing a TV Spec Script episode of *The Walking Dead*.

CPSIA information can be obtained
at www.ICGtesting.com
Printed in the USA
FFHW022251180119
50220797-55196FF